Praise for Larissa

The Maizie Albright Star Detective Series

View To A Chill
(A Cherry Tucker & Maizie Albright novella)

"An engagingly entertaining drama. It was like having the best of both characters in the same story, yet separated by their roles. " — Dru Ann Love, Dru's Book Musing

"If you love southern settings with plenty of sweet tea and eccentric characters, the meet up of these two heroines is epic." — Barb Taub, humor writer and author of the *Null City* series

"If you love short mystery stories or novellas, this is the book for you." — Map Your Mystery

16 MILLIMETERS (#2)

"The author so brilliantly creates an environment where Harvey Weinstein-like behavior could exist, and demonstrates how actresses must walk a delicate line in order to stay employed and still not be victimized. Maizie's missteps make each of her successes an absolute joy, and I encourage readers to delve into this lively, funny, and genuinely satisfying series." — Cynthia Chow, *Kings River Life Magazine*

"With visually descriptive narrative, humorous quips, witty repartee and a quirky cast of characters, this was a such a fun book to read. This was an engagingly entertaining book" — Dru Ann Love, Dru's Book Musing

15 MINUTES (#1)

"Larissa writes a delightful book. Suspense, romance, and some funny situations. [Maizie's] a teen star grown up to new possibilities." — Sharon Salituro, Fresh Fiction

"I love Larissa Reinhart's books because they are funny but they also show the big heart of the protagonist." —Lynn Farris, Hot Mystery Review

"Hollywood glitz meets backwoods grit in this fast-paced ride on D-list celeb Maizie Albright's waning star. Sassy, sexy, and fun, 15 Minutes is hours of enjoyment—and a wonderful start to a fun new series from the charmingly Southern-fried Reinhart." — Phoebe Fox, author of *The Breakup Doctor* series

"Maizie Albright is the kind of fresh, fun, and feisty 'star detective' I love spending time with, a kind of Nancy Drew meets Lucy Ricardo. Move over, Janet Evanovich. Reinhart is my new "star mystery writer!"— Penny Warner, author of *Death Of a Chocolate Cheater* and *The Code Busters Club*

"Child star and hilarious hot mess Maizie Albright trades Hollywood for the backwoods of Georgia and pure delight ensues. Maizie's my new favorite escape from reality." — Gretchen Archer, *USA Today* bestselling author of the *Davis Way Crime Caper* series

"Boasting a wonderful cast of characters, witty banter blooming with southern charm, this is a fantastic read and I especially love how this book ended with exciting new opportunities, making it one of the best book in this delightfully endearing series." — Dru Ann Love, *Dru's book musings*

"This is a winning series that continues to grow stronger and never fails to entertain with laughs, a little snark, and a ton of heart." – *Kings River Life Magazine*

The Body In The Landscape (#5)

"Cherry Tucker is a strong, sassy, Southern sleuth who keeps you on the edge of your seat. She's back in action in *The Body in the Landscape* with witty banter, Southern charm, plenty of suspects, and dead bodies—you will not be disappointed!" – Tonya Kappes, *USA Today* Bestselling Author

"Anyone who likes humorous mysteries will also enjoy local author Larissa Reinhart, who captures small town Georgia in the laugh- out-loud escapades of struggling artist Cherry Tucker." – *Fayette Woman Magazine*

"Portraits of freshly dead people turn up in strange places in Larissa Reinhart's mysteries, and her The Body in the Landscape is no exception. Because of Cherry's experiences, she knows that—Super Swine notwithstanding—man has always been the most dangerous game, making her the perfect protagonist for this giggle-inducing, down-home fun."— Betty Webb, *Mystery Scene Magazine*

Death In Perspective (#4)

"One fasten-your-seatbelt, pedal-to-the-metal mystery, and Cherry Tucker is the perfect sleuth to have behind the wheel. Smart, feisty, as tough as she is tender, Cherry's got justice in her crosshairs." – Tina Whittle, Author of the *Tai Randolph Mysteries*

"The perfect blend of funny, intriguing, and sexy! Another must-read masterpiece from the hilarious Cherry Tucker Mystery Series." – Ann Charles, *USA Today* Bestselling Author of the *Deadwood* and *Jackrabbit Junction Mystery Series.*

"Artist and accidental detective Cherry Tucker goes back to high school and finds plenty of trouble and skeletons...Reinhart's charming, sweet-tea flavored series keeps getting better!" – Gretchen Archer, *USA Today* Bestselling Author of the *Davis Way Crime Caper Series*

Hijack In Abstract (#3)

"The fast-paced plot careens through small-town politics and deadly rivalries, with zany side trips through art-world shenanigans and romantic hijinx. Like front-porch lemonade, Reinhart's cast of characters offer a perfect balance of tart and sweet." – Sophie Littlefield, Bestselling Author of *A Bad Day for Sorry*

"Reinhart manages to braid a complicated plot into a tight and funny tale. The reader grows to love Cherry and her quirky worldview, her sometimes misguided judgment, and the eccentric characters that populate the country of Halo, Georgia. Cozy fans will love this latest Cherry Tucker mystery."– Mary Marks, *New York Journal of Books*

"In HIJACK IN ABSTRACT, Cherry Tucker is back—tart-tongued and full of sass. With her paint-stained fingers in every pie, she's in for a truckload of trouble."– J.J. Murphy, Author of the *Algonquin Round Table Mysteries*

Still Life In Brunswick Stew (#2)

"Reinhart's country-fried mystery is as much fun as a ride on the tilt-a-whirl at a state fair. Her sleuth wields a paintbrush and unravels clues with equal skill and flair. Readers who like a little small-town charm with their mysteries will enjoy Reinhart's series." – Denise Swanson, *New York Times* Bestselling Author of the *Scumble River Mysteries*

"The hilariously droll Larissa Reinhart cooks up a quirky and entertaining page-turner! This charming mystery is delightfully Southern, surprisingly edgy, and deliciously unpredictable." – Hank Phillippi Ryan, Agatha Award-Winning Author of *Truth Be Told*

"This mystery keeps you laughing and guessing from the first page to the last. A whole-hearted five stars."– Denise Grover Swank, *New York Times* and *USA TODAY* bestselling author

Portrait Of A Dead Guy (#1)

"*Portrait of a Dead Guy* is an entertaining mystery full of quirky characters and solid plotting...Highly recommended for anyone who likes their mysteries strong and their mint juleps stronger!" – Jennie Bentley, *New York Times* Bestselling Author of *Flipped Out*

"Reinhart is a truly talented author and this book was one of the best cozy mysteries we reviewed this year." – *Mystery Tribune*

"It takes a rare talent to successfully portray a beer-and-hormone-addled artist as a sympathetic and worthy heroine, but Reinhart pulls it off with tongue-in-cheek panache. Cherry is a lovable riot, whether drooling over the town's hunky males, defending her dysfunctional family's honor, or snooping around murder scenes." — *Mystery Scene Magazine*

NC-17

Maizie Albright Star Detective #3

LARISSA REINHART

Past Perfect Press

NC-17, Maizie Albright Star Detective #3

Copyright © 2018 by Larissa Reinhart

Paperback: 978-1-7323516-6-0

Hardcover: 978-1-7323516-7-7

Library of Congress number 2018913129

Author photograph by Scott Asano

Cover Design by The Killion Group, Inc.

Past Perfect Press

This is a work of fiction. Names, characters, places, and incidents are either the products of the author's imagination or are used fictitiously, and any resemblance to actual persons, living or dead, business establishments, events, or locales is purely coincidental.

Printed in the USA

Books by Larissa Reinhart

Maizie Albright Star Detective Series

15 MINUTES

16 MILLIMETERS

A VIEW TO A CHILL

NC-17 (2018)

18 CALIBER (2019)

A Cherry Tucker Mystery Series

PORTRAIT OF A DEAD GUY (#1)

STILL LIFE IN BRUNSWICK STEW (#2)

HIJACK IN ABSTRACT (#3)

DEATH IN PERSPECTIVE (#4)

THE BODY IN THE LANDSCAPE (#5)

A VIEW TO A CHILL (#6)

A COMPOSITION IN MURDER (#7)

Novellas

"A CHRISTMAS QUICK SKETCH"

in SLEIGH BELLS AND SLEUTHING (box set)

THE VIGILANTE VIGNETTE

Audio

PORTRAIT OF A DEAD GUY

STILL LIFE IN BRUNSWICK STEW

Box Set

CHERRY TUCKER MYSTERIES 1-3

A Finley Goodhart Crime Caper Series

PIG'N A POKE (prequel, short story)

THE CUPID CAPER

Claim Your Free Story!

PIG'N A POKE, A Finley Goodhart short story (prequel)

When a winter storm traps ex-con Finley at the Pig'N a Poke road-house, she finds her criminal past useful in solving a murder.

To keep up with Larissa's latest releases, contests, and events, please join her newsletter: http://smarturl.it/larissanewsletter and receive *Pig'N A Poke* as a gift. Note: Larissa will not share your email address and you can unsubscribe at any time.

Thank you!

Larissa

Acknowledgments

To Ritter Ames, Kim Killion, and Terri L. Austin, a huge debt of thanks for their support and patience with me in getting *NC-17* published. I couldn't have done it without their help.

I also need to thank my review team for their patience! To my newsletter pen pals for their support. Also thank you to my Facebook group, The Mystery Minions, for your continual cheering.

Minion Agnes Hoepker (Gladys) for being a good sport for not only using her name as a slightly corrupt probation officer but for also letting me use her office nickname.

And to Kristine Zepf for her advice on coma victims.

To David and Melinda Bakara of EXPEDITION: BIGFOOT! in Blue Ridge, Georgia. Your museum is amazing and you were incredibly hospitable. Thanks for telling me so many great stories!

Thanks to Peachtree City, Fayetteville, and Senoia for their continual inspiration in my "The Devil (Hollywood) Came Down to Georgia" theme for the Maizie Albright stories.

Thank you to my friends and family for all your support, particularly Mom, Gina, Bill, Hailey and Lily! And as always, Trey and the girls. And Biscuit. xoxo

To Sophie & Luci & Hailey & Lily
Study hard but don't forget life's best mysteries aren't meant to be solved.

Preface

The **Motion Picture Association of America (MPAA) film rating system** is used in the United States and its territories to rate a film's suitability for certain audiences based on its content.

NC-17 – Adults Only

No One 17 and Under Admitted. Clearly adult. Children are not admitted.

Maizie Albright's newest clients:
Ages 15, 14.75, and 14.5.
Grade 10 at Black Pine High School
Home of the Tree Toppers
in Black Pine, Georgia.
Also home to Bigfoot.
#Allegedly

ONE

#MeTwont #HesDaBomb

---

*S*takeouts are not all they're cracked up to be. Unless you have a more realistic vision of a stakeout than I had. Or maybe a different mentor. One would think sitting in a truck together for hours on end might lead to scintillating conversations. An intimate bonding through shared experience, cold coffee, and stale donuts. Even a little nookie.

Depending on your mentor, of course. But not Wyatt Nash of Nash Security Solutions.

I had high hopes for such stakeouts. But I've had high hopes for many things in my life. With twenty-five years of life experiences that mostly didn't meet expectations, I should've learned to lower the bar a bit. But with this man, hope —high or low— was all I had.

Nash was not only my boss and mentor. Nash was my dream guy. He's built like a demigod, with intense Paul Newman-blue eyes and a flash of dimple from his rare sexy smiles. A dry sense of humor. Loyal. Caring. Intelligent. Brave. Chivalrous to a fault.

A really big fault. As long as he's my boss, he won't date me, let alone share intimate bonding. Or nookie. And I get it. As an ex-actress who's had twenty years of Hollywooding, I've been

#metoo'd beyond recognizing what's normal for inappropriate behavior. When your personal self was a brand, "pimping" takes on meanings both literal and figurative. And thanks to my manager, my moral code included exception clauses.

But with Nash and me, the situation's different.

I know you've heard that before, but it's true.

Our mutual (I hope mutual) desire was born from respect as much as an attraction. Granted, that desire has been barely mentioned and not really acted upon in the few months we've known each other. Nash put the brakes on anything romantic until my two-year mentorship ended and we can officially partner.

That's a long time for mutual desire without action. Particularly for a red-blooded twenty-five-year-old such as myself. Nash is thirty-two. Which is like twenty-five in man years. Maybe less.

I believe, these brakes frustrate us equally.

I know I shouldn't be thinking about nookie during stakeouts. But I can tell Nash's thinking about it, too. It's in the way he grips his binoculars. Runs a finger in the neckline of his Lynyrd Skynyrd T-shirt. Rolls down the window of his truck to gulp fresh air. And cuts me the occasional gaze so heated, I get flash burns on my cheeks.

Also, because we live in Georgia and even though it's fall the temperature still feels like July. I have skin pale enough to guide ships to safe harbor on moonless nights. Like literally. It happened at Black Pine Lake once when I wasn't wearing bronzer.

This was also probably why our conversations were not so scintillating. The blood our brains need for conversation had been diverted to other areas of our bodies.

Like today, as we sat broiling in Nash's Silverado pickup, waiting for crazy Roger Price to finish his shift so we could follow him around town. This week we'd followed him to a variety of fast food restaurants, Walmart, Tractor Supply, and thirteen gas stations. (Roger's a scratch-off nut.) And I couldn't come up with anything more scintillating than talking about my ex-manager's (and still mother's) stupid wedding.

Stupid because she's marrying my ex-costar on *All is Albright*. My ex-fiancé. Unbeknownst to me, he was hired for that role. And now was hired to marry my mother. For the show.

Or so I keep telling myself.

As you can tell, I have issues when it comes to men. Maybe more so than with carbs. And that's saying something.

"Roger Price at eleven o'clock," said Nash.

My phone chirped. I gave eleven o'clock a glance, confirming Roger Price's quick stride from Radio Shack to his Nissan Sentra. Checked my phone. Another text from Vicki.

"This wedding is going to kill me," I said, my eyes back on Roger Price's Sentra. "Now she wants assorted safari animals. Non-carnivorous."

"What does that mean? Giraffes?"

"Maybe a zebra? Elephant? Her wedding planner is crazy. He already ordered the floral. The animals will eat her decorations."

"Better the decorations than the people. The guests are already at risk from Vicki's fangs."

We shared a grin. My heart tripped. A rush of blood shot through my veins and smacked my cheeks.

"Do you want to be my plus one? For the wedding?" I asked in a voice that I hoped sounded cool and not desperate. "I know it's not your thing at all. It'll be a zoo, regardless of the animals. All those photographers. Celebrity guests. And they'll be filming for *All Is Albright*...But the food will be good. Unless an animal gets into...Never mind."

"It sounds like a nightmare. But if you really want me, I'll go."

"Want you? Of course, I want you. To go. To the wedding. With me."

"Only for you, Miss Albright." He shook his head, but the bare glimmer of a smile hovered on his lips.

"For me?" I cut the excitement in my voice, tried to play it cool. "But you'll have to wear a tux."

"Stop trying to sweeten the deal."

Nash cut his eyes from Roger Price's car to me. Our gaze held.

His pale blue meeting my sea glass green. His eyes warmed, like a glacier melting. Mine probably darkened to the color of a jungle spring, considering the heat rushing through my body.

He leaned forward, placing his hand on the seat between us. My heart pounding, I adjusted my posture. Turned toward him with my knee on the seat. Licked my lips and tasted Rapture.

My Urban Decay lip gloss. Thankfully, I wasn't wearing Obsessed.

Nash took a deep breath. Reached behind him and zipped down the window. A breeze swirled inside the cab. It carried the scent of hot asphalt and burger grease, but also a refreshing gust of hope.

"Miss Albright," said Nash. "Maizie."

A car's motor started. Nash glanced out the windshield. Stiffened.

"What?" Roger Price was ruining our moment. Of all times to start his car. "What were you going to say?"

"He's leaving."

That was not what he was going to say. Or if it was, my desperation was worse than I thought. If I only I could woman up, get a spine, and confront him about our imaginary relationship.

Roger Price's car puttered from the parking lot. Nash jerked the gear shift of the Silverado and pulled out of the lot.

Instead of a spine, I searched for a non-scintillating conversation topic. Deflection was more in my wheelhouse. "I hope Roger goes to Chick-Fil-A again." I flipped my ponytail off my neck and fanned. "I'm starving."

"You just ate a bag of donut holes."

"Donut holes are more of an appetizer than lunch. Besides, Lamar gave me day-olds. I think their potency declines with freshness."

"Whatever you say, Miss Albright. But it'll have to be drive-through."

My heart thumped. Both at Nash's sweet acceptance of my food logic. And the thought of Chick-Fil-A.

Roger Price sped past Chick-Fil-A. I held back my disappointment. This day was turning out to be one long letdown. But I held
on to hope. For Roger to appease his hunger. Among other things.

"Hinky," said Nash. "Did you notice the Sentra doesn't have
plates? It had plates yesterday. Why would he take off the plates?"

"Roger is a weird guy. If he wasn't, his mother wouldn't have
him investigated."

An alarm shook my phone. I checked the time. "Shizzles. I have
to go."

"You can't go. We're tailing a guy."

"It's my probation volunteer work. I told them I'd be there at
three. I got the sweetest volunteer position. Assisting at the
community theater. I can't tell you how many phone calls that
took. They thought I wasn't really Maizie Albright. And when they
realized I was Maizie Albright, they couldn't believe I didn't want
to get paid. It took a lot of womansplaining about judge's orders,
probation, and whatnot to convince them to let this be my charity
work."

"I don't think your probation community service hours count
as charity."

"Are you sure?"

Nash nodded, focused on pacing the Silverado at a fair distance
from the Sentra. Black Pine wasn't very large. Tailing someone in
town was harder than you'd think. Unless you don't mind
appearing obvious.

"Roger looks like he's headed downtown," I said. "You could
drop me off at the office and I could walk to the theater."

"You need to schedule your volunteer hours after work."

"But—" My phone chirped. "Now Vicki wants a fitting
at four."

"A fitting?"

"Probably for my bridesmaid dress."

"You're working," said Nash. "We have a tail on Roger Price.
You're staying with me."

My toes curled at that declaration. I thumb-typed Vicki. Three texts popped onto the tiny screen of my flip phone before I could hit the send button. "Hells. She wants me to go to Giulio's fitting. That's totally awkward."

"Forget Vicki." Nash gritted his teeth. "Price is slowing."

I looked up. Price had pulled into a bank. Parked in front of the sidewalk. And exited the running car wearing a cow mask. "He certainly loves Chick-Fil-A. But that's a little strange, even for Roger. Wait, what is he carrying?"

"Miss Albright, call the police." Nash cut the wheel, blocking the drive into the bank's parking lot. He reached across me to pop open his glove compartment. "Stay in the truck."

"What was Roger carrying? It looked like—"

"A bomb."

"A bomb? For what? To rob the bank? Can you do that?"

"Apparently." He slipped his .38 Special from the glove compartment, checked the chamber, and opened his car door. "Wait for the police. Move the truck when they come. For now, don't let anyone else into the parking lot."

"I could give you back up."

Sliding out his door, he leveled me with a glance. "No, Maizie. Stay here."

"But Nash—"

"That's an order." The door slammed. Nash ran across the parking lot, slipping the .38 into his belt holster.

Used to taking direction, I didn't argue but dialed 9-1-1. Stayed on the line, as dictated by the dispatcher. Typed an answer to Vicki, as she demanded. Kept my eyes glued to the front door of the bank. Listened for sirens with my other ear. Checked my watch.

I was late for my charity — I mean, community service — work. But wouldn't a probation officer understand tardiness as the result of stopping a crazy bank robber? Even if I wasn't actually stopping the robber myself. Just sitting in a truck, waiting for the police to show so I could move the truck. While my partner was inside a bank that might blow up.

My gut tightened. *Please don't blow up the bank, Roger.*

Could you make a working bomb at Radio Shack? Roger Price excelled at making robots. And playing video games until three or four in the morning with people from "foreign parts." According to his mother. She had shown us a multitude of robots. His massive collection of gaming paraphernalia. His bedroom welding equipment.

Hells.

Roger's recent interest in gardening really worried his mother. He wasn't much of an outside guy. Or one to get his hands dirty, unless it was from model paint. But he'd been stockpiling fertilizer. Worried that her son was going to start a "drug farm," she hired Nash to watch Roger. She thought he was meeting dealers in his off hours. Not scarfing chicken sandwiches and robbing banks.

I hopped out of the truck to pace the parking lot. No one exited the bank. Wouldn't customers flee upon seeing a man enter wearing a cow mask? I chewed my lip. What if the security guard saw Nash's piece and thought him an accomplice? Except this was Black Pine, Georgia. The security guard was probably a distant relation of Nash's. Or at least recognized him as Wyatt Nash of Nash Security Solutions. There was probably a security arm of the Rotary Club or something.

Should I call Roger's mother?

Maybe after he's arrested.

And on that note, where were the police? I lifted the phone back to my ear to ask the dispatcher. A horn honked. I peered around the Silverado. A man in a Lexus rolled down his window. A man looking irritated and harried. Before I could explain, I heard the double buzz of another call. Checked my ID and saw it was my probation officer.

Hells to the shizzle.

"Move your damn truck," hollered Mr. Lexus.

"Just a minute and I'll explain," I called and heard the approaching sirens. I did need to move the damn truck. But not for this guy. "Sir, you need to back up."

"Get off your damn phone and move your damn truck."

In my ear, the buzzing of my probation officer continued. On the other line, the 9-1-1 responder asked me a question about what I could see. Although I didn't think she meant an irate man in a Lexus.

"Hold on," I said to 9-1-1 and pointed a finger at Lexus. "You hold on, too."

"Move your fat ass. Or I'll do it for you." Mr. Lexus opened his car door.

"That is so totally uncalled for, sir. I'm still in an adjustment phase to living in Georgia. I didn't get to eat like this back in California. And I no longer have a trainer. Thank God for small favors. But still, it's hard to control my eating and exercise unless I have someone berating me." I ran a hand over my ponytail. Off track again. And my spine still seemed to be playing hide-and-seek. "If you could please get back in your car, the police—"

The dispatcher spoke again. The buzzing from my probation officer cut off. My phone chirped six times. Texts from Vicki. The sirens grew louder. I shoved the phone in my pocket and turned toward the truck. Saw Mr. Lexus stalking toward me.

"I'm going to move, but you can't go into the bank right now. You need to back up and drive away. Please believe me, sir."

"Why the hell not?"

Beneath my feet, the ground rumbled a millisecond before I heard the explosion. The door of the bank blew open. Tore off its hinges. Sailed through the air. And slammed into Roger Price's Sentra.

TWO

#NoExcuses #YetAgain

---

*T*he next morning, while my head felt like it would explode — shooting off my neck and slamming into the ceiling, much like that bank door did to Roger Price's car — across from me, my probation officer, Gladys Hoepker calmly read the official report detailing the horrible blunders of my past. Probably current blunders, too. Although Gladys had the air of a much older woman, I guessed she was in her mid-thirties. Glossy blonde hair cut into a neat bob. An unbecoming, yet efficient suit. Nails trimmed and not painted. A smartwatch that caught her eye every three minutes. On the floor behind her desk, she had a bag of knitting supplies.

I focused on these details, trying to find the calm that Gladys so wonderfully maintained. I squirmed on the molded plastic chair. Pulled air through my nose and let it whoosh from my mouth. The ujjayi breath was supposed to be calming, but it made me lightheaded.

Okay, Maizie, that's because you're hyperventilating. Slow down your breath. Repeat your mantra. Nash is not dead. He's injured, but not dead. Everything's going to be okay.

"Everything is not okay, Miss Albright."

I stuttered out the last breath and blinked at my probation officer. "I'm sorry?"

Gladys glanced from me to her computer. "You keep saying that, but you're in serious jeopardy of breaking the terms of your probation."

"I didn't mean for you to hear that."

"Then quit talking while you're breathing." Gladys frowned. "The breathing itself is seriously annoying. But the chanting? That's got to stop. I'm about to ask for a psych counsel. You're lucky your drug tests are clean because my first inclination is you're on something."

"I'm trying to calm myself. My therapist Renata taught me—"

"What's your new therapist taught you? Oh right, nothing. Because you don't have one. Which is one of the conditions of your probation." Gladys pulled a sheaf of papers from her printer, then dropped them into the folder on her desk.

"I'm sort of working on that? Therapy is sort of expensive?"

"Listen, Maizie. This is not California. We don't bend rules for hotshot stars in Georgia. It's hard to believe a judge would let you leave the state when you're on probation. These guidelines he delivered should be a cake walk. And still, you screwed it up. Live with your father. Get a job. Stay clean. Seek therapy. No jobs associated with the TV or film industry. Community service. Check in weekly with your probation officer. How hard can that be?"

"I'm not a hotshot star. At least not anymore. And I don't think anyone ever called me hotshot?" I wasn't sure if anyone said "hotshot" in this century, but that wasn't pertinent. "Some events have been just out of my control—"

"Like a bank robbery."

I drooped in my chair. "Exactly."

"Let's see…" Gladys peered at the paper on her desk. "Or missing your last appointment because you were serving 'a subpoena to a woman whose pit bull treed you in her front yard' and you 'had to wait for a fireman to get you down.'"

"Yes. When you're chased by a dog ordered to 'kill,' there's a lot of motivation to get up a tree. Getting down is much harder."

"Appointment before that, you were up all night on a surveillance op at the Tiger Lounge and overslept."

"The husband was cheating with a stripper. The pictures inside the Tiger Lounge came out dark and grainy which isn't good for court, so we were waiting for him to exit the back for a rendezvous in the alley. Which, I mean, *ew*. At least wait until she gets off work, right? This guy was a real—"

"I don't care that this guy is a real anything, Maizie. I care about you meeting the terms of your probation. And one of those terms is making it on time to your weekly meetings. Another is to meet with a therapist. And do community service. None of which you've complied."

"I had my community service set up, Miss Gladys. But the play rehearsals didn't start until this week and—"

"And you still missed the first appointment." Gladys folded her arms and leaned back in her chair.

"Because there was a bank robbery and my partner was—"

"You know what this job gets me, Maizie?"

I shook my head.

"Excuses. I've heard so many excuses over my time, I could load a U-Haul and dump them on my employer, friends, and family anytime I don't feel like doing something." Gladys placed her hands on her desk and leaned forward. "You know what I don't do, Maizie?"

I had a feeling I knew, but I shook my head anyway.

"Give excuses for things I should be doing. I just do whatever I need to do. Because I'm supposed to do it. Like an adult does. That's why you're on probation, Maizie. You want the easy way out. If you don't feel like doing something, whether it's making it to your community service or—" Gladys tapped the paper "—saying no to a boyfriend when he wants to sell narcotics, you wimp out."

"I didn't know Oliver was selling Oxy. And I really wanted to make it to my community service, but by the time Roger Price blew up the bank—"

Gladys held her hand up. "Excuses."

I slid back in my chair and twisted a lock of my hair.

"Maizie, do you want to return to Judge Ellis in California and give these excuses to him? I don't know Judge Ellis, seems like a real nice guy to make these probation requirements so easy for you, but I don't think he wants to hear these excuses. You know what I think?"

I sighed.

"I think he'd rather revoke your probation than hear excuses. The only thing a judge wants to hear is 'yes, your Honor. I can testify that my client fulfilled the terms of her probation.'"

"Yes, ma'am."

Gladys pushed a piece of paper toward me. "Since you're unable to deal with the responsibility of finding therapy and community service work, I have done it for you. You will report to your community service work in one hour. And to make it even easier on you, your appointed psychologist, Dr. Trident, will assign the community service work."

"Trident like the gum?"

"No, Trident like the doctor of psychology who will be treating you." Gladys narrowed her eyes.

"I meant just in terms of spelling." I refrained from another deep breath. "Is Dr. Trident expensive?"

"He's doing it pro bono. Which means you need to make a doubly extra effort to work with him and make it to your sessions, Maizie. He's moving to the Wellspring Center. You will help him with the move today."

I wrinkled my nose. "I'm moving furniture?"

"And boxes. Cleaning. Painting. Whatever he needs to get his new office situated. Then for your community service, you'll be assisting at Wellspring wherever they need help."

"Where?"

"Black Pine Wellspring Center on Black Pine Mountain. It's

been remodeled by the new owners. At the turn of the last century, the original buildings were used by summer visitors for a European spa or something. It's changed hands a few times. I think it was a chicken farm for a while. Anyway, now it's back to the original idea. A health and wellness retreat. Which is why Dr. Trident moved his office there."

"Okay. The community theater was more in my wheelhouse than moving boxes, but I'm happy to volunteer." I studied the paper she handed me and folded it into a square. "Just an FYI, before I get to this I need to see my boss. He's in the hospital and if I don't mind the office, we could lose business. His ex-wife has a competing private investigation's office and—"

"No excuses, Maizie." Gladys stood, folded her arms, and leaned over me. "Here's an FYI for you. You're in violation of your probation right now. And FYI, I haven't reported you. Yet."

Yet. The most ominous word in the English language. Maybe followed by FYI.

THREE

#PresumedNotMissing #BigFootBelievers

---

*D*espite Gladys's dire warnings, I stopped at our office before going to the Wellspring Center. I needed to gather a few things — mostly my wits — and to check in with Lamar. Lamar owned our building and the Dixie Kreme Donuts shop under which Nash housed his private investigations office permanently and himself temporarily.

Nothing is better or worse than working in an office that smelled like donuts. Nothing is better or worse than finding your boss's Hugo Boss briefs in a file cabinet.

At least for myself, in both cases.

Lamar was also an ex-cop and silent partner of Nash Security Solutions. Or would be as soon as Nash's evil (generally) ex-wife, Jolene Sweeney, would sell her half of the business to him. Currently, Jolene had two security businesses. Half of Nash's and her own, Sweeney Security Solutions. Meaning she competed with herself. Spite does not provide good business acumen. It does, however, do an awesome job of ruining an ex-husband's business.

Which I guess, was the point.

I stopped in the Dixie Kreme shop — a habit I pretended was more about neighborliness and less about donuts — to give my hellos to the staff. I'd missed Lamar. He'd already gone to the hospital.

Wishing I had that option, I trudged up the stairs to Nash Security Solutions. As I climbed, I skipped the squeaky step that sounded like a gunshot and realized, in only a few months, how well I knew this building. I'd memorized the pattern of bricks peeking through the cracks in the plaster walls. Learned how to jiggle the key in the old brass lock because the humidity (and dirt) made the gears stick. Then to pull the door shut before pushing it open. I knew the water stains in the ceiling and the low spot on the wooden floor that made you trip and stub your toe on the metal leg of the desk. How to lift the drawers on the file cabinets so they wouldn't catch on their dented sides. The time of day the sun slanted through the blinds and heated the couch's wooden arm. It would singe your arm hair if you weren't careful.

Familiarity breeds endearment towards the contemptible, IMHO.

I loved the office. Despite its propensity toward grime. But today its familiarity gave me a sense of homesickness. Maybe similar to the first visit home from college. (In all honesty, I'd attended U Cal, Long Beach, as a commuter. But I assumed it would have that same bittersweet feeling.) Nash Security Solutions had become a home of sorts. And like a family, Nash Security Solutions had given me hope for stability and security, something an actor rarely feels.

Even at the pinnacle of my career in the starring role of *Julia Pinkerton Teen Detective* — when we were pulling in awards and the best prime-time spots — there was always the niggling feeling it could all disappear in an instant and without warning.

Because it could. And it did.

Acting was a career of risk, chance, and optimistic determination. You bet on the short odds. And when you get to a point where you could place your marker on a long shot for the big career boost, you'd best have a safety net. My manager, Vicki, was wise enough to understand this. Knowing the vagaries of child stars and their potential to screw the pooch, she invested in a platinum parachute.

For herself, apparently.

Leaving me with nothing but legal fees, student loans, and no understanding of real-world finance. But whatevs. I was still young. Vicki, not so much. I'd voluntarily (and by judge's orders) given up acting. I had chosen a new career. And still had a kick-ass wardrobe of designer outfits. For now.

This job was really hard on my clothes.

And the job had only Roger Price's mother as a client. That realization made my stomach clench and my lungs seize. I grabbed the edge of Lamar's La-Z-Boy, gripping the wooden frame that had wormed its way past the padding to the worn corduroy fabric. A paroxysm of weeping threatened to overtake me. But I couldn't cry and hyperventilate at the same time. I doubled over and let the blood rush into my head and clear up the mess.

A knock on the door threatened to tip me forward. But knocks (generally) meant business. I pinched the skin between my thumb and pointer finger hard enough to shut off the waterworks and force a gasp of pain.

"Come in," I wheezed.

The door swung open and three pairs of sneakers entered. Our clients didn't generally wear sneakers. I tipped my head up, following the denim-clad legs to T-shirts and three teenaged heads. Two girls and a boy. Adorbs, all three. Fresh and still young enough to not have become embittered with dashed dreams and threadbare hope. They were iGeneration.

I think embittered with dashed dreams was more of a Millennial thing.

"Are you okay?" said a girl with long brown hair. Cute freckling across her pert nose. Brown eyes. Total girl-next-door look. Except for the black tee featuring a cat with an evil grin, stating, "We're all mad here."

The teen who babysat my six-year-old half-sister wore mostly pink tees that spoke of pride in her Southern roots. And her love for hair bows, dogs, and lake hair.

To each his own.

I rose. Whooshed out a long breath. Slowly inhaled. And hiccuped. "I'm fine, thanks. What can I do for you?"

"We saw your online ad."

"We have an online ad?" Hope swelled and washed away the doubt and fear. "I didn't know Nash had made an online ad. That's great."

"This wasn't the place with the online ad," said the boy. He had rumply brown curls. Shorter than the girls, he jutted his chin in the air. Maybe to make himself feel taller. Or less short. His T-shirt featured a zombie eating a brain burger. Gross. But boys were gross. So, they say.

"Oh, right," said the girl. "The other place had the ad."

Doubt and fear returned. Particularly at the implication of "the other place."

"Who had the ad?" I said.

"Sweeney something-something," said the third teen. "We saw your sign when we were walking to the other place."

Sweeney Security Solutions. Jolene. Right around the corner. Of course, she had online advertising. And of course, we didn't.

"Shouldn't you be in school?"

This girl had a halo of tight, brown curls and beautiful olive skin. She probably didn't even need a six-step cleansing and moisturizing routine. The girl unfolded her arms and placed her hands on her hips. Her tee read, "Dead Inside."

I really hoped these kids were into irony. They certainly weren't into pink hair bows. I took a tiny step back and bumped into the La-Z-Boy.

"It's Saturday," said Dead Inside.

"Oh, right." I rubbed my head. "My days are a bit mixed up. I was at the hospital and the police station all night. I feel kind of jet-lagged."

"Police station?" said Cheshire Cat.

"Hospital?" said the zombie boy. "For a case?"

"Sort of. It's been a long twenty-four hours." I glanced at my watch. "And I need to get going. What can I do for you?"

"I'm Mara," said Dead Inside. She hooked a thumb at the other two. "He's Fred and she's Laci. We need a detective."

"For a school project? I'm short on time today, but you can come back later."

They shook their heads.

"No, it's for real," said Mara.

"How much do you cost?" said Laci. "As a detective?"

"If you're wondering how much a case runs, it depends on the type. For example, if you need a security evaluation on your home or business—"

"Not security. A missing person," said Laci.

"That's not as cut and dry as a security evaluation. That sort of work's hourly, but there may be incidental costs. Court documentation. Expenses. I'd have to look it up since we don't get a whole lot of missing person cases."

"You don't have any experience on missing person cases," said Fred, disappointment dusting his voice.

"I have some experience if you need an interview or something. Is it an article for your school newspaper? I'm really good at giving interviews. I've had a lot of experience in my past career as—"

Laci cut in. "Can you give us references?"

"References? For you?" Actually, I probably couldn't. Not with those cases. And where was this going? The clock was ticking. I needed to meet Dr. Trident before he called Gladys. If she didn't like my dog in the tree excuse, she really wasn't going to like the teenagers in the office excuse.

"My two most major cases had missing persons in them," I said quickly. "They were also murder—" I stopped myself, remembering to whom I was speaking. "But why don't you come back later? I'm sorry but I really—"

"You were going to say murder cases," said Mara. "That's

perfect. We need you to investigate a murder."

"We don't know if he's murdered," said Laci.

"He's probably murdered," said Mara.

"Hold up," I said. "What's going on with you three? You have a missing friend who may be murdered? And you want to hire me to investigate?"

They nodded.

"Are the police also investigating?"

They shook their heads.

I slowed down my speech and took another step back, rocking the chair. "You don't have anything to do with this missing proba- ble-murder, do you?"

"We were camping together." Mara glanced at Fred. He nodded. "And that's when Chandler disappeared."

"Oh my God. Why didn't you tell the police? What did Chan- dler's parents say? They must be out of their minds with worry."

"We don't really know his parents," said Laci.

"Holy shiz, that doesn't matter." I checked the tone of my voice and forced myself to calm. "You have to tell his parents. And the police."

They shuffled back a step, glancing at each other.

"We'll do it now." My thoughts hopped from every teens-in- the-woods horror flick to every teen-murder-pact news story I'd seen. I couldn't hide my shudder, but I maintained the even keel to my voice. A benefit of acting. Staying calm among possible teen killers. Surely Gladys would allow me the excuse of reporting a teen homicide if it included turning in the main suspects. "I'll go with you. It'll be okay. The police will appreciate you reporting it."

"We already went to the police. A week ago," said Fred. "They're not interested."

"What do you mean they're not interested? It's their job to be interested in missing and murdered people. Did you give them all the facts?"

"Of course," said Laci. "Our parents went with us and we filled out a report detailing everything that happened that night. And everything we knew about Chandler."

I watched them side-eye each other. "What about Chandler's parents? His parents must have noticed he's missing and gone to the police."

"He's not a minor," said Mara. "He's like twenty-something. We don't know his parents."

"You were camping in the woods with a twenty-something-year-old man?" My stomach turned over. I licked my lips and wondered if Chandler was missing because he was in jail. I hoped he was in jail.

"Chandler's the producer of our YouTube channel."

"Your YouTube channel has a producer?"

Mara nodded. *"Bigfoot Trackers.* Chandler's also the star. Fred and Laci are research and hosts, too. I direct. I prefer behind the scenes."

I would, too, if I had a Bigfoot show, but whatever. "Let me guess, you were vlogging on your camping expedition."

"Of course," said Laci. "Right behind the new Wellspring Center."

"Wait a minute. I'm supposed to go to the—" They didn't need to know that. "And Chandler struck out on his own, looking for Bigfoot, while you were..."

"Making s'mores," said Fred.

"Chandler was actually investigating Wellspring," said Mara. "Not Bigfoot."

"We're always investigating Bigfoot," said Fred. "That's our job."

"It's not a job unless you actually get paid," I said. "Back to Chandler..."

"We get paid. Ad revenue," said Laci. "Our Kickstarter blew the roof. And we have sponsors." She turned so I could read the Bigfoot logo patch on her backpack. Next to an even bigger logo for a camera. And one for a sports drink. Plus a patch for a s'mores-flavored protein bar.

"Way to rock the product placement," formed on my lips, but then I remembered I was adulting. I cleared my throat. "Anyway, you were making s'mores. Near the Wellspring Center. Why were you near the Wellspring Center?"

"We believe Bigfoot — Ouch. I have this theory about chickens — Stop kicking me, Laci." Fred rubbed his chin. "It's a good spot to look for Bigfoot."

"And Chandler never came back? Did you look for him?"

The teens cut their eyes to the ground.

"He told us not to leave the campsite," mumbled Fred.

"He never said goodbye or came back to get his stuff," said Mara. "That's why I know he's murdered."

"We looked the next morning," said Laci. "We couldn't find anything. And the police looked. They used a dog, but the dog traced his scent back to where he parked. His car was gone and they put out an APB. But they couldn't do much else."

"The police think he just took off?"

The three nodded, tight-lipped. Then glanced everywhere but at me or themselves.

"What else did the police say?"

"That he drove to the Atlanta airport and bought a ticket to Mexico," said Mara. "Chandler wouldn't do that. At least without telling us. The police said we were confused. But how could the three of us be confused at the same time?"

If they convinced themselves into confusion, that's how. A very teenager-y thing to do. I should know. I spent most of my teenage years in confused convictions.

"How close were you to the Wellspring Center?" I said.

Mara dragged her toe across the floor. A loopy line appeared in the dust. "Very close."

"Were you trespassing?"

More toe dragging. Laci stared at Fred. Fred focused on the dust trail pattern.

"If we weren't inside the fence, I don't think it counts as trespassing," said Mara.

Okay, then. "What do you think happened to Chandler? Fred, you answer. And no kicking, Laci."

Fred ran a hand through his curls, grabbed a handful, and squeezed. "Well...we've been investigating this area for a while. I have a hypothesis that Sasquatch would be attracted to the chicken farm. A perfect source of food, right there in his habitat. He might want retribution for humans tearing up the mountain to build stupid things like spas—"

"In any case, we have evidence Bigfoot's been there," interrupted Laci. "The Wellspring Center opened recently, and we were worried that they may be adversely affecting Bigfoot's habitat. But—"

"But then..." Fred gave Laci a side-eye. "Watching the construction and fortifications, we started thinking there may be another reason for the Wellspring Center to build there. Chandler was convinced of it. We began a plan to see if we were right."

"Fortifications?" I said. "I thought this place was like a health retreat or something."

"Okay, fences."

"Fences are not so unusual. Actually, they're pretty common."

"To keep people out?" said Mara. "Or to keep something in?"

"Wait, you think the Wellspring Center has something to do with Bigfoot? And Chandler got...kidnapped? Murdered? By the Wellspring Center? Like a *Stranger Things* plot? Or *Twin Peaks*?"

They refused to nod, but I could tell by their steely-eyed expressions that I'd hit on their suspicions. Teenagers hated being told their opinions weren't valid. They also didn't like to be patronized.

I wasn't left with much else to say.

"And hiring me to look into Chandler's disappearance would mean..."

"You need to help us investigate the Wellspring Center," said Fred. "To see if they're behind Chandler's disappearance."

"I have to do community service—I mean, volunteer work at

the Wellspring Center. And there's a Dr. Trident—" I wasn't going to get into the details of therapy with them. "Who needs my help."

"It's a perfect cover," said Mara, hopping in place. "That means this is meant to be. You're already there."

"Wait," said Fred. "We don't know if she's working *at* the Center or *for* the Center. You can't trust the first detective you find."

"Stop saying 'detective.' We're private investigators. And I'm not getting paid by the Wellspring Center. I've never even been there. Although I was supposed to be there about fifteen minutes ago."

The conversation had a "Who's on First Base" quality that made me dizzy. Or maybe I was still dizzy from hyperventilating.

"Anyway," I continued. "My working at the Center doesn't mean anything. It's a coincidence built on the fact that the Wellspring Center just opened. I'm going there because...Dr. Trident needs my help. Moving in."

"You're helping a doctor move their stuff in?" Mara's eyes slid to Fred. "Like moving furniture?"

"Possibly. And maybe painting." I controlled my shudder. My phone beeped. I glanced at the incoming number. Gladys. Shizzles. "I'm sorry. I've got to go."

"We'll talk later," said Mara.

I gave her a tight smile. I didn't have the heart to tell these kids that I didn't have the time or patience for a missing person-Bigfoot hunt. I had to seek out actual paying jobs. Deal with the disappointingly tangible demands of a business. And fulfill the terms of a genuine probation mandate.

Plus help a very real-life Nash. As long as he kept on living.

FOUR

#TridentGleam #TeenAgeMutantNinjas

---

*B*lack Pine Wellspring Center smelled like its chicken farm days hadn't been too far off in the past. Unfortunate for a beautiful tract of land cut out of the forest near Black Pine Mountain's peak. The main building had that gothic stone architecture popular more than a century ago with the turrets, heavy wood decor, and sweeping staircases. And the creepiness. I'm sure in its spa days, the rich carpetbaggers seeking to avoid the heat of a Southern summer thought it stately and comforting. Now it had the look of an old mental hospital favored on those ghost-hunting reality shows.

The teens' Bigfoot reports weren't helping.

While parking my dirt bike Lucky (because thus far, luck had kept me from dying in a hideous crash), I spotted several new buildings that looked modern and not-so-creepy. I hoped Dr. Trident would have an office in one of the smaller buildings.

No such luck.

Main building. East wing. Suite thirteen. It was like the gods of creepiness had conspired against him.

I found the suite, expecting heavy drapes, oriental rugs, and *The Haunting of Hill House* wallpaper. Instead, it had white plaster walls, plantation shutters on the windows, and bamboo floors. Not unlike many of the California therapist offices I'd visited over the years.

The bamboo floors soothed me. I'd been surrounded by pine and oak since my move to Georgia.

Except for a desk, no furniture yet. Which, I guessed, was why I was there. Or at least one of the reasons. I knocked on the suite thirteen doorframe to alert the man sitting behind the desk.

The knock echoed in the cavernous room, startling the doctor from his phone thumbing perusal. He jerked his head up, then adjusted his glasses and peered at me.

"I'm Maizie Albright," I said. "I'm your pro bono. And your community service volunteer. Happy to help. But I'm also in a hurry? My boss is in the hospital and I need to see him."

Dr. Trident rose from his desk and crossed the room to meet me. He looked older than me, though young to have his own office. He and Gladys had that in common. Unlike Gladys, he didn't dress the part to signify age and wisdom. Instead, he rocked a dreadlock man bun and beard. He also wore the loose pants and mandarin-cut top I recognized as a martial arts uniform from my years starring in *Kung Fu Kate*.

He patted my wrist while we shook hands, then gave me a short bow. Coming from California, I didn't find it odd. Many of the psychologists I knew liked to give their patients an East-meets-West psyche mashup.

"Excuse my attire, but I find it comfortable for moving day," he said. "The Center has a brand-new gym. I did my meditative exercises before arriving. Do you do meditative exercises, Maizie?"

"I like yoga breathing." I wasn't sure if that counted as exercise. But it sounded like something Dr. Trident would like to hear. I left off the part about my recent tendency to hyperventilate during yoga breathing which probably defeated the purpose. My ex-therapist, Renata, would call that a topic for the couch.

"Excellent. We'll work on that."

Which left me confused. Unless he guessed I hyperventilated.

"I understand you're a television star," he said.

"Not anymore. I started working in the industry when I was a toddler and had a lot of success in my teens. *Julia Pinkerton, Teen Detective* was my big breakout role." I shifted, not sure if I was supposed to delve into couch topics or if this was just a community service work introduction.

"I work exclusively with celebrity clients. One could say it's my calling." He smiled, showing me a beautiful set of veneers. "I'm here now that the entertainment industry has set up in Black Pine."

"Yes, it's kind of ironic for me. Since my probation sent me home to get away from the industry."

"Many industry professionals need help. Maybe you've heard of me?"

To be polite, I gave him a faint smile instead of a head shake.

"Selfie?" He held up his phone. "We can Instagram our first meeting. Hashtag-doctor-celeb-meet-and-greet."

Startled, I smiled up at the camera he'd already tilted above us. I wondered which meeting he'd post, community service or therapy. Neither did me any favors. Both smacked of all kinds of patient-doctor confidentiality issues.

But at least he knew how to hold a camera to get the most flattering shot.

*D*r. Trident gave me a quick tour of the main building, then walked me to the parking lot. We stopped for "photo ops" along the way.

"How long will this take?" I said.

"According to your probation officer, you need a lot of hours. But don't worry. I talked to the manager and he feels there's a lot of work here to keep you busy. You'll accumulate time in a jiffy."

I was pretty sure time accumulated whether one was doing community service or not. In fact, an accumulation of time was something I needed to acquire, not spend. Lamar waited for me at the hospital. And Roger Price's mother waited for her debriefing.

Which I wouldn't mind putting off. At the police station last night, our conversation had an accusatory ring. Kind of screaming ring, too. Somehow, I had to convince her to pay for our services. My breath tightened, and a squeezing pain lit my chest. I stopped to yoga breath and repeat my mantra.

Dr. Trident halted his forward stride to glance over his shoulder. He rushed back. "Are you all right?"

I held up a finger. Leaned over until the blood funneled back to my brain. Straightened. And gulped air. "Fine."

"Is it the children? Do you find them distressing?"

"Why would I find children distressing? Wait, what?" I jerked my head up. Mara, Fred, and Laci loitered against a moving truck, watching me.

I eased closer to Dr. Trident and lowered my voice. "What are they doing here?"

"Same as you. Helping me move in. They're just volunteers. Are they a trigger? Pediaphobia?"

"Pedia-whasit?"

"Fear of children. It's not uncommon. Shall we try some behavior therapy?"

"My behavior's fine. I'm more concerned with theirs. Hang on." I strode forward and stopped before the three, accosting them with a fierce whisper. "What are you doing here?"

"Helping you," said Mara.

"I don't need this kind of help."

"Maizie," said Dr. Trident. "Don't waste our time."

I glanced over my shoulder.

"You'll have a chance to get to know each other in a moment. I have a meeting and I hate to remind you, but you were late."

I sighed and slid in line next to the reason I was late. Then scooted several steps to my left, leaving a gap between us.

For someone in a hurry, Dr. Trident spent an inordinate amount of time explaining how to carry boxes and furniture. How to bend our knees. How to measure doorways. How to use an elevator.

I found myself leaning against the truck with crossed arms,

gazing into space. Trying not to think about Nash. Or roll my eyes at Dr. Trident's excessive mansplaining. I glanced at the teens. And realized we all had the same posture and glazed eye syndrome.

Old habits die hard.

But didn't they have homework to do? People their own age to stalk? Bigfoot to capture?

Dr. Trident clapped his hands and our small group simultaneously straightened. "Can you repeat what I just said?"

The kids and I mumbled something about elevators, safety, and knees.

"Good," he said. "Are we cool?"

We stared at him. Then gave him an almost imperceptible nod that we understood his archaic slang.

"Great. We'll get ice cream when you're done."

I felt my spirits rise.

"And no worries, it's gluten and dairy free."

And crash.

As Dr. Trident strode into the building, I turned to the teens. "Seriously, why?"

"Dr. Trident said you're here for community service," said Laci.

"That does not answer my question."

"What'd you do?" said Mara.

"Again. Why are you here?"

"We want to get to know you," said Fred.

"Google me. I have work to do."

"We know," said Laci. "You seem kind of busy, so we thought this would be a good way to—"

"We thought you were a detective," said Mara. "But community service? Really?"

I'll admit, hits to my vanity still stung like nettles. Luckily, acting builds up a thick skin of wounded pride. "It's a long story. It was in the news."

They wrinkled their noses.

"It's not that bad. Entertainment news mostly. Look for the *Julia Pinkerton, Teen Detective* fan blogs if you want a gentler read."

They blinked at me.

"Julia whatta?" said Laci. "Is that someone for your references? Wikihow said we should ask for references."

"You don't know *Julia Pinkerton*? What about *Kung Fu Kate*?"

Nothing.

I wasn't going to go through my list of TV movies. *Julia Pinkerton* wasn't on that long ago. How could they not know *Julia Pinkerton*? It'd won Teen Choice awards and was nominated for an Emmy. "What about *All is Albright*?"

Laci snickered.

Of course, they'd seen Vicki's reality show. "If you've seen *All is Albright*, you know why I'm here." They shook their heads and I tried to hold back the surprise from my voice. "Really? I'm Maizie Albright."

They shrugged.

"I was an actress. Until I was on the reality show, *All is Albright*. Although that's also acting."

"Have you done anything lately?" said Mara. "Like on Netflix? Prime? Hulu?"

After my head shake, she shrugged. "Sorry. We mostly watch YouTube. I've heard of *All is Albright* but I've only seen a few clips. Pretty funny."

It was a reality show, not a comedy. But I supposed one could argue, that sort of reality show was one and the same.

"Doesn't matter," I said. "Now I'm a private investigator. But maybe that didn't make the YouTube clip. Well, I'm training to be a private investigator. It takes two years of apprenticeship in Georgia to get a license."

"That means you don't have references." Mara pulled a folded paper from her pocket and shoved it at me. "Here's Chandler's picture, anyway."

I glanced at the photo of a mid-twentyish blond man in full hiking gear. The picture looked like they'd made a screenshot from a video frame. Did they even know him?

"Thanks." I slipped the the paper into my pocket. "Since you're here, let's focus on moving these boxes now. The faster I get it done, the quicker I can get out of here."

"Yes, we should start." Mara jumped into the back of the truck. Began pushing boxes toward us.

I was surprised at their willingness to help. Teens had changed a lot since my day.

Fred pulled off a box and dumped it into my arms. "Here you go."

"Thanks."

I trudged toward the side door of the Wellspring Center's main building. Shifted the box in my arms to grab the handle. The box was too heavy. I turned to ask for help.

The kids had disappeared.

FIVE

#NiceCream #ChickenDance

I set the box down and considered reporting the teens. They were obviously using my community service to play the Bigfoot equivalent of *The Goonies*. Which meant they were trespassing. However, my short visit with Dr. Trident caused me to doubt my ability to explain to him the young YouTubers stalking tendencies without considerable time and effort. It'd be much easier to find them myself.

Jogging through the building, I glanced down halls and unlocked doors. Exited out the back into a lush garden with winding paths leading to the other buildings. Asked a couple sitting on a bench if they'd seen the kids. At their no, I turned around and reentered the building. Tried a side door in the west wing that exited to the parking lot. Reentered. Rode the elevator, asking the few people I passed if they'd seen the kids. Poked in more unlocked rooms.

Nothing.

Okay, then. They must have bounced. They'd judged me on my community service and my lack of references and bailed.

I admit to being a teensy bit hurt. I'd built a previous career on being a teenager and appealing to teens. Or so I'd thought. I had a soft spot for them, particularly considering I never got to experience the rites of passage typical to American high schoolers. If I'd had the chance of participating in Bigfoot hunts on the weekend instead of *Teen Vogue* shoots, I would have become a stronger person. I was sure of it.

Part of me wanted to help them look for their friend. Too bad they hadn't come to see me before my life literally exploded.

*F*inished with unloading the boxes — by myself — I sat with Dr. Trident in the Wellspring Center's cafe, Café. Café was one of the new buildings set in the back garden, or the plaza as Dr. Trident called it. We sat at a patio bistro table, gazing at the stone monstrosity called the "Center," housing the main offices and suites. I tried not to think of *The Shining*. Or if the Center had eaten the children.

"What do you think?" Dr. Trident sipped distilled water while I ate.

"You need more volunteers. Or more mature ones."

"I meant the ice cream," he said. "You don't consider yourself mature?"

I made a play of snorting and waving off the mature comment. "The ice cream's not bad. It has a slightly gummy texture and kind of a menthol flavor, but it is refreshing."

"We use an herb blend that has carminative qualities similar to menthol. Good for your stomach. Our chef developed the ice cream from soy milk, protein powder, and monk fruit sweetener."

It saddened me when chefs developed instead of cooked. But at least the healthy choice had a calming effect. I placed my mantra on hold for a minute and enjoyed the stillness of the Wellspring Center. For a newly opened place, the stillness was surprising. I supposed the guests were retreating. In silence.

"Feeling better?" he asked.

"You noticed?"

"It's my job to notice." He shot me a Trident-styled grin. "But it's not hard when your breathing is so labored."

"I'm worried about my boss. He was recently hurt in an accident. Well, not exactly an accident. More like a work-related catastrophe. But still, I hate to think of him lying in the hospital alone. Lamar will be there, but he has to supervise the donut shop. And there's no one else but me to watch over my boss."

Dr. Trident patted my hand. "Why do you feel responsible for him?"

"I guess I feel responsible for the office. We're on shaky ground financially. Our new competitor is my boss's ex-wife, so that's been rough on him."

"You're worried about your job?"

"I need my job. But the office is all my boss has. His ex-wife already cleaned him out of everything else. I have to make sure we stay afloat while he recovers."

"You have a lot of animosity toward his ex-wife."

"I do?"

"I can tell. Is it her ability to undermine your financial security?"

"Um." I think it was her ability to undermine my relationship with Nash, but that was for the couch.

Wait. Were we doing the couch here?

He gripped my hand. "Maizie, don't let someone else's success compromise your future triumphs."

"Okay?" I slid my hand out. Renata hugged, but we didn't do a lot of hand-holding.

A man stopped before our table, thankfully ending this non-couch confab. Like my father, he had the beard, ruggedness, and camouflage favored by local mountain men who "dealt" but didn't "fraternize" with Black Pine's nouveau wealth. The three teens stood behind him, shifting glances between the man, us, and themselves.

"Are these yours?" The man jerked his thumb behind him. "I found them nosing around the back buildings."

"They are, Everett." Dr. Trident motioned for the three to sit. "Did you get lost?"

"Yes," said Mara. "We were lost."

They were so not lost.

Everett agreed. "They were snooping."

"We're interested in architectural history," said Fred. "We're taking AP Art History."

"This area is an important landmark, you know." Laci tossed her long, brown hair behind a shoulder and raised a brow.

"That's a crock of bull," said Everett.

"It's true," I said, meaning the crock of bull but intimating their fake class. "My probation officer told me the Wellspring Center was originally a spa for rich Southerners. And then a chicken farm."

"We were looking for chickens," said Mara.

"It does smell like there could be chickens." Wait. Why was I helping them? "But I haven't seen any chickens."

"Stay away from the outbuildings," said Everett. "We're in the process of tearing them down. We're liable if you get hurt. These old buildings could kill you."

"That is sage advice," said Dr. Trident.

We watched Everett stomp off, and Trident grinned at the teens. "Who wants ice cream?"

They shook their heads.

"We have a lot of homework," said Mara. "It's getting late. We just wanted to say goodbye to Maizie."

Yeah, right. I jerked myself out of the post-ice cream stupor. "I need to get to the hospital before visiting hours close."

"Remember what I told you," said Dr. Trident. "I'll see you tomorrow."

I'd already forgotten what I was supposed to remember, but I promised myself to pay better attention during the real couch session. I took the brick path toward the castle. The teens trailed behind me. Raised gardens filled with a mix of wildflowers, herbs, and bushes nestled between junctures in the path. Small wooden signs pointed to various buildings among the flowers. The largest building was called "Physical Life." A glorious multi-storied structure fronted with a wall of glass, so viewers could see the evidence of guests getting physical. Although none were currently.

We strolled the paths and stopped beneath the back portico of the castle. The area had lost its creepiness. And smelled less like chicken. More like flowers.

"I think I like this place," I said, opening the heavy oak door. Flowers had been carved into the lintel and the wrought iron handle was shaped like a ginkgo leaf. I got the vibe now. Seeing how it would appeal to celebs who dug quirky, historic places. The Wellspring Center made you feel like an appreciator of quirky and historic.

Mara rolled her eyes, suggesting my IQ had been lowered by brick paths, carved lintels, and flowers. "When can you start working?"

"I just finished working. Remember? Me with the boxes? While you were snooping? That's your freebie. I distracted Dr. Trident with actual work while you were free to snoop."

Their adorable faces looked less adorable when sneering.

I released the handle. "I'd really like to help you. But if your friend is missing, the police are your best bet."

"We told you about the police," said Fred. "There are bigger forces at stake."

"I think that's a mixed metaphor. And there is nothing sinister about the Wellspring Center other than that weird chicken smell. Which may not be chickens, by the way. Because I'm pretty sure this place is vegan."

"Don't you care that Chandler disappeared? He could be dead," said Mara. "Or hurt."

"Of course, I care." Although I wasn't sure if Chandler was real. But I wanted to care. "How are you getting home?"

"We biked."

"On the mountain road? Are you crazy? The SUVs take those

corners way too fast. I'm scared I'll be run off the mountain."
Seeing their look, I checked myself. "I drive a dirt bike. For now."

"We take mountain trails in the forest," said Fred. "Is the dirt
bike part of your probation?"

"No." My cheeks heated. "It's a long story."

"You have a lot of long stories," said Laci.

"My life is a little complicated," I said stiffly. "And that's why I
can't go all *X-Files* with you. I'm super busy."

"Everybody's busy," said Laci. "You have to make time for
what's important."

"Exactly." I'd gone all day without visiting Nash at the hospital. Talk about important. The sharp edge of panic ripped at my
lungs. I yanked open the heavy door before the teens could
witness me hyperventilating again. Timing my breath to my steps,
I fought for self-control and wormed through Oriental-carpeted
halls hung with botanical prints. Found the front lobby with its
turn-of-the-century heavy wood decor.

I'd parked Lucky on the far side of the lot. Close to the forest
where I wouldn't have to experience a pea gravel kick-start.
Rolling Lucky onto the dirt, I heard a call from one of the teens. I
left Lucky and moved closer to the woods, wondering if I could
find my way to whatever dirt bike track or old logging road they'd
used. Riding mountain roads on a dirt bike did scare me. Nash
often lectured me on turning into road kill.

Nash.

I leaned over. Mantra'd. Rose and studied the forest to draw
my focus away from my wounded boss. And spotted the teens.
Without bikes.

Decidedly skulking.

SIX

#TheNotQuiteSecretGarden
#RazorWhyre

---

*H*ells. They were going to get into trouble. I should've made the kids come with me. Or gone with them to the mountain trail shortcut. I'd just left them to trespass on their own.

Adulting sucked.

Leaving Lucky, I crashed into the woods after them. Switched to stealth mode and picked my way through trees, brambles, and thick vines until I heard the high schoolers again. Talking about chickens.

"Carcasses would show…" Fred's lecture was drowned in a gusted rattle of leaves.

"I'm not looking for a chicken burial mound," said Mara. "That's stupid."

"What if they used the chicken mound to bury other…you know?" said Laci. "Like Chandler?"

"They didn't have a graveyard for the chickens," said Mara. "Besides *he* would've eaten everything."

"You don't think there would be a bone cache?" said Fred.

"Possibly. But not here. It'd be deeper in the woods."

Were they looking for Chandler or chickens?

The teens stopped talking. I halted, fearing I was lost. Hugged a tree and talked myself out of a panic attack. Spotted the Physical Life building to my right. I scurried through the woods to the outside of Wellspring's rear grounds. Behind the huge sports facility was a wooden privacy fence. It continued its run alongside the forest ending somewhere in the distance. The fence rose above my head, but I could see the far-off top of a greenhouse somewhere inside.

Likely, a vegetable garden. Dr. Trident had said Wellspring grew their own produce and herbs.

Stepping out of the forest, I scoped for the little delinquents. Spotted them about a football field away as they darted from the forest toward the fence. Fred leaned over. Laci helped Mara climb onto his back. Mara hoisted herself over the fence. Fred and Laci took off, running alongside the fence toward the far reaches of the property.

I hollered, but they were too far away. Or ignoring me. I knew I couldn't catch Fred and Laci. I also knew I wouldn't get over that fence. But I might find a gate and Mara before she did whatever they were doing.

The passage between the garden fence and gym was a tighter fit than it looked from the woods. The fence has been built at the edge of the gym's cement slab. Giving me about a one-foot gap. I slipped in sideways. Right arm. Right shoulder. Right leg. And felt the crush of the softer parts of my body between wood and wall. I sucked and straightened, then inched along with my back against the sports facility.

Getting stuck between a gym and vegan garden seemed an apropos fate.

I changed my mantra to one vowing exercise and healthy eating if I could squeeze out with all my parts intact and within the next hour. I scraped along, popping crystals from my Dries Van Noten Haidet T-shirt like a Hansel and Gretel breadcrumb trail.

I hoped my future mammograms would be more comfortable.

Eventually, my right shoulder connected with open air. Like a sausage freed from its casing, I oozed from the passage. Dusted my shirt of loose threads and dangling crystals. Checked my surroundings. I was on the back side of another fence. This one chain link. And hidden by a series of hillocks covered in shrubbery.

Behind me, there was the ridiculously long and tall garden fence stretching into the distance where it looked like it made a right and traversed the back of the property in an L shape. No pretty gardens or paths here. Cleared land that had yet to be used. An open field with crumbling buildings, scrubby vegetation, and a bit of timber in the distance.

I followed the wooden fence, searching for the garden entrance. Twenty yards ahead, I spied a gate. Much panting later, I stood before the wooden gate. This handle was steel and not decorative. And locked with a high-tech security panel.

Meaning Mara should really not be in the garden.

Calling for Mara, I followed the tall fence to where it cut right and stretched along the back of the property. A couple football fields-sized walk-jog later, the wooden fence ended on the east side of the property. No gate on this end. But another fence began.

Chain link trimmed with rolled razor wire.

I studied the east fence and wondered why a holistic wellness resort needed razor wire. Beyond the chain link, the dense forest climbed the mountain. The razor wire could protect celebrity retreaters from paparazzi. Or keep out local ne'er-do-wells looking to score a free spa day.

But the woods appeared thick. The trespassers would have to be determined to break in. They'd do better squeezing between the gym and garden fence. Which, I realized, was my only exit unless I found a way back into Wellspring's plaza area.

And no way was I scaling razor wire. I'd already ruined my top. I didn't need to tear up my jeans.

I studied the barren area of the Center's back property. If I followed the chain link, I'd eventually reach the plaza. Thick timber grew around the fence farther down. The Center's imposing castle-like towers rose in the distance. The flower hills hid everything else. They reminded me of the grassy dunes used to create a windbreak at a beach. Minus the sand.

I hiked back, wondering why the Center left this acreage deserted. What was the point of running the fenced area like an L when there were all these old fields in the middle? And why only one gate into the garden? That must be totally inconvenient.

I tell you what's totally inconvenient. Forcing myself to hike along a garden fence that ended in nothing. For no reason. When I had a man in the hospital waiting for me.

Why did I do this?

Right. Mara, Fred, and Laci. Who were probably home by now. Not studying for their AP-whatever. Maybe Nash would have an opinion on the juvenile delinquents and their suspicious ways.

Wait. Nash.

I felt the oncoming rush of anxiety. Placed a hand on the garden fence to catch my breath. And heard an odd squeak and thump combo. I squinted, searching the barren wasteland, then the flowering hill barrier. The Wellspring Center's local redneck, Everett, had emerged between the giant flower mounds, pushing a wheelbarrow.

With a rifle holstered over one shoulder.

SEVEN

#McEverettsGarden
#TheKidsAreNotAlRight

*E*verett Lawson with a rifle and a wheelbarrow did not make for an inviting figure. In fact, he looked like he came out of the old Wellspring Center's central casting.

His eyes were on the wheelbarrow. I did a quick dance, then shot off toward the crumbling remains of a Gilded Age (or Chicken Age) barn. Mostly collapsed. Probably the type of building in his warning to the kids. The shack smelled like it had once been inhabited by a very old cow. And might have had bats living in it more recently, judging by the condition of the floor. Also by the absence of most of the roof. I didn't want to examine the ceiling's beams too closely.

I cowered near the open doorway. My shoulders hovered near my ears in expectant bat mode. My hand covered my mouth. Peering out, I watched for Everett Lawson.

At the wooden fence's gate, he parked the wheelbarrow. Adjusted the rifle. And craned his neck, looking around the back forty.

I ducked inside the nasty barn. Held my breath. And peeked again.

The gate was open. But no Everett. What kind of vegetables demanded a high-security gate?

I could think of a plant that wasn't a vegetable that warranted privacy. A plant popular among celebrities that could easily be sold at Wellspring. But most celebs had prescriptions for such vegetation. And people to fetch their 'scrips. That's a lot of trouble to hide a pot farm unless it was some extra-fabulous blend.

The Wellspring Center was going to be a very popular celeb hangout if that were true.

But more importantly, how was Mara going to get out? I now understood why the kids were focused on the garden. Looking to score. Possibly to sell. Which might also explain their "missing friend."

They seemed like such nice kids. Albeit a skosh weird. But not the type to be involved in a high school drug ring.

I wondered if people had thought the same about me as a teen. Growing up on sets, it was harder to stay away from drugs than it was to find them. Vicki tried to curtail that issue. She helicoptered, telling any and all I had enough trouble focusing on work.

And unless it was diet drugs, we weren't interested.

Unfortunately, there were enough sirens in the deep blue of Hollywood, they'll eventually drag you overboard with the right call. My particular song was a mixture of "you look like you need to relax" and "this will really piss off your mother."

Maybe these kids were facing a similar kind of pressure in a different way. Maybe Mara deserved getting busted. But a fifteen-year-old does not want to get caught pilfering from a drug farm by a testy redneck toting a rifle. Particularly fifteen-year-olds who took AP classes and grew up in a nice mountain town. Instead, I could probably give her a scared-straight testimonial and snap her out of this phase.

I ducked from the shed and jogged across the field. Inside the gate, I halted. Furrows lined the open field in neat rows. A small tractor had been parked on the far side. No cute, curly-haired fifteen-year-old skulking in the background.

And the pot looked a lot like tomatoes.

I craned my neck, trying to see farther into the acreage. Drying corn stalks and old bean teepees. And were those…peppers? The greenhouse was situated at the crook of the L-shape. Maybe Mara had gone there? I imagined her trapped like a rat in a bizarre tomato-pot farm maze.

Moving toward the greenhouse, I paused to ease around the piled fertilizer bags. The same brand Roger Price had stockpiled.

My breath jerked. I gasped and felt my lungs snatch for air.

Craptastic. Now I couldn't even look at a bag of fertilizer without hyperventilating.

My brain ran like a movie reel I couldn't turn off. From Roger's fertilizer collection to watching him waltz into the bank. To Nash grabbing his gun and running after him…

Grabbing my chest, I bent over. A bad idea. The smell caused my stomach to clench. My lungs fought to expel the noxious air as they pulled more in. Spots danced in my eyes. My hands shot out and hit the bags as my knees buckled.

Something prodded my back. Everett Lawson's voice broke through the paroxysms.

But the barrel of his gun was more effective at snapping me out of it.

"What in the hell are you doing?" Lawson repeated. "This is private property. You're trespassing."

Bent over, I swung one arm out and held up a finger.

"Get the hell out." The barrel of his rifle poked me again. "I'll not tell you again."

"A minute," I gasped. "Having a fit. Please."

The barrel pushed against my hip. "Have your fit outside. Who are you?"

I looked over my shoulder. "Maizie Albright." I pushed out the words between breaths. "I work for Dr. Trident. Just met you in Café. Can't breathe."

The barrel eased off my hip. "You shouldn't be back here."

"Okay." I slowly turned around and straightened, my hands out. "Please. I didn't mean anything."

"Move."

Carefully, I eased past him, keeping my back to the fence.

"Stay out of here."

"Sorry." I slipped out the gate and pulled it not quite shut.

Hopefully, Mara would find her way to this gate and skedaddle before Everett found her. Maybe she'd already gotten out. They'd given me the slip several times today already.

I had a bad feeling about this. The teens. The fences. Everett Lawson and his rifle.

I'd just left a girl to a man who seemed like he'd shoot first and ask questions later. Over a plot of tomatoes.

Something was amiss at Wellspring. Maybe the kids were right after all.

EIGHT

#VisitingHours #ComaToast

I walked the outside perimeter of the fence before giving up. My anxiety over Nash overrode the guilt I felt abandoning the kids. Aside from storming the garden or trying to convince Dr. Trident that a lunatic had been let loose in Wellspring's vegan paradise, I didn't know what else to do.

Per ushe for Maizie Albright.

My drive to Black Pine Hospital included pondering over how to locate the teens plus the odd fencing and gun-toting situation at Wellspring. But mostly I focused on staying alive. Dirt bikes on trafficked mountain roads don't mix well. As soon as I made more money, I'd trade Lucky in for an actual vehicle. But first I had to keep my job. Which meant finding more jobs for Nash Security Solutions. Since our only job had been a literal bust.

Seeing Nash was not going to be easy. My chest felt prepped to spasm as I parked at Black Pine Hospital. But the thought of the time I'd already wasted kept panic at bay. I sucked air slowly and fast-walked to the building.

I'd had my share of experience at Black Pine Hospital. My autographed picture with the third-floor nurses still hung in their station. I stopped to give them my greetings, then moved toward room 313. Outside the door, I found Lamar and met him with a hug. He handed me with a bag of day old Dixie Kreme Donuts from his shop.

"How is he?" I asked.

"Same," said Lamar. "Where've you been?"

"The meeting with my probation officer that I'd previously missed. She sent me to Black Pine Wellspring Center to meet my new therapist. And work for him as community service."

"That's not a conflict of interest?"

I shrugged. "As long as my therapy isn't done while we're working, I guess. Although I get confused knowing when we're on the couch and when we're off."

Lamar's eyebrows crept higher.

"Therapy slang. Do you know anything about the Wellspring Center? The grounds are amazing. It looks like they've done a major remodel. I also met some teens who seem obsessed with the place. Which is odd, but they may have a point—"

"You were doing community service with teenagers?" Lamar frowned. "That's not right. They should keep the juveniles separate from adult offenders."

"I'm don't think I really count as an offender," I said. "It was just a big mistake. That I'm now correcting. And the kids weren't doing any kind of service that I could tell."

"Is your probation officer with the city?"

"No, a private company. Black Pine Probation. Not so creative in the name department, right? But I guess it serves a purpose."

"They can't all be Dixie Kreme Donuts." He patted me on the shoulder. "Did you speak to the ATF investigator yet, hon'?"

I shook my head. "I've been at the Wellspring Center most of the day. These teens—"

"She'll be contacting you about Roger Price. Just a heads up. Make sure your paperwork on Price is in order. Sorry to cut you off, but I've got to check on a few things at work. You can tell me about the kids later." Lamar's lined face furrowed. "I know Nash'll be glad you're here. Tell him about the community service but keep it mellow. Nash worries about you. Even in his…current state. And we don't want to make his current state worse than it already is."

I felt my skin heat. "Of course."

"Bye Maizie." Lamar hugged me again. "Sorry to be in such a rush. I'm glad you're finally here."

Taking a deep breath, I entered the room. Nash lay in a hospital bed near the windows. More like occupied than lay. His massive body threatened to spill off the bed. They'd left his gown untied, but it still stretched snugly against his brawny shoulders. I'd searched for pajamas in the office but couldn't find any.

Which, at another time, would have provoked some interesting thoughts. But late last night, it made me cry, thinking about Nash catching a cold.

He appeared to sleep peacefully. But I'd never seen him sleep. I'd rarely seen him not in motion. Never lying down.

I approached the bed, wanting to stroke his rugged face. But with all the tiny cuts, I feared causing him pain. More scars to add to his collection. He wasn't a beautiful man. But even asleep, he had a swarthy, action-hero quality. A quality for which many leading men would give their eye teeth. (Many had. By filling them down.) The bandage taped to the back of his head covered the horrible gash I'd glimpsed before they'd put him in the ambulance.

After I'd found him in the smoke-filled bank.

I felt panic rise and squeeze my chest, but I drew out a shaky breath. Battened down the panic. Took his large hand in mine and squeezed.

"I'm sorry I wasn't here sooner. My probation officer took me off theater work and had me hauling boxes. I broke one nail and ripped another, but I'll have Tiffany at LA HAIR fix them. I could use a manicure anyway."

The monitor above his bed beeped. I glanced at it, then at his face, searching for a sign he'd heard me. "And we had a visit from these high schoolers looking for their missing friend. It's a real dilemma. Taking on a case with so much else is going on. A case I'm not sure pays. A case the police already rejected. But I'm worried about these kids. I need your advice on this one…"

I remembered what Lamar had said about worrying Nash. Stalking teenagers and getting caught by a gun-toting gardener would probably trouble him.

"Never mind. How about Roger Price? You saved that idiot's life. His arraignment is Monday, but they'll keep him in jail. The ATF is on the case now. How about that?"

Was Roger Price an okay topic? I bit my lip. Talking to an unconscious Nash was harder than I thought.

"Speaking of Roger's mother, she's fit to be tied that he used her new instant pot to hold the bomb. She'd never even opened the box. Won it in a white elephant drawing at her company's Christmas party. She's still convinced Roger was involved with drugs."

Shizzles. I probably shouldn't be talking about the instant pot. The lid caused the gash in Nash's head. We might not get paid because of that instant pot.

"And don't worry about the business because I've got that all under control. I can fit in the community service work in with the other work. My real job."

Work we didn't have. And I didn't think chasing after the YouTube teens counted. Lamar could give us a pass on the rent for a month or two, but what about everything else? Much of the software was billed monthly. The equipment needed constant updating. There were taxes. Nash had two mouths to feed, now that I mentored under him. And who knew how much this hospital bill would cost.

The high-paying clients used Jolene's office because she could afford things like online advertising. She also talked potential clients into a more expensive security system at every new home sale (her other business was real estate). My own mother was using Sweeney Security Solutions for her wedding security detail.

I whooshed out a shaky breath. *Okay, Maizie. Don't talk about the business. If it's upsetting yourself, it would definitely distress Nash.*

Hells, what else could I talk about?

"Remi is about to lose a tooth. She's setting up traps for the tooth fairy. I got caught in one this morning and it took me an hour to untie myself."

Great. Now he'd worry that I'd get trapped by my six-year-old sister and couldn't get to work. Was there nothing in my life that wasn't dangerous or distressing?

"Speaking of Remi." I opened my backpack and pulled out a stuffed armadillo. "She thought you'd want Steve while you're in the hospital. But once you get out, she wants him back."

I took a deep breath. And pinched my thumb to stop my tear ducts from getting any bad ideas.

"Which I'm sure will be very soon. Swelling on the brain's not so bad, the doctor said. It could be a lot worse. There's no bleeding and it's not too severe. He said you should wake up soon since your Glasgow Coma Scale is a seven. Congratulations on that."

Oh my God, I was congratulating him for being in a coma.

I took a deep breath, repeated my mantra, and felt the waves of panic blossom into full-grown hysteria. I bent at the waist, hit my head on his bed rail, and fell on the floor.

"I'm fine, Nash," I wheezed from under his bed. "And you're going to be fine, too. Everything's going to be okay. Just wake up soon?"

NINE

#YouTubeIn' #BelieveTheBelievers

To get my mind off Nash and the office woes, I let curiosity win over my good sense and tuned into the teens' YouTube channel. After a few hours of viewing *Bigfoot Trackers* footage, I was not a convinced believer. But I felt better about Chandler's relationship with the kids. He looked about my age, mid-twenties. He had a matched enthusiasm for all things Bigfoot and monster-y. Treated the kids as respected partners, but with the affection of an older brother. And he was super cute. Had a face the camera loved.

Chandler also had decent videography and editing skills. *BFT* was a well-produced channel. With a massive fan base. There were multiple fan blogs dedicated to their vlog.

The four also had much to say about the Wellspring Center. Much to say that might be construed as libel. Wellspring was way more likely to strike Chandler with a defamation lawsuit than kidnap him.

Although Everett Lawson had been carrying a gun when Mara slipped into the garden.

"That's the kind of jumping to conclusions Nash doesn't like," I told Remi, my six-year-old half-sister. The better half, having sprung from the union of my Daddy and Carol Lynn. His second wife cooked like butter couldn't kill you — I hoped she was right — and checked all the boxes on the "appropriate mothering skills" list. Like not carting her two-year-old to live in California after one successful diaper commercial.

Remi was curled up next to me on my bed, entranced with *Bigfoot Trackers*. Actually more entranced by the ads leading to *Bigfoot Trackers*. Something about a Bigfoot family selling mattresses in the forest. Remi was single-handedly paying for the Bigfoot kids' s'more bills through ad revenue.

And it looked like others were, too. Their most popular episode had over seven million views. Their least popular video had fifty thousand.

"I could catch him." Remi slipped off the bed and turned a cartwheel.

"Chandler? I don't know if he's actually done anything wrong. Although the high schoolers hinted at trespassing."

"Not Chandler. Bigfoot." Remi blew her bangs off her face and stuck her hands on her scrawny hips. "I know exactly how to do it. He can't be much bigger than the Tooth Fairy."

"I always imagined the Tooth Fairy as small. You know fairy-sized. No bigger than your pinkie. If you adjusted your Tooth Fairy traps accordingly, it'd save me a lot of pain and frustration."

Remi rolled her eyes. "You obviously haven't seen the movie. The Tooth Fairy is big. He looks like Mr. Nash. In a tutu."

I couldn't picture Nash in a tutu. "That's not what the Tooth Fairy really—" I stopped myself from arguing with a six-year-old over the size of a creature who traded coins for baby teeth. "Bigfoot isn't real, Remi."

"I thought you wanted to help Fred, Mara, and Laci find Chandler."

I shrugged.

"Then you must believe in Bigfoot."

"I don't have to believe in Bigfoot to find Chandler."

She gave a disgusted sigh and pirouetted to the door.

"Where are you going?" I called.

"You ain't a believer, I don't need to tell you nothin'." Hiking up her nose, she crossed her arms, and stamped out of the room. In the hall, a whistle pierced her absence. A second later, three Jack Russell terriers squirmed out from under my bed and darted after Remi.

I gave my own sigh and turned my attention back to Chandler and the Bigfoot dilemma. Using the Nash Security Solutions passwords, I checked our databases for information about Chandler. No criminal records. (Thankfully.) No debt. No recent social media posts. His car was found in Atlanta airport parking. His last known whereabouts were Black Pine.

The police would have checked hospitals and jails, so I didn't bother. If the kids were so insistent that he was missing, maybe there was more to the story. I wasn't going to ask Lamar to field that question with his cop buddies. Lamar had too much to worry about.

After a slight hesitation, I called a friend on the force, Detective Ian Mowry. We'd gone on a few lunch dates in the past. He was nice and good looking. Had a daughter Remi's age. We had a mutual enthusiasm for lunch. And crime. And pie. But we both knew my heart lay elsewhere.

Even if that elsewhere didn't want to do anything about it. At least until my apprenticeship was over.

"Hey, Maizie," said Mowry. "What's going on?"

"A missing person, Chandler Jonson. BPPD investigated this recently. He disappeared from a campsite on Black Pine Mountain near the Wellspring Center. He was camping with some teens."

"Right, the Bigfoot kids." Mowry chuckled. "It wasn't my case, but I heard we had an ATL — Attempt to Locate. We used dogs, but never found any sign of anything gone wrong. They tracked him from the campsite through the woods to his car. Looked like he drove off. We checked around, but nothing turned up."

"The kids think..." I was looking for something more astute than "he's more than missing" but Mowry beat me to it.

"Bigfoot got him?"

"Or somebody else. And he disappeared near the Wellspring Center. Which is also...weird."

"You're becoming more Black Pine every day, Maizie." Ian laughed. "But I'd think if anybody understood what's going on at Wellspring, it'd be you. Heath spa run by folks from California?"

"I get that kind of weird. But have you seen the layout?"

"I haven't been myself, but the officers-on-call did speak to those folks and checked the place out. Listen, Chandler's got a history of taking off. I think the responding officers spoke to a family member. The ATL would get a crazy idea and bug out without telling anyone. Once they didn't hear from him and months later learned he was in Alaska. No one else seemed concerned he was missing."

"These kids are very concerned."

"He had charged a ticket to Mexico the same night he went missing. Don't know for sure if he made the flight. Homeland Security's a massive amount of red tape. The officer in charge felt there wasn't enough evidence to seek further action."

"But Chandler has a YouTube channel with the teens. They have new shows regularly."

"Everyone's got a video blog. Ask the kids to detail what happened that night. I don't know the full story, but I remember our officer saying there was some kind of argument before he left."

"Those three are always arguing. I don't think they know how to have a conversation without arguing."

"I don't know what to tell you, Maizie. The missing person report was filed, and appropriate actions taken, but there's not much more we can do."

"Thanks, Ian."

"Anytime." He paused. "How's Nash doing?"

"Same." I held in a shuddering breath and ticked off seconds. Released. Progress.

"Don't give up hope, Maizie. He'll need you for that."

"You're a good guy, Mowry."

"I'm a patient guy, too. Keep that in mind if anything…changes."

TEN

#WhatIfs #ObiWannaDoIt

*A*fter a night of googling "cheap online ads" — I don't recommend, unless you're ready to boil your eyes — followed by a bout of not-sleeping, I rose early. Avoided another Tooth Fairy trap. Grabbed a leftover sausage biscuit from the fridge (with a prayer of gratitude for giving my father a wife who could cook). And headed to the office in downtown Black Pine.

The sun had not yet fully risen, but donut vapor already steamed off the Dixie Kreme building. The neon "Fresh and Hot" sign burned in the window. I stopped in to greet Lamar and the donut folks. Grabbed a cup of joe and two donuts (pumpkin and apple spice in honor of the autumn we were not yet experiencing) and hiked up the wooden stairs to the office.

I jiggled the key in the lock, held my breath it wouldn't stick, and hovered my knuckle above the glass before opening. I'd gotten in the habit of knocking after catching Nash half-dressed. At the thought of not finding Nash dressed or undressed in his temporary home (but hopefully not temporary business), my spirits plummeted. Not even the pumpkin or apple spice donut cheered me.

In the front room, I straightened the pile of magazines — *PI Magazine*, *Fraud*, and a *People* (my contribution) — for our (non-existent) clients. Ran a feather duster over the dented file cabinet. Scooted Lamar's scruffy La-Z-Boy toward the corner for better chi.

In the back office, I checked for new messages (zero), new payments (zero), and new leads (zero). Wrote up our notes on the Roger Price incident to send to his mother (and the ATF). Wrote a personal note on her bill about Nash's courage and continued coma that (hopefully) guilted her into paying. Inventoried our subscription renewals for the month. And ran out of ways to help the business.

The front door opened. I hopped from the desk then fell back into the office chair.

"Were you expecting someone?" Lamar ambled into the inner office, holding out a white paper bag. "Thought you could use another."

I slid forward from my droop. I'd been hoping the teens would return. I'd left a comment on their YouTube channel page asking them to contact me again. And prayed they hadn't been caught by Everett Lawson. "Just thought you were a client."

"Little early for clients. Why don't you go see Nash while I watch the office?" Lamar dropped the bag on the desk. Turning back, he surveyed the reception room, ambled to the La-Z-Boy, and scooted it back to its original spot. Satisfied, he fell into the chair and kicked back. "I'll hear the phone or the door. Even with my eyes closed. Woo-wee, the shop was busy this morning. My day started at three thirty and didn't let up until now."

"I've got to do community service again." I placed my elbows on the desk and thunked my chin onto my folded hands. "It seems I'm way behind on hours. What a time for volunteer work."

"I don't think it's volunteering when it's court-ordered, hon'."

"In any case, I'll pop in on my way to and from the Center to check on Nash. Maybe he's awake."

The first night, I'd imagined Nash waking with me at his side.

I'd wear my favorite Dolce & Gabbana, Givenchy Le Rouge lipstick, and an expression of optimism crossed with concern. Something my directors called "hopeful apprehension." Like in the TV movie I'd done, *While You Were Shifting*, a teen-werewolf twist on the rom-com.

The first night I'd been afraid to leave Nash, so I didn't run home to change. At this point, even Nash waking alone in the middle of the night would've been a relief.

Hope plummeted again at the shake of Lamar's head. "Talked to the night nurse already. Not yet awake. But soon."

I bit my lip. "Lamar, what if—"

"I don't do 'what ifs,' Maizie." Lamar's voice was firm but gentle. "And you shouldn't either."

"But Lamar, if word has gets out that Nash is…incapacitated, more clients will go to Jolene. What will we do if—"

Lamar shook his head. "Do your community service and see Nash. Talk to him. I know he'll like that. We'll come up with a plan. Just focus on what's important for now."

*A*t the hospital, I gazed down at Nash's sleeping, non-beatific but still ruggedly handsome face, and listed everything I'd eaten since the last time I'd seen him. It seemed a safe topic until upon reaching the end, I feared he'd start worrying about my heart health.

Or my weight.

I told him that I'd come up with a new topic after my community service work. I resisted kissing him, which seemed creepy when he couldn't reciprocate. (Not that he would.) Tried not to cry. And gave the nurses a bag of donuts.

Then felt guilty for putting their heart health in jeopardy.

The day was clear, a bonus when one drives a dirt bike up steep mountain roads. A quarter mile from the Wellspring Center, something popped out of the woods on the opposite side. My heart leaped into my throat. I veered close to the drop-off, swerved into the other lane, and skidded to a halt on the opposite shoulder. I hopped off the bike, sucking in breath faster than I could let it out, and stuck my head between my legs. Footsteps approached.

Three pairs of sneakers.

"Why aren't you in school?" I gasped.

"You do this a lot," said Fred. "This head between your legs thing."

"I'm under a lot of stress right now. The threat of falling off a mountain does not help." I whooshed out a breath and looked up at Fred. "Don't ever do that again."

"Sorry."

"School?" I wheezed.

"It's Sunday," said Mara.

"Sunday school?"

"We need to talk to you."

"I need to speak to you, too." I let out a final whoosh and straightened. "What were you doing in the Wellspring Center's vegetable garden?"

"Not about that," said Mara. "We tried the other detective. She wouldn't even look at us."

"I tried to warn you." Pulling off my helmet, I shook out my flattened hair. "We should really chat about your trespassing habits. Were you looking to score?"

"Score on what?" said Laci.

"We're not keeping points or whatever. It's not a game," said Fred. "This is for real."

"Are they growing pot in that garden?" I said. "And are you trying to steal it?"

"Pot? Like marijuana?" Mara wrinkled her face. "In a vegetable garden?"

Either they were naïve or very good at improvisation. I was going with naïve. For the moment. "How did you get out?"

"We had a rope." Fred drew himself up and squared his shoulders. "Laci and I tossed it over the fence and held it while Mara scaled it from the other side. Pretty ingenious."

"We saw it on YouTube. You googled how to scale a fence," said Laci.

Fred shrugged. "Still pretty cool."

"I couldn't see much more than vegetables," said Mara. "What kind of place would have a big fence for vegetables?"

I also had many questions about the fence. And the guy guarding the vegetables. But that was not the point. "The point is you shouldn't be skulking about the Wellspring Center. It's trespassing and against the law whether you have a missing friend or not. And by the way, unless he's Peter Rabbit, Chandler wouldn't be held in a vegetable garden."

"We didn't know it was a vegetable garden until Mara scoped it out," said Fred. "We have to take into consideration all the possibilities."

"You need to consider what will happen if you get caught, the Wellspring Center presses charges, and you end up in juvie instead of college."

"Is that what happened to you?" said Laci.

"I'm way too old for juvie." I jerked. "Again, not the point."

"You're doing community service," said Fred. "You're on probation. I googled you like you insisted. You got kicked out of California."

"Not kicked out. A judge…Anyway, I made some mistakes in friendships. And a relationship. I made bad choices. But now I'm making amends. Who better to tell you to stop making bad choices?"

The teens crossed their arms and stared off into different directions.

"I need to do my community service. So…stop stalking me?"

Mara's face crumpled. Fred glanced at her, then looked away.

Laci's lip quivered. "We're not stalking you. We just don't know what else to do." Her voice broke. "We need help. We keep trying, but nothing's working. And we don't want to get in trouble."

Guilt prickled my conscience.

"You're our only hope to find Chandler." Mara covered her face in her hands. "As soon as we mention Bigfoot, everyone ignores us. Even though everyone online totally believes us."

Laci's quiver turned into a full tremble. She wiped her eyes with the back of her hand and turned away.

I could handle the snark. I couldn't take tears. My eyes watered.

"Once you file a missing person's report, if it's an adult and there's no evidence of anything really bad, the police won't do anything. We can't get anyone to take us seriously." Mara sniffled. "And you seem—"

"The least serious," said Fred. "In a good way. Please, help us."

Should I be offended or flattered? In either case, their tears inflected new wounds on my already aching heart. But I'd never handled a case without Nash. I didn't know how to find a missing person without his guidance. I was no real *Julia Pinkerton, Teen Detective*. I was just Maizie Albright, still youngish investigator-in-training.

I had to pull my adult card. "I'll do what I can. But it's just a really bad time for me right now. I've got a lot going on."

"Whatever." Mara sniffed and jerked her chin toward the forest. They climbed over the embankment into the woods.

"Breaking into the Wellspring Center is not going to help you any," I called after them. "I'm serious. You're going to get in trouble."

I rubbed my forehead, then slid my helmet back on. Hopped back on Lucky and continued up the mountain to Wellspring.

My old therapist, Renata instructed me that guilt wasn't an issue if I were being honest with others and with myself. I might have been too open with the teens, but I hadn't been honest.

Come on, Maizie. Luke Skywalker hadn't known what he was doing either, but he still manned up.

Wait. Was I Luke in this scenario? Or...OMG. Was I Obi Wan Kenobi?

Now I really felt old. Old and completely unprepared. Either way, I was their only hope.

Did Obi Wan ask for permission slips from Luke's parents?

ELEVEN

#SelfieSolutions #DigTheKicks

I found Dr. Trident at his office desk. Today he wore another loose cotton outfit. In keeping with his Tai Chi image, I supposed. Or maybe I'd caught him post-meditative workout again.

"Come in, Maizie," he said, glancing up from his phone.

He rose and waved a hand at the conversational furniture grouping in the corner of his room. I trotted to the couch and waited while he chose a chair opposite. Couch time. After that talk with the teens, I really needed this. I hadn't been looking forward to therapy with Dr. Trident. Loyalty to Renata persisted. I tended to bond fast and deep and had trouble letting go. Yet another reason for the couch sessions.

But I needed help sorting this mess. I had people who required my help and I couldn't even find time to breathe properly.

"Where would you like me to start? I find it's easiest to begin with Vicki since everything tends to fall like dominoes after that."

"I was thinking of the files first," said Dr. Trident. "I'm behind on my documentation. But it's such a lovely day, I'd much rather be outside. Wouldn't you?"

"So, we'll do this outside?"

"I'll take you. I could use a brisk walk."

While we strolled the empty halls to the plaza door, I thought about myself as Obi Wan.

"Remember those kids from yesterday?" I asked. "Caught looking at the old buildings?"

"Curiosity is a virtue, isn't it?"

Not when it came with trespassing, but I was no virtue expert. "They're looking for someone…or something."

"Hopefully, wisdom. Maybe an inner peace."

"I'm talking about something more practical," I said. "You see, they told me—"

"You can't get more practical than inner peace, Maizie." Dr. Trident stopped us at the back door to square me fully in his gaze. "Look at me."

"Okay."

"No, really look at me."

I squeezed my eyes shut and opened them, hoping that would help.

"Do you see this?" Dr. Trident waved a hand before his face.

"Yes?"

"What is it?"

"Your face?"

"No, Maizie, it's inner peace. I have it. You need it. Repeat after me, 'Nothing is more practical than inner peace.'"

"Nothing is more practical than inner peace."

"Do you feel better?"

I did a quick inner peace check. Mostly found a stew of confusion mixed with simmering anxiety. As well as some gas from the sausage biscuit-donut mix. "I'm not sure?"

"Tell yourself you're sure. Only you can tell yourself how to feel, Maizie."

"I'm sure I feel better."

"Good." He patted me on the back and opened the door. A ray of sunshine followed by a light breeze swept inside. "Refreshing, isn't it?"

Unsure if he meant my feelings check or the fresh air, I nodded.

"Let's do a selfie." He held his phone above us. I automatically drew my arm back to settle on my hip, looked up, adjusted my chin angle, and smiled. He snapped, and we strolled from under the portico to the brick path. "A selfie does some good for evaluating your day-to-day feelings."

"It does? I thought it fostered self-absorption and self-centeredness. At least that's what Renata said when she told me to stop—"

"It's all relative, isn't it, Maizie? It all depends on how one uses the selfie."

I didn't want to promote a battle between therapists, so I nodded.

"For example, I have a client who's...shall we say, famous for being famous? All due to their life on social media. He composes beautiful pictures of himself. A wonderful photographer. Very creative. Thousands of people follow him. And he's never been happier or felt more complete. All due to my help. Why?"

"Because you double tap his pictures?"

"No, because I showed him there's a difference between selfies and selfies. Do you understand?"

"I don't have a smartphone right now, so maybe I need a different kind of help?"

"Everyone needs a different kind of help, Maizie."

We veered from the Café path to one that pointed toward the meditative labyrinth. Which brought me back to thoughts of *The Shining*, but the Wellspring Center had grown on me. The heavy stone edifice still appeared slightly sinister. I chalked that up to the teens' *Stranger Things* anxieties. But the flowers and brick paths gave it an Oz vibe. I'd grown used to the old chicken farm scent. Hard to believe the Wellspring Center to be an underground government facility meant for the capture of Bigfoot while pretending to be a celebrity wellness retreat.

Which is why I didn't believe it.

"Mazes are good for meditation," I said. "Is this going to help me with the inner peace selfie thing?"

Dr. Trident looked up from his phone. "I certainly hope so. Do you see that wheelbarrow? Why don't you grab it?"

The wheelbarrow held gardening equipment. "Is this some kind of Zen thing?"

"What a wonderful idea." The sun sparkled on Dr. Trident's grin. "Do that."

Hang on. This was no couch session. This was more community service.

I let out a long sigh and pushed the wheelbarrow to the maze. Dr. Trident pointed behind me. I turned around and pushed it down the path running along the maze. We stopped before a raised bed bare of flowers. Not as tall as the hills I noticed the day before. But large enough to inflict some major manicure damage.

"Enjoy planting." He pointed to the trays of pansies and pots of shrubs and roses. "When you're done, you can have ice cream again."

"But I don't know how—" I stopped. Dr. Trident had already jogged away.

In the distance, a rooster called. I shivered, wondering if the Bigfoot-chicken theory had some merit. Then gave myself a mental facepalm.

I glanced around, looking for gardening assistance or at least another flowerbed to study. We'd taken a path away from the main grounds. About one hundred yards away stood the remnants of the Center's bygone days, a long, single-story structure with a stone facade. No brick path led to it and a rope fenced it off. I wondered if it had been the building the kids had investigated when Everett caught them. Some of the stones had fallen off the outer walls, leaving crumbling mortar and plaster behind, but the roof looked in good condition. The cedar-shake shingles appeared new.

I wandered from my gardening duty toward the building to read the sign, hoping it would give some details to its history or the purpose of the renovation. But it was of the "no trespassing" variety.

Nothing made the building particularly interesting except that it was forbidden. Behind it lay a line of flower hills. And I knew what was behind those hillocks.

Nothing.

I plodded back to my gardening and evaluated the mound. Twenty minutes later, I had pit stains in my Splendid tee, more broken nails, and dirt mixed with my Nars "Risky Business" lip gloss. I also had two holes dug in the large mound. Midway into the third hole, my shovel had struck an object. The *Kung Fu Kate* script writers loved nothing better than buried treasure — aside from an intricately choreographed kung-fu battle — and incited by those memories, I applied real enthusiasm to my digging. A few minutes later, I unearthed a shoe. Actually, a man's hiking boot.

Disappointed, I took a break to cool my chafed palms and emotions. I considered calling Gladys to complain about my community service and new therapist. And determined it would net negative results. For me, in any case. I tried to look at the brighter side. I was in the sunshine (despite my pale skin), breathing fresh air (possibly chicken toxic), and doing good for the community (by beautifying an exclusive retreat supported by the wealthy and celebrities).

Perhaps I did have a case to make with Gladys.

I checked my messages. No updates on Nash. No forwarded calls from the office, either.

Breathe, Maizie.

I jerked out of my panic and stared at the boot. Cast my mind away from the business and wondered if it was a chicken-farm-days boot or something newer. Using a watering can and the bottom of my shirt, I cleaned it off and examined it more closely. A Keen, size ten. Leather and mesh upper. Rubber sole. I didn't know if Keen was favored by chicken farm employees, but Keen was a favored brand of hikers. REI always had tons of Keen footwear. I learned this in my previous life. I'd spent many afternoons shopping at REI with first ex-fiancé, Oliver. He loved puttering about all the new climbing and hiking gadgetry.

More so than actually using the equipment, IMHO, but that might be spite speaking. His arrest led to my apprehension as an accessory and my subsequent probation. I wouldn't have dirt in my lip gloss if it weren't for Oliver.

I placed the boot in the wheelbarrow. Took a long drink of water to clear my head. Thought about Everett Lawson and his gun, razor wire, and the plot to *Stranger Things*. I had my doubts that Chandler had been abducted by evil Wellspring employees and buried in a garden — despite what the kids thought — but one doesn't find a buried boot every day.

I decided to dig for the matching boot. For no reason other than it was a lot more interesting than digging for plants. And I'd kill two birds with one stone.

Twenty holes later, I had no match. But I did have chapped palms. And a godawful mess.

I quickly shoved plants into holes, squirted them with a hose, and galloped off with the boot in search of a place to clean up. As for the flower bed, Wellspring paid for what they got in terms of my help.

By way of wooden signs, I wound through the brick paths and flower gardens toward the fitness facility. Or "Physical Wellspring" as they called it. A complete departure from the Wellspring's historic buildings, its facade was a giant wall of glass. This facility alone must have cost at least a million to build. I searched for guests in the fishbowl but only saw two.

Maybe that was why I'd been chosen as hired help. Besides a lack of visitors, there wasn't an ample amount of employees either.

Inside, slate floors and stone planters held a jungle's worth of foliage and mini waterfalls. Programmed bird calls chirped and wind chimes tinkled from hidden speakers. The lobby directory told me I could find a pool, gym, juice bar, and locker rooms besides the track, weight rooms, and classrooms.

I chose locker rooms and trudged forward, trying not to drip mud on the beautiful floors. I hurried past the juice bar, separated from the lobby by a wall of waterfall glass. Then stopped at the edge for a double-take. A champagne blonde in Lily Lotus had caught my eye. I inhaled, searching my olfactory senses, and recognized Chanel No. 5 amid the wet vegetation and faint chlorine scenting the lobby.

Vicki.

I squinted through the wavy distortion of the waterfall. She wore sunglasses, but I recognized her by the dark red lipstick. Not many women had the balls to wear Dior's "Sulfurous" during a workout. I tried it once and finished my exercises looking like I'd been punched in the mouth.

Why was Vicki at the Wellspring Center? A pre-wedding spa retreat? But that meant the film crew would be nearby. *All is Albright* hadn't wrapped for the season yet. Besides that, Vicki had never met a spa retreat she couldn't write off for the show. Which is one of the reasons she learned to wear lipstick without it bleeding down her face. She even sauna'ed in lipstick.

Vicki was the only woman I knew who could wear moist.

I quickly did a slow scan, searching for our usual camera crew. And spotted the three-person team on the other side of the bar. Al's Panasonic HDX900 pointed toward Vicki's table. Behind him, our sound guy, Otto, sat at the juice bar with headphones clamped to his ears, his eyes on the bag in his lap. Lori, the director, peered into another bag, this one holding a monitor. She also wore headphones, listening to the conversation at the table.

Glad I was out of the camera's lens, I refocused on Vicki's table and studied the back of the man's head sitting across from her. I'd glossed over him previously, assuming it was Giulio, but this was not Giulio's head. Giulio had thick, dark, wavy hair and well-defined narrow shoulders. This man had a shaved head and massive shoulders. Giulio might turn to implants and workouts to bulk up, but he'd never shave his head.

Giulio had perfected the masculine head toss. His waves could bounce and catch the light with a technique subtle enough to not look like a sixteen-year-old girl on a vanity trip.

Through the waterfall, it almost looked like Vicki was juicing with Nash. My breath hitched. Realizing I was steaming the glass, I forced my pant to slow. Besides Dwayne Johnson, there was only one other man Vicki knew who had a shaved head and beautifully massive shoulders.

And that was also impossible because Oliver was in prison.

TWELVE

#NoBootAboutIt #FullOutFugitive

*B*efore I embarrassed myself — like hyperventilating, passing out, and crashing into a waterfall wall where Vicki would find me with dirty lip gloss and clutching a muddy boot — I hurried away from the juice bar to the hall leading to the locker rooms. In my previous life, Vicki did everything in her power to limit my humiliations from reaching the limelight. (A Herculean task, I admit.) Now that I'd quit my part of our actress-manager power team, she seemed to revel in my disgrace.

Which is disconcerting for a daughter. Probably something to add to my couch sessions. If I ever got them.

I pushed my thoughts away from Vicki and focused on quickly finding the locker room before I was caught by the *All is Albright* crew.

"My darling, what has happened to you?"

Not quickly enough. But at least it was only Giulio.

I turned to give him a dirty (literally) smile. "I've been gardening."

Giulio skipped the head toss to bend at the waist in an effort to control his laughter. "My dear, what do you know about gardening?"

"Pretty much zero." I curled my arm holding the boot into my side in order to grasp Giulio's elbow and yank him to standing. "I'm doing volunteer community service. I'm a little behind on the terms of my probation."

"I see." He sobered to study me. "I understand now why they dress prisoners in the orange jumpsuits. This community service is bad for your wardrobe."

I glanced at my white tee and grimaced. No amount of dry cleaning would bring it back. "I think I need to dress smarter in the future. Yesterday I was hauling boxes and lost my embellishments. Today I went with no embellishments and found myself knee-deep in dirt."

"Then why are you orange?"

"Georgia has colorful dirt." I shrugged. "Is the show doing a spa day?"

Giulio gave me a un-patented Latin sigh. "In a way. Your *madre*, Maizie." He gave his head a shake, not enough to toss his hair, but one that conveyed his deep-seated sorrow.

"You made your choice. Career over sanity. Assuming you chose to marry Vicki for your career." I bit my lip, tasted dirt, and used it as a palate cleanser at the thought of Giulio and Vicki's marriage.

"I should have married you when I had the chance." His dark eyes were mournful, seductive. Another talent. That look had made Giulio famous on soaps before he achieved greater notoriety as my (hired) lover. "I would be an Albright and have the happy life instead of the one I now face. With beautiful children. Green eyes and dark hair. They would photograph so well."

"I think I'm flattered?" I paused to evaluate. Maybe not. Vicki also had green eyes. "In any case, that ship sailed long before this marriage scheme. It's like a third-rate telenovela or a Korean TV drama. Engaged to my mother after a —thankfully very short — engagement to me? Even if our relationship wasn't real, it's still disgusting."

"It was real to me."

"Are we on camera now?" I said. "Because you're channeling emotion harder than a silent film star. Between the voice and the expressions, I'd think you were going for an Emmy."

Giulio smiled. "Do you really think so? I am feeling dejected by Vicki, of course, but I think I should appear more so on camera. When our breakup happens, the audience will have seen the fore-shadowing."

I sucked in a breath. "Vicki's breaking up with you? What about the wedding?"

"She does not know yet."

"*You* are breaking up with *her*?"

"I can't continue with this farce, Maizie. It's too hard. Besides she has found this *testa di cazzo*, this man she calls 'old friend.' But he is not so old. And I do not trust him. *Che stronzo.*"

"Calm down," I spoke soothingly while my chest tightened and stomach clenched. If Giulio skipped out before a sweeps week wedding, there would be hell to pay. And knowing Vicki, she would somehow blame me. Or I might find Giulio buried in one of the Center's gardens.

Hold that thought.

"Maizie, why are you staring at that boot? Do you not care how horribly your mother treats me? I could have become your step—"

I jerked my gaze off the boot and onto Giulio. "Please don't say those words. I'm too old to have a step-anyone. I'm sure Vicki isn't interested in this old friend. An old friend could mean anything from her Mercedes dealer to the girl who does her eyelashes. She doesn't need to know someone's name to call them 'friend.'"

"He is no dealer." Giulio paused. "I take that back. But not of cars. You of all people should know this."

"Wait, what?" I clutched Giulio's arm. "Is this old friend doing a juice bar scene with Vicki right now?"

"He has more screen time than I do lately. Can you believe?"

"Yes, I can believe." My stomach knotted, and acid fizzled up my throat. "Giulio, who is the man? Is it Oliver? Please say it isn't Oliver."

His almost over-plucked eyebrows squeezed together. "Of course. I am such the idiot. Sorry, my darling. I should have not been thinking of only myself. This is terrible for you, too."

"How is it possible?" My chest constricted, and I gasped. Gasped again. I couldn't catch a breath. Or I was catching them too fast. I dropped the boot and clutched my chest.

"Maizie, what is happening to you? Is it a heart attack? I told you those fried pickles would kill you." Giulio's arm slipped around my waist. "Breathe, my darling. Or stop breathing. You are going to explode."

I doubled over, taking Giulio's arm with me.

He leaned over me, rubbing my back. "What is it, my darling? Is it some kind of attack from the garden? Were you bitten by the snake? Do you need me to suck venom from you?"

I shook my head hard. Held up a finger.

"What are you doing here?" Giulio's voice sharpened. "Go away. *Via.*"

"Maizie?" said another man's voice.

I recognized the voice. And chose to continue hyperventilating rather than look up.

"Maizie, do you need help?" said Oliver. "What's wrong?"

"*Vaffanculo,*" said Giulio. "I am taking care of her. She is fine. She is not bitten."

"Bitten?" said Oliver. "What do you mean bitten? Should we get a doctor?"

"What's going on?"

I sucked in Chanel No. 5, hiccuped, and felt close to passing out. Giulio's arm tightened, and he yanked me closer. I hung like a rag doll, my breath baking the mud to concrete on my Golden Goose sneakers.

"It's about time you showed up, Maizie," said Vicki. "She's going to your fitting, Giulio."

"Vicki." Giulio grunted with the effort of keeping me off the floor. "Maizie will not go to my fitting. There is no fitting."

Not now, Giulio. I couldn't add my mother's unhappiness (or wrath) to all my spinning plates. I pushed out one long breath, held it, and jerked upright. Sucked in one long, slow breath. Skidded a glance over Oliver. And focused on Giulio. "No wedding talk yet," I wheezed. "I can't handle any more stress."

"What do you have to be stressed about?" said Vicki. "You're not the one getting married."

"She's obviously stressed," said Oliver. "Remember the panic attacks she had during the trial? This looks like a panic attack. Sweetheart, are you having a panic attack?"

"Oliver, I'm surprised to see you." I tossed my hair to prove Oliver wrong. Dirt rained on the slate floor. My eyeballs danced, but I kept myself from swaying. Slipped the boot behind my back and cocked a hip. My voice came out in breathy spurts. I hoped it sounded more sultry than panic attack-y. "Why aren't you in jail?"

"Why are you covered in dirt?" said Vicki.

"She is gardening," said Giulio. "For the community."

"Community service." I glared at Oliver. "Because I'm on probation. Because of you. Again, why aren't you in jail? How did you get out of California? Are you even allowed to cross state borders?"

I sucked in a breath and almost hyperventilated again. "Oh my God. Have you escaped? Are you hiding in the Wellspring Center? Wait, I don't want to know. This could really get me in trouble with my probation officer."

"Let me explain everything," said Oliver.

"That's what you said when they came to arrest us." My lungs compressed. I leaned over, scooped up the boot, and ran half-bent. And hoped I had enough breath capacity to get out of the building without keeling over.

That's all I needed. The camera crew catching my mud-encrusted floor flop in their B-Roll footage.

*a*fter running out of the Physical Wellspring building, I'd continued to sprint. Down brick paths, through the main building, and to the parking lot. My intention was to get far away from that crazy train before it loaded me on board and took me someplace I didn't want to go.

Like jail.

Instead, I decided to see Gladys. My probation officer would want to know about a possible fugitive from the law. A possible fugitive involved in my case. A possible fugitive who pleaded the fifth and therefore could not testify that I had no way of knowing he was selling narcotics to geriatrics.

I should talk to a therapist about this residual resentment for Oliver that I couldn't shake. Renata said forgiveness was the first step toward moving on with your life. However, I feared Dr. Trident might have a different therapeutic method. Like healing through Snapchat.

Worse, Snapchat with Oliver.

But before I arrived at Black Pine Probation, I found myself at the hospital. I knocked my mud-caked sneakers against the curb, shook myself free of any clinging dust, and snuck into the hospital. I slipped into the hospital, skirting the nurses' station. Worried I'd be identified as too dirty to visit, I felt compelled to see Nash nonetheless.

"I finally have something we can talk about," I said to sleeping Nash.

It bothered me that Nash's large body appeared to be in the same position since my earlier visit. I raised his arm — the one without the tubes and wires attached. Flexed it. Massaged the muscles. Lingered on the bicep for a minute longer than deemed appropriate. Curled his fingers in mine and wiggled our hands together. I laid the brawny arm gently on the bed. Glanced at his legs. And thought I should probably get permission before touching any covered parts.

"Vicki doesn't know it yet — and I want to be far away as

possible when she does — but there might not be a wedding," I said. "No exotic orchid bouquets. No riding to the altar on a baby elephant. No leaving the ceremony in a rose-petal, helicopter flurry. You're off the hook. No tux and no nightmare date."

I bit my lip. "If it counted as a date. I wish I knew what you were going to say in the truck. Before Roger Price—never mind."

Pulling up a chair, I sat down. Then stood and rubbed his other shoulder. Out of fairness. But not the whole arm. I didn't want to accidentally knock out an important tube. I patted his bicep instead.

"Anyway, Giulio wants to break up with Vicki. He says it's because she's into Oliver, but that's not it. I think he finally figured out that Vicki isn't interested in Giulio's career whether he's her husband or not. Can you believe it? I mean the part about Giulio figuring it out. Obviously, she proposed to him for the ratings."

I smoothed the sheet over Nash, folding it under his arms. Placed Steve the armadillo on the bed, so he was tucked up in the crook of Nash's arm. Then moved to his feet, figuring they were safe enough to touch. I began massaging, starting with his toes.

"Oh right, Oliver. Remember him? My ex-fiancé who tricked me into thinking he cared about serving the community and left me doing community service. That's some irony, right? I'm afraid he's escaped from prison and fled to Black Pine."

Whoops. Likely not a good topic for a coma victim.

I smoothed the sheet over his feet. "Don't worry about Oliver. I'm turning him into Gladys after I leave the hospital. Giulio, Vicki, and Oliver were at the Center for a spa day. I won't have to see Oliver again. But while I was doing my community service, I found something interesting. A boot. Which doesn't sound so interesting, but those teens are looking for a missing friend. They wanted to hire us, isn't that…"

No business talk. I bit my lip. Tasted less dirt than the last time.

"This may sound crazy, but I think there's a possibility this boot could be from the missing man. Maybe he was killed. Not by Bigfoot himself, but in a Bigfoot related-death."

I waited, watching for eye movement behind his lids. Or for suppressed laughter.

"It sounds even more ridiculous outside my head. Only Bigfoot-related because they were looking for Bigfoot at the time. And that's a long shot. The police said Chandler, the missing guy, drove off in his car then flew to Mexico. But it does make you curious, doesn't it? Why just one boot? If you look at it objectively, the flower bed hadn't been planted yet. And the boot is new-ish. It hadn't deteriorated at all. There's no mildew yet. Keen makes a good boot, but I doubt even they could prevent mildew after a long burial. That soil has a lot of clay in it and you know, clay retains a lot of water."

By his expression, I could tell he wasn't impressed.

"Okay, I cheated and looked that up. I really don't know anything about mud or gardening. And I don't know if I believe the boot belongs to the missing YouTuber, but I am worried about these high schoolers. I know you think I worry too much about people I shouldn't worry about. But Nash, they're kids. They're going to look for Chandler either way. I need to help them. And what if something really did happen to Chandler?"

Nash often used silence to convey his feelings. It was almost like we were having a regular Maizie-Nash confab.

"The boot isn't too impressive. What should I do next? What would you do if you were me? I chased him online as much as I could. The police spoke to his brother. He and his family live in Black Pine…Okay, that seems logical. I should talk to Chandler's family. Go to his apartment. Speak to his friends. Duh, of course."

I wrapped my fingers around his and squeezed. "I knew you'd help me."

What was I saying? Whatever. Didn't matter. I was speaking to Nash. And not passing out.

"But enough about me. When are you going to wake up?"

THIRTEEN

#TalkDirtToMe #StalkingBigFootStalkers

---

*A*s I suspected, Gladys was not amenable to my Wellspring Center plight. I should've led with Oliver instead of Dr. Trident. Or taken a shower before I'd arrived. She'd curled her lip at my dirt-encrusted attire and asked me not to sit. I stood before her desk, monitoring my breathing and trying not to "Pig Pen all over her cubicle."

"Here's what I think, Maizie," said Gladys. "I think you don't like to get dirty."

"Who likes to get dirty? I mean, aside from my six-year-old sister, Remi. And it's not the getting dirty she likes as much as the not bathing." I could tell by Gladys's expression, she didn't consider Remi a suitable example. "It's not the dirt. Or the sun on my pale, pale skin. Or the broken nails and ruined clothes. Truly."

"Right."

"I admit, at first I wanted to complain. But not about the dirt. There's some confusion of whether I'm doing therapy or just working. Because I don't think it's a Zen thing. And then there's Dr. Trident's proclivity for selfies. We're not making progress on the therapy checkbox of my probation. And then there's the razor wire fence in their back forty. And a gardener who threatened me with a gun. Probably not a good environment for an adult offender, am I right? But really, I'm mainly worried about a certain person who may or may not be a fugitive hiding at the Wellspring Center. And getting me into a lot of trouble."

"Uh huh."

"I mean, seriously, think of the possibilities. If I'm not around Oliver, I can't be harboring, right? Or an accessory, if it's Vicki who's doing the harboring? Or would that be aiding and abetting? Although why would she harbor Oliver? His arrest and my subsequent arrest caused her a lot of problems. Namely, losing the star of the reality show she produces. I mean, so really, what's she doing with him?"

Gladys blinked. "Are you done?"

"Sorry, I guess you wouldn't know why Vicki is all of the sudden besties with my former fiancé. But then, I was as shocked as anyone when she engaged herself to my other fiancé. I'd ask Dr. Trident for help on this, but I'm afraid he'd want me to work it out in tweets or something."

"You can stop anytime."

"I'm stopping."

"Maizie, maybe you didn't understand our meeting yesterday. In order to not be in violation of your probation, you need to do two things that you are not doing. One is community service. The other is seeing a therapist."

"And this is one of the areas where I'm confused—"

"It's not confusing, Maizie. It's actually very straightforward. You do your community service at the Wellspring Center. And you see Dr. Trident as a therapist."

"But are selfies really that healthy?"

"I am not a therapist, Maizie. I am your probation officer. I am the person standing before a door. The door that says, 'Go directly to jail. Do not pass go. Do not collect two hundred dollars.'"

I thought that might be a mixed metaphor, but I didn't have the heart (or guts) to tell Gladys.

"Are we clear, Maizie?"

"Yes, ma'am."

"Good. Dr. Trident expects to see you tomorrow morning. He was disappointed you didn't stay for ice cream."

"I bet," I mumbled but refrained from the teenage eye roll. I glanced at the dirt clods in front of her desk, secretly smiled, and walked out.

*A*t the office, I found Lamar sitting at Nash's desk and peering at the ancient computer monitor through a pair of half readers. He looked up, took off the readers, and cocked his head.

Before he could start the "what happened to you?" speech, I held up a hand. "Volunteer community service at the Wellspring Center. Gardening. I got a little crazy with the shovel." I dropped the boot on Nash's desk. "But I found this."

Lamar gave me a look.

"I know. It's a boot. Here's the thing, those teenagers from yesterday…" I gave him the hand again. "I know, I'm an adult offender and they are juveniles. Anyway, they weren't doing community service. They're looking for a missing man. I want to help them. He's the star of their YouTube show."

"Missing man?"

"They hunt for Bigfoot with this guy, Chandler. He's in his twenties. They were camping…" I held up my hand. "I know. Anyway, Chandler went missing near the Wellspring Center while the kids were toasting marshmallows. They're sincerely worried even though Black Pine PD has basically closed the case. Chandler's an adult and tends to flake out. But now I found this boot. I talked to Nash about it. We think I should look into it, beginning with Chandler's family and friends."

Lamar looked at me.

"You can speak now," I said.

"Maizie, sit down."

"I'm dirty."

Lamar waved his hand at the dusty office. "We'll apologize to the maid later. I can barely understand you, you're talking so fast. You talked to Nash about this?"

"I talked, he listened. But don't worry, I kept cool. I don't think Bigfoot will cause Nash any anxiety. I stopped myself from talking about Oliver, my ex-fiancé who should be in prison. Or at least, too much about Oliver. He's definitely not in prison. I found him at the Wellspring Center. With Vicki. And an unhappy Giulio."

Lamar frowned. "This is a lot of drama."

"Tell me about it. What do you know about the laws of harboring fugitives? If I saw Oliver and reported him to my probation officer, am I clear? Or do I need to go to the real police?"

"Is he a fugitive? How did he get out?"

"I have no idea. If he were going to *Shawshank Redemption* his escape, I think it would have taken longer."

"What was his conviction charge?"

"Possession. Police found Oxy and Vicodin at the private community center he owned. He'd been accused of selling it to some of the elderly people who frequented the center. Also, he had a masseuse who turned out to be more than a masseuse. But they dropped the pandering charges to focus on the possession for sale. The older people loved Oliver and refused to say he sold or gave it to them. His attorney was able to get it knocked down to possession."

"Oliver might not be a fugitive, Maizie. Chances are with a good attorney he might be out, time served. As sensational as the trial was, the prisons are overcrowded with drug offenders. Could he afford to pay fines for a reduced sentence?"

"His family owns half of Catalina."

"I don't know what that means, but I'm going to guess he's been released."

"It's so unfair," I said. "I didn't do anything but date him and now I'm covered in dirt and he's hanging out in a spa? How can this be? Someone should've warned me that he was out. Or don't they do that for ex-fiancées?"

Lamar shrugged. "That's why I like selling donuts better than walking the beat."

"I don't think Black Pine has much of a beat."

"It's all relative." Lamar smiled. "Don't worry about Oliver getting his just deserts, hon'. It won't help you any. Get your obligations done and move on."

"I wish you were my therapist, Lamar." I released a long pent-up sigh. Which didn't lead to any irregular breathing. Progress. "But how could Oliver show up here? Shouldn't he be doing probation back in California? I'm here because Daddy is here, and Judge Ellis felt I needed to get out of California in order to rehabilitate."

"Maybe his judge felt similarly."

"If all the judges felt that way, California is going to depopulate quickly." I scowled. "Oliver must be here because he knew I moved back to Black Pine. What does he think he's doing?"

"Maizie, don't let him distract you." Lamar leaned forward in his chair. "Now what's with the kids?"

"They want me to look for the missing guy, Chandler."

"I got that. But they're minors. And you really need to focus on getting real clients. Paying clients."

"They seem confident they can pay us—" I stopped at Lamar's look.

"Have you spoken to the ATF agent yet? Or Mrs. Price? Nash could really use that check in his bank account."

I shifted my feet. "I mailed the invoice and the report to Mrs. Price. I'll talk to the ATF agent soon. I promise."

Lamar steepled his fingers together. "I've been thinking. Maybe we should stick fliers in boxes."

"About Chandler?"

"No. Not a missing person flier. For the business. Advertising the services Nash Security Solutions offers."

"Okay?"

"Can you make something like that?" Lamar ran a hand over

his head. "I'd try to figure it out, but I'm not so hot on the computer."

"Sure." In forcing my tone to sound upbeat, the quality sounded more kazoo-like. "No problem."

"If only we could get back some of that business Jolene's swiped from us." Lamar sighed. "No use crying over spilled milk, though. I'm glad Nash has you here, Maizie. I don't know what I'd do without you."

I hugged Lamar. "I'll do whatever I can."

"You're going to have to turn down the kids for now. Nash needs real clients. Just stick to your to-do's." He gently pushed me away. "But maybe push a shower to the top of that list."

FOURTEEN

#TrapperKeeper #CainsNotAble

I always found the shower an opportune place to cry. I was already wet. No one could hear me. The steam kept my sinuses from clogging. Aside from the risk of razor cuts, I could still multitask effectively. And with all the tasks on my to-do list — Make fliers. Collect payment from Mrs. Price. Steal Jolene's clients. Finish my probation community service and non-therapy. Be angry about Oliver. Find Chandler Jonson (and don't tell Lamar). — I seriously needed to multitask. And release my anxiety over Nash in a safe place.

Safe as in private.

I had filled my loofah with my Ouai body scrub and allowed the first few sobs to escape when a pounding on the bathroom door began and continued until I had slopped through my final rinse without the repeat. Toweling off, I called through the door and when no one replied, cracked it.

Allowing a six-year-old and four Jack Russell terriers to squirm through.

"What are you doing?" said Remi.

I didn't answer as I knew this was a rhetorical question as so many were with Remi. Also because I was too busy trying to fend for myself. The dogs were licking the moisture off my legs.

"I caught something. But it got away."

Not sure if this was a good or bad thing, I nodded and skipped moisturizing to pull on clothes before I got any real questions.

"Daddy said even if I caught Bigfoot or the Tooth Fairy, I couldn't keep them."

"He's right," I said. "You shouldn't keep wild creatures. They're meant to live in nature."

"Like penguins. We don't have the right kind of fish in the lake."

Used to Remi-logic, I nodded and began my multi-step hair and skin care regime. Something I used to get at the salon. These days, I could barely afford the product let alone the salon treatment. Luckily, my only girlfriends in Black Pine worked at LA HAIR. Lucky for me, not so much for them. I added "call the girls for an appointment" to my mental to-do list and realized Remi still spoke of her traps.

"But what do you think Bigfoot eats?"

"Some say they like chicken. But I don't really know."

"Chicken?" She stuck out her tongue.

"Who doesn't like chicken?"

"What about candy bars? You think Bigfoot eats 'em? I know the Tooth Fairy don't. Momma said he thinks sugar is bad for your teeth."

"I suppose everybody but dentists and the Tooth Fairy like candy bars."

"That'd explain the wrapper." Nodding, Remi grabbed a bottle of Sisley Hair Rituel. Smelled it, squirted some on her tiny fingers, and applied it to the tail of one of the dogs. Who immediately tried to bite it off. Thus began chasing its tail. Causing the other three dogs to get in on the action. Dog hair flew through the air, sticking to my skin. Tiny paws — that felt more like horse hooves —trampled my bare feet. Wayward claws and tails scratched my shins.

I screamed and climbed inside the shower stall.

Remi chased the dogs out, then returned. "Can I have this?" She held up the bottle of hair oil.

"No." I snatched it back from her. "That costs like a hundred dollars. I need to make it last. You can't use it on the dogs."

"Why would I use it on the dogs? And can you get me some candy bars?"

"Remi, I'm up to my ears in work. And I'm meeting Chandler's brother soon."

"Chandler from *Bigfoot Trackers*? Can I meet his brother?"

"No can do, Remisita. This is a 'professionals only' visit. I have no idea what this dude is like." For all I knew, he was like Chandler. Maybe into Tooth Fairies. We'd never be done with the traps.

Opening the door, I ushered her out. Her tiny yet determined chin rose. "You are no fun anymore."

"Tell me about it." I sighed, shut the door and caught my reflection. Not long ago, this mug could be found on the cover of magazines. Now I only looked worthy of a *National Enquirer* exposé.

Giving up on glamour, I pulled my hair into a ponytail and hurried outside to Lucky.

*L*ike Roger Price, Crispin Jonson still lived with his parents in Black Pine. Unlike Roger, he didn't blow up a bank and my boss. Therefore, I could speak to him without passing out.

The Jonson's lived in a large brick home in an upscale neighborhood in Black Pine. Crispin was twenty-one and worked at a local tubing company. It seemed floating on a river was popular with the seasonal guests.

"I've never gone tubing," I told Crispin. "It sounds like fun."

"It sucks," said Crispin, flipping a fan of light brown hair from his face. "Especially when tubers get stuck and I have to rescue them. Have you ever hauled out a fat dude who's wedged between two giant rocks?"

Obviously not, but I shook my head anyway.

"They always get wedged between the same two rocks. It sucks. I wanted to be an outfitter, but they make you work your way up. Chandler's so lucky."

"But Chandler's missing," I said. "Kind of not lucky, IMHO."

"He's not missing. Chan's just gone. If he were really missing, we would have heard something."

That sort of logic was difficult to argue against. I switched topics. "When was the last time you saw Chandler?"

"Every time I turn on the friggin' TV. I'm so sick of that stupid show. Friggin' algorithms. Because Suz and Mike watch his channel, it's all over our recommended and watched lists."

Suz and Mike were Susan and Michael Jonson, his parents. Of course, Chandler's parents would watch their son's show. I nodded approvingly, then frowned at Crispin. "I meant in real life. The last time you talked to him face-to-face. Or even on the phone? Messaged? Snapchatted? Whatsup'ed?"

"No clue. I don't talk to Chandler. He talks to my parents some-times. But he's not, like, the reliable son. Look who's here. Helping them. Someone's got to watch this house." He waved a hand at the kitchen table where we sat. Next to his phone and laptop, energy drink cans, chip bags, and other wrappers littered the table. A pizza box and empty jug of milk sat on the counter. Cereal boxes graced another counter.

He spotted my critical kitchen gaze. "The cleaning lady doesn't come until tomorrow."

I had my doubts about the help Crispin proclaimed. Still, prodigal son and all. I pulled out the boot from my Campomaggi backpack. "Does this look familiar?"

He pulled up his pant leg and showed me the Keen currently ensconcing his foot. Unfortunately, the matching one appeared on his other foot. No Cinderella here.

"Could it be Chandler's? What shoe size was he?"

"I don't buy his shoes, so I don't know."

Interviewing was a lot harder than I thought. "Where are your parents? Do they know he's missing? I'd like to talk to them, too."

"I don't know where they are. Went somewhere for work. Suz and Mike talked to the police too. I'm telling you, Chandler takes off and doesn't tell anyone. All. The. Time. Anyway, he drove to Atlanta and flew to Mexico. Police confirmed it. Nobody's worried."

"But has he bounced since *Bigfoot Trackers* started? It looked like his show's been uploaded consistently over the last year. And it's really popular." I quoted the kids, "'Viewers expect constant content.'"

Casting me an aggrieved look, Crispin mumbled something about letting him "think" and looked to the kitchen ceiling for help. I let my gaze wander the room again. Family pictures hung on one wall. Outdoorsy fun. The brothers as children on trails, rivers, beaches, and skiing. Arms around each other, laughing and smiling. But nothing recent.

"I can't remember when I talked to him. But the last time Chan took off, he went to Alaska."

I glanced back at Crispin. He'd been watching me study the pictures.

"That was about two years ago?" he continued. "Chan worked at a fishing camp while he researched the Yeti. He finally called us three months later."

"He didn't have a YouTube channel back then?"

"Just a blog. He's had a blog for a long time. But no one does that anymore." Crispin ran his hands through his long brown hair. "Guess he got tired of doing the Bigfoot show and moved on to something else."

At the height of its popularity?

"I'd really like to know more about Chandler, the person," I said, trying a different tack. "It could help me locate him. Even if he's not really missing, I'm sure everyone would like to know where he is."

Crispin snorted. "Okay."

"At least the *Bigfoot Tracker* team would like to know."

"They're kids. Probably can't figure out how to do the show without him."

"They're worried about your brother. He left them at the camp-site and never returned."

"Typical," said Crispin. "Wait. Are you really a private inves-tigator?"

I nodded, crossing my fingers beneath the table.

"Because he does get stalkers. Crazy women. Most of them don't look like you, though." Crispin raised one brow and gave me a side smile. "You want to go tubing sometime? I get a company discount. We could bring a cooler—"

"Let's keep this professional," I said in my best professional private investigator voice. This wasn't going anywhere. I stood. "Do you have a key to his apartment? I'd like to check it out. I'd also like to see his room."

"The police already looked but whatever." Crispin dragged himself from his chair drape. "I think we got a key around here somewhere."

He rummaged in a bowl near the kitchen door, looped a key on his finger, and walked it to me. I held out my hand. He grabbed my wrist. "You sure you're not interested in Chandler because of the show?"

I yanked on my wrist and his grip tightened.

"I'm only interested in finding him."

"Okay, then. You never know about peeps." Crispin dropped the key in my palm. "Like I said, stalkers."

I shoved my hand into my pocket, gripping the key. "Where's his room? Upstairs? I'll find it."

"I think I better keep an eye on you."

I mentally rolled my eyes and followed him up the back stair-case and down a hall. No family pictures here. The walls were lined with film posters. "I guess your family are movie fans?"

"Mike's a producer. Mostly indie stuff. Used to direct. Suz directs, too."

"That's where Chandler gets—"

Crispin spun around, fists clenched. He stepped toward me. "Don't even."

"What?"

"You were going to say, 'Chandler takes after them.' That would be *me*. Chandler goofs off in the woods, playing with a GoPro. I write and know how to direct. One of these days I'll get something made. I've always been interested. Not Chandler. He could've cared less. I've gone to the sets with Mike and Suz since I was able to look after myself."

"So," I said, trying for casual and not creeped-out. "Where are your parents again?"

"I told you, I don't know. We don't check up on each other." He sneered. "Not like Georgia parents, hovering over their kids. I see it on the river all the time."

"There's nothing wrong with caring about children…" Realizing I was about to take a segue into Maizie-couch-issues, I stopped.

"Whatever. You don't understand."

"I get it and still think you're being insensitive to your brother's situation." I cocked a hip and mustered a Julia Pinkerton glare. One raised and one lowered eyebrow with a slight lip curl. "And I wasn't raised here. I was raised on sets in California. Ex-actress."

"What sets?"

"*Julia Pinkerton, Teen Detective.* And some other work I'd rather not mention."

"Never heard of it." He shook his head. "What's it on? Microcable?"

"Network—never mind." I refused to be disappointed at my lack of fame with the youth in Black Pine. The middle-aged in Black Pine certainly knew me. Which meant I had rapidly aged or marketing had gotten the demographics all wrong.

Okay, Maizie. Not supposed to care about that anymore. You have a real job. Even if it's going sideways at the moment.

I strode past Crispin, looking through doorways. Found what I thought to be Chandler's and entered. Framed prints of the mountains hung on the walls. King size bed neatly made.

"Not his room. It's a guest room."

I pivoted. Crispin stood in the doorway, crossed arms.

"So, like any other acting? Why are you back here? Couldn't make it? Do you want to do this indie project? I'll need a screen test and I can't pay you, but…"

I ignored him to march into the next room. Framed movie posters. Bedding wadded and rumpled. Energy drink cans and crumpled chip bags scattered throughout. I began to back out and bumped into Crispin.

"Sorry, I guess this is your room." My eyes carried over the mess and landed on his dresser. A small cardboard box stood open on its side. A bag of brown capsules had spilled out of the box.

Crispin pushed past me and swept the bag into the box. "Do you smoke?" He turned around holding another box. A wooden cigar humidor. "I've got good stuff. Vape or pipe? I've got papers, too, if you're into that."

"I'm good, thanks."

He followed me into the room across the hall. "It's medicinal. My doctor in California sets me up. I have a 'scrip. For anxiety."

"I'm not DEA. Just looking for your brother." Another bedroom. Less lived-in than Crispin's, but it held a similar man-boy vibe. Cleaner. Chandler's movie posters were more *Creature from the Black Lagoon* than Crispin's art-house flicks. The dresser was covered in trophies and childhood knickknacks.

"Academic bowl?" I said. "Chess?"

"Chan was a total nerd in school, yeah." Crispin sidled up next to me. "When I Google you…"

"Don't Google me." I opened the closet door. Ski equipment, winter wear, and flannel shirts. A shelf of boots. None missing a leftie, but the size was correct. Of course, size ten was like a woman's eight. He probably had trouble finding good deals, too.

I sighed and closed the closet door. I wasn't learning anything new other than Chandler was a high school brainiac, monster nerd, and outdoorsy. And he had an annoying younger brother.

Crispin hung in the doorway. "Not finding anything?"

I held in my glare and opened a dresser.

"Do you think pawing through his tidy-whities is going to find him?"

Crispin had struck one of my many raw nerves. I didn't know enough about investigating (yet) to get any good leads on Chandler. And he was right. Chandler's underwear was not going to help me. No secret diaries hidden beneath his boxers. "Why does he have so much stuff here when he has his own apartment?"

"I don't know. He crashes here sometimes. Maybe when the stalkers get too crazy."

I turned to see if Crispin was kidding or not. "Do the police know about the stalkers?"

He shrugged.

How could he be so blasé about his missing brother? "Where do you think your brother is?"

"Hell, hopefully."

FIFTEEN

#GoldishGirls #OnMyOwnAgain

*I*t was hard for me to believe a brother could have so much animosity toward a brother. I guess that was the whole thing with Cain and Abel, but as Vicki never took me to church, I didn't know much about that. As someone who didn't have a sibling until six-and-one-half years ago, I couldn't image hating a brother enough to wish him dead. Or not caring if he was. It made me want to bundle Remi up and smother her in hugs.

Too bad Remi wasn't the cuddly type.

I needed to talk out my suspicions about Crispin Jonson. Nash would have a terrific opinion. I pulled my helmet on, ready to jet — an impossibility on Lucky, but still — to the office.

And caught myself.

Pinching my thumb, I refocused. Now, who else would listen to me hash out my feelings about Crispin and sort mountains from molehills?

I didn't want to bother Lamar. Particularly when he didn't want me wasting time on this case. Ian Mowry? Probably would tell me the police already interviewed him and got nada. Although he might be interested in Crispin's pot…

I had no time for police witness paperwork for a possession charge.

That left me with the girls. They would also understand the plight of my nails. And would commiserate about Oliver. That's what friends were for. Venting and dishing snarky comments about your exes. Tiffany and Rhonda of LA HAIR were like *The Golden Girls* except much younger and more ghetto.

If the strip mall housing LA HAIR had been in LA, I would have considered it sketchy. The parking lot had potholes and most of the lines had faded. The door of LA HAIR looked like cracked marble. Or broken glass. Black with a gold crackle finish, so take your pick. Inside, the black and gold theme continued from the open shelving to the hair stations. The stylists also wore black. Black with bleach freckles masked with Sharpie ink. But their hearts were pure gold.

For the most part. Sometimes I worried about Tiffany.

To the disgust of the other stylists, Rhonda and Tiffany left their stations — reception and nails — to greet me. I had a *Steel Magnolias* moment and almost cried. Then Tiffany dragged us outside, using me as an excuse for a cigarette break, and I got over myself.

In the alley behind the salon, Rhonda took in my hair, nails, complexion, and outfit. Gave me a solemn and disappointed, "Girl."

"I know," I said. "It's been so bad I can't even take care of myself properly. But I did shower today. It's been a while since I slept, though."

"When celebrities go to hell, y'all fall completely apart," said Tiffany.

"Not all of us," I said thinking about Giulio and Vicki. "You will never guess who I saw today. Someone who is probably not a fugitive. And had the nerve to show up in Black Pine. Particularly at a time when I look like this."

Rhonda clapped her hands. "This is going to be good. Who?"

"Oliver Fraser?"

She danced in a circle. "I can't believe it. It's like you're cursed."

"Don't sound so excited."

"Oliver, your ex-fiancé?" said Tiffany. "I thought he was in prison."

"Not so much. I found him at the Wellspring Center juice bar with Vicki and Giulio."

"Lord Almighty, Maizie." Rhonda exploded with laughter. "You have the worst timing of anyone I know. And we have the scoop even before *TMZ*. I can't wait to say I knew it first."

"You can stop being so thrilled," I said. "This is horrible. He has no right to be spa'ing while I'm digging in dirt and moving furniture. He's supposed to run into me in Saint-Tropez after I've lost twenty pounds, have a perpetual tan, and own a successful private investigation office. With my adorable three children — Jemima, Astrid, and Carter — and my loving husband. Who's incredibly wealthy, handsome, and gently wakes me in bed with a tray of donuts and coffee every day."

Tiffany blew out her laughter in a plume of smoke. "How d'you plan on losing twenty pounds and eat a tray of donuts every day?"

"What did you say when you saw Oliver?" asked Rhonda.

I gritted my teeth at the memory. "Not much. I was too busy having a panic attack. And trying to keep Giulio from breaking up with my mother. Not that I have an issue with that, but I really can't handle the fallout. She's already texting me sixty times a day about the wedding."

"Giulio did what?" said Rhonda. "What is going on? Is it the season-ending of *All is Albright*?"

"It did have the season-ender-cliffhanger vibe," I said. "But Giulio seemed sincere in his contempt for Vicki and the situation with Oliver. I don't blame him. Although Giulio brought it on himself. I do blame him."

Tiffany shook her head. "I swear Jerry Springer needs to do an episode on you. It'd really help his ratings."

"It is a lot of drama at once." I sighed. "And it does seem absurd when you're not living through it."

"I'm sorry," said Rhonda. "Oliver ruined your life. You deserve to be living your dream before seeing him again."

"Thank you. He picked the worst week of my life to show up."

"How's Mr. Nash?" asked Rhonda soberly.

I began to cry.

"He passed? Oh Lord, I am so sorry I was cutting up so hard. I had no idea."

I shook my head, wiped my eyes. "No. But he hasn't woken up…" I couldn't admit how much I missed Nash. He was my boss. The girls had enough to say about my usual ineptitudes. I wasn't getting into that kind of stupidity. "…and we're in financial jeopardy."

"Bankruptcy?" said Tiffany. "Dump that place and get yourself another job before you land back in jail. Don't risk your probation, girl. I know this for a fact. We could hire you here to sweep hair. Except Rhonda's supposed to do that."

"I am?" said Rhonda.

"But…" I wasn't ready to give up on Nash. These women were practical by design and always kept it real. Which I liked. Although sometimes they could get too real. Which could be a little painful.

"I do have one case. But the clients are teenagers."

"Are you kidding me?" asked Tiffany. "Get a real case. Hang out at the Cove and pass out business cards or something. Some drunk, rich guy will hire you, for sure. To do what, you probably don't want to know, but still. Money's money."

No one wanted me helping the kids. As I had the same initial instinct, I didn't correct Tiffany. Instead, I explained the night of Chandler's disappearance and the fruitless police search. "These high schoolers are sort of a big deal. They have a YouTube channel with the missing guy, Chandler Jonson—"

"*Bigfoot Trackers*? Lord Almighty, do not tell me that hottie Chandler Jonson is missing." Rhonda placed her hands on her braids and shimmied, causing her considerable curves to undulate. "Chandler Jonson is dreamy. It's so cute when he thinks he sees Bigfoot and goes chasing off into the woods."

Tiffany snorted.

She shot a look at Tiffany's snigger. "That's legit, Tiff. Better than all the *Tasty* videos someone else watches who doesn't even cook."

"They're called satisfying videos for a reason. It's how I relax."

I just might be the only American who didn't YouTube.

A glow appeared in Rhonda's cherubic cheeks. "If you saw Chandler, you'd watch him, too. We do live in the heart of Bigfoot country. They've found—"

"Hold up." I sensed the brewing of an epic believer battle. Epic battles were as much a part of their friendship as makeup tips and GNOs, but time was of the essence. "Before we get into Bigfoot drama, I wanted to get your opinion on another kind of drama. I just met with Chandler's brother, Crispin. He doesn't believe Chandler is missing. He doesn't even seem to care. But he did mention that Chandler has a lot of female fans. Stalkers."

I glanced at Rhonda, who shook her head and mouthed, "Not me."

"He thinks stalkers kidnapped Chandler?" said Tiffany.

"He thinks Chandler bounced. That's Chandler's M.O. But the brother definitely had suspicious vibes. Couldn't tell me much about Chandler. Couldn't tell me where his parents were. Didn't even know his brother's shoe size."

"Who knows their brother's shoe size?" said Tiffany.

"Size thirteen," said Rhonda. "Twelve, thirteen, and a seven."

Tiffany rolled her eyes. "It proves nothing. Men don't pay attention to that stuff. The police interviewed Crispin, didn't they?"

"Yep," I admitted. "Though Crispin might've been high when I talked to him. Maybe he gets paranoid. He offered me a toke and I spied some kind of pills on his dresser."

"Sounds like you were killing his buzz," said Tiffany.

"I don't know." I blew out a long sigh. "I want the new me to be the strong *She-Ra* type. But I feel like I can't do this job properly without Nash. I'm so indecisive and unsure. I ask the wrong questions and I don't know what clues to look for. All I got from Crispin was an offer for a date and a screen test."

"Screen test?" Rhonda wrinkled her nose.

"He wants to do indie films like his parents. And he's way jealous of his brother's success." I tapped my chin. "But the stalker situation is worth exploring, don't you think? If Rhonda is crazy about Chandler, there must be even crazier women who are interested."

Tiffany shook her head, making the blue tips of her angled bob swing. "You got nothing else, do you? Stalkers and a suspicious brother?"

"I have a boot." I opened my backpack to show them.

The girls looked in the bag, then glanced at each other.

"Listen, Maizie, if the office is in danger of closing, maybe you should focus on looking for another job," said Rhonda. "This sounds like a dead end. If the police couldn't find anything—"

"But I'm the kids' Obi Wan."

Their foreheads wrinkled.

"I'm their only hope. No one believes them."

"They believe in Bigfoot," said Tiffany. "That should tell you something."

SIXTEEN

#Miseryable #Bikeaboom

*T*he end of the day approached, and I needed something. Some kind of evidence (other than a boot and a suspicious brother) to prove the Chandler situation more serious than it seemed to get the police to resume their investigation.

Or if Chandler had bounced, I needed to find him and put the teens' minds to rest.

Chandler's apartment was located on the other side of town from his parents' subdivision. A modest block of six small flats on the edge of town. Judging by the trucks and small sedans in the parking lot, the other tenants were working class. I was surprised he didn't live in a tree house in the forest. Or a tiny home on the lake. Or anywhere more glamorous than this.

Inside Chandler's second floor one-bedroom, more creature feature posters hung on the walls. He had simple, clean-lined furniture and a crap ton of camera gear. What he didn't spend on his housing, he did on camera and sound equipment. Two desktops and a laptop on one giant desk, covered in trailing USB cords. His bedroom revealed a crazily mixed pile of camping and hiking supplies. The kitchen, mostly trail mix and protein bars. The bookshelf was an encyclopedic array of cryptozoology.

But no evidence of stalkers. No perfumed letters, gifted undies, or amputated ears.

Of course, the police would have confiscated any amputated ears. Another question for Ian Mowry.

I had no hacking skills and I couldn't guess his computer passwords. While I poked around his shoes, I heard the rumble of an engine. I scooted to the window and peeked through the blinds. A motorcycle had pulled into the gravel parking lot. Absently, I watched the helmeted man park his bike and study the apartments. I returned to the shoes, letting my thoughts drift back to my clue-search. What would Nash look for? The clues in *Julia Pinkerton, Teen Detective* had been hidden but obviously useful.

I supposed real-life clues were not so obvious.

Alrighty. If I wasn't good at looking for clues, maybe canvassing was more my thing.

I left the apartment to knock on doors, starting across the hall.

"Hello," I said, in my best professionally investigative voice. "I'm looking for Chandler Jonson, your next door neighbor. He's missing. Have you seen any suspicious people around lately? Or Chandler?"

The woman who answered the door raised an eyebrow and squinted at me.

"Aside from me," I said. "And I'm not suspicious. I was hired to look for Chandler."

The door shut before I could step back. I squelched a "Hey" and moved on.

"Good evening. My name is Maizie Albright and I'm with Nash Security Solutions. My clients are worried about your neighbor Chandler Jonson. Have you spoken to the police about him recently? When was the last time you saw him?"

"No *policía*." The door swung closed.

The next apartment, I skipped the police and waved a crumpled five dollar bill.

"I know Chandler," said the tenant, smoothing out my Lincoln.

The large guy wore flip-flops and a Salt Life T-shirt. The scent of garlic and onion drifted from his apartment, making my stomach growl. "He's a cool dude. You know he's got a YouTube show?"

I nodded. "I heard it's very popular with the ladies."

"It is?" The man leaned back in his doorway. "No way. That's totally cool."

"Have you seen any ladies hanging around here? Maybe of the stalker-ish variety?"

"Stalking Chandler? Dude, no way."

"His brother thought it was a problem."

"Whoa. A crazy fan. I can see that." Big Dude held out his hands, framing the scene. "So, like this chick takes Chandler."

"Yes?" A prickle of excitement ran through me. I danced on my toes, ready to dash the information to Ian Mowry. I could finally have a solid lead. "Did you see her?"

"Kind of an old chick. Maybe middle-aged. Total nut job. She lives in the mountains. On a farm."

"On Black Pine Mountain? That's where he was last seen."

"Not sure what mountain. He had an accident and she takes him home. And chains him to the bed. And when he tries to escape, she takes a sledgehammer—"

I held up a hand. "I think that's *Misery*."

"Yeah, have you seen it? Totally awesome."

"But Chandler?"

"You think something like that could happen to him?"

"I hope not," I mumbled. "Thank you for your time."

Apartment five was empty and no one answered at six. Feeling the acute grip of disappointment, I wandered back to Lucky. And noticed a puddle underneath her. A puddle that hadn't been there earlier. A few feet away, I spotted something on the ground and pocketed it. I felt queasy. But decided to try rational and logical before hysterical and crazy.

I returned to apartment four.

"Hey," said Big Dude. "Did you find Chandler?"

"Not yet," I said, wondering if the oregano in his tomato sauce was really oregano. "Do you know anything about bikes?"

A minute later, we gazed at Lucky. He bent over her, straightened, and folded his arms. "Someone clipped your fuel line."

"Why would they do that?" I covered my mouth with my hands, backing up. "Oh my God. Is Lucky going to explode?"

"Dude. Did you see the explosion in *The Godfather*? *The Dark Knight* had a good one." He squinted. "*Casino*. Dude, totally *Casino*."

"Were they dirt bikes? Are we in danger?" I yanked my phone from my back pocket ready to dial 9-1-1.

He shook his head. "Nah. You just can't start it. Those were bombs, dude. Someone was probably trying to steal your gas."

"Oh." My relief was almost as great as Big Dude's disappointment that there wouldn't be an explosion. "You must watch a lot of movies."

"Dude, I'm a key grip. But I really want to get into special effects."

Of course. I couldn't get away from the industry.

But that didn't bother me so much as the object the motorcycle rider had dropped was a lighter. One explosion in my life was enough.

"It's been a day," I said to Nash. Visiting hours were almost over, but we needed to talk.

Or at least, I needed to talk.

I gazed at the man lying in the bed. I'd brought him one of his concert T-shirts from the office and laid it on top of his hospital gown. I figured the nurses needed him in the gown, at least until he could move around on his own. But it was easier to talk to Nash with a Metallica logo draped over his chest than light blue cotton.

"By the way, it looks like you lost weight. Which is totally unfair since you've barely moved a muscle since getting here. I tried this new workout called digging and exercised muscles I never knew I had. But when I got on the scale before my shower, I'd gained two pounds. How is that right?"

Someone had moved Steve the armadillo back to the table. I settled him under Nash's arm. Stroked Nash's forehead. Just for a second. Noted the growth of stubble on his cheeks that had begun to hide his cuts. And original scar.

Original to me, anyway.

I sank onto the chair next to his bed. In the open door behind us, the bustle of hospital life continued. I scooted closer and pretended he didn't smell more like hospital and less like Nash.

"I've been busy since finding the boot. It seems the only people who are worried about Chandler are the YouTubers. And maybe his neighbor. But the more I look into this case, the more I find his disappearance odd. Chandler might be flaky, but I really don't think he'd abandon the kids in the woods to suddenly run off to Mexico. It doesn't make any sense."

Taking Nash's hand, I squeezed. "Don't worry, I'm not leaving you to run around Mexico to look for Chandler. Yet. I did talk to his brother. He's a piece of work. But no real evidence I can take to the police. Yet. Other than the boot. Which I'm giving to Detective Mowry. As soon as I get my bike working again."

I forced a chuckle. "I guess the neighborhood where Chandler lives is sketchier than I thought. Not that Lucky would have exploded or anything. Easily fixed. Daddy said he can replace the fuel line tonight. And Ian Mowry's going to check the motorcycle database for a matched description of the vandal's bike. I'm going to see him tomorrow."

Probably bike sabotage was not a good coma topic. Nash didn't like me driving Lucky as it was. And I had my doubts that the motorcycle rider was trying to steal Lucky's fuel. Although my number one suspect for that prank — Crispin — didn't own a motorcycle. At least I hadn't seen one at the house.

I paused to ease my voice from anxious to carefree. "Anyhoo, it's been a full day what with my friends telling me to quit work and seeing Oliver and finding...not very good evidence. But don't you think it's important I keep trying for the sake of the teens?"

We sat on that for a minute.

"I promise I'll get us some other clients, too. And do my volunteer community service. And therapy. In any case, I don't have time for Vicki's possibly-non-wedding, right? And helps me to avoid Oliver. Not that I'm dwelling on Oliver. No worries there. It was just a shock to see him. And so totally unfair that I'm here, dealing with—"

I was surprised by the vehemence in my voice. Switched to a better-for-coma-patients tone.

"I mean, he was my fiancé, Nash. I know that doesn't sound like much when I was also engaged to Giulio, but I really thought I loved Oliver. And he wasn't who I thought he was. He betrayed me." My anger collapsed into self-pity. I sniffled and pinched my thumb, not liking that feeling any better. "How can he just show up here like nothing ever happened?"

Steve stared at me impassively.

"Let it go. You're right. I should be glad that I learned the truth about Oliver even if it got me in so much trouble. I mean, look where I am now."

I was in a hospital, talking to the man I secretly adored. Who was unconscious. And in serious financial jeopardy. And as much as I wanted to help him, I couldn't seem to do anything right.

An unexpected sob bubbled from my chest. I pressed Nash's hand against my cheek then laid it back on the bed.

"Don't worry. Not going to lay all that on you. Back to a safer topic. I wish you could help me with the teens. I'm not sure how to proceed. I've been relying on your guidance up until now."

The steady beeping of his monitors gave me comfort. I felt my shoulders relax. Allowing blood that had been constricted in my neck to flow properly to my brain.

"Of course, I should go to Wellspring and ask around there next. They were camped nearby. I have to go there tomorrow anyway. I never met the manager. I could talk to the other staff.

Not that there are many at the Wellspring Center. But I guess it just opened and without many guests…"

I laid his palm against my cheek again and sighed. "I don't know what to do without you, Nash. Why don't you wake up now?"

SEVENTEEN

#CircularFile #AsGoodAsItGets

---

*T*he next morning dawned full of promise. Even if the night hadn't brought any sleep. I had a new to-do list. Fuller and longer than I'd like. But there was hope that Nash would wake, and I applied that optimism with the last of my Tom Ford shimmering body oil. With Lucky repaired, I motored to work, keeping an eye out for motorcycles.

Thankfully, it proved too early for marauding cyclists.

Upon arriving at the office (today's donut was frosted maple), I realized I had no way to contact the kids. I needed them to check out the boot before I took it to Ian Mowry. See what they knew about Crispin and stalkers. Or any other non-*Stranger Things* theories that I could investigate. I didn't know the teens' last names, but I knew a place that might have taken their basic info.

They'd asked the other private investigator for help. Sweeney Security Solutions.

The thought made me shudder. And almost put me off the donut. But I couldn't let Jolene Sweeney have the upper hand. I crammed the frosted maple in my mouth and set off for Sweeney Security Solutions. On foot. It was one block over from the Dixie Kreme Donut building. Another slap in the face.

Instead of a second floor (dusty) two-room office, Sweeney Security Solutions had a first-floor suite in a beautifully restored historic brick property. With parking that wasn't overrun by donut shoppers. Flowers grew in decorative urns by the door. The big front window sparkled, as did the glass in the wooden door. The gold letters naming the business weren't chipped or peeling. And when I opened the door, the room smelled like fresh laundry and sunshine. Not men and donuts.

You couldn't have everything.

The girl at the front desk — young, pony-tailed, and eager— glanced up from her coffee. "You're Maizie Albright."

"Guilty as charged." I held up my hands and chuckled. "Is Jolene here?"

"Not yet."

Thank God for small favors.

"Jolene said you used to be on TV. Can you do something?" At my bewildered look, she added, "Like a line or something?"

I pointed my finger at her. "I'll make it happen."

She stared. A little blankly for my taste.

"Did you want something other than Julia Pinkerton? That was her catchphrase."

"Who's Julia Pinkerton?"

If only Vicki wasn't so wrapped up in *All is Albright* reality land, *Julia Pinkerton Teen Detective* would have sold to Netflix by now.

Then I reminded myself I didn't care about that anymore. "Never mind. What's your name?"

"Sienna." The girl glanced behind her as if Jolene made a habit of sneaking in through a back door. "I have a protocol I'm supposed to follow if you come in. Are you armed?"

"Totally not my thing."

"Are you alone?"

"Yes?" I twisted to confirm the small reception room was empty. The *All is Albright* film crew had orders not to follow me, but sometimes they surprised me.

"Are you paying for something? Or dropping off a payment of any kind?"

"No. Why would I pay Jolene?"

Sienna shrugged. "Then I need to ask you to leave. If that doesn't work…" She opened a drawer and pulled out a small revolver. "I'm supposed to threaten to shoot you."

I held up my hands. For real this time. Took three steps backward and stopped.

"Listen, Sienna. I'm just here to get some information. Did some teenagers come in yesterday? About a missing person? And possibly Bigfoot?"

"Yes." The pistol wavered.

"Can you put the gun down? I promise to leave in a minute. I just need the teens' phone numbers."

"I think that's private information." Sienna looked at the gun uncertainly.

"It's not worth shooting me over." Hells, Jolene. Arming a kid who didn't know how to use a gun. Against me. "Just set the gun on the desk. I'll go away in a minute. I promise."

"What if you try to take the gun from me?"

"I'm not interested in shooting you either." I slid backward, stopping at the door. "How's this? Jolene isn't taking the teens' case, is she?"

"I don't think so. She wasn't here when they came in. But when I told her they were teenagers, she laughed and told me to put their info in the circular file." Sienna laid the revolver on the desk. She flicked a glance over her shoulder, then dropped her voice to a whisper. "All our filing cabinets are rectangles."

"The circular file is a euphemism for a trash can."

Sienna frowned at me and cut her eyes toward the gun.

"Google it. Are you getting paid to work here?"

She nodded and her ponytail bounced. "I'm an intern. Jolene's my cousin. I'm getting paid in experience."

"Why aren't you in school? This is Monday, right?"

"It's a work-study program. I'm a senior. I only go to school for half the day. Although Jolene didn't say which half."

Oh boy. "Did you know the students who came in?"

She cocked her head. "Not really. They're younger than me. And they're not in the same classes as me."

Considering she didn't seem to be in any classes, that made sense. "But you recognize them."

"I know their show. They're in Communications, which mean they run the morning announcements. Sometimes they put on their own clips, which is totally unfair since Avery Manning has a way better show and they never show her clips." She cocked her head, flipping her ponytail. "Avery does makeup tutorials. The cosmetic companies send her makeup for free, hoping she'll talk about it on her vlog. I mean, how lucky can you get?"

That did sound pretty cool. "What's her YouTube channel called?" Wait a minute, I was getting sidetracked. "What do you think of Mara, Fred, and Laci? What's their rep?"

"They're like super popular. But not at school. They have a total attitude. Like they think they're smarter than everybody else."

Maybe they were. But I didn't want to make Sienna feel bad. "Do you know their vlog partner, Chandler? Did you hear he's missing?"

"He is? Did he quit? Chandler's so hot. He's the best part of the show. Avery is so going to want to hear about this."

Great, I started a high school vlog war. "About their contact sheet. Why don't I help you with that circular file issue? We have one in our office."

She opened her desk drawer and pulled out a single sheet of paper. Glanced at the gun.

"You followed protocol. If I see Jolene, I'll tell her you did a good job with that."

"Thanks." She handed me the paper. "You're not at all like Jolene said you'd be."

Taking the sheet, I folded it and shoved it in my pocket. Moved toward the door and stopped. I shouldn't want to know what

Jolene thought of me. I had a pretty good idea. But curiosity got the best of me. I turned to look back.

"What did Jolene say I'd be like?"

"'The dumbest B-list, non-talent who ever walked the face of the planet.' And 'a fat slut who used T and A to get her face plastered on TV and magazines.'" Sienna tapped her chin. "Um, a 'brat who doesn't deserve all that's been handed to her.' And 'Maizie couldn't get a clue, let alone find one, because her head is too far up her…'" Sienna's face reddened. "Well, you know where."

I winced.

"Oh, and, 'If anyone says otherwise, it's only because Vicki Albright paid them.'" Sienna noted my expression, placed her hand on the gun, and slid the revolver to the edge of the desk. "But I'm sure she didn't mean it."

Poor Sienna. Jolene meant every word even if she was wrong. For the most part.

*B*ack at the office, I sank into the desk chair to look at the Sweeney Security Solutions contact information. Noted the teens' fake names — Tony Stark, Carol Danvers, and Wanda Maximoff — and hoped the phone numbers were real.

I texted the kids, telling them I had information about Chandler and asking them to meet. Thought about how shady that sounded from an "adult offender." Qualified it with a text, asking them to meet at the office for an appointment. Followed by a text that their parents were invited to attend.

They didn't respond.

I chewed my lip. Remembered they were in school. Texted again, asking them to wait to text me until school was out.

Their three-way text arrived in swift, confusing swoops. Silly me, to think they wouldn't check their phones during school hours.

"Two fifty-five."

"Human geography quiz."

"Take it tomorrow."

"Can't. Orthodontist."

"After school."

"Marching band practice."

"Skip it."

"Orthodontist, dude. Use tomorrow's ortho slip. He'll never check."

I didn't want to know about that one.

"Wait. Gotta take notes."

At least someone was halfway paying attention in class.

Emojis paraded across a text bubble, followed by three animated GIFs. I tried to decipher their meaning then gave up.

"My office. After school. No skipping," I typed. During which six emojis and three more band excuses popped up. But I had a flip phone and no keyboard. "I need to talk to your parents." I added a happy face. Made from punctuation marks.

I received a thumbs up emoji and three phone numbers.

Satisfied, I closed the phone and readied my bag with a new Nash shirt for the hospital. And a pair of jeans. The tightest ones. Since he'd lost weight. Not that I'd noticed which pair were tighter. Much.

Hearing the door open, I turned. Lamar sauntered in and collapsed into the La-Z-Boy.

"You look a little hellish," I said.

"One of the big mixers shorted. I've been helping in the back. We're also short-staffed in front. The new girl wasn't working out. Sweet as anything. Cute as a bug. But dumber than a bag of rocks. She couldn't make change to save her life."

"Her name wasn't Sienna by any chance?" I held up a hand. "Never mind. I'm headed to the Wellspring Center."

"Community service?"

I jerked a nod, remembering his feelings about teen clients.

"How are those flyers coming?"

"Um, yeah. Great." Dangit. I'd spent the night searching *Bigfoot Trackers* for crazy stalker comments. After six hundred "Chandler, you're so hot. Swipe me sometime," I had a list of names to research. Out of thirty hundred sixty-eight different avatars, only sixteen lived within in a hundred mile radius of Black Pine. And of those sixteen, only three could legally drive. And of those three, only one wasn't in prison. And she turned out to be a Black Pine soccer mom. Who had pictures of a soccer tournament in another state during the time Chandler disappeared.

And then it was time to get up.

"Good. Don't know what we'd do without you, Maizie," said Lamar, closing his eyes. "Did you get that check from Mrs. Price yet?"

"Not yet, but I'm sure it will be fine." It didn't feel fine, but it always helps to be optimistic. "I'm going to see Detective Mowry today. I'll make my appointment with the ATF agent then, too. I have the case notes ready to go."

"Boy, it'd be nice if we had more income coming in right now. I'll see what I can do." Lamar yawned. "In a minute. Three thirty has never felt so early as it has this week."

"Have a little rest. I'm hoping to hear about a paying job this afternoon. Clients rejected by Jolene." I chewed my lip, feeling guilty that I deliberately misled Lamar. But I did hope the teens would pay. And then I could assuage Lamar's doubts with that happy news.

"Nash doesn't know how good he got it when he hired you."

One could always hope.

EIGHTEEN

#HashtagHealingRevolution
#StupidIstTheNewDumb

---

*A*fter a quick hospital visit — I spoke to the nurses about shaving Nash, but they said with his injuries it was better to let the beard grow, even if I was right about him waking up scratchy — I arrived at Dr. Trident's office, prepared to deliver Gladys's ultimatum.

For better or worse, he needed to therapy me. For reals.

But Dr. Trident was with a patient. Or so the sign on his door said.

Of course.

But that meant I was free to canvas the staff about one missing camper. I wandered the halls, looking for the manager's office. Following the signs, I found it in the west wing on the first floor. The old-timey accessories and oriental carpet had been removed in this hall. With white plaster walls, the heavy dark wood didn't look half as spooky as the rest of the building.

I entered the small waiting area. No receptionist. But like Dr. Trident's office, they'd gone cool California with the bamboo floors and sleek, modern furniture. I knocked on the manager's door. At the beckoning of the male voice inside, I entered.

Then began backing out the door.

"Wait, Maizie," said Oliver, hopping up from behind the desk. "Don't go."

"What are you doing in here?" I hissed. "Where's the manager?"

"I'm the manager."

The bottom of my stomach dropped to somewhere around my knees.

"Why are you doing this to me?" I said. "You're supposed to be in prison."

"I was pardoned."

"Why would they pardon you?"

"Because some legislators believed I was really trying to help the senior citizens. They talked to the governor. Lack of healthcare for things like pain medication is a real thing, Maizie."

"Not in Beverly Hills, Oliver. Did your parents donate to their campaigns?"

"That, too." He shrugged. Moving around the desk, he stopped in front of me. "I owe you an apology. Several. Please, don't leave yet. I need to apologize as part of my therapy. Could you just hear me out for one minute? Please?"

The pain registering in Oliver's face made me want to cringe. I'd seen it when he first told me stories about the people he helped. I'd thought it was an empathetic pain. I'll admit, it was attractive to see such compassion in a man so handsome and virile. Oliver had a high Hollywood hotness rating for a local celebrity. But it was the sensitivity that had hooked me. And then we'd hooked up. And gotten engaged. And it wasn't even during a sweeps week, like with Giulio.

However, the whole selling of drugs and masseuse-whatever had turned me off. Big time.

For good.

But, as someone who'd been through many bouts of therapy, I knew the struggle of needing to apologize to someone who didn't want to hear it. I planted my feet on the beautifully polished bamboo. And forced myself to listen to a litany of "never wanted to" and "never intended to" that began with an "I" and ended with a "you."

Like with Dr. Trident, I found it easiest to nod my head.

If I stayed much longer at the Center, I might need to see that healer about neck acupuncture.

"I really loved you, Maizie. I never meant to hurt you like this."

Nod.

"I shouldn't have listened to my lawyer and spoken up at your hearing."

Nod. With the help of all my willpower.

Which wasn't saying much. But still.

"And when I heard about this job, managing the Wellspring Center, it was like a dream-come-true. This is my niche. A place where I can really help people. With all kinds of holistic services. And to be here, close to you. It felt like the universe was giving me a second chance."

The universe did not seem to feel the same way about me.

"That's a really weird coincidence, Oliver. You don't even need to work. Not like in a real job. Does your probation officer know where you are? Why would they let you leave California?"

"Don't worry so much, Maizie. I got all the red tape cleared. Vicki helped me."

Vicki. I should have known. "When?"

"About a month ago. With all the new film industry activity here, it seemed like the perfect destination for a healing retreat. The South needs to catch up with California when it comes to the benefits of holistic healing and who better to introduce it than well-known personalities…"

I stopped listening to do a quick math check. About a month ago, Vicki had gotten engaged to Giulio. Was this more punishment for ditching my old career? I really needed to talk to my therapist about this.

Then remembered who my therapist was.

Thank you, universe.

Oliver held out his arms. "Do you want to hug it out?"

"Not really." I turned, then pivoted back. "I actually came here to talk to the manager about a missing person."

Oliver grinned. "That's me. Do you want to sit down?"

I shook my head. "Did the police come by last week about a young man who went missing nearby? He was camping with some local teens. Did anyone see him?"

"Sorry, I wasn't here yet. I can ask my staff and get back to you, though."

"Thanks."

"Maizie, I want to make all this up to you. Anything you want, it's yours."

"Just the information about the camper would be great."

"If you think of something else you'd like, let me know."

I'd like Oliver to return to California ASAP. But I just nodded.

I really needed a talk with the universe and find out what I'd done to tick it off.

I'd planned to ask Everett Lawson about missing Chandler Jonson. The guy had suspicious vibes, but I wanted to remain open-minded. My daddy walked around his property with a gun. And was often surly. It was kind of a mountain man thing. Although Everett took it to an extreme. I also wanted to ask other staff about Chandler. Hopefully, someone had seen something.

And maybe I'd slip in a few questions about what Oliver was really doing here. It wasn't like he needed a job.

I had an idea of why he took the position at the Wellspring Center. And why Vicki had encouraged it. It was a way to pull me back into her fold. Not that she ever liked Oliver that much when we were dating. He was "tolerable" as a local A-lister. She'd rather I marry a director. Or better yet a director who had the money for producing. Someone who could do more for our career.

I mean, my career.

And people thought arranged marriages were dead.

At reception, I asked for Everett Lawson.

"Who?" said the young man working behind the desk. "He's on staff? I don't know him."

"Maybe he's the gardener. I'm not sure of his official title. But he seems to be garden-y, caretaker-y."

"Check the groundskeeping office."

I leaned on the desk and tried a new lead. "Do you know anything about Chandler Jonson?"

"Is he a gardener?"

"No, he was camping nearby and went missing. Last week."

"Sorry." The man shook his head.

"How's your new manager? Is Oliver Fraser on the up-and-up?"

He took a breath. "Did you just come from the juice bar? Sometimes if you mix certain herbs, they can make you feel a little confused."

"Thanks for the advice." I would skip the juice bar. I didn't need any more confusion in my life.

In groundskeeping, I found a sign listing the landscaper, lawn service, and pool service personnel. I didn't know if they were on break or working elsewhere, but they weren't in the office. In either case, Everett Lawson was not listed among their numbers. Which was weird.

I wandered the resort — from the pool to the gym to Café, and even to the massage huts — and spoke to very few people. None knew Everett except by sight but could not tell me his title or where to find him. None knew of Chandler, although several remembered the police asking about him. Everyone seemed to like Oliver.

Just my luck.

I also didn't see many guests. But the place was new. They needed some casual (paid) mentions in the right magazines and on social media to get the ball rolling. Free stays for the right people. A luxe hookup for a notoriously finicky and privacy-conscious celeb. With some captured candids of the celeb enjoying the Center sent to the right media outlets.

Or at least, that's how I understood how celebrity marketing worked.

In any case, it didn't take long to return to Dr. Trident's office. My sticky note had been removed and the "in session" sign had been taken down. I knocked and entered. Found Dr. Trident with a couple. A man in a business suit and a woman in a lab coat.

"Do you know Maizie Albright?" said Dr. Trident. "She's one of my patients. She used to be on TV. I'm helping her through a difficult period."

"Wonderful," said the business man.

"Nice to meet you." I held out my hand, hoping the wonderfulness had been paired with "helping me" and not "difficult period."

"Sam Martin. Call me Sam." Sam's smile didn't evoke the expectation of animated sparkles like Dr. Trident. But it was still nice. "What do you think of the Wellspring Center?"

"It's impressive. Are you a guest?"

"An investor and founder. Have you tried the spa? The rejuvenate waters are amazing. That was the original use back at the turn of the twentieth century. That's where the Wellspring name came from."

"I had no idea."

"Trident." Sam turned to the doctor. "You haven't told her about the waters?"

"I begin inward and then work outward, Sam," said Dr. Trident. "Maizie needs a lot of inward help. Starting outward. Although Maizie, mixing traditional cures with new methods is trending. We must look to our past to see our future. Don't you think so?"

"I'm no expert—"

"Of course you're not." Dr. Trident beamed. "That's why I'm here for you."

Dang universe.

"We're very proud of what we've done," said Sam. "We want

to give our clients everything they could need in a health resort. Physical, spiritual, and emotional healing. That's why Dr. Trident's on board. He's made quite a name for himself. And now Dr. Sakda's here, too."

I glanced at the woman still standing a few steps outside our small group.

"Nice to meet you, Dr. Sakda." When she didn't respond, I burbled. "You remind me of Lucy, one of my posse on *Kung Fu Kate?* On the show, Lucy was supposed to be Chinese but in real life, Lucy's name was Sunisa Sakda. She's Thai. Are you Thai?"

Dr. Sakda's eyes widened. *"Kung Fu Kate?* What? Just because I'm Asian doesn't mean I do martial arts."

"Of course not," I stammered. My cheeks heated. "I didn't mean to imply that or stereotype you. Actually, on the show, they made sure my posse was diverse. We had…Oh, God. What I mean is…You see I was an actress. And on children's TV shows these days, they are very careful…as well they should be…Although why I was the star when I'm…Anyway, I love bubble tea. And curry. But especially pad thai. Unless that's not really Thai?"

Her eye roll was completely justified.

"I don't suppose you're a therapist, are you?" When she shook her head, I wasn't sure whether to be relieved or disappointed.

"Dr. Sakda is like a nutritionist," said Dr. Trident.

"Ethnobotonist," said Dr. Sakda. "My degree is in biochemistry, not nutrition."

"She and I are working together. We're creating herbal blends for the juice bar. It's going to revolutionize healing." Dr. Trident rocked back on his heels, smiling. "Oh, I like that. Hashtag-healing-revolution."

"That's very interesting," I said, hoping to redeem myself. "I'm sure the difference in each person's biochemistry means they each need a different—"

"I don't make herbal blends," said Dr. Sakda. "I'm a molecular scientist."

"Um, that's interesting, too?"

Dr. Sakda was going to hurt her eyes with all that rolling.

I changed the subject. "Did any of you hear about a missing camper? His name is Chandler Jonson."

"Sorry," said Sam. "Is he a friend?"

"Friend of a friend. He and some teens were camping nearby on Black Pine Mountain. He disappeared on them."

"Really?" said Dr. Trident. "Did they go to the police?"

"The police hit a dead end. The K9 unit tracked him to his car and the car was found at the Atlanta airport."

"That's good news isn't it?" said Sam.

"Except no one's heard from him."

"Did you try the Atlanta police?" said Dr. Sakda. "If he's in Atlanta, wouldn't that be the logical place to look?"

"I'm going to…check into that. I'm sort of helping these kids. The ones who were camping. And they're really upset. And…"

"Maizie, look at me," said Dr. Trident. "I can tell by the sound of your voice you are feeling unsure and confused."

"Those are kind of normal feelings for me? I think I'm just worried…"

"Of course, you're worried. And you know what worry does?"

"Causes panic attacks?"

"No, Maizie, you cause panic attack."

"I think—"

"You shouldn't think. Maizie, look at me. Worry does nothing."

I widened my eyes. It seemed to work better than speaking.

"Repeat, after me, Maizie. 'Worry does nothing.'"

I gritted my teeth, feeling the pile-on of humiliation. I couldn't look at Sam or Dr. Sakda but felt their embarrassment for me. "Worry does nothing."

"Do you feel it, Maizie?" Dr. Trident held out his hands and waved them before me. "Feel the energy?"

"Energy…" I spoke slowly. "From your hands?"

"No, from the words, 'worry does nothing.' I'm just very physically expressive." Dr. Trident held up his hands, twisting them.

"But you could be right. I knew a guru who said my chi was strong."

"As entertaining as this was, I need to go," said Dr. Sakda.

Dr. Trident gave her a short bow. "Of course. Until our next meeting."

She shook her head and strode from the room.

"Maizie." Sam clasped my hand. "I've heard a lot about you. I'm so glad to finally meet you. We'll get you involved in our programs."

"Where did you hear about me? From Dr. Trident?"

Dr. Trident beamed.

"No," said Sam. "Actually, from our new manager."

Oliver. Damn universe.

NINETEEN

#MicroabrasedEmbrace #BookinIt

$\mathcal{M}$y eyes were on my to-do list when the universe
called out for the third time that morning.

"Darling, there you are. I've been looking all over for you," said
Giulio. "Why haven't you returned my texts and calls?"

I took a massive ujjayi breath and counted down my blessings
before releasing. It didn't take long considering my week. Shoving
my to-do list into my pocket, I turned to face Giulio. He wore a
plush white robe, Fendi slides, and possibly nothing else.

"Because I'm busy," I said. "I don't want to hear about the
wedding. And, hello, clothes?"

"Someone needs to listen because your *madre* will not." He
flung his arms out, exposing his sculpted and waxed chest. "Look
at what the stress is doing to me."

I sniffed. He smelled like La Mer and San Pellegrino. "You're so
shiny. Exfoliated?"

"I just came from the water treatment. And a body micro abra-
sion. It was necessary for the stress. But if my skin was not glow-
ing, you would see what your mother is doing to me."

"Are you both staying at the resort?"

"We are guests of *il stronzo*." Giulio swung his arm toward the west wing. "He is up to no good, I tell you. This Oliver. Good riddance for you. But unlucky for me."

"Stop gesturing. Your robe keeps opening."

"Lucky for you, then?" His dark eyes gleamed. Much like his skin. "Darling, join me for a massage? Deep tissue."

"Gotta go." I turned back toward the exit.

"Wait, Maizie. You have to help me. Your *madre*'s wedding plans are growing the more insane. Why animals and helicopters? What is she thinking?"

I pivoted. "I'm sorry, Giulio. I just don't have time for this. With Nash in the hospital and this new case plus the community service and therapy? You want to see stress? Look at me. The bags under my eyes have their own circles."

He sidled forward. "It's true. You look terrible, my darling. Really wretched. Come with me. You can relax in my room. If your mother sees us?" He shrugged, and the robe parted. "What can we say?"

"We can say no, Giulio. We say no," I said and stalked off.

*B*efore going back to the office, I puttered Lucky toward the Jonson house. I wanted to know if Crispin housed a red, fast-looking motorcycle. Which would save Detective Ian Mowry a lot of time in arresting him.

I parked Lucky on the street before the Jonson's. Noted which neighbors didn't look home (all of them) and cut across a lawn to the side yard. Walked nonchalantly to the garage window. Covered by shades. Crossing the driveway, I zipped around to the front porch and rang the bell.

No answer.

I took a minute to think about the empty house and the dutifulness of the self-professed dutiful son. Hurried around to the backyard, pulled up the latch on the pool fence, and hiked up the deck stairs to the back door. Tried the knob and entered. The Jonson's had an alarm system that — thanks to my Nash Security Solutions training — I knew was unarmed.

Thank you, prodigal son.

I took a left into the kitchen, found the garage door, and spotted a golf cart, and a Honda CRV full of Taco Bell bags and empty energy drink cans. Probably Crispin's car. Either he drove one of his parent's (likely much nicer) vehicles or he sported around on a red motorcycle. I toured the garage, looking for motorcycle evidence — No extra helmets or motorcycle handbooks — before returning to the house.

In the kitchen, I detoured up the back stairs to Crispin's room. No helmets or motorcycle jackets in his closet. The room still held the qualities of a pigsty. Gladys would not approve. She'd also not approve of his stash. Crispin had even left his TV and computer on. So much for his environmental footprint.

I slid into the gaming chair before his computer and clicked the mouse to wake the dark screen. Password. Glancing at the indie posters on his wall, I took a gamble and typed, "Frank."

Bingo.

Thank you *Donnie Darko*.

Hoping to find a picture of the motorcycle, I searched his files. No photo uploads. Tons of unfinished scripts. I glanced at his email. Rejections from film schools, amateur movie awards, and agents. I clicked on another window. A paused game appeared. In the upper corner, a text box blinked. I studied the screen and felt a stirring of recognition. Then fought off a wave of nausea. My lungs contracted and I dropped my head between my knees.

Same stupid shoot-em-up game that Roger Price played.

I waited for the moment to pass, studying the wires and dust bunnies beneath his desk. And the brown box he barely attempted to hide. I nudged the box with my foot, then used the toe of my sneaker to open it. The top of a baggie peeked out. Reaching in, I pulled out a capsule. I didn't recognize the brown color. No printing on the capsule either. It didn't appear manufactured by a big company. But then most people didn't get their drugs by the baggie in plain brown boxes.

Crispin's pharmaceuticals weren't my business.

Letting out a disgusted sigh, I thought about how badly I sucked at finding clues.

The stairs creaked and the light from the hall blinked on.

Craptastic.

I slid out of the chair, onto the floor, and crawled to the far side of the bed. Peeked underneath. Shuddered at the thought of sharing the floor with Crispin's boxers and pizza boxes. A shadow blocked the doorway. I wiggled an arm and leg beneath the bed. My shoulder slipped in, but my butt had issues.

Once again, my body shape failed me.

The shadow entered the room. What would Crispin do if he caught me? Call the police? Invite me to spark up?

Holding my breath, I stilled my wriggling. I heard him at the dresser, rummaging around, then cross to the computer.

Shizzles. I'd left the computer screen on.

While he clicked, I clenched and squirmed, trying to get under the bed. Giving up, I slid my leg and arm out and considered my options. The closet stood open. The adjoining bathroom was across the room. I could crouch by the bed until he caught me.

The clicking had stopped. The gaming chair sighed and shuffled.

Slowly, I slid my legs beneath my body. Rested my hands on the carpet, ready to spring. Kept my head ducked below the bed until the last possible minute.

The footsteps moved closer and stopped.

I bounced to my feet, an excuse ready to tumble from my lips. A book hurtled across the room. I covered my face and ducked. The book glanced off my shoulder and fell on the bed. Shaking off my surprise, I barely registered the man's shape before he leaped through the bedroom door. Footsteps pounded down the hall and clattered on the stairs. I ran after him.

"Crispin?" I called. "It's me, Maizie Albright. Sorry to scare you."

At the top of the stairs, I paused to listen. A door slammed. I pounded down the stairs and glanced left and right. Chose the living room, then darted through the hall into the kitchen. Outside, a motorcycle engine cranked. I pelted back into the living room toward the front window. The helmeted rider zoomed down the drive and cut a hard left into the street.

The front door stood ajar. I turned the lock and closed it behind me. Cutting across the yard, I ran for the street, hoping to get the make and model of the cycle.

The cyclist was gone. Crispin didn't seem the book throwing type. He seemed the "I found you hiding in my bedroom, now you have to do my indie project and introduce me to all your insider contacts" type. Which meant...

Hells, I had no idea. Per ushe. It was probably Crispin.

I jogged back to Lucky. She'd been knocked over. But she still worked.

"I'm sorry this keeps happening to you," I said. "Not that you have feelings, but it does seem like someone doesn't want me looking into Chandler's disappearance. Or they have a strong animosity toward dirt bikes."

Which made no sense. But neither did anything else this week.

I retrieved my helmet which had rolled farther down the curb. Pulled my phone from my pocket and considered calling Ian Mowry. To report someone had thrown a book at my head and knocked over my bike...during my breaking and entering?

Probably not a good idea.

Or to narc on Crispin? I slipped the pill from my pocket and studied it. Brown powder inside a clear capsule. It looked like something from a health food store. Which was probably why Crispin was buying it in bulk. The weed was another story — prescription or no, it was still illegal in Georgia — but a drug bust over a dime bag could tie up my investigation if he had anything to do with Chandler's disappearance.

My investigation. I snorted. I had a boot and a hostile brother. And some kids who really believed an evil scientist (or evil developer) at Wellspring had kidnapped their friend.

Both favorite villains in *Kung Fu Kate* and *Julia Pinkerton, Teen Detective*. Which didn't help their case much at all.

TWENTY

#KidsTheseDays
#MyPeopleAndYourPeople

---

*L*amar heard me enter the Dixie Kreme building — I forgot to skip the step that sounded like a gunshot — and met me in front of the office door. He handed me a donut. "There are high schoolers here for you."

"Sorry."

"I gave them donuts. Maizie…"

"I know, I know. I just found something and…Don't worry, this won't take long. And as soon as they're gone, I'll call Mrs. Price and see what's taking so long with the check."

Nodding his head, Lamar plodded down the stairs to the donut shop. I jiggled the office knob, pulled the door forward, pushed it open, and halted. Eyes on their devices, Laci, Fred, and Mara had sprawled across the floor and furniture. Donut debris, backpacks, and camera equipment littered the coffee table and floor.

"OMG. I just cleaned this place," I said. "How do three people take up an entire room? And would a hello kill you? I mean, what if I were an armed robber or an ax-murderer? I could have walked in and taken you out and you wouldn't even have noticed. Get off your phones."

Three sighs floated toward me. Three phones, one laptop, and an iPad clicked off. Mostly.

"We noticed you," said Fred. "We're doing homework."

"On your phones?"

"I have a paper to write," said Laci.

"With your thumb?" I shook my head and opened my backpack. "Do you recognize this boot?"

A hesitant yes resounded. So hesitant, I wasn't sure who said it.

"I'll turn the boot into the police as evidence. However, I asked around today and nobody knows anything at the Wellspring Center. It's so fenced off, I doubt anyone saw Chandler. I also looked in his apartment and talked to his brother. I keep coming up empty. I think we need to try other avenues of investigation." I held up my hand to stop their protests. "At least for now. I want your play-by-play of that night. Detailed play-by-play. And everything you know about Chandler."

"We already told the police what happened," said Laci.

"I'm not the police." I narrowed my eyes at the fake "obviously" cough.

"It had to be something to do with the Wellspring Center," said Mara. "And they had to have taken Chandler. They must have driven his car to Atlanta. Maybe they left prints on the car?"

"Everyone knows not to leave prints," said Fred. "They would have worn gloves or wiped the car down. But they might have left DNA evidence. Maybe the police could sweep his car for hair and fibers. That doesn't take any time."

"Real life is not a *CSI* episode. I'm going to tell you right now, the likelihood of the police doing DNA tests on Chandler's car is extremely low. Unless we have real evidence that he's gone. That's what I'm looking for. Real evidence so we can help the police."

"We're not hiring you so we can go to the police," said Laci.

"But first," I continued. "I need to talk to your parents."

They groaned and flopped around on the floor.

"If you want my help, we're doing this my way," I said, then remembered that was a line from *Julia Pinkerton*. Not Julia's line.

Her teacher's line in season one, episode eight, "Trust No One." Causing Julia, the teacher, and her class to get trapped by an evil land developer. Julia saved the lives of all his students, but the teacher had died. After apologizing for doing it his way instead of following Julia's advice.

I looked at the teens and chewed my nail.

"Listen, I need to understand Chandler better," I said. "To figure out the motive for his disappearance, I need to study the victim. When we have a logical motive, we'll be able to figure out the means for who did this. Does that make sense?"

They nodded.

"Walk me through that night."

Fred looked at the girls and picked up his phone.

Exasperated, I snatched his phone from his hand. "Fred, I'm trying to talk to you."

He held out his hand. "We're going to walk you through the night. But I need to ask my mom's permission first."

I found Lamar in the donut shop kitchen, wrestling a giant mixer with a screwdriver and a pair of pliers. He set down the pliers and looked over the top of his readers. "I thought you told the kids you needed to spend your time getting new accounts."

"I know," I controlled the frustration seeping into my voice. "But they're good kids. And they only have me. And I think they'll pay us. I'm going to talk to their parents. But don't worry, I'm still working on new clients. And everything else."

Lamar kept his eyes steady on me.

"Now that Giulio is breaking up with Vicki, I don't have to deal with the wedding. That's some bonus time. Of course, Vicki doesn't know that, so she's getting irritated when I don't respond to her Outlook invites. And I already did my volunteer community service for the day. Sort of."

"I guess that's good." I always admired how Lamar steeped his doubt in patience. "Did you hear from Mrs. Price yet? Has she paid up? I saw y'all have some bills due."

"Mrs. Price isn't returning my calls. I think she's avoiding me," I said. "But I did steal the missing camper case from Jolene. Although she didn't want it, so technically I didn't steal it."

"And technically it isn't a case."

"Right. But I do have an in with Jolene's receptionist now. It's possible she'll give me leads without even knowing. If Sienna doesn't shoot me. Jolene gave her a derringer."

Lamar slow blinked.

"Seriously. I should report Jolene to the police except I don't want to get Sienna in trouble."

Lamar sighed, took off his glasses, and rubbed his eyes. "Maizie, have you slept since the bombing?"

"It's been kind of hard to sleep with all the tooth fairy snares. I snuck to the kitchen for a water, stepped in one, and found myself tied to the kitchen table until Daddy got up. Luckily, he gets up around four. The girl used some kind of flexible wire."

Lamar pushed out of his chair and circled the desk to stand before me. He placed both hands on my shoulders. "Maizie. You need some rest."

I shook my head. I still needed to see Detective Mowry about the boot and my bike. And then take the teens fake-camping. But I didn't want to worry Lamar. He had enough with the shop and worrying about Nash. "I just need more coffee. I'm sorry. I'm babbling."

"Why don't you go home? Or better yet, go upstairs and take a nap. It's quiet there."

"That's the problem. It's too quiet. We need clients. I'll go to Jolene's office right now. I know I can talk Sienna into giving up some files. And I'll make Mrs. Price—"

"Maizie, you're no good to Nash if you can't think straight."

"Lamar, I can't sleep, so I might as well work." I gulped. "Every time I close my eyes, I see Nash in the bank. I just can't."

His lined face grew more furrowed. "Hon'—"

"It's okay, Lamar. I can handle it. It's only been three days. And Nash will wake up soon."

*T*o placate Lamar and to prevent us from being sued, I called the three's parents. They agreed to meet immediately at Fred's mom's house. Which was "so embarrassing."

According to Fred.

Mrs. Hernandez served *polvorones* cookies and sweet tea as an after school treat. I immediately liked her.

"Thanks for meeting with me," I said, handing out my Nash Security Solutions business cards. "I just wanted to make sure you were okay with your kids hiring me to look for Chandler Johnson."

Laci's dad sighed. "It's their money, I suppose."

Off to a good start. They knew an investigation cost money.

"And don't worry about them riding with me in a car. I drive a dirt bike."

The parents looked at each other.

"How old are you?" asked Mara's mom.

"Twenty-five. I'm an apprentice to the owner, Wyatt Nash. He's…indisposed. But I have his full support." I crossed my fingers behind my back. "A little about me, I've been working most of my life. Not as an investigator. But I did play one on TV."

"TV?" Laci's dad cocked his head. "Who was your agent? Do they do referrals?"

"They're not going to need an actor's agent," said Mara's mom. "An entertainment lawyer would better serve them. Didn't you hire one to look at their sponsor contracts?"

"I'm a lawyer," said Laci's dad. "I don't need to hire entertainment law to read a contract."

"So, Chandler Johnson." I segued to get us out from under the excruciating weight of the entertainment industry. "How well did you know him?"

"I give Chandler props for his vision," said Laci's dad. "He's got a great face for the camera. But I think it's our kids' response to Chandler that really makes the show popular."

"He did teach them a lot about videography," said Mrs. Hernandez.

"That's nice," I said, thankful that at least Fred's mom thought about the victim.

"But Federico taught Chandler how to do an ad campaign," she continued. "Fred got ten thousand likes on their last Facebook and Instagram ad. I think he's really good at choosing clips that go viral."

"Mara wrote the copy for that ad," said Mara's mom. "And it was her video they chose."

"Yes," I said quickly. "That's all wonderful. But I'm really interested in Chandler as a person. To, you know, help me find him."

"Chandler's flaky," said Laci's dad. "He also knows how to live off the grid. Good luck with that."

"I'm going to be pissed if Chandler left to start a new channel," said Mara's mom. "We're invested. He's the star."

"Not necessarily," said Laci's dad.

"NYU's film school wants current work and Mara won't be applying for another year. You can't seriously think they'll have this kind of popularity without Chandler? He's got the young male and older woman demographic."

"They already know how to do everything on their own," said Laci's dad. "Mara's a great director. Fred knows the tech. And Laci's something else on the screen."

"Do you think Chandler just took off?" I said. A little sadly, I'll admit.

"That's what the police told us. To Mexico." Mrs. Hernandez curled her lip. "His family said Chandler can be irresponsible like that. If I had known that from the beginning, I don't think I'd let Fred do this project."

"I thought the kids were doing the YouTube thing because they really believe in Bigfoot?"

"You know kids. They like to geek out." Mrs. Hernandez turned to Mara's mom. "Isn't that what they call it?"

She nodded. "They certainly do. Mara's always loved Bigfoot stories. But now she's able to transition that into a film career. I'm so excited for her."

"Back to Chandler," I said. "Your kids really like him. And — on camera, at least — he seems fond of them. It surprised me that he would ditch the three in the woods. It seems out of character."

"It was rude," said Mrs. Hernandez. "But Fred's working toward his Eagle Scout badge, so I'm not worried about him. But to leave the girls? And to take off without saying goodbye?"

"Mara can handle herself," said Mara's mom. "She's been camping since she was a baby. Just because she's a girl, doesn't mean she can't take care of herself."

"Of course," said Mrs. Hernandez.

"It's not a big deal," said Laci's dad. "They meet up, do the shoot, then separate. Particularly if someone has homework. I can't have Laci out all night if she's got an exam the next day."

"They often meet up in the woods and leave each other there?"

I didn't want to judge their parenting skills — especially as a non-parent — but I felt judgy. However, I also didn't understand camping. Or wanting to be in the woods. Or Bigfoot.

The teens were right about one thing. Nobody else seemed to care about Chandler's disappearance.

"Your kids are very concerned," I said. "I feel like I need some evidence for them — one way or another — to confirm what happened to Chandler."

"Federico's very attached to Chandler," said Mrs. Hernandez. "He's like an older brother. But Fred doesn't understand that sometimes young adults are selfish."

They looked at the young adult in the room for confirmation.

I shrugged. "I suppose that's true. But —"

"We appreciate your willingness to help our kids," said Laci's dad. "We think it's a waste of time, but they have their own money available to them. To be honest, I advised against this, but they're being stubborn."

"It can't interfere with their school work," said Mara's mom.

"If you find him," said Mrs. Hernandez. "Tell Chandler that he owes them at least a final episode."

"They should have signed a partnership contract," said Mara's mom. "We can't threaten to sue now."

"We still can," said Laci's dad. "We can argue that it was an oral agreement."

Poor Chandler, already facing a lawsuit. Unless he was kidnapped and murdered like the kids thought. Then maybe the parents would cut him some slack.

TWENTY-ONE

#GrizzlyTeddy #DetectiveDoGooder

*N*ow that I had secured one case for Nash, I needed to score more. Knowing Sienna's directive, I approached Sweeney Security Solutions cautiously. Fortunately, Sienna had a customer. Unfortunately, the customer was my former fiancé.

The first one.

Before I could escape, a tinkling bell had announced my entrance. Oliver turned from his stance before Sienna's desk, did a double take from his initial quick glance, and crossed the room in what seemed like one stride. "Maizie, it's so good to see you." He stopped a few feet from me, looking unsure as to how to greet me.

"What are you doing here?" I flicked a glance at Sienna to check for the derringer.

"I'm helping Vicki. She decided to hold the wedding at the Wellspring Center. Her previous venue didn't allow elephants. I'm not sure what that means, but we're happy to accommodate her. This place is providing extra security."

Which meant that Jolene would lose the project when Giulio dumped Vicki. I hadn't thought about that piece of the breakup. I couldn't help a satisfied smile. "Great."

Evidently, Oliver mistook my smile. He stole closer. "Do you want to get a coffee? Just to talk. I found a place that makes great donuts. I know how you love—"

I quickly shook my head. "No, thank you. I came to talk to Sienna. Hello, Sienna."

"Hello, Maizie." Sienna put her hand beneath the desk.

"Jolene would not want you shooting me with witnesses present. Did she mention that?"

"Let me check my notes."

"What did you mean, shoot you?" said Oliver.

"Never mind. I'm working." I moved around Oliver to approach the desk. Then glanced back. "Actually, Oliver could you stay a few minutes? Don't get any ideas. Just so Sienna doesn't shoot me."

"Of course." He wedged his large frame into a chair.

I turned back to the receptionist desk. "Sienna, I've been thinking about that circular file problem you have. Do you have more cases you need help filing?"

"Actually, I have a bunch," she said. "Jolene showed me how to do a credit check and if the score doesn't meet her number, I'm supposed to dump it. Or if the clients don't photograph well. Unless their credit score is one hundred points above her cutoff."

"I'll take those off your hands." In my head, I drummed my fingers together and cackled. Jolene's snobbery would save our business. Outside my head, I kept it cool. "We don't photograph the client, only the person they want watched."

Sienna dropped her voice to a whisper. "Most people who come here don't photograph well because they're, you know, old? And they get kind of angry when I ask them to Airdrop me their selfie. They don't know how to Airdrop. Or selfie. This job is so hard."

"I can only imagine."

Sienna pulled open a drawer.

"Please don't shoot me." I backed up. "I just thought if you were going to throw them away—"

Oliver shot out of the chair and darted in front of me. Sweeping an arm behind him, he crushed me into his back, then lunged toward the desk. "Drop it, Sienna."

Sienna screamed and dropped the pile of folders on her desk. Her chair rolled backward and hit the wall.

I peered out from behind Oliver, pushed his arm away, and stepped out. "I'm sorry. When she opens a drawer, I get nervous."

Oliver whooshed out a breath and turned to face me. "Man, you scared me."

"No, you scared me." Sienna's eyes had gone all anime — so large and rounded, they seemed to take up her entire face. "You're so big and your voice sounded so mean and scary."

"His voice is deep," I said. "It just sounds worse than it is."

"I wouldn't hurt anybody." Oliver was doing that thing with his face again. Mixing hurt and hope. Making me uncomfortable. "I just want to help. Please, Maizie. Let me make everything up to you. I'll do anything."

"That is so sweet," said Sienna. "You're like a teddy bear inside a grizzly bear. Or a polar bear. Except polar bears are so cute. Grizzly bear. And you photograph really well. Super well. You're actually kind of hot."

"Yes," I said. "Oliver's been photographing well for a long time. But it's too late. I have moved on with my life. I'll just take the files—"

"But he was willing to take a bullet for you," said Sienna.

"Yes, I would," said Oliver. "And I'd do it again."

"Sienna wasn't going to shoot me, so it doesn't matter." I darted to her desk and grabbed the files.

"I could still shoot you," said Sienna. "Just to make you see how much he cares about you."

"That's okay. I got the point. Not necessary." I ran for the door, calling over my shoulder. "Thanks. Glad we could help each other. Later."

I wasn't sure who I hated more. Jolene or the universe.

*A*s much as I wanted to return to the hospital — Not to reassure myself that Nash's shoulders were bigger than Oliver's. To get advice on using night vision goggles. — I forced myself to stick to the to-do list. Mrs. Price wasn't answering her phone, but I wanted to catch Detective Ian Mowry before he left work. I had a boot to deliver. And I could also ask him about night vision goggles. Without having to deduce the answer.

The Black Pine police station was not my favorite place — it ranked near the bottom of my list, somewhere between the gym and Vicki's nip and tuck clinic — but at least I wasn't there to give witness testimony. Or victim testimony. Or suspect testimony. After speaking to the officer behind the bulletproof shield in the waiting room, I only had to wait a minute before Mowry opened the door to the back offices.

"Maizie." He grinned. "Good to see you. Come on in."

"Thanks, Ian." I followed him through the door, past the fingerprint/storage room and into a larger room of cubicles. The station buzzed with a mix of anticipation and tension. Mowry hurried me past groups of officers talking in hushed voices. We took a right down a row of cubicles.

Ian lowered his voice. "A body was found on Black Pine Mountain. That's why I've been so busy."

"What happened? An accident?"

He shook his head. "Suspicious death. Gunshot. A hiker found the body few days ago."

I placed a hand on his arm. "It couldn't be Chandler Jonson, could it?"

"No, hon'. Different ethnicity. But we still don't have an ID. GBI is running his fingerprints for us. We sent him to the bureau in Atlanta for the autopsy." Ian waved me to a chair by his desk. The cubicle walls were covered with sticky notes and drawings made by his daughter. Adorbs. "But never mind that. What do you have for me?"

"I found a boot at the Wellspring Center. It feels silly, but it's newish and was buried in a new flower bed. The teens think they recognize it from the missing camper. Anyway, I just thought I'd hand it over as evidence." I handed him a shopping bag.

"I'll give it to the officer who handled the investigation. He'll call you later with questions." Ian placed the bag on his desk. "How're you doing? How's Nash?"

"Still in a coma." I sighed. "I'm okay. Roger Price's mother won't pay us. It's totally awkward asking for money from a client whose son was arrested for almost killing my boss."

"Price is lucky the bomb didn't hurt anyone else. Nash deserves a medal." Ian rocked in his chair. "Did the ATF agent tell you they think Price was working with someone?"

"No." I frowned. "To us, Roger appeared quite the loner. The typical geeky gamer. Who evidently likes to make bombs and blow people up. His mother thought he was into drugs, but we didn't even find evidence of that, either."

"I don't know any details. Just water cooler talk. We gave ATF a cubicle while she's investigating, but Agent Langtry's not very friendly. At least not to me." He shook his head, then waved off the comment. "Doesn't matter. I just wish I knew more."

"It's possible Roger was working with someone. We'd only been following him for a few days. He didn't meet with anyone during that time, but the officer could have pulled dead files off his computer we hadn't accessed. We were watching his phone and the other usual stuff. He was on social media a lot, but it was mostly gaming talk."

Ian nodded. "How's your bike?"

"Daddy fixed it. Good as new." I hadn't told him about Lucky's second mishap since it involved a bit of illegality called Breaking and Entering. I suspected Ian wouldn't view my run-in at the Jonson home as "no harm, no foul." I busied myself with finding a smaller bag inside my backpack. "I almost forgot. The motorcyclist at Chandler's apartment might have dropped this. I can't say for sure."

Ian peeked at the lighter and cocked his head. "This was near your bike? With a cut fuel line?"

"I don't want to do paperwork, Ian."

"Neither do I." He studied me. "If you're not sure, I'll just hang on to it for now."

"Is stealing gas a problem on that end of town?"

"Not really. But that kind of crime can be random. I don't have a number on the motorcycle yet. Can you remember the make or model?" He smiled. "It'd be helpful to have more than "red" and "fast-looking.""

"Sorry." I sighed. "An investigator should be better at paying attention to details. I didn't realize how badly I sucked at investigating until I had to do it alone."

"You're in training. You shouldn't expect to handle a full case by yourself." Ian scooted his chair closer, then leaned forward, placing his forearms on his knees. "Maizie, I'm worried about you. You look really...tired or something."

"This heat does a number on my skin." I flushed, knowing guilt did the same thing. "And I could really use a keratin treatment. A manicure and facial, too. Plus, community service is hard on my wardrobe."

Ian shook his head. "It's in your eyes. Don't get me wrong. You look as beautiful as ever. But I recognize that kind of exhaustion."

"Oh, that." I rose from my chair. "I'm not sleeping."

"You're a little young for insomnia. Maybe you should see a doctor."

"I have one. He's part of the problem."

TWENTY-TWO

#ThePriceofthePrices
#UnaBombaMomma

---

*A*s much as I wanted to return home, eat Carol Lynn's food, and pretend to sleep, I couldn't let Nash down. We had a client overdue for payment. I had procrastinated long enough. Mrs. Price would continue to ignore my letters, emails, and calls. It was time to play my most despised role: collections agent.

Add in the double whammy that I was collecting on the mother of the man who left me breathless and awake all night.

In a bad way. A very bad way.

I parked Lucky in the Price driveway behind Mrs. Price's car and next to Roger's Sentra. I stared at the gash in his roof and crumpled frame. A garbage bag had been duct-taped over the driver's side window. Another garbage bag covered the roof gash, but the door had buckled. No amount of duct tape was going to keep rain from seeping in.

Good luck getting insurance to cover that, Roger.

I tore my eyes off Roger's car and meant to slide a leg over Lucky, but I couldn't make myself get off the bike. Instead, I gazed at the brick ranch with the silk flower wreath on the door and wondered how such a normal-looking home could raise a bank bomber. Roger grew up in a one-parent household, but then so did

I. Was it all the video games he played? Or a chemical imbalance that pushed a tinkering inventor into an evil scientist? Maybe he was into drugs and we had completely missed it.

I didn't care. I wanted Mrs. Price to pay us, then I never wanted to see her or Roger again. Except in court. Where I had no choice but to go. With or without Nash.

A mist settled over the house. I was hyperventilating inside my helmet. I yanked it off, tumbled from the bike, and sat on the driveway with my head between my knees.

After mantra'ing and wheezing back into semi-normal breathing, I pushed off the driveway and ambled to the door. Knocked. Rang. Waited.

I opened the screen door and banged on the wood until the wreath shed a few silk flowers. "Mrs. Price," I called. "I really need to talk to you."

Nothing.

From my previous visits, I knew Mrs. Price spent most of her time in the kitchen. She'd served Nash and me sweet tea in Superhero glasses. Mine had a cracked picture of Batman. The ice sweat had looked like rain and Batman was missing a finger and his nose.

Mrs. Price didn't want to speak to me any more than I wanted to talk to her. Her son was in jail because Nash and I hadn't caught him in time. But her son had blown up my boss. I knew she was home. Both cars sat in the drive.

I had things to do. A lot of things.

I'd tried calling and knocking. I could cross this off my list and move on to the next item. I thought about Lamar working two jobs, trying to keep Nash Security Solutions afloat. And Nash waking up to an empty office (and residence) because Lamar and I couldn't pay his bills.

Adulting really sucked sometimes.

Julia Pinkerton wouldn't allow Mrs. Price to hide from her. Of course, Julia Pinkerton never had to act as her own collection agency. But if Mrs. Price was a valuable witness or even better, a suspect, Julia would have already kicked the door in and forced her to speak.

I was pretty sure kicking in the door was against the law. Instead, I marched around the house, onto the back slab of concrete that served as a patio, and knocked on her sliding glass door.

Inside, Mrs. Price jerked her head from the magazine she'd been reading.

Placing my hands on my hips, I raised my brows and chin and mustered all of Julia's swagger. "Open the door, Mrs. Price."

She glanced at her magazine, then at me. Her mouth set in a grim line.

"I'm not stepping off your patio until you talk to me."

Her eyes shifted to the cord dangling on the inside of the door.

"And if you shut the shades, I'll lawyer up."

The last thing we needed was attorney fees. But I'd found the threat of litigation worked better than actual litigation.

She placed her hands on the table and pushed off her chair. Lumbered to the door and grabbed the cord to the vertical blinds. We eyeballed each other and exchanged a mutual feeling of "you're not my favorite person."

Or at least, that was what I was feeling. Maybe her feelings ran a little harsher.

"I didn't hire y'all to watch my son allegedly blow up a bank. If you were doing your job you would have caught him." She yanked on the chain and the blinds zipped across the door.

"All right. If that's how you want to play it." I pulled out my phone, flipped it open with a flourish, and paged through my menu of about twenty numbers. None of which were an attorney. I held the ringing phone up to my ear. I could sense her standing on the other side of the glass. I hoped she sensed my phone. "I'm calling my lawyer."

"LA HAIR," said Rhonda. "We're full up right now. But you can make an appointment. Or try your luck. Your choice. It's a free country."

"Hi there, Rhonda. It's Maizie Albright of Nash Security Solutions. We have an issue here with a client refusing to pay. Not only refusing to pay but refusing to speak to me. She signed a contract. Even if services weren't rendered in a favorable outcome, she still has to reimburse us."

"I'm on this," said Rhonda. "What d'you want me to do?"

Rhonda and Tiffany loved shakedowns. "As my attorney, I would like you to speak to Mrs. Price."

"Price? As in the dude who blew up the bank?"

"The mother of Roger Price who used her instant pot and a lot of fertilizer to make a bomb. A bomb that would have killed Mrs. Price's son if my Nash — I mean Mr. Nash — my boss and your client hadn't saved him. And saved the rest of the victims of Roger's failed robbery at First National Bank."

"Alleged bank robbery," said Leslie Price from behind the blinds. "He wasn't trying to rob the bank."

"In which," I continued. "Mr. Nash suffered a horrendous head injury and now lies in a coma. Due to her son."

"Alleged."

"That coma is not alleged," I said. "It's totally for real. You should be ashamed of yourself."

"Hang on, Maizie," said Rhonda. In the background, a muffled argument played out. "Just a minute, Tiffany. This is Maizie and she wants me to play her lawyer...No, she asked me to do it...I am too fierce...I know you have experience with lawyers, but as a receptionist at LA HAIR, I have experience with phones."

Actually, of the two, Tiffany was more fierce. But lawyers generally didn't threaten bodily harm. I sensed a Battle Royale for the phone. And backpedaled. "Rhonda, as my lawyer, I know you'd like to handle this matter immediately. But no need to speak to her now. Have your secretary make an appointment to get Mrs. Price's testimony."

"I'll talk to your lawyer right now. Because I'm not talking to you." Mrs. Price yanked open the sliding door and shoved her hand through the blinds. The blinds swung and thwacked her arm.

Hells.

"Rhonda, Mrs. Price would like to speak to you," I spoke quickly, fought my way through the blinds, past her arm, and into the kitchen. "Do not let your partner handle this matter."

Scuffling sounded through the phone. Which did not bode well. Lawyers didn't scuffle. As far as I knew.

Leslie Price turned toward me, hand still held out.

I swept my phone behind my back. "Before I have you speak to my attorney about payment, I heard Roger might have been working with someone else. Is that true?"

When Nash woke up, he'd want to know if we'd missed Roger's accomplice. And now that I'd called my fake lawyer, I had the brilliant idea of suing Roger and his partner to pay for Nash's hospital bills.

Feeling more Vicki than Julia, I placed my hands on my hips and gave Leslie a hard stare. She backed a few steps from me and sank onto a chair. Crossed her arms and looked away.

I put the phone to my ear. "Looks like you're going to need to subpoena Mrs. Price."

"What does that mean?" said Rhonda. "Lawd, Tiffany, back the hey up. You can't listen in if it means breathing down my neck. You know I can't stand that vape stank."

More scuffling ensued. Followed by heavy breathing.

"Maizie, it's Tiff. What's going on? You having trouble with someone?" said Tiffany. "Ask her where she gets her hair done. I've got dirt on most stylists in town. Next time your woman goes in for a highlight we apply bleach and threaten to not rinse until you get what you want."

I cleared my throat. "That seems a little extreme? I'm sure my client will comply without the need for…additional measures. May I speak to Rhonda again?"

"Legal mumbo jumbo will not get you—"

"This is Rhonda speaking," said Rhonda. "To whom do I have the pleasure of conversing? Legally-wise?"

"It's still Maizie." This was so not working. I looked at Leslie

Price. Or maybe it was. Her pallor had paled and her eyes had grown red and teary. "Let me get back to you."

I flipped the phone shut and sat in the chair across from Leslie. "I know this must be hard for you. I can't even imagine what you're going through. But Mrs. Price, Wyatt Nash is in a coma. He almost gave his life to save your son. You have an obligation to pay us even if the results weren't what you wanted. We certainly didn't want it to end this way. We were just doing surveillance."

She blinked back tears. "The bomb wasn't meant to go off."

"But it did." My heart felt bent and twisted. A small part of me empathized with Mrs. Price. Her only son arrested and likely to spend the majority of his life in prison. Nash and I hadn't figured him out in time.

But a bigger part of me — the part that made me feel smaller — just wanted to be done. We'd only had a few days to follow Roger. She'd had his whole life. "Mrs. Price, please just pay us so I can go."

She nodded, rose, and lumbered to the counter where her purse rested. Bringing back her checkbook, she sank heavily into her chair and gusted a sigh. Tears rolled off her cheeks and plopped onto the checkbook, smearing the ink. She ripped off the check and handed it to me.

I folded it and stuck it in my pocket. "Thank you. I am sorry about Roger. Was he working with someone else? It might help his case."

Her eyes darted to the side, but when she looked back, she shook her head. "Leave me be."

"Fine." I exited through the blinds and asked the universe to please cut me some slack and not let the check bounce.

The ride home — despite the usual lumbar pain and burning sensation to my thighs — was almost pleasant. I had finally accomplished a task. We were one step closer to not losing the business.

Back in the office, I pulled out the check. And noticed Mrs. Price had written, "Help us" in the memo section.

Shizzles.

TWENTY-THREE

#ThePriceIsNotRight #HighNoonAtSix

"I'm so confused," I said to Nash. "I want to deposit that check. Bad. But why would Mrs. Price write 'help us' on it? I should probably go back to Black Pine PD, but I'm late for camping. And to be honest, I think Ian Mowry might only be tolerating my style of hot mess because he'd like to go to lunch again."

Nash's monitor blipped. I glanced at the steady heart line, then back to Nash. He looked pale. His five o'clock shadow was a beard. Hair had begun to grow where he usually kept his head shaved. My chest tightened. I focused on Steve the armadillo, whom I'd placed on his stomach.

"I called Mrs. Price, but she won't answer. Again. The woman is so frustrating." I squeezed his hand. "Fine, I'll go back. But after my camping reenactment. I promised the three. And I can't let kids down, right?"

Steve stared at me impassively.

"Okay, the truth is, I don't want to see Mrs. Price again. I don't even want to think about the Prices. I hope there's enough evidence that I won't even have to appear at Roger's trial."

I blew out a long sigh. "Nash, never in my life have I felt the way I feel about Roger Price. I think I hate him. And I've dealt with some petty, malicious backstabbers. People willing to physically hurt me to prevent me from getting a part or to slow production enough to get me fired. Once a stage mom actually sent her son into my dressing room to lick my water bottles and cough into my makeup. Her daughter was my understudy for a teen deodorant commercial. Her son had chicken pox."

I winked. "Joke was on her because I'd had chicken pox when I was six. And gave it to all my costars. On accident. But even with all the Tonya Harding-isms, I mostly felt sorry for that kind of desperation. It's a brutal industry."

Sucking in my breath, I shook my head. "But Roger? He took a bomb into a bank where there were innocent people. And look what he did to you. I can't stand—"

A tear dripped off my cheek and splashed onto Nash's knuckle. I slowly rubbed it in and swallowed the lump in my throat.

"So, I don't think I can help Mrs. Price."

I could feel Nash's look. His eyes were closed, but I knew what he was thinking.

"I'm acting like a princess? Okay, fine. I'll see what's wrong with Mrs. Price." I kissed Nash's hand, stood, and moved the stuffed armadillo to Nash's feet. "Steve, make sure Nash sees you when he wakes up. Tell him I'll be back soon. I've got a mother of a bank robber and a scene of the crime to visit."

*A*s I drove back to Leslie Price's house, I couldn't help but feel the anger and resentment toward her build again. I had business flyers to make. Sixty-five texts from Vicki to delete. Two mysterious texts from Giulio to ponder. One from Oliver to ignore. A Nash to worry about. And a crime scene to reenact. In the woods. But first I had to figure out why Leslie Price had written "help us" on her check.

Thank you, Roger Price, for blowing up a bank, my boss, and giving me more dealings with your mother.

The Price street was quiet at dinner time. I parked Lucky in the driveway behind Leslie's car, avoided looking at Roger's Sentra, and skipped the front door for the patio. The vertical shades were closed, but the kitchen was lit. I knocked on the glass, hoping it wouldn't give Leslie a heart attack. A moment later, the shades jostled, and an eye peered through the blinds.

A man's eye. I was pretty sure. Certainly not Leslie's. Roger was in jail. And as far as I knew, there were no other men in the household.

The eye squinted. I hopped back a step. The blinds swung back. My heartbeat quickened. I slipped to the side of the door. A second later, the kitchen light cut off. I caught the slight movement of the shades slithering.

I flattened against the side of the house, wondering why I was weirded out. It was perfectly reasonable for someone to be suspicious of a backdoor caller. Maybe he was visiting family, come to care for Leslie in her mother-to-alleged-bank-bomber time of need. Or a neighbor. A friend. Maybe Leslie was dating. It wasn't like we'd been watching Leslie. Just her son.

A son who might have had an accomplice. A woman who had written "help us" on her check's memo line.

Shizzles.

The lock clicked. The sliding door scraped along the track. The plastic blinds clattered. I scooted around the corner of the house. And squatted to peer around the edge.

A young man stepped through the doorway. Turned slightly away from me, he studied the backyard. He wore the uniform of Black Pine's working class: jeans, work boots, and ball cap. He held something in his right hand. The blunt edges looked like a handgun.

Before he turned my way, I scooted backward. Rose despite the trembling. I darted across the front yard toward Lucky. Rolled her backward into the street. Pushed her across the street in a sprint. Tripping to avoid running over my own feet.

I dropped Lucky's kickstand next to the jacked-up truck backed into the drive. Snuck behind the truck to catch my breath. With my heart hammering in my throat and my lungs seizing, I peered around the truck toward Leslie's house.

Young dude stood in the front yard. Still looking like he held a gun.

Holy hellsbah.

I jerked back and flattened against the garage. Had he seen me rolling Lucky out of the drive? Maybe he hadn't seen me. Or not a good glimpse of me.

Okay, Maizie. What would Julia Pinkerton do?

Jump on Lucky, rev her up, tear across the street, and take out the dude with one booted kick. Then hop off the bike (with it still running) and onto his chest to demand answers.

However, I did not have the skill nor the stunt double to pull off such a trick.

What would Nash do?

Wait, watch, and take pictures. A much better plan. I sank to the cement, lay behind the truck, and peered out from beneath. A handy benefit of jacked-up tires that I'd not previously considered. Using my phone, I took photos. Likely, the pics of Leslie's visitor would come out as grainy as a Bigfoot shot.

Young dude had moved from the front yard toward Leslie's garage. Crossed the drive to glance inside Leslie's car. Ignored Roger's. (Understandably.) And moved around the drive to the other side of the house.

Clambering to a squat, I grabbed the tailgate to hoist myself to standing. Setting off flashing lights and a shrill wah-wah that had all the subtleness of a giant's alarm clock combined with a blare horn.

I froze. Except for my heart which had leaped into my throat. And the flop sweat that had broken out on every inch of my body.

Who puts an alarm on their tailgate?

Behind me, something moved inside the garage. I deliberated between outing myself to the armed dude across the street or an irate truck owner.

Who might also be armed. This was Black Pine, after all.

The garage door's motor rumbled. I bounded from behind the truck and onto Lucky. Jamming my helmet over my ponytail, I fired her up and accelerated. Sped out of the driveway and down the street. Not risking a backward glance. Mainly for fear of losing control and crashing.

Turning the corner, I stopped but left the engine chugging. Swiveled to look behind me. Movement told me that truck owner had left his house to check on his truck. No movement at Leslie's house.

Should I leave Leslie Price to her fate?

Roger Price had kicked off the most hellacious week of my life. And now I had to save his mother?

Pulling off my backpack, I yanked out my phone. Left the backpack and Lucky near the corner. Trudged down the desolate street, my eyes on both houses. Feeling exposed and vulnerable. Like a gunslinger, moseying down the center of town to his shootout. No *High Noon* citizens watched me. Leslie's neighbors didn't pay any attention to the woman awkwardly trolling their street. Perhaps to her death.

Although I wasn't going to think about that.

Next door to Leslie Price's house, I cut across her neighbor's drive to the side yard. Wondering how I could get to Leslie without young Jesse James seeing or hearing me. I had my phone at the ready. I heard but didn't quite register the footsteps behind me. In one quick movement, I flipped the phone open and hovered my thumb above Ian Mowry's speed dial number.

And was tackled from behind.

TWENTY-FOUR

#TakeDownDowner #OfferingSpite

With my head shoved into the ground, it was hard to assess who was doing the shoving. Hard, really, to do anything other than inhale dirt.

"Keep your mouth shut," growled my assailant.

The pressure eased. A hand gripped my arm, yanking me to my feet. Spun me around. And backed me into the neighbor's garage wall.

I blinked, refocused. "You're not the dude. You're not a dude at all."

The woman standing before me raised her eyebrows. "Why are you skulking around the Price house?"

"I'm Maizie—"

"I know who you are. Agent Langtry. ATF." She pointed to a badge attached to her belt. "Again. What are you doing here?"

"I came earlier to collect payment for service rendered. Just because we didn't catch her son doing drugs but instead caught him as he blew up a bank—"

Agent Langtry spun her finger in the "hurry it up" sign.

"Mrs. Price had written "help us" in the memo section of the check. I returned to ask why, because she won't answer my calls.

And this youngish thug was inside. He's packing heat. I wanted to see if she needs help."

"You're trespassing."

"Not really," I said, hoping Agent Langtry didn't sense my recent proclivity to break and enter. "I think the area between houses is a kind of a no man's land. Technically, I haven't broken any laws."

"No. It's private property. You're trespassing."

Shiztastic.

"I planned on throwing rocks at Leslie's bedroom window. Like in *Say Anything*. Except, instead of playing a Peter Gabriel hit, I'd ask her if this dude is holding her hostage. Then I'd take that information to the police. Actually, I'm working with Detective Ian Mowry."

Langtry's eyebrow lowered a fraction.

"Not working-working, but he's helping me. With another case. Sort of. We've gone on a few dates, but I'm not that interested. I mean, Ian's a really nice guy. Good looking. We have similar interests, like crime and lunch. I like him. But my boss—"

Langtry whipped her head to the right, then shoved me to the ground.

"Am I arrested?" I said through a mouthful of dirt.

"Shh," said Langtry, flopping next to me. She drew a camera from the pocket of her jacket.

In Leslie Price's backyard, footsteps crunched on pine straw and what accounted for grass in Georgia. A figure moved in and out of the shadows, easing toward the house. Langtry's camera whirred. The figure paused — I held my breath — and reentered through the sliding door.

We pushed off the ground and hurried from the side yard to the street. I took Agent Langtry's cue of silence as we trudged toward Lucky. Rounding the corner, she stopped and placed her hands on her hips.

"Is Leslie Price being held hostage?" I said.

"This is an active investigation. I appreciate your concern. Go home."

I blinked. "Do you want the pictures I took earlier? Or to see the check memo? I really need to cash the check, but after I do that, you can have it as evidence. Oh God, you haven't put a hold on Leslie Price's bank account have you? Because we really, really need to get paid. Like—"

"Go home."

"Am I in trouble? You might have heard I'm on probation..."

Langtry had excellent facial expression skills. Some actresses never mastered that kind of control.

"I'll just go home then."

"Do that." She waited while I climbed on Lucky and adjusted my helmet. "I met Detective Mowry. You could do a lot worse."

I'd done worse. He was now the manager of an exclusive healing resort.

*A*t the Dixie Kreme building, Fred, Mara, and Laci sat on the wooden stairs leading to the office. Donut crumbs, sprinkles, crumpled napkins, and Styrofoam cups littered the stairs. Backpacks and equipment bags had been dumped in the hall leading from the donut shop.

I sucked in a breath, then let it out slowly. "We don't have a cleaning service, so could you—"

"You're late," said Mara. "We have to get to the site before it's too dark."

"Right," I said. "I have to do one more thing. I should probably make a call to my probation before an ATF—"

"Your last text said you had one more thing," said Laci. "Is this the same last thing or another last thing?"

"Something came up on the next-to-the-last thing," I said. "It's important."

"More important than a missing person?" said Mara.

"The thing is—"

"We have to go now," said Fred. "It's going to be dark soon. After our reenactment, I've got to study for a chemistry test."

"OMG, you didn't study yet?" said Laci. "Why did you wait until the last minute?"

"Why would you study early?" said Fred. "I've got other stuff going on. Do you have nothing better to do?"

"Okay." A nerve hammered above my eyebrow. "I'll do the last thing after this thing. Did you tell your parents where you'll be? Did they sign my permission slips?"

They pulled crumpled papers from their backpacks and handed them to me. I smoothed the papers, read the signatures, then studied the kids.

"Fred, your mother signs her name, 'Mrs. Hernandez?'"

Mara elbowed him.

"My mother is very traditional," said Fred.

"We should really go." Laci pointed to her watch. "It's almost sunset."

"I'm leaving these slips as evidence where Lamar can find them." I climbed the stairs. "And when I come back, this place better be cleaned up or no s'mores. Do you hear me?"

*W*e hopped off our bikes on the side of the mountain road leading to the Wellspring Center. I followed the three into the tree line, pulling Lucky with me. The trail through the woods wasn't apparent from the road, but within the trees, the dirt path became obvious.

"An old logging road," said Fred. "Actually, it's perfect for your dirt bike."

"Totally," I said. "Except I have a fear of hitting a tree. Or a root and getting flipped off the bike. Or being decapitated by a low hanging branch."

"Anyway," said Mara. "You should leave your bike here. We don't want the engine scaring off any Sasquatch."

"Good idea."

"We should check the offering site," said Laci.

"Offering site?" That didn't sound spooky. At all. I yanked on the straps of my Campomaggi backpack. "Is this part of the reenactment? Let's not get sidetracked by Bigfoot. We need to focus on you showing me exactly what happened. Because Fred has a chemistry test tomorrow."

"We all have a chemistry test tomorrow," said Laci. "Just follow us."

We hiked the winding trail that was all uphill. My hiking boots grew heavy. My hair stuck to the back of my neck. And the backpack rubbed against my lower back, creating a sweltering furnace between my butt and shoulders.

A metal rebar flecked with a scant amount of paint marked the first quarter-mile.

"Almost there?"

The three laughed.

At around the third quarter mile, the teens veered from the path and into a thicket. Giant chunks of granite covered in moss and bushes jutted from the ground. We moved around an outcropping and the path disappeared.

"Aren't there a lot of snakes?" I said. "And I'm not getting a signal. What if we get lost?"

"We know where we're going," said Fred. "And you're making too much noise for snakes."

"Snakes don't have ears," I said. "I think there's poison ivy. And poison oak. What about spiders?"

"Spiders don't have ears either," said Laci.

"The offering site is just ahead." Mara stopped to pull off her pack. "Are y'all ready?"

From her backpack, she carefully opened a case holding a video camera. Fred and Laci pulled small cameras from their packs and attached them by straps to their ball caps.

"Why are you getting out cameras?"

"We always take footage when we get to this point," said Fred. "You never know what you might see. Laci and I wear GoPros and let them run continuously. Mara uses the Canon 70D, so she can capture what we're doing. The continuous autofocus is amazing."

"Although we do a lot of voice-over during the edits," said Laci. "You want continual narration. And flashbacks."

"You're vlogging our reenactment?"

"Yeah, we need content for the channel," said Fred. "With Chandler missing, especially. Our viewers expect it."

"We could lose our advertisers otherwise," said Mara. "It'll help spread the word about Chandler."

They spoke of live streaming versus upload. Then argued about viewer versus sponsor expectations.

I couldn't escape the industry. Not even deep in the woods with the *Scooby-Doo* gang.

"Okay, I get it. The entertainment business is twenty-four-seven-three-sixty-five. Even if you're a teenager. Been there, done that, and got that ugly T-shirt." I hunched my shoulder under my pack and tromped from the group. Why couldn't kids be kids anymore? They should be sneaking off to the woods to drink and make out, not creating professional videos about secret woodland creatures and worrying about viewer stats.

"You're going the wrong way," said Laci.

Straightening my shoulders, I turned and followed them.

We eventually stopped near a hollowed out tree. Mara held her camera steady, filming Laci and Fred as they bent before the tree and pulled out the bucket.

"My sandwich and baggie of pretzels are gone," exclaimed Fred, dumping out the bucket. "He left a thank you. Some acorns and a wrapper."

"We don't know if the Sasquatch is a he," argued Laci. "We can't assume a sexual identity."

"You also can't assume Bigfoot ate your food," I said. "It could have been hungry squirrels. Or a hiker."

"Squirrels can't carry a lighter." Fred waved the lighter. Then stared at it. "Y'all, look at this. Does this look like Chandler's lighter?"

Laci snatched the lighter from Fred's hand while Mara moved in for a tight shot.

"Hang on," I said. "That could be evidence."

Laci turned to the camera, holding the lighter in the palm of her hand. "He made contact. He's trying to tell us something about Chandler."

"How can you be sure it's Chandler's lighter?" I'd already found one lighter. On *Julia Pinkerton,* we never used the same clue twice. "And why would Chandler have a lighter?"

"Adults use lighters," said Laci.

"Many adults don't carry a lighter. Unless they often do things that need a lighter."

"Like light a fire?" said Fred. "In case you get stuck in the woods? Or if you're—I don't know—camping?"

He had a point. But still.

"How do you know it's Chandler's lighter?"

Laci tapped on the Bigfoot silhouette. Printed above the insignia, "Hide and Seek Winner."

"But why would Bigfoot have Chandler's lighter?" What was I saying? "I mean, who else knows about this offering place?"

"People who watch our channel," said Mara. "Although it'd take some time to track down the offering site without help."

"I need to think about this." I held out a paper bag. "Please put the lighter in here and I'll take it to the police. And the wrapper. Leave the acorns." I pretended not to notice Fred shoving the acorns in his pocket. "Do you recognize the wrapper? It's a protein bar."

"Chandler eats those," exclaimed Laci.

"We all eat those," said Mara. "But Chandler probably carried them in his pack."

"This could mean several different scenarios. Chandler could have lost them on a trail before or after he disappeared," I said. "Or he left them here himself, so you wouldn't worry about him. To prove he's not really missing."

"He could prove he's not really missing by telling us that in person," said Laci.

"True." I shoved the paper bag in my backpack. "Maybe Chandler littered, and someone dumped them in the bucket, thinking it's a trash can."

"Or someone kidnapped him and during the struggle, Chandler dropped the lighter and wrapper," said Fred. "And a Sasquatch wanted to leave us a clue."

IMHO, my trash can theory made more sense.

"Or someone could be messing with us," said Mara.

"What do you mean?" I turned to face her, then ducked my head. She still had the camera running.

"We get hate mail all the time," said Mara. "People leave ugly comments about the show. Everyone who watches our channel knows Chandler's missing."

"You should have told me. It's important."

"All shows have haters," said Laci. "You have to have a thick skin and ignore that kind of stuff."

"If Chandler is really missing, we have to look at all motives. Even non-Bigfoot or show-related motives."

The kids looked at each other and shrugged. It was hard to tell if the shrug was an "I don't know" or a "don't talk about it" movement.

"Let's move on," I said. "I'll check the channel's comments again when I get home."

One more thing for my to-do list. Added to dropping off another lighter with Black Pine Police. Ian was going to love that. I had also forgotten to make the flyers. And to vet Jolene's rejects. But I hadn't forgotten Vicki's wedding emergencies. I had deliberately skipped those.

"We should hurry," I said. "I also have homework."

TWENTY-FIVE

#Unglamping #HiddenHugging

*W*ith the sun setting, the forest grew creepier. Mara removed her camera lens to mount a night scope, then reattached the lens. The other two took off their GoPros. We hiked in rising switchbacks on a barely discernible trail until we reached a clearing. An area half-hidden by a granite outcropping and a thicket of trees. A crude stone fire pit had been left in the center of the clearing.

"The sun is setting," said Mara. "We still have a little light. Action."

Laci and Fred stepped in front of the camera.

"Chandler Jonson is still missing," intoned Laci. "We know y'all are as worried as we are. Tonight, we're recreating what happened the night he went missing for our private detective, Maizie Albright."

The camera panned to me.

Startled, I waved. "Hello." Cocking my hip, I planted my hand on it before I realized serious private investigators probably didn't pose.

Old habits.

Mara zoomed in, then angled back to Fred and Laci.

Fred — sounding like a mini-Rod Serling — walked through the campsite, pointing. "Imagine a tent here. A fire flickering in this pit. Three trackers sitting on logs, roasting marshmallows. Discussing what had been a disappointing day in their attempts to collect evidence of nearby Sasquatch."

I rolled my finger in the air, hurrying him along.

"Chandler had said he wanted to check out the fence line," said Laci. "For the past year, there'd been a lot of activity in the old chicken farm ruins. Like the construction of a giant fence and whatever was going on inside it. History tells us this area had always been an excellent find for indications of Bigfoot presence. During the chicken farm days, there was a noticeable uptake in sighting stories as well as other proof like footprints and sounds. The unique moans, whines, and grunts associated with Sasquatch. But with the new Wellspring Center's hostile takeover—"

"I thought the chicken farm had been abandoned a long time ago?" I said. "And Wellspring bought it. Which isn't necessarily hostile."

"Yes, I meant hostile as to what they are doing to the land." Laci glowered. "And since Wellspring acquired the land, the Sasquatch stories have declined. Evidence proving that Wellspring is invading their habitat."

She pointed a finger at me before I could speak. "Anyway, Chandler wanted to check out the fence line, to see if anything new had been built."

"Fair enough." I sank onto a log before the empty fire pit.

"And we were enjoying our marshmallows." Fred sat on a log.

"The police said you had an argument before Chandler left."

Laci and Fred glanced at each other.

"We wanted to go with him," said Laci. "And he wouldn't let us. Chandler never acted like that before. We've always checked the fence line together."

"And look what happened," said Fred. "If we had gone, maybe he wouldn't have disappeared."

That thought made my stomach hurt. If something had really

happened to Chandler, the opposite would have been more likely. The three might have suffered the same fate. "Do you think Chandler knew something would happen?"

Laci crossed her arms and stared at her feet. Fred found a sudden interest in a stick.

"He shouldn't have brought you here at all if he thought something was going to happen."

"Chandler wouldn't have put us in danger," cried Laci. "We always followed safety procedures. We've had survival training."

Considering in three days I'd had a book thrown at my head, a gun shoved in my back, and my bike nearly blown up, there were many types of danger. But was I any different than Chandler, following the kids to the scene of the crime when the crime hadn't been solved?

Not that we still knew if there had been a crime.

"Okay, so you argued, Chandler left, then what happened?"

"After about thirty minutes," said Laci. "We got worried."

"I hopped up," said Fred, hopping up. "And ran to the edge of the trees." He demonstrated peering through the trees. "But the girls called me back."

"Not because we were scared," said Laci. "Because it was super dark, and Fred hadn't taken a flashlight. We were worried he would trip and hurt himself. Safety first."

Fred returned to shoot a death glare at the girls. "My fellow searchers were getting anxious, so I stayed with them. I could tell they were nervous."

Oh boy. I held up a hand before Laci could argue. "Show me the route to the fence where Chandler disappeared."

*W*ith Mara recording, we navigated through the trees and into another clearing. A man-made area before a large wooden fence. Of the vegetable protection kind. The top of the greenhouse peeked above the fence. We were facing the back of the Wellspring property.

"When you 'check out the fence,' do you walk around to the side where you can see in?"

The kids nodded. The incline here was steeper than inside the fence. The Wellspring Center must have leveled their land back in the heyday.

"Have you hiked to the top of Black Pine Mountain?" I asked, gazing up the steep mountain slope. "To the lookout?"

"You've never done it?" said Laci. "There's not much of a view. But there is a plaque bolted into the side of a rock and a bench. I think it was put there in the twenties. It's a rough hike and the trail has mostly disappeared. You can reach it by a road from the other side of the mountain, so the trail here has been abandoned."

"I haven't done much touristy stuff in Black Pine," I admitted. "When I'd visit, we mostly stayed at my Daddy's property. He's not much for going into town."

We clambered along the fence line, rounded the side and walked until the wooden fence ended in chain link. Mara panned up, focused on the razor wire, then on me.

"Yes, that's odd. But not *Supernatural* odd. I don't think it has anything to do with Bigfoot. You've not seen what lengths paparazzi will go to take photos of celebrities without their makeup on."

"It's not just the razor wire." Fred pointed through the fence to the banks of greenery, hiding this area from the Wellspring lawn. The Center's towers rose in the distance. "There's something going on in the old building near the maze."

"I saw that building. They're working on it. It's cordoned off because it's hazardous."

"We think that's where they do scientific experiments," said Fred. "It also has several junction boxes and more wiring than normal. Extra exhaust stacks in the roof. If they were going to capture Sasquatch and do experiments, that's where they would do it."

They sounded intelligent until his point ended with "Sasquatch experiments."

I kept my IMHOs to myself and turned my back on the fence. "Do you know where the K-9 unit tracked Chandler's movements?"

Fred pointed up the mountain. "From here, they said he followed a trail into the woods. But not far. He eventually cut around the campsite to another trail back to his car."

"Bypassing your campsite? Why would he do that?"

"We think the dog picked up an old scent," said Laci. "We're in these woods a lot. We tried to explain it to the police, but they ignored us. They also didn't take the police dog on the Wellspring side of the fence. They said there wasn't enough evidence for a warrant."

"Okay, Mighty YouTubers, I assume the police have already scanned this area for any evidence of Chandler. It's getting dark. Unless you have anything you've left out — like you know how Chandler might have snuck into the Wellspring Center from here — I say we take his trail back to return to study for chemistry tests."

Mara switched off her camera.

Laci pointed farther down the chain link. "There's a gate. They could have snatched him and taken him inside."

"Show me the gate," I said.

We trooped alongside the fence to an area that became overgrown with scraggly bushes, prickly vines, and thin pines. The kids wormed between the fence and trees, pushing away vine tendrils that whipped my face and shoulders.

"Here it is," said Mara.

We stopped in a huddle. Thick metal bars fastened the fence to a heavy gate reinforced with rods and more razor wire.

"Why put a gate here?"

"If they captured Bigfoot—"

"Fred, can you humor me and try a theory that's not Bigfoot related?"

He scratched his chin. "To hide the gate?"

"Obvs," said Laci. "But why?"

"See how the dirt's scraped away by the gate and everything is mangled on this side," said Mara. "Like they were moving something heavy."

"Like—"

"Don't say it, Fred." I followed the line of trampled foliage with my eyes. "Where does it lead?"

"Someone's coming," whispered Mara.

I squinted through the trees. Lights bobbed along the rough terrain. As the vehicle drew closer, I saw it was a golf cart. By the size of the figure behind the steering wheel, it didn't take much to guess who was driving.

"Craptastic," I muttered. "Oliver."

"You know him?" Fred's whisper pitched higher. "What will he do to us?"

"You, I don't know. But he may try to hug me."

Fred grabbed my arm. "Hug as in…"

"Wrap his arms around me and squeeze." I glanced at Fred's face. "Like in a literal hug."

Laci grabbed my other arm. "We can run."

"He's already seen us. There must be cameras watching the fence line. Besides, I am not running through these woods. It's like an obstacle course for spider webs."

"Maizie?" called Oliver, parking near the gate. He swung out, rocking the golf cart. "What are you doing here? And who's with you?"

He strode toward us, squinting. Pulling out his phone, he switched on the flashlight function and shone it along the fence, highlighting our faces.

I blinked and shielded my face, feeling like the Von Trapp family in the cemetery scene. "Hey there, Oliver. Nice evening for a hike, right?"

"You don't hike," said Oliver. "All those times I wanted to hike the hills, you'd said your ankles weren't strong enough. Or have you changed that much?"

"I have changed considerably." I folded my arms over my chest. "Ankles included."

"She still doesn't hike," said Fred.

"Stay out of this, Fred," I hissed, then turned back to Oliver. "We're looking for clues from the missing camper."

"I've been asking about him for you." Oliver leaned toward the fence, raising his hand to grasp the link. "Do you want to come in?"

"We're good. Anyway, why is this gate hidden? And what's with the razor wire?"

"And what are you keeping in the chicken coop?" said Fred. "Or should I say, who?"

"What do you mean by 'who?' I don't think we have a chicken coop. Wellspring is vegan. Wait." Oliver chuckled. "Did you think the camper's in a chicken shed?"

"If not Chandler, what about Bigfoot?" said Fred.

I mentally face-palmed.

"Seriously?" Oliver grinned and crossed his bulky arms over his amply muscled chest. "Is this like *E.T.* or something? That's so cute. Maizie, your friends are adorable."

I felt tempers flare around me and sought to get us back on track. "We mean, why is the Wellspring Center so overly concerned with security? The place is odd, Oliver."

"Maybe for Georgia," said Oliver. "But you know what kind of security is needed for our guests, Maizie."

"Yes, but—" He had a point. A point I had made a few days ago. And a few minutes ago. Which, for some reason, made me resentful. "Come on, guys. Let's go. He's not going to help us."

"Maizie," Oliver's voice pitched. "I'm sorry. You must be worried about the missing camper. Why don't you all come inside so we can talk?"

"No way," said Fred. "You just want to hug her."

I could feel Oliver's embarrassment more than I could see the flush that must have heated his well-defined, high cheekbones. "Friends hug."

"I'm not your friend," I said. "I'm an unfortunate event in your past. And we're going."

"The event may have been unfortunate, but our relationship wasn't," said Oliver. "I'll ask more questions. I'll check the security footage for you. Let me help you."

I turned back to look at Oliver. "Really?"

"We can look at the security videos together. Tomorrow morning?"

"He just wants to get you alone so he can hug you," whispered Fred. "Don't do it."

Laci smacked Fred. "If she watches the footage with him, he won't have a chance to delete it."

"If it's not already deleted," murmured Mara.

"Make him take you to the old chicken coop," whispered Laci. "We want to know what's inside. Why they need all that equipment."

"This is about Chandler, not Bigfoot," I reminded her.

"It's too risky," said Fred. "Maizie, don't spend time alone with him."

"Are you jealous?" Mara whispered-squealed. "Oh my God. Fred, you're so jealous."

"Don't be ridiculous, Mara, because *ew*. I'm old enough to be Fred's...sister." I hushed them. "Okay. I have to see Dr. Trident anyway. Why don't you suggest that I'm doing community service with you? That'd be super helpful."

Two stones, one bird. I was so happy with my cleverness I almost forgot I'd have to spend the morning with Oliver.

*L*eaving the gate, we pushed through the timber to attempt to follow Chandler's route. It still didn't make sense to me why he wouldn't have gone back to the campsite. From the teens' reports and what I saw on their videos, Chandler cared about the kids and their show. As for their argument, it made sense he would want them to stay at the campsite if he thought there was some danger. But what kind of danger could there be at a health spa? Had he gone to confront someone about Wellspring encroaching on Bigfoot habitat?

Maybe Everett had accidentally shot him. And buried him in the tomato garden.

I didn't like the direction of these thoughts. Nash would say I was jumping to conclusions. I should discuss it with Nash. Before I confronted Everett about how he really fertilized his tomato patch.

The trail from the gate was overgrown but discernible enough to see the tire tracks and broken branches of recent activity.

"Probably police," I said. The kids didn't argue. But then, there was no evidence of Bigfoot knowing how to drive.

"Someone's following us," whispered Laci. "Do you think it's that Oliver?"

"How can you tell?" I said.

"We're trained to listen," murmured Fred. "Chandler taught us how to tune our ears to the sounds of the forest."

My ears had been tuned to any slithering in the underbrush, not to the stalkings of ex-fiancés. We stopped to focus on the murmuring of any non-woodland fauna. Caught the light swish of footsteps on leaves. I grabbed Fred and Laci's arms. The camera swept the forest from side-to-side as Mara panned the deepening gloom.

Something moved in the shadows. I jerked and tightened my grip on their arms. Mara focused on the spot, adjusting her lens.

"I have a bad feeling," I murmured. "And not an Oliver bad feeling. Let's go."

"But what if—" whispered Fred.

"Not tonight." I yanked, pulling them along the trail. "I need more information about Chandler before I trust that it's safe for you to be out in the woods alone."

"You're with us," whispered Laci.

"I don't count. I shouldn't have brought you here in the first place." I glanced over my shoulder. Mara hung back, filming over her shoulder as she walked. "Mara, put the camera away. Come on."

"I might capture something," she said.

An object thudded the ground near my feet. I leaned forward and searched the path, praying it wasn't a hefty spider. Nothing but forest debris. Before I could righten, something smacked the tree above me, winged off, and thumped my backpack. The force spun me sideways. I cantered right. Regained my footing.

A palm-sized rock lay on the ground where I had stood.

Another stone slammed into a tree a few feet from Mara. Dust rained. She waved her hand before the video camera, coughing.

"What was that?" said Laci. "What's going on?"

"Watch out," I screamed. "Mara, get down."

A rock slammed into the tree above Mara. Her camera flew out of her hand, hitting the ground at her feet. She stood frozen, her hand still hanging in mid-air.

I shoved Laci and Fred to the ground. Vaulted toward Mara. Before I could reach her, another stone whizzed through the air. I tackled her from behind, bringing her to the ground.

"Crawl," I whispered. "Get to Fred and Laci. Stay down. And keep going."

Mara's eyes teared. "But, my camera."

"I'll get it," I said. "When you get a little farther away, run. Stay ducked down, but run to the campsite."

"Where are you going?"

"I want to know who's doing this."

"That's stupid."

"Believe me, I know. But better me stupid than you three." I watched her scuttle backward. Laci and Fred rowed their arms, urging her to retreat. When Mara reached the pair, they took off.

I scooped the camera into my pack, then scurried into the undergrowth. Off the trail, I angled back to where the rock thrower might have stood.

Whoever it was had a fairly accurate and strong throwing arm. And ample material to use in the forest.

Off the trail, my fear of creepy crawlies and turning an ankle intensified. But I figured half of my DNA was forest-friendly. I focused on that half, trying to remember anything useful from summers with Daddy. If Vicki's DNA helped me slay a prêt-à-porter, Daddy's could help me to stay forest fierce.

I picked my way among the tangle of bushes, vines, and fallen limbs, trying to slip from tree to tree. Twilight deepened. I longed to use the keychain flashlight dangling from my belt, but I didn't want the rock thrower to spot me. I thought my off-the-beaten-path paralleled the actual trail, but I kept losing sight of the barely cleared track as I veered from tree to tree. I stopped behind a tall pine, closing my eyes to listen. The forest echoed with small sounds. Popping sticks and leafy shuffles grew into the patter of feet.

I opened my eyes and peeked around the tree. The forest seemed darker. And the footsteps had stopped. A rush of birds flew, chattering. Behind me, something moved through the forest. I glanced over my shoulder and spotted a shadowy figure.

And then it was gone.

I squinted, peering into the timber. Heard more rustling behind me. I half-turned. And was knocked back. Shoved against the tree.

My scream shook more birds from their perches.

In my peripheral, I caught a swinging motion. I ducked and curled my hands around my head. An intense pain slammed into the back of my shoulder. I fell forward. Felt the scrape of bark. The sponginess of foliage.

And my Campomaggi getting ripped from my back.

TWENTY-SIX

#DownAndOutAndNotInBeverlyHills
#ToSleepPerchance

*L*uckily, the tree caught my fall. With my forehead. Before I slid into the softer leafy vines at the base. Which I feared were poison ivy.

As I lay there — dazed, aching, and frightened — my assaulter clomped off, plowing through the forest at top speed.

I'm not saying it was Bigfoot. But when the kids found me — like the disobedient children they were — they had some theories that sounded almost relevant.

Relevant if Bigfoot was into muggings.

"It had to have been him," said Fred. "Who else could throw those rocks like that? Or bash you with a stick?"

"Someone with Little League experience?" I skipped my flying book incident. Although there were similarities to our forest friend.

"He thinks we're from Wellspring and that's why he attacked you. He hates Wellspring. They're destroying his habitat."

"By building a giant garden of organic herbs and vegetables? Does Bigfoot also hate hipsters?"

"What did he look like?" said Laci.

"I had my face shoved into a tree." I stared at the ground, shaking my head. "And I was too busy cowering to look."

"What about my camera?" said Mara.

"They got it along with everything else in my backpack. Sorry." I patted my pockets. "No phone. I stuck it in my backpack. My probation officer is going to love that. And my keys."

I buried my face in my hands. I had to be the worst investigator in the history of investigators — real and fiction. I'd risked the kids' lives for what? I had zero evidence that Chandler wasn't in Mexico. All I'd done was possibly incite his brother to acts of vandalism against my bike. It'd probably been crazy Crispin following us. He was as outdoorsy as Chandler, after all.

Maybe Tiffany and Rhonda were right. I should quit this job. At least then Nash would have one less payment to dole out.

Except Nash was in a coma. I couldn't give up yet.

Wait. Was I trying to be something I wasn't because of my feelings for Nash?

How humiliating. I was supposed to be a feminist.

As if they sensed my despair, the three circled around me, draping their arms around my shoulders.

"You still have your mini flashlight," said Laci.

"Don't forget about the lighter and the protein bar wrapper," said Fred. "And the boot. Those are great clues."

Maybe for Sherlock Holmes. Too bad I hadn't played an adult investigator.

"Don't worry," said Mara. "We believe in you. You'll find Chandler. Or at least what happened to him."

I wanted to believe in me, too. I didn't want to disappoint them. But the list of people I didn't want to disappoint was ever growing. And the time I needed ever shrinking.

I hugged them back. You had to love kids and their optimism. I'd lost mine somewhere in that bank.

· · ·

*F*red insisted I take his bike. When Mara and Laci refused to let him ride on the back of theirs, I deemed it inappropriate to share a mountain bike with a fifteen-year-old boy and borrowed Mara's. I told Fred he could do the chivalrous thing and let Mara ride with him. Which spouted an argument from the girls. After suffering through a long speech about the post-post-modern feminist concept of chivalry from Laci, the girls discovered Laci couldn't support Mara's weight.

Mara rode on the back of Fred's bike.

I followed the three into town to make certain they actually went home. At least riding a mountain bike felt safer than riding on Lucky. Albeit a lot slower and with a lot more effort.

Silver linings.

I pedaled myself to Black Pine Police, hoping to speak to an officer connected to Chandler Jonson's disappearance. I had a lighter and protein bar wrapper to not turn in. And a stolen back-pack to report. Much worse than a vandalized dirt bike.

I was moving up in the criminal world of victimization.

The police station hummed with activity. After answering multiple questions about Nash's condition, I was left in the waiting room to stare at my ragged nails and wonder if my Mother cropped jeans would ever recover from woodland trauma. Detective Ian Mowry arrived thirty minutes later. Whom I wasn't expecting. But it was always nice to see Ian.

"What about your daughter?" I asked. "It's a school night."

Ian smiled. "She's with her mother. I told reception to notify me if you needed anything. And you looked like you had an accident. What happened?"

"I went hiking." Ignoring his look of surprise, I continued. "I had more evidence on the Chandler Jonson case for you. Until it was stolen. Actually, a lot has happened since this afternoon."

"I think we should sit down." He herded me in the back to his desk. "Start over."

"The evidence was a lighter and protein bar wrapper believed to be Chandler's. Found at a Bigfoot offering site. A bucket inside a tree. The kids had identified the lighter positively and the wrapper semi-positively."

"Semi-positively?"

"A brand he favored. But to be honest, it's a popular brand."

"Gotcha." Ian leaned forward. "I'm really more interested in the theft and why you look like you've been run over by a truck."

I sighed. "The kids took me to the campsite where Chandler was last seen, then we hiked to the back gate of the Wellspring Center. Had a chat with Oliver Fraser—"

"Oliver Fraser. Your ex-fiancé? The one who got you in all that trouble?"

"He's sort-of managing the Wellspring Center."

"He moved to Black Pine?" Ian leaned back in his chair and crossed his arms.

"Don't worry, I made sure he's not a fugitive. Anyway, I just learned Wellspring has security cameras posted in the area of Chandler Jonson's last known location. Did the officer handling his case look at the Wellspring CCTV footage? Oliver invited me to watch surveillance videos tomorrow morning, but I wanted to know—"

"Oliver Fraser invited you to watch security footage?"

I nodded, not liking the look settling into Ian's normally easygoing features.

"I'll ask about the videos." Ian's arm dropped to his desk and his fingers drummed the laminate. "Skip forward to the part where you were robbed and ended up looking like you do."

"Okay." I squirmed in my chair, relieved to get beyond Oliver's part because Ian was making me uncomfortable. Ian had never made me anything but comfortable. Too comfortable. Which was why dating him didn't work out. The men that tended to catch my interest were more Harley Davidson than Honda Accord.

Of course, one is more likely to receive a traumatic injury on a Harley than in an Accord. Something to think about.

"The teens and I were trying to trace Chandler's path that night through the woods—"

"On Black Pine Mountain?" He skewed his lips to the side. "Did their parents know they were on the mountain?"

"They filled out my permission slips—"

Sighing, he mopped his face with his hands. "Lord love you, Maizie, but merciful heavens, you're a hot mess."

"I tried to warn you."

That shut him up for a moment. "What happened to you? How were you robbed?"

I chewed my lip. I wasn't sure how to explain this without telling Ian about Crispin. I didn't want to lose the Bigfoot case. The three were counting on me. And then there was "Do Not Pass Go" Gladys waiting for me to screw up. Ian would be required to report me if he figured out I had broken into the Jonson house.

I lied. "I tripped and fell in the woods. And — I'm trying not to scratch — I think I might have poison ivy, too. On my face. I can feel it flaring."

"And the theft of your backpack?"

"I...uh...left it by my bike." I squirmed. "And someone took it."

"What else happened today?"

I performed a breaking and entering, stole an herbal remedy, tricked a young girl into giving me her unwanted clients, and intimidated Mrs. Price into payment. Whereupon she wrote me an SOS. And when I returned, I found an armed man at her house but was taken down by an ATF agent before I could find out if the armed man was holding her hostage.

None of which I said aloud. "I met Agent Langtry."

"I know." Ian massaged his mouth. "Did you want to fill out a theft report?"

"I don't think so. I'm pretty tired. I should go home for calamine and ice."

"Before you go..." He drummed his fingers against the desk. "Promise me that you and the kids will stay off the mountain for the time being."

"I have to do volunteer community service and therapy at Wellspring."

"That's fine, just stay out of the woods. We still don't have an ID on the victim we found near the peak. And no motive."

"I have no intention of returning to those woods. I'm not a woodsy sort of person anyway."

"I figured." He gave me a tight smile.

Slowly and painfully, I rose from the chair. "Thank you. I'm sorry I wasted your time."

Ian watched me, then followed. "Come on." Placing a hand on the small of my back, he walked me down the hall, through reception, and into the parking lot. He frowned at the mountain bike I pulled from the bike rack.

"It's a loaner," I explained. "Lucky's keys were in the backpack."

"Someone stole your backpack with the keys but not the dirt bike?"

"You know criminals..." I gave the shaky laugh of an actress unconvinced by her character's motives.

"I'll give you a ride home." Ian walked the bike to his truck. As he opened the passenger door, he studied me. "Why did you really come here, Maizie?"

Because I foolishly thought I could report a woodland assault and robbery without screwing up more than I had already done.

I closed my eyes for a moment. "I don't know. I'm a little lost without Nash's help, I guess. I'm really sorry I wasted your time."

"I want to help you, Maizie. But don't forget. I'm law enforcement."

I knew that too well. But gave him my Covergirl smile anyway.

*V*isiting hours were over, but after a major dose of acetaminophen and Neosporin, I borrowed Carol Lynn's minivan and sped to the hospital. I'd made friends with an admitting nurse who understood that coma patients needed mental stimulation as much as they needed rest. Particularly from loved ones who had odd working hours.

In his room, I placed Steve the armadillo under Nash's tubed-up arm. And after a quick (impersonal) massage, I dropped into the chair beside Nash's bed. Took his hand in mine.

"It's been a long day. I'm a little dinged up, but aside from possible poison ivy, I think I'll be okay." No need to worry Nash about the woodland assault and battery.

If there was a timberland mugger, the police would find him while looking for their mountaintop shooter. And if it was Crispin harassing me, I'd have to figure that out for myself.

I stroked Nash's hand with my thumb. Yawned. Blinked hard. My shoulder and forehead throbbed. I focused on comparing Nash's pain to mine.

"The Bigfoot kids and I hiked to their campsite where Chandler went missing. Like literally next to the Wellspring Center's vegetable garden. I didn't want to make a big deal of it in front of the three — particularly because I was on camera — but I think Chandler must have been meeting someone. My guess is Everett Lawson, the gardener with the gun, and something terrible happened to Chandler. Why is it that nobody at Wellspring knows Lawson? What if he shot Chandler?"

I studied Nash's face and thought I could sense the flicker of a frown.

"I know. Jumping to crazy conclusions. But none of this makes sense. Why would Chandler disappear? The *Bigfoot Trackers* show is really popular. I checked the stats and just in ad revenue alone, Chandler probably pulled in more than a million a year. That's like a Millennial's dream, getting paid to hang out and do stuff you wanted to do anyway. And if the teens are making a percentage, it's no wonder their parents let them go to the woods whenever and with whomever they want."

I fought the sting of jealousy that snuck through my exhaustion.

"How has TV changed so much so quickly? Even on reality

shows we're forced to do stuff you don't really do because your usual stuff is pretty boring. Anyway, I can't believe Chandler would give that up without saying anything. It doesn't make sense."

I scooted closer, leaned an elbow on the bed, and rested my cheek on my fist.

"Tomorrow, I'm going to look at Wellspring's video surveillance with Oliver." I yawned, lulled by the steady blip-blip of his monitors. "Oliver's really aggravating. And he's making Fred jealous. Which is disconcerting, too. And Giulio is driving me bonkers with threats to call off the wedding, which I normally would support except I don't have time for that kind of backlash. I'm going to make Lamar's flyers, too, just as soon..."

My head slipped off my fist and landed next to his arm. I remained bent over, resting my cheek on Nash's bicep for a long moment.

"I'm so tired, Nash. I don't know how much more insomnia I can take."

The heaviness in my limbs resisted the awkward stretch. With the ache in my shoulder, the discomfort felt unbearable. Exhaustion battled with the pain. Without giving it much thought, I dragged myself onto the bed, curling into the tight space between his arm and body. Breathed in the scant Nash scent that still remained on his skin. Awkward if someone found me, but I was too drained to care.

"Just for a minute," I told Nash. "You won't even know I'm here. I'm just so tired..." My thoughts liquified into a blend of Bigfoot, Oliver, and baseball.

I heard the even keel of my breath. Felt my limbs loosen, flex, then relax.

And Nash's arm draw around me.

TWENTY-SEVEN

#KeepingItTooReal #DonutDolt

---

espite the sign reading "closed," the front door of LA HAIR swung wide. I smiled at Tiffany just before Rhonda pulled me into a deep hug.

"Oh, my stars," said Rhonda, releasing me from the cushioning of her body. She smelled of Happy, Hydrox, and hope.

This was the real reason I had begged for an extra-extra-early appointment. I needed hugs and encouragement after all my disappointment and despair.

Not to mention, my nails looked like I'd let beavers gnaw on them. And my hair? Don't even get me started.

"Lawd, it's early. I don't know why you always want an appointment at the crack of dawn." The blueish circles beneath Tiffany's eyes almost matched the blue tips in her dark asymmetrical bob.

"Habit. Hair and makeup on the set were always early. And I have to be at the Wellspring Center first thing." I waved the paper bag in my right hand. "I stopped by Dixie Kreme on my way here."

Tiffany's hand shot out and snatched a coffee from the paper tray I carried. Rhonda grabbed the donut bag from my other hand.

I deposited the tray on the counter and sank into a salon chair with a coffee. Back in the day, I always brought treats to hair and makeup. I hadn't wanted to be seen as one of those stars who took services for granted. It also got me extra keratin treatments and quickie facials, which was a nice bonus.

"You look like hell," said Tiffany. "When's the last time you slept? And what happened to your face?"

"Tree bark scrape. I had a mishap in the woods." I lied. Again. But I couldn't handle anything but hugs, light, and love today. No arguments about my job or possible lack thereof. "When I got home I needed to research and make flyers. I just couldn't get to sleep."

I pulled a folded piece of paper out of my back pocket. Not an easy task when wearing the Jean Atelier slim-fit. For me, anyway. "How does this look?"

Rhonda studied the flyer. "I think when you say, 'we'll fulfill all your needs,' you might want to be more specific about the needs. Particularly because your picture looks a little—"

"Slutty?" said Tiffany, eyeing the flyer over her shoulder.

Rhonda pursed her lips. "I was going to say glamorous."

"That's my headshot. I don't have anything recent. How is that slutty?"

"Your eyes are half-closed and your lips are puckered and pouted," said Tiffany. "How is that not slutty?"

My face burned. "It's normal for a headshot."

Tiffany shrugged and turned her attention to the donut bag.

"What are we doing today?" Rhonda lightened her voice and busied herself at the counter behind me. "Highlights and trim? Girl, your nails need fixing something terrible."

"I don't have time for highlights," I said. "Whatever you can do quickly. I'm meeting Oliver to look at security footage this morning. I can't face him looking like this."

Rhonda spun my chair around. "Hold on, now. Whys the hells? That boy got you a ticket to jail."

"I don't *want* to see Oliver. This is just business. At the Wellspring Center. Where it turns out he's now a manager." I shoved my arms through the holes of the plastic cape Rhonda held.

"And how's Mr. Nash?" said Rhonda.

"The same," I said, feeling a twinge of guilt about climbing into his hospital bed. I had been woken by a nurse thirty minutes into a beautifully deep sleep. The best I'd had since the incident. Despite my cramped position.

Still. Awkward.

"You look kind of funny. Still have feelings for him?" asked Tiffany. "Because I thought you said nothing was doing while y'all were mentoring or whatever."

"Nothing is doing. You are correct."

"What about that cop?"

"Nothing is doing there, either. Ian Mowry is a friend who helps me on cases."

While Rhonda brushed out my hair, she studied my face. "Don't go back to Oliver. Even if you're lonely. That man is bad news."

"No worries there. He may try, but he will not succeed."

She jerked the brush from my hair and whirled the chair around. "What'd you mean, 'he may try?' What happened?"

Tiffany grabbed the chair and spun it to face her. "Did he put the moves on you?"

"No moves. He's just being nice. Apologetic. Helpful. That sort of thing."

Tiffany snorted.

"Help you with what?" said Rhonda.

"Help me with…" Wait. There was an accusatory ring in the air again. I was so not in the mood for "keeping it real." No more than I had been with Ian the night before. "My community service."

"Uh huh," said Rhonda with all the sarcasm she could muster. She returned to brushing.

"What's going on with bank bomber's mother? Did she pay you?" Tiffany cracked her knuckles. "Or are you going to let me at her?"

"She paid with a check. And wrote "help us" in the memo." I sipped my coffee. "When I went back to ask what she meant, there was an armed man at her house. And I can't get a hold of her. Who knows what's going on there?"

"What?" Rhonda's brush hung in mid-air.

"ATF thinks Roger was working with someone. I guess the armed man was his partner. Anyway, not my problem." I settled my coffee on the mirrored station stand. "How about a trim and blow out? Do you do Olaplex? And my nails…we better go with a nude, considering the volunteer work I've been doing. Maybe OPI's 'Taupe-less Beach' or 'Feeling Frisco?'"

Rhonda set down the brush. "Not your problem? Did you just say a woman who personally asked you for help is not your problem?"

"What the hell is Olaplex?" said Tiffany. "And I think 'Berlin There Done That' is more appropriate considering who you're seeing this morning."

I averted my eyes and snatched the last donut from the Dixie Kreme bag. Sour cream.

Touché donuts.

"Put down that donut, girlfriend," said Rhonda. "Roger Price's momma needs you. She called your agency to deal with her crazy ass son. She wrote 'help us' on a check she gave to you. Obviously, this is your problem."

"It is the ATF's problem. It stopped being my problem when Roger Price blew up my boss. No matter what she wrote on that check."

"I don't think so." Rhonda crossed her arms. "You need to talk to Roger."

"I am hells-to-the-no not talking to Roger." I ripped a chunk off the donut with my teeth. And almost choked swallowing it.

"Rhonda surprisingly has a good point," said Tiffany. "Roger might know something that could help his mom."

"He blew up Nash—I mean the bank," I said. "When I think about Roger, I forget to breathe. I can't do it."

"You're breathing just fine now." Tiffany raised her brows. "Listen, Roger is not going to tell the cops anything because his lawyer told him to keep his trap shut. But Roger might tell you something. It's worth a shot."

I shook my head. "You just don't get it."

"I thought you were all about becoming a new, stronger person," said Rhonda. "You're saying no because you're afraid of Roger Price?"

I hiked my chin higher. "I have to meet Oliver soon. Can we get started?"

"It is too early in the morning for this, Rhon," said Tiffany. "Let me do her nails, get paid, and go home to nap before I really have to work."

Their disapproval hung in the air like a misting of Aquanet.

"I already have an almost-dead boss on my conscience. And a missing Bigfoot YouTube star to find. My boss's business to save. A ferocious probation officer to pacify. And a wedding to keep in place. At least until I get the rest of this stuff done. Stop making me feel bad. Do you see the bags under my eyes? The state of my skin?"

Rhonda stuck a hand on her hip. "Maizie, I tell it like it is. You do your thing. But this is no time for fabulous hair when Roger's momma needs you."

"She has a thing about mommas," said Tiffany. "Me, I don't trust cops. I agree with Rhonda. You want something done, you do it yourself."

"I thought we were friends." I felt a pout appearing and forced my face to neutral.

"Friends don't let friends off the hook," said Rhonda. "Talk to Roger before it's too late."

"You know," I said. "I don't think I have time for hair and makeup."

"Who said anything about makeup?" said Tiffany. "And you better have time after getting us here this early."

"May I remind you, I brought donuts," I spoke stiffly, hoping my TV crew slip-up wasn't Freudian. I thought real-life friend-ships would be easier. Not full of the blame-game. I had Vicki and Giulio for that.

"I thought the donuts made up for you insisting on an appoint-ment four hours before we open. Now you're sounding all uppity." Tiffany cocked her hip and settled her hand on it. "You better have brought cash, because we know your credit is no good."

"If that's how you feel." I fought the flush that clashed with my forehead bruise.

"That's what we know," said Tiffany. "Remember, you're broke? You're no longer *Maizie Albright*. You're just Maizie Albright, a broke girl on probation who needs a real job. And who needs to get her shit together."

I gasped like I'd been punched in the stomach.

"Tiff, have more coffee," said Rhonda quickly. "You are so testy when you're not decently caffeinated."

I yanked the cape off, fished out a twenty and tossed it on the counter. "I have a long bicycle ride in front of me. I'm sorry I wasted your time. But I can't do this. Not this week."

"If that's how *you* feel." Tiffany grabbed her coffee and strode to the back door.

"Y'all, don't do this," said Rhonda.

I biked home, stopping first at SaveMo for the only hair supplies I could afford. Then attempted to color my hair and paint nails. With the help of Remi. Who was not helpful at all. Neither were the five Jack Russells who decided to join us in the bathroom. One of which now had an orange streak down his back.

"That's alright," said Remi. "He's the only one who didn't get caught in my Bigfoot traps. The other dogs will feel better about themselves since he looks so silly."

With that logic, I felt more than silly. I'd been caught in Remi's traps. I was also orange. And my face was brown. I'd used too much self-tanner trying to cover the scraped bruise.

Plus I thought I might have broken up with my only friends. And I wasn't sure why.

At the office, Lamar stared a few seconds too long. It took a painful amount of thumb pinching to not burst into tears.

Lamar checked my reaction and lightened his voice. "Thank you for the flyers. They're very...interesting. I'm sure we'll get a lot of attention with these."

"Do you think I look skanky?" I chewed my lip.

Lamar studied me. "I would not use the word skanky. It'll grow out, won't it?"

I closed my eyes and swallowed. "I meant the flyers."

"Oh. Well. They're very...interesting."

He'd already said interesting.

"I'll try again later. I have to get to Wellspring. When I return, I'll go through all the files I stole from Jolene. I'm sure we'll have new clients rolling in by this afternoon. That's great, right?"

"Sure, hon.'" Lamar's doubt rang with less patience than previously. He held up a finger and pulled his phone from his pocket.

I circled around him to the desk and started a new to-do list. I wrote "watch videos with Oliver" at the top. Followed by "make new flyers." "Research Jolene's clients." "Tell Giulio to suck it up for another week." And "find new salon" at the bottom. In small letters. Then wrote "for emergency purposes" next to it.

Not that I was fooling anyone but myself. Rhonda and Tiffany had always been real with me. I could take all the "stop acting Hollywood, you don't have the cash to back it up" statements. But combined with "quit Nash Security Solutions and get a real job?" Not with Nash in the hospital. And "drop the teens" when I was their Obi Wan? And this business about talking to Roger Price? The man ruined my life more than Oliver Fraser ever did. At least Oliver never almost-killed someone I (maybe) loved. It was so not fair of the girls. Even if I had asked them to come in four hours early for nothing.

Some friends.

"Yes, it is," said Lamar to the caller. "What's the news?"

I looked up from my list and mouthed, "hospital?"

Lamar nodded. "That's real good....Okay....How long?" He smiled and raised his brows at me.

I dropped the pen and felt tingles in my toes. The sensation shot an electric current up my feet, through my limbs and trunk. My head buzzed. My face contorted. I patted my cheeks and realized I was smiling. Hard enough to hurt.

Bobbing on the balls of my feet, I waited for Lamar to finish his phone call. "Mr. Nash's awake? Is he okay? What did they say? He's not going to die? He's not going to die. He's awake and I'm leaving." I rammed my hip against the desk, took a quarter turn, and stumbled out of the office.

He was alive. Nash was alive, and I didn't care if I had to spoon feed him for the rest of his life. He was alive and awake and that was all that mattered.

Wait, spoon feed what?

Whatever. He was awake.

"Hang on," called Lamar. "They're keeping him to run tests. And he has a visitor."

"I don't care."

TWENTY-EIGHT

#WhileYouWereSleepingWithTheEnemy
#JoleneDontTakeMyMan

The nurses and I exchanged grins as I raced past their station to Nash's room. Reaching his door, I forced myself to stop, take a breath (without hyperventilating), and do a mirror check. I'd cried off my mascara and eaten off my lip gloss. And I still had the coloring of a Halloween decoration.

But I'd burned off ten million calories biking to the hospital along the county highway, so my glow was healthy.

I made a quick hallway touchup and took another ujjayi cleansing breath. When I didn't pass out, I grasped the doorknob and pushed through.

The bed back was raised, allowing Nash to sit up. His right arm was still tubed and monitors still blinked, but the atmosphere had changed completely. His body no longer looked shrunken, the blue gown stretched taut over his large frame. The stubble had grown into a light beard, hiding the little scar on his chin, giving him a swarthy ne'er do well vibe.

His head turned slowly. Nash's gaze moved to roam over me, then stopped. Paul Newman baby blues met my bloodshot, mascara-smeared sea glass greens. His lips pursed, then opened, and quickly shut. He glanced at the person sitting on his bed.

Holding his hands.

OMG.

I had so fixated on Nash awake I had totally missed Jolene. I felt the blood drain from my face, then rush back to lick my cheeks. Props to Jolene. Her blue sheath dress was totally fetch. Hugged her lithe body and set off the sheen to her auburn locks. It looked better than the red *While You Were Shifting* Dolce & Gabbana I had envisioned.

"Maizie? What are you doing here?" Jolene stopped, then sniggered. "What happened to your hair? And your face?"

My fingers automatically stretched to comb my orange, cornhusk-dry flyaways. Realizing it was a lost cause, my hands dropped.

Kind of like my heart.

And my self-esteem.

"Um..Undercover...work," I stuttered.

Shizzles, another lie.

Nash's head jerked. "Lamar?" he croaked.

"Lamar's at the office now...He, uh...later? We made some flyers? And um..." I felt unsure of safe conversational topics again. Patted my hair. Felt my eyes grow hot. Pinched my thumb and took a breath. And started to hyperventilate.

Holy shizzles. What in the hellsballs was wrong with me?

My breath intake accelerated. Spots danced around the room. I doubled over, smacking my head on my knee. Stifled a groan. And focused on the fat tears plopping onto my mud-stained Golden Goose sneakers while I counted seconds between breaths.

"Miss Albright?" said Nash.

"Don't get up, Wyatt," said Jolene. "It's too soon. You're supposed to rest."

"No," I gasped. "'S'kay."

Doubled over, I shuffled backward. Bumped into the doorframe and sidled into the hallway. Smacked into a cart and sent it spinning. Sending the candy striper running after it.

Giving me time to make my escape before I totally lost it.

*T*he pain in my chest ached so acutely, I almost made a right turn into the ER on my skedaddle to the parking lot. But knowing my weakness and recognizing the ensuing agony, I ignored the pain radiating from my core to my extremities. My head pounded with each step I took.

Which it deserved since my head could've stopped me from this pain in the first place.

Never in my life had I felt so low. Even after my arrest, when I was a running joke on *TMZ* and *E! News Daily*. Not only was my heart shattered, but I also had no money. No home of my own. No car nor even a dirt bike. No friends to comfort me. My family support was dysfunctional at best — except for Remi and there was only so much you can get from a six-year-old intent on capturing mythological creatures — and perhaps soon, I'd have no job.

I couldn't even make a flyer to save my boss's business because I was so fixated on making him fall in love with me. While he was unconscious.

Even my character in *While You Were Shifting* hadn't been that stupid. And she'd been stupid enough to fall in love with a were-dolphin in a coma.

What kind of fool had I become? I'd always had issues with falling for the wrong men. My therapists had a lot of explanations for this. Office romance syndrome. Absent father syndrome. Mommy Dearest syndrome. (Joke. Sort of.)

And I had immediately gone and done it again. Fallen in love with Nash. And imagined he reciprocated.

Sure, there'd been a few times where we'd been in tight situations and relieved the stress with a little face mashing. But we hadn't rounded any real bases. To a guy that didn't mean anything. And according to the proclamations of my celebrity gal pals and *Cosmo*, it shouldn't mean anything to me either.

But it did.

Hells. Nash had clearly said he wasn't interested in dating while he mentored me. How did I take that as a future relationship together?

Why did I constantly paint my life vision in pink rainbows?

Rainbows weren't even pink.

The humiliation grew as I sped from the hospital toward Black Pine Mountain. I swallowed hard and concentrated on not dying on the winding road. Told myself I deserved the agony of pumping uphill on a six-speed. Gasping and sweating, I trudged into the Center, past reception, and down the über modern hall leading to Oliver's office.

The door swung wide at my knock. "Good morning," Oliver exclaimed.

Startled, his arms dropped from the reach to hug. Probably at the sight of my face. Meaning my expression. But possibly from the brown tree rash and demented hair color.

"Are you okay?"

"Fine." Calling on Julia Pinkerton's unswerving sassiness, I tilted my chin up. "What could be wrong? Certainly not my love life."

"Your love—Giulio said you weren't dating anyone."

"Which is why there's nothing wrong there. If I were dating someone, I'm sure it would be very wrong indeed." I stopped, troubled at the *Downton Abbey* lilt I'd adopted. "Anyway, I'm here to look at the surveillance tapes. And get a tour of your unoccupied buildings and fenced vegetable garden."

"Unoccupied buildings?" Oliver shrugged. "I'll do my best. I'm really glad to see you, Maizie. Do you want to grab a cup of coffee before we start?"

Yes, I did. But I wouldn't bow to temptations from beautiful men with gorgeous physiques any longer.

Although I could really use another shot of caffeine. "Only if it's takeout."

TWENTY-NINE

#DowntonInTheDumps #ShineMoOnMe

*O*liver ushered me into security, a first-floor room down the hall from his office. A bank of monitors lit one wall. Beneath it, a long workstation housed computers, a two-way radio system, and other apparatus. I noted the locked boxes behind me. Keys. Emergency equipment. And an unmarked cabinet that looked suspiciously like a gun safe.

Por qué-why guns at a health spa?

But more importantly, the room was empty. Except for me and Oliver.

"Where is your staff?" I asked. "Shouldn't someone be in here? Supervising? Us?"

He rolled out a chair and sat in the one next to it. "We have CCTV cameras everywhere on property. All staff has an app on our phones that can access the monitors. Having security visible instead of cooped up in here, helps to deter any unwanted visitors. You can never be too careful."

That's how the kids and I were spotted outside the fence.

Oh, shiz. Dr. Trident could have been watching me half-ass my volunteer work for him on that flippin' phone he always had out. And here, I thought the therapist was just addicted to social media.

I'd curse the technology, but as an industry insider, I couldn't help but admire the advancement in security solutions.

Hang on. Someone might have also seen me skulking the back forty on their phone. And would have seen the kids and Chandler during their reconnaissance trips. Prickles of unease crept up my spine. I shivered.

"Are you chilly?" asked Oliver. "Do you want a blanket? You could cuddle while we look at the videos."

I held up my coffee. "Did you see us last night, Oliver? Or did someone else report us?"

Oliver looked at the monitors and scratched his neck. "There was a memo. I recognized you, so I said I'd take care of it. Find out what you were doing."

"A memo?"

"Text message to check the back gate CCTV." He shrugged. "I know. It feels a little creepy, but we have to protect our guests, and this is the most efficient way. Our guests want to know their privacy is protected. What's tricky is maintaining the illusion that we're not hyper-vigilant."

He reached to squeeze my elbow. "You know how it is for people like us, Maizie. You can't be too careful."

I slid my elbow back. Thought of the bodyguards I had known back in my day. And how much safer I'd felt in Black Pine. With Nash. Until the bank…

"Maizie, are you all right? What's wrong, sweetheart?" Oliver rolled his chair closer to take my hands in his. "What happened? What can I do?"

I shook my head, slipped my fingers from his large hands, and pinched my thumb.

Oliver watched me, concern making cute little indentations between his eyebrows. "Maizie, I'm worried about you. You look…not so good. And you seem…super sad. I know finding me in Black Pine is a shock, but I've never seen you like this before."

I swallowed hard and sniffled. "I'm fine. Thank you. You have an amazing security feature. Very good. Let's access the night that Chandler disappeared, shall we?"

Back to *Downton Abbey* mode. I had never done a British period piece. I didn't know how I channeled this character but whatevs.

Oliver nodded and reached for a binder, paged through it, and followed the instructions to click through to an application on the computer.

"You know me. I can barely text." He flashed me a stunning smile then returned his attention to the computer screen. "Okay, I put the date in here…I think."

He was taking forever. "Do you want me to type it in?"

"By all means." He nudged his chair a few inches to the right. I hopped from my seat to stand next to him. Typed in the date, approximate time, and clicked enter.

Above us, the largest monitor blipped, then showed a field of camera views. At the bottom of the screen, the date and time blinked beneath the fifty tiny windows.

"Oh wow," I said. "Is that everywhere in Wellspring?"

"I think so." Oliver studied the binder, then reached around me with one arm to type on the computer. "I'm just putting in the back fence location…"

He was also squeezing me closer. My hip was precariously close to his face.

Before he could press enter, I dropped my left hand to cover his on the keyboard and pointed to a screen with my right. "Wait. What's going on there?"

In one of the tiny viewers, two tiny people in white doctor coats left the alleged old chicken coop. Keeping his hand beneath mine, Oliver half-rose next to me and leaned forward to peer at the screen.

"Looks like the nutritionist and Dr. Sakda had a meeting or something." His hand slipped from the keyboard to settle on my hip. He turned me to face him. "Or it could have been the Bigfoot autopsy."

I sucked in my breath.

He winked.

I smacked him.

"I couldn't help it." He chuckled. "The kids last night. They were so cute."

"They'd hate that you thought they were cute."

"I know. They're not the only one who's cute." He looked down at me, his forehead crinkling in that adorable way. Again. "What's going on with you, Maizie?"

I sighed. "Oliver, I don't want to talk about it. I just want to see the footage from Chandler—"

He slipped a finger beneath my chin and tilted my face up. "Is that a scrape? Did you get that last night? Babe, what happened? Why are you wincing? Are you hurt?"

I rolled my aching shoulder and adopted my *Downton Abbey* voice to steady my nerves. "If you must know, someone attacked the children and I. Me. Last night. In the woods. Behind Wellspring. After we left you."

"What?" Oliver gripped my shoulders. I cringed, and he released me. "Are you okay? Is that why you look like you do? Who was it? Why?"

I placed my hands on his chest to push him back. Tried not to think about all the muscles beneath my fingers. Or any memories of those muscles I had successfully suppressed.

Or so I'd thought.

"It's all in a day's work for an investigator."

"This isn't you, Maizie." Oliver placed his hands over mine. "You're talking strangely. You're acting strangely. And you look like...not you. I knew I was right to be worried."

Shizzles. I kept my eyes on our hands.

"But there's more going on, isn't there?"

I looked up. His face hovered close to mine. In a dark room lit only by security monitors. I sucked in a breath. And another when his eyes inadvertently slipped to watch my lungs fill.

What in the hellsbah was I doing? This was Oliver. He was the enemy. He was just one of the many who had ripped my heart from my sleeve to tromp and mangle it under their feet. But the only one who almost sent me to prison.

I winced again, thinking of Nash and Jolene. A tear squeezed from my tear duct. I pulled in a mouthful of air, hoping my eyeball could somehow inhale the tear before Oliver got the wrong idea.

Pretty sure he got the wrong idea.

His eyebrows quirked together. The full lips that had been pressed relaxed. And the big brown eyes turned their sympathetic gaze to mine. "Oh, Maizie."

He crushed me to his chest, then ran his hand up my back. Lucky for me — or unlucky, depending — his giant hand pressed the massive bruise given to me by the Pitching King of the Forest. I shrieked and shoved off.

Oliver backed into a shelf of binders, knocking it askew. Binders rained around his feet.

Clutching my arm, I panted. "Just show me the surveillance footage."

"What was that?"

"I told you I was attacked in your forest," I snapped. "Someone tried to beam us with rocks. Then walloped me with a stick. On the exact spot you just touched."

"A rock and stick?"

"I think a stick. He obviously wasn't decked out with Wellspring equipment." I pressed the heels of my fists against my eyes to stop the tears. "Can you just show me the missing camper footage now?"

"Of course."

Clicks sounded on the other side of my fists.

"Craptastic."

That was my line. And it wasn't a good one. I pulled my fists off my eyes and blinked at the fuzzy monitor. "Where's the footage?"

"Um…" Oliver consulted the binder. "I can't seem to pull up that area."

"It's been deleted?" I scooted in next to Oliver, reading the binder over his shoulder. "Are you sure you typed in the right code?"

"I think so."

"You think so? What if you deleted it?" I felt my chest tighten. "No, not again."

"What's wrong?" Oliver spun around in his chair. "Are you having a panic attack? Babe, slow down your breathing. It's okay. Maybe the police took the footage."

"Right, the police." I sucked in a breath and another. "Except if they saw something, they wouldn't have given up on Chandler. I've got nothing, and these kids are depending on me, Oliver. Teenagers are paying me to look for a missing person. They're successful YouTube stars, but they're still children. I'm acting like I know what I'm doing but I don't actually know what I'm doing."

"It's okay, Maizie. Breathe."

I gripped his shoulders. "Oh God, can't I do anything? The only thing I seem to succeed at is failing. I can't even manage the terms of my probation. I skipped Dr. Trident to see you."

"That's kind of sweet," he whispered.

"It's not sweet, Oliver. It's stupid. Just like it was stupid for me to try to follow some dude who was chucking rocks at our heads. And look what happened. I almost got my head bashed in by Bigfoot. He stole my backpack, my phone, and the keys to my dirt bike." Tears splashed onto Oliver's massive forearms. "I drive a dirt bike because I even failed at keeping a car. It was repo'd."

"Oh, babe." Oliver shook his head sorrowfully. "You should see Dr. Trident."

While I gulped air and sobbed, Oliver kept one hand on my elbow and walked me to the east wing. At Dr. Trident's door, Oliver pressed a kiss to my forehead — expertly missing the bruised skin — knocked on the door and walked back to the elevator.

The door swung open. Dr. Trident peered through his glasses at me, frowning. "Maizie, you're late. Again."

"I need help." I gasped and pressed my hand against my chest. "I'm such a mess I can't even breathe. I don't know who I am anymore. I feel like I have nothing."

His man bun bobbed. "I've been waiting for this."

"You have?" I looked up at him from my half-bent position of vulnerability and pain. Hoping my initial impressions had been wrong. Maybe beneath the man bun and selfies, there lurked a new Renata.

"You are like the fragile bird with the broken wing who keeps trying to fly but can't make it more than a few hops," he pronounced.

"Oh my God. I'm the wounded bird." I felt a renewed burst of pain. "I always thought I wanted to date wounded birds. But it was me all along."

"Come in." He swung the door wide. "Lie down on my couch and catch your breath. We have work to do."

An hour later, I knocked on the door to Oliver's office. "Sweetheart, are you better?"

"I had a breakdown," I admitted. "And a bad color rinse. But Dr. Trident actually helped me feel better. He made me tea and it really calmed me down."

"I'm so glad." He pulled me into a slightly smothering hug, and this time I didn't try to stop him. Instead, I sank into the familiarity of his powerful body, letting his firm planes and contours mold against my soft (too soft) curves. His arms tightened around me until I gasped for air.

"Sorry," he said, drawing me away. "I just feel so bad about everything. I missed you so much. You're my biggest regret. I've been seeing a therapist, too. I can't get over what I've done to you."

"That's good," I said purposely vague. "I'm supposed to selfie, so I can 'see incremental improvements in my emotional state' that will 'manifest in my features.' Selfie therapy. Who knew? Except I my phone was stolen."

"I'd love to selfie with you," said Oliver.

Something Wyatt Nash would never dream of saying, I thought, but forced my thoughts from Nash. If near-death brought him and Jolene back together, I could be happy for him. How many times had I wished my parents had gotten back together before Daddy married Carol Lynn? Nash was my boss. I needed my job and the mentorship. I could find romance elsewhere. Anyway, everyone always said to separate work and pleasure.

The thought still made me want to cry. But baby steps.

Oliver held up his phone.

"Can you wrap your arm around my head or something to hide my hair?"

I felt Oliver's thick forearm settle on my head. "How's this?" He chuckled. "Smile."

I felt Oliver's fingers tickle my ear. Tipping my head back, I slipped my arm around him and smiled at the phone he held above us. "Thanks."

His arm dropped from my head to my shoulders. He studied the picture. "Not bad. You want me to tag you somewhere?"

"I'm not on social media anymore. Rules of my probation." I slipped out of his arm to take the phone. Cringed at my washed-out features that contrasted with the dark circles. Oliver's arm cast a shadow that hid any glimmer of a real smile. Selfie muscle memory had kept me from looking totally wrecked. This was the purpose of Selfie Therapy. To see how mega awful I looked. Supposedly.

At least I could check therapy off my probation list. If this counted.

"I sent a memo to all the staff asking about the camper. If you had a picture of the guy, that'd be helpful."

"I appreciate that Oliver. The dogs tracked his scent to your fence."

"Then away into the woods and back to his car."

"How did you know?"

"Like I said, I've been asking around. Listen, do you want to do lunch after the tour? Is there a restaurant in town that serves Southern food? I've wanted to try something authentic."

I brightened at my favorite conversational topic. "There's this place that looks like a shack. Like, literally the roof is rusted and the porch is condemned. It's roped off. And it doesn't have a name. But oh my, do they have the best vegetable plate ever."

"Vegetable plate? I figured you want something less healthy."

I grabbed his arm. "The best thing about a vegetable plate is you don't have to have any vegetables. I mean, I do. Get vegetables. Usually fried okra. Along with mac and cheese and cornbread. Fried okra would hit the spot. It's been a long day. And it's not even ten o'clock."

"Babe," he said with all the sympathy I'd been missing from my friends.

"Oliver, you have no idea how hard it's been starting over. If I wasn't living with Daddy, I'd be homeless. That's how little I make. The investigation agency is barely staying solvent. We've been scrambling for cases because my boss's ex-wife blackballed him in the community. She's horrible. She opened her own agency just to spite Nash. I mean Mr. Nash. To put him out of business."

"I'm going to close our account with her. I don't care what Vicki says." Oliver slid my hand off his arm. Raising it, he touched his lips to my knuckles. "We'll hire your agency for her wedding."

There probably wouldn't be a wedding, but I didn't want to disappoint Oliver when he thought he was making me feel better. I focused on venting instead. The words tumbled from my mouth faster than I could properly annunciate them. Particularly from my sob-thickened lips.

"Then this morning, the girls — who I thought were my real friends — told me I had visit Roger, the guy who blew up the bank and put my boss in a coma. As if. That is not my job. The ATF is on it. You know how I feel about jail." Oliver squeezed my hand apologetically. "Anyway, I never want to see Roger Price again. Every time I think of him, I almost pass out. He nearly—" I bit my lip.

Oliver brought my hand to his lips again. "Babe."

"I did my own hair with something called Color'n ShineMo. Bought from a store called SaveMo." My voice cracked into a small sob. "It's so cheap it doesn't have all the letters in the name."

"Oh babe, I'm sorry."

"What's even worse? Jolene Sweeney. She and Nash are—" I closed my eyes. "It doesn't matter. Dr. Trident pointed out that I've focused on all the wrong things. I have made my happiness from trying to make other people happy, thinking they will...like me more. I've always done that with Vicki and Daddy. And producers and directors. Co-stars. Friends. I'm still doing it here. I can see that now."

"You need 'me' time," said Oliver. "Everyone needs 'me' time."

"I can't afford me time. I need to see those buildings. I need to make new flyers. And vet Jolene's rejected clients. I don't even have time for lunch."

"I can give what you need, Maizie. I used to make you happy. Let me try again."

THIRTY

#HeartRemedies #NoBustBusted

---

*I*nside a candle-lit room smelling of lemongrass and lavender, I lay on my stomach beneath a blanket. Naked and sated. Barely awake but finally resting. And ignoring my ex-therapist Renata's call for introspection. I didn't want to think about anything but basking in the afterglow I was currently experiencing.

Oliver really knew how to seduce a girl. I could seriously get used to this again. It'd once been part of our weekly routine.

Outside the door, I heard the rumble of Oliver's voice, then the door opened quietly and someone padded in. Half-asleep, I quirked a smile. "Is that you?"

"Yes." He sank onto the padded table and I slid over to make room. One of his large hands touched my back. "How are you feeling now?"

"Much better."

"Your hair looks much better, too. Back to its usual color." He ran his fingers through my trimmed, colored, and Olaplexed locks. "So soft."

"Thank you." I stretched my arms then folded them beneath my chin. "Hair, nails, facial, and deep tissue massage. It's been so long since I've felt this good. Too long. And you brought me a vegetable plate without vegetables. Just what the doctor ordered."

"You know, I could get you a job on security at Wellspring." He played with a lock, twisting it around his finger. "No more worries about money. And spa treatments whenever you like them. The perks are nice."

"I miss perks," I said. "I've been telling myself I don't need perks. But it's the first time I've never had perks."

His fingers trailed down my spine. "There's nothing wrong with liking perks. That's human nature."

I wasn't ready for those kinds of perks. But I wasn't foolish enough to know I might need a job in the immediate future. "Maybe after my probation is done. I've got enough confusion with having my community service and therapy here. And now I really need to get back to work. Chandler isn't going to find himself. Unless that's what he's doing. Which is kind of a sucky thing to do to his young YouTube partners."

"I want to help you find Chandler."

I rolled over. "You do? Because nobody else thinks he's really missing."

Oliver laid a hand on my bare shoulder. "Of course. I'm all about helping people. Besides, he did disappear outside my health facility. I have every right to know what happened to him."

Conscious of my nakedness beneath the thin blanket — not to mention Oliver's powerful hand lightly caressing my shoulder — I stilled. "I don't know about your rights, but fine. You can help. Show me the old buildings and the greenhouse."

"Now?" Oliver's eyes appeared unfocused. His finger stroked my arm.

I jerked upright, pulling the blanket with me. Slid off the table and from under his hand. "Yep. I've wasted enough time. I'm a professional."

Considering my state of undress, professional seemed a poor choice of words.

. . .

"*T*he greenhouse," I said, ticking off my tour of Wellspring buildings. "The old chicken coop. And any other buildings that seem mysterious."

"Sure, babe." Oliver led me from the spa and into the back plaza. "Whatever you want."

The thrill of a possible bust spiraled through me, something I used to channel for Julia Pinkerton episodes. She constantly broke into condemned buildings and secret labs, exposing criminals and charlatans.

However, Oliver's nonchalant attitude tempered my mood. He acted like Wellspring was just an over-the-top health spa.

Which it probably was.

"You can see everything," said Oliver. "Except the basement."

I stopped. "Why?"

"That's where we keep Bigfoot." He winked. "And we don't have a basement."

Chuckling, he rested a hand on my back and detoured me toward another path. We passed the meditation maze and the flower garden I'd destroyed.

"I found a boot in that garden," I told Oliver.

"Really? That's weird."

I frowned, wanting him to be more curious. Or defensive. Something. He was so agreeable. That's what people always liked about Oliver.

What I used to like about Oliver.

Nash was disagreeable. Downright ornery. But always curious.

Not great attributes in a boss, I told myself. Except for the curiosity. For an investigator, that was a plus.

I needed to stop thinking about pluses. My imagination had invented too many pluses that had gotten me into this state of unrequited passion in the first place.

"You're quiet," said Oliver. "Those kids are getting to you, aren't they? Are you a Bigfoot believer now, too?"

"I'm not sure what I believe." I looked beyond the Wellspring property to the mountain slope. I had convinced myself Crispin had followed us and for some reason — probably my snooping — he'd attacked us. But I'd sensed someone or something else on the mountain, too.

Oliver followed my gaze. "I wish you hadn't gone into the woods. It's dangerous at night. I sent one of our security personnel to search the forest to see if they could figure out what happened to you."

"That's not necessary," I said but felt secretly pleased.

"It's not safe." Oliver placed a hand on my elbow and stopped our walk. "The police were here. Someone was killed on the peak. Nothing to do with us, but there is a hundred-year-old trail leading from the Wellspring property. The old spa used the path for their guests."

"I heard about it." I was surprised Oliver knew. Ian hadn't told me the police had been to Wellspring, but it made sense. "My friend in the police department told me someone had been shot."

"All the more reason for you and the kids to stay off the mountain trails. I should've warned you last night, but I didn't want to scare them."

He turned us off the path to a covered pergola used for golf cart parking. We hopped in a cart and gently motored through the plaza to the planted hillocks in back. A path had been concealed between hills. We emerged behind the hills before a gate in the fence that separated the back of the property. Oliver pulled out his phone and tapped in a code. The gate swung open and we drove through.

"What about the buildings back here?" I said as we passed the old cowshed. "And this empty land. Why is the garden so far away?"

"We're still restoring. It's a lot of acreage." He parked the golf cart near the garden fence. Used his phone to electronically unlock the gate. We entered and strolled through the tomatoes, passed the drying stalks of corn and beans.

"And what about those?" I pointed at the piled bags. "That's an extraordinary amount of fertilizer."

"Maizie, it's a garden. I've never seen you so suspicious." He laughed. "I can't wait for you to see what we're doing."

Oliver continued to the greenhouse, once again using his phone to unlock the door. The air was hot and moist and smelled fresh and dewy. Glass walls rose to the pitched glass roof. Rows of potted trees with big glossy leaves lined the walls. Smaller plants shelved in hydroponic trays were grouped in the center.

"That's our herb garden." Oliver pointed at the shelves of hydroponic trays. "All the typical kinds you find in vitamin shops and for cooking."

"No pot?" I scanned the room, looking for something to bust.

"Sweetheart, weed is illegal in Georgia," said Oliver. "Aren't drug tests part of your probation?"

"Not for me." I gave him the side-eye. "I'm just checking. What are those trees?"

"Kratom. They're subtropical."

"Wait a minute. Isn't kratom illegal?"

"Not in Georgia." Oliver grabbed my hands. "This is why I'm so excited, Maizie. We're going to treat patients at Wellspring. Dr. Sakda's overseeing the process into making it into a real pain remedy people can use."

I gazed at Oliver, recognizing the gleam in his eyes and fervor in his voice. He had the same reaction when he operated his Beverly Hills community center and spoke of helping people there. Throughout Oliver's childhood, his grandmother had been in and out of the hospital, dealing with incurable pain. Unfortunately, her daughter — Oliver's mother — bore the brunt of her misery when her pain meds didn't work. His dad, a philanthropist and amateur bodybuilder, also dealt with chronic pain.

I understood why he felt so strongly about holistic health treatments. I sort of understood why he gave Oxy to the elderly. He didn't need the money. It made them feel better.

I didn't grasp why he thought he could get away with it. Or

why he ignored the dangers of addiction. Especially since his father struggled with it.

Or why he risked our relationship for it.

Everyone had their blind spots, I supposed. But maybe Wellspring was the answer for him. "I'm happy for you. Really." I slipped my hands from his and patted his arm.

"It's a dream come true. Especially now that you're here to share it with me."

*H*appy for Oliver but disappointed in my non-bust, I kept my thoughts to myself as we drove back to the plaza. I directed us toward the condemned chicken coop with the new roof and "extra exhaust stacks," as Fred had noted. We parked the golf cart and left the path to walk into the roped-off area before the old building.

"And this is where we do our experiments," Oliver said in his best Frankenstein voice. Followed by an evil laugh. He sobered. "We don't want guests in here because they could contaminate our work. That's why we've kept the condemned signs."

I had a feeling I would get no busts today.

Using his phone, he unlocked the door to the lab. We stepped inside, onto a smooth concrete floor in a long, open room. It smelled pungent, musty, and slightly floral at the same time. The outside stone walls were drywall inside and fitted with shelving. Heat lamps hung from the ceiling. Work tables held computer equipment, beakers, boilers, microscopes, and test tubes. A giant machine whirred in one corner. A big glass-fronted fridge took up another wall.

Explaining the need for extra electrical boxes and smokestacks. It was a secret laboratory. But the only surgery being done was on plants.

Sitting at a work table near a window, Dr. Sakda looked up from her computer. She pushed her glasses to the top of her head and glared at us. "What are you doing in here?"

"Giving Maizie a tour," said Oliver. "Go on with your work, we won't interrupt."

"Making more juice blends?" I grinned, then caught her look and held up a hand. "I know. You're a molecular scientist."

"Ethnobotanist. I'm examining the cell structure of a plant in order to reproduce its chief characteristics chemically."

"Very good." My *Downton Abbey* voice was back. I gazed up at Oliver, giving him a "help me not to say anything stupid" look.

He placed a hand on my elbow, then took me on a quick trip around the room. We looked at the food dehydrator where herbs dried. A grinder for pulverizing. And a capsule filling machine where the powdered plants were compressed into pills. Plain brown capsules.

Identical to the ones Crispin had.

"Are those for sale?" I asked. "What are they?"

"The kratom supplement. The nutritionist and the doctors give them to their guests. Totally homeopathic."

"But not for sale outside Wellspring?"

"I wish." He sighed. "If we could get FDA approval, I think we could do a lot of good. For now, we don't make them for the retail market."

I turned to Dr. Sakda. "What do they do?"

She glanced over her shoulder. "Helps with pain. Anxiety. The usual."

Oliver grinned. "See what good we're doing here, babe?"

"But why the extreme fencing?" I said to Oliver as we left the building. "And drastic security precautions? I saw the gun cabinet. Are you sure you're not growing drugs? Many start out as plants you know."

"Babe, it's not like we have a poppy farm. Why are you so worried?" He wrapped an arm around my waist. "Wellspring is awesome."

Why was I so worried?

Chandler. Missing security footage. The mysterious Everett Lawson prodding me with a gun. Crispin had a box of Wellspring pills. Pretty sure he wasn't a guest. And I'd been walking along the path with Oliver's arm around my waist.

I'd almost forgotten he was the enemy. The ruiner of my life. Part one.

Craptastic.

I wriggled out from under his arm. "You can help me find Chandler, but let's keep this professional, shall we?" I wished I had done a period piece. I would have rocked the accent.

"Of course."

"I want to speak to Everett Lawson. I've been unable to find him, and he's not listed as a caretaker or gardener. No one seems to know him."

"That's weird. Are you sure he wasn't a guest?" Oliver rubbed his lip, then pulled out his phone.

"Definitely not a guest. And can you ask security what happened to that missing security footage?"

He nodded.

"One more thing, can I have one of those supplements? I'm curious about them."

Oliver stilled his typing. "You probably shouldn't take them. Not if you're on probation."

"Why?"

"You know." He winked. "Herbs can throw off drug test results. Like poppyseed muffins."

"You're sure they're not drugs? Oliver, you got in trouble for this before."

He shoved his phone in his pocket and took my hands. "Babe. Those were prescription medications that I made accessible to the elderly. Medications that they needed, but whatever. I learned that lesson the hard way. The stuff we grow here is natural remedies. Homeopathic. Like the spa waters. You know what one of our main garden crops is? Arnica. Mountain daisy. Used in first aid and in sports medicine. We also grow chamomile, St. John's wort, and windflower."

"Why would those brown pills make me fail my drug test?"

"I don't know if they would make you fail. Dr. Sakda is the better one to ask, but the chemicals in that plant mimic other pain relievers. I'm just trying to help you. I don't want to ever cause you trouble again." He kissed my knuckles. "Maizie, you know how much I love you."

Too little, too late, said my head. But my heart thumped like it was jamming to Gangsta Rap. The gaping wound left by my unrequited Nash love ached to be filled.

Stupid heart.

THIRTY-ONE

#Bambioozled #FreeFalling

I'd find another way to get the brown capsule. Unfortunately, the pill I'd stolen from Crispin had been taken when Bigfoot mugged me. If Crispin had the same kind of pills, he'd gotten them illegally. Maybe taken them from Wellspring. It could be a lead. And my only link between Chandler and Wellspring, other than Bigfoot.

If his brother's love of herbal supplements could be considered a link.

I really did need more sleep.

If only I could talk to Nash about this. Now that he was conscious, he was much harder to approach. Namely, because I was humiliated by my man-crush. And Jolene probably hung in his room, helping him with his recovery. With her evil temptress powers.

And their shared history as husband and wife.

Where had she been when he was unconscious? Unless she'd been the one who kept moving Steve...during real visitor hours.

Why would she not visit her ex-husband when she thought he might die? Jolene would have regretted the way she treated Nash while he was alive and gone to make amends. Take him back and make it up to him. Like by becoming real partners again. In Nash Security Solutions. And in life.

No way would she keep me on as an apprentice.

Craptastic.

I worked so hard to save a business that would get me fired anyway.

Instead of seeing Dr. Trident, I used the house phone to call Daddy. A girl needs her daddy when her heart was broken. Although that wasn't the reason for my call. I was just in no mood to ride a mountain bike.

I also needed to get away from the Wellspring Center before Oliver found me again and sweet-talked me into something greater than a spa date. I couldn't waste any more time. Despite the fact that Oliver wanted to help me, he wanted to spend a lot of time holding hands and hugging.

Sneaking into a dark corner of Wellspring's lobby, I checked my to-do list while I waited for Daddy. Flyers. Jolene's clients. Talk Giulio down from the breakup. Interview Everett Lawson. Check in with Gladys. Report to the teens.

I crossed off "watch videos with Oliver" and "find new salon" (guilty, but not too sadly as I was now Olaplexed). Added "steal brown pill from Wellspring" and "look up Wellspring CCTV's system to learn about deleted feed." Then wrote "sneak into hospital and check on Nash" in tiny letters. Scribbled it out. And wrote it again.

At the bellow of my name, I looked up from my to-do list and turned to the Center's front doors. A giant stood in the doorway wearing a camo sports coat, handmade ten-thousand dollar boots, and Wranglers. His long beard once retained the same color as my Olaplexed locks. Now he looked like a colossus Santa.

"Daddy," I called, running to him.

He hugged me, then pulled me off his giant frame. "Have you gotten in with these yo-yo's? This place is the talk of the town. California hippies have taken over the old chicken farm."

He glanced around. "Although it does look like they've done a nice job in restoring the old place."

"Yes, they've done a lovely job with the historic preservation." I pushed him out the door before Oliver heard him from his office. He'd want to apologize to Daddy. That's all I needed. Daddy had strong (negative) feelings about Oliver. It was better *not* to tell Daddy that Oliver now resided in Black Pine.

A big not.

In the parking lot, Daddy turned a slow circle, searching for Lucky. "What's wrong with your bike this time?"

"Missing its key. It's down the mountain on a path leading into the forest. I rode a mountain bike here."

"Did you now? Good for you." He mansplained the benefits of hard labor and physical effort while we retrieved Mara's bike and walked it to his King Ranch truck.

I refrained from rolling my eyes about twenty times.

We drove down the mountain while I relaxed in his leather seats, enjoyed his air conditioning, and relished the lack of helmet I needed for the ride.

"Your sister's in a hell of a lot of trouble," said Daddy. "You know she's been setting traps out back? She's been using candy bars as bait. Caught one of the dogs. And another one's orange for some damn reason."

"Remi's a little obsessed with Bigfoot," I said, avoiding the orange comment.

"Well, that obsession needs to stop. She knows dogs shouldn't have chocolate. The poor thing was sicker than all get out. Had to take him to the vet."

"Oh no." Guilt stabbed at me. "I didn't pay attention when she asked what Bigfoot ate."

"Remi's in trouble for lying. Said she didn't put out the chocolate."

"Oh," I said faintly. I'd been doing so much lying lately, I feared it'd rubbed off on little Remi. I really needed to do a better job in big sister-ing. "What can I do?"

"It'd be a big help if you could help dismantle her dang traps before another dang dog gets caught."

"I'll add it to my list." Recognizing the teens' logging trailhead, I called out for Daddy to stop. He pulled over, then asked me how I lost my keys.

I lied and said my backpack had been robbed. I couldn't stop with the lying. Now I understood the whole slippery slope thing.

But explanations were never easy with Daddy. Particularly when I couldn't tell him that the loss of my backpack resulted from a rock and stick attack. He'd do his own Bigfoot hunt with his Remington Sendero. That's all the police needed with a shooter on the loose.

"Girl, someone who didn't know you would take you for stupid," said Daddy. "What kind of fool leaves their backpack with their bike on the side of a road? And for mercy's sake, look at the state of your bike."

Daddy hefted the bike upright and walked it to his truck. "What are you doing to this poor thing? Fuel line was cut, now this?"

"I need better wheels. And I can't afford anything."

"How about a Gator? You can borrow one of mine."

"Is that even street legal?"

"Not on public roads."

"Which is where I drive, Daddy." I blew out a breath. "Now is not the time for learning a life lesson on living within my means. I have no means because I'm about to lose my job."

"I'm sorry to hear that. Maybe you should take better care of the things you do own. Like your dirt bike. And whatever else was in your backpack." He folded his arms and gave me the eyeball.

I closed my eyes. "Can you at least fix Lucky and get me a new set of keys?"

"Yes. If you get your mother off my back about her damn wedding."

I opened my eyes. "What?"

"Vicki said she wants me to send a herd of deer down the aisle.

She said she's 'rethinking the safari for a *Bambi* motif.' What in the blue blazes does she mean?"

Considering Daddy was a hunter, not a herder, I had no idea what she was talking about. Unless she was reenacting Bambi's mother's fate. Which was not wedding appropriate. Daddy's company made apparel scented with deer pee. Which I think, one would not want at one's wedding.

But Vicki had also wanted elephants and I couldn't imagine them smelling much better.

I had a feeling she was forcing my hand, not Daddy's. Particularly now that I didn't have a phone and couldn't respond to her texts.

"I'll talk to her," I said. "I'll put it on my list."

I climbed into the pickup which retailed at a similar price to my repo'd Jaguar. I missed driving in comfort with luxuries such as cup holders, radios, and engines that didn't make my legs numb.

But beggars couldn't be choosers. Lucky was better than a mountain bike. And according to the girls, my position in society had fallen to that of beggar.

And if Jolene had her way, I probably had a few more rungs to slip down.

THIRTY-TWO

#BigfootStalker #MakeMeABeliever

*G*ladys was happy to hear I finally had therapy. She was not happy to hear my phone had been stolen. But as owning a phone was not listed in the terms of my probation, I didn't worry about it too much. She had the numbers for the office and Daddy's cabin, after all. Not that I was ever at either place much.

But as I was currently at the cabin, I worked on the new flyers, then went out to dismantle Remi's traps. She followed behind me, kicking at dirt clods and pine straw with her little boots. In a six-year-old pique with her family, the world at large, and Bigfoot.

"He's the one poisoning our dogs with candy bars."

"Uh huh." I was not going to get in the middle of a standoff between my father and Remi. Both were as stubborn as belly fat. "How many traps do you have?"

"I lost count."

Great.

She hooked a thumb at a large oak. "That's where Bigfoot watches the house."

"You better tell Bigfoot to find a better hiding place. If Daddy sees him, he might shoot him for trespassing."

"Not under the tree. That's where I found the wrapper. Up there." She dashed to the tree and began to climb a ladder nailed onto the trunk.

I followed the ladder with my eyes. "In the deer stand?" Prickles of unease broke across my flesh. "Hang on, Remi. Let me go up there first."

"It's only big enough for one person," she called over her shoulder. "It's a stand, not a sit."

"Remi, get down. Now."

My voice contained some quality that made her pause, then slowly back down the tree. She glared at me, crossed her arm, then stomped off to poke at one of her traps. I climbed hand over hand, my stomach fluttering and my nerves prickling. The tree-stand was little more than a three-foot metal platform with a small padded chair attached to the tree above it. A safety harness was also anchored to the tree.

"I bet you anything you're not allowed up here, Remi," I called.

"You better not snitch," she snarled.

The stand easily held my weight, although the altitude made me want to vomit. I doubted it'd hold Bigfoot, but it could hold Daddy and he was not a small man. I sat in the chair. Got a view of tree tops. I turned halfway and saw the house between the trees. My window was dark but visible. As was the kitchen and family room. A dog squirmed through the kitchen doggy door. Three more followed. They darted off the deck. Immediately spying me, the Jack Russells went nuts.

I looked down and saw Remi standing below me, staring up. The Jack Russells circled her, yapping and jumping at the tree.

"I'm coming down." I stood slowly and gripped the chair arms. And spotted something in the fold between the seat back and cushion. I pulled out a cigarette filter.

My father was not a smoker.

Another wave of unease washed over me. I shoved the butt into my jeans pocket and focused on climbing down the tree ladder. At the bottom, the dogs barked and sprang at my legs. Catching my scent, they took off into the woods.

Remi folded her arms and gave me her best glare. "You get to have all the fun."

"Where did you find that candy bar wrapper? Right here, under the stand?"

She nodded grimly.

"And where was the dog caught when he got sick? Which one was it?"

"Itty took sick."

We walked to a spot deeper into the woods. I turned. The stand was clearly visible. I took a deep breath. "How long was Itty stuck here?"

"I don't know." She turned her back on me and scuffed her boot into the dirt.

If Itty had been caught in a trap and saw Bigfoot in the tree-stand, he would have gone berserk. Alerting the other dogs and eventually, people in the house. I had a feeling it wasn't chocolate that made Itty sick.

Nor was it Bigfoot in our deer stand.

I told Carol Lynn that it wasn't a good idea to let Remi play out back for a while. I didn't want to scare Remi's mother, but I showed her the cigarette butt and explained the candy wrapper. Said I was going to report it to the police. Then packed a bag and moved to the office.

I felt reasonably confident that Daddy would take residence in that tree stand. And put the house on lockdown. I didn't like scaring my family, but I was spooked. Someone was watching our house.

Lamar was not around, so I left my suitcase and drove Lucky to the Black Pine police station. I waved to the woman behind the window and didn't wait long before Ian Mowry ushered me to his desk. I gave him the cigarette butt and explained where I found it.

Ian looked at the ceiling. Then at me. "Nash is awake. I stopped by this morning."

"Yep." I gave him my *Young Miss* smile. Upbeat. Wholesome. Grateful. Hoped it didn't look too fake. "Great news."

Cocking his head, he waited for a beat. "You look different."

I smoothed my hair. "I had some work done. All natural, of course."

"You still look like you haven't slept."

My smile fell. "I've been busy."

He cast his eyes to the evidence I'd given him. "Looks that way. I don't like what's going on, particularly with the murder victim on the mountain. We still don't have an ID. It takes some time to go through the databases. The ME said he was probably shot on Friday, midday. The perp is probably long gone. Doesn't make sense they'd be interested in the Spayberry's, but you can't be too careful."

"Doesn't make sense to me, either," I said.

"You didn't notice a delivery truck or big van nearby? We think that's what the perp or victim had been driving. Victim's vehicle wasn't left at the scene, but we found the tracks. Several ATV tracks, too, but that's circumstantial. Plenty of people take ATVs up the mountain for riding."

I shook my head. "The only vehicle I've noticed is the motorcycle involved in cutting my fuel line."

"Still don't understand that one. It's not like your dirt bike holds much gas. I'm sorry that happened to you," said Ian. "I'm going to send someone out to look at your daddy's property. Boomer's got a nice cabin. One of the best properties in town. Someone could be casing the house for a robbery, I suppose."

"I moved to the office."

"We don't have the manpower to cover Nash's office and the cabin. I know Boomer has a great security system, Maizie. You're better off staying there." Ian rapped his fingers against his desk. "You think it's a stalker or something from your TV days?

"If it's a stalker, it's not one of mine. No one seems to know my shows anymore." I tried another *Young Miss* grin and felt more *Awkward Family Photo* than cover girl. "But they could be one of Chandler Jonson's. I was told he had stalkers."

"I think we looked into the stalker theory. Nothing credible turned up. A soccer mom in the area is a big fan, but she had an out-of-town tournament when Chandler disappeared."

I suppressed the frustration from my voice and aimed for private investigator professional. "I really think this is related to the Chandler Jonson case. Someone doesn't like me looking for him."

"That seems a little…extreme."

But because I hadn't told him all the truth behind the Bigfoot case — illegally entering the Jonson house for a big example — it was getting increasingly difficult to explain. "Like maybe the same person who stole my backpack. And cut Lucky's fuel line. I'm worried about the teens on *Bigfoot Trackers*. If some stan — stalker fan — is upset Chandler's missing, they might take it out on Mara, Fred, and Laci."

Ian leaned forward. "Maizie, I think you should stay at your father's cabin. I don't want to draw any conclusions on why someone might have been in your tree-stand—"

"And poisoned Itty."

He nodded. "But knowing Boomer, he'll lock the gate, turn on the alarms, and patrol the woods. Now that Nash is awake, you can relax a little. Go home and try to get some rest."

My to-do list still wasn't done. I couldn't afford to be on lockdown. Nash might be awake, but I was still running the office. At least until Jolene took over. "Can you have someone check on the teens? Drive by their homes while they're on patrol?"

"Of course." He stood. "You told them to stay off the mountain?"

"Yes. But I seem to have no authority over them."

"They're teenagers." He smirked. "Get used to that feeling. Wait until it's Remi."

Remi as a teenager. What a scary thought. Daddy would definitely need to ramp up his security.

Ian fiddled with the bag holding my cigarette evidence, then looked up. "Did you meet with Oliver Fraser today? You said you were going to look at the security tapes."

"Do you know anything about the Wellspring Center's CCTV system? I tried to watch footage of the night Chandler disappeared and it was deleted."

"That's odd."

"Right?" I leaned forward. "Ian, I know the police investigation didn't net any results, but I really think there's something going on. With the Wellspring Center and Chandler's disappearance."

"Uh huh."

"Chandler's brother, Crispin, had a big box of herbal supplements that looked like they were from Wellspring."

"And you know this because?"

"I saw a box of them in Crispin's room when I toured the Jonson house with Crispin. He's a little…I don't know…" Could I say creepy? Was that professional? "Jealous of his brother and not really concerned about Chandler's disappearance."

"Sibling rivalry stuff. Because Chandler's famous?"

"I think there's a weird family dynamic. But my last therapist was all about family dynamics so maybe I'm just sensitive to them."

"How's your new therapist?"

"He doesn't really care about my family dynamics. He has an outside-in philosophy. Look good to feel good. Which I guess has its merits. I do look better after Oliver took me to the Wellspring Spa."

"He took you to a spa?" Ian's eyebrows notched together. "As long as you're feeling better, I guess."

I think I was a long way from feeling better. But I flashed him another *YM* smile anyway. "Are you going to reopen the investigation into Chandler's disappearance now that I've collected all this evidence?"

He sank back in his chair. "The thing is Maizie, we're not a big police department. With this murder and the ATF investigation into the bank bombing, it's all hands on deck. Even if Agent Langtry doesn't want me involved....Anyway, there's a lot going on."

"You still don't think Chandler's missing."

"Hon', it's not that I don't think he's missing. It's just that I don't know if he wants to be found. I've looked at the file."

"His credit cards haven't been used. And his phone's been off. Who leaves their phone off that long?"

"Someone who likes to live off the grid. He's done it before, Maizie. Alaska. He might be researching for a new show. How long can you track Bigfoot on Black Pine Mountain without results?"

"Then why wouldn't he tell Mara, Fred, and Laci?"

"Because he's myopic and obsessive? Why wouldn't he tell his family and friends he was going to Alaska?"

That thought deepened the abyss in my already cracked heart. Fred, Laci, and Mara would be crushed. "But the show. He has sponsors—"

"Face it, Maizie. YouTube isn't regular TV. You upload whenever you want. He's not beholden to anyone. He's leaving those kids high and dry, but it isn't the first time that he's skipped town on a whim. You said yourself the Jonson's have weird family dynamics. It also wouldn't be the first time someone with star quality had a few screws loose."

Been there. Done That. But that old T-shirt fit a little too tight.

*B*ack at the office, I dialed up a four-way with the teens' parents. The more I thought about Bigfoot in the tree-stand (especially knowing Bigfoot didn't smoke Marlboro's), the more I worried about Fred, Mara, and Laci.

I detailed the case in my most professional private investigator voice. "Not to alarm you, but I have a fear that there might be reprisals from *Bigfoot Trackers* fans because of Chandler's disappearance." I felt a *Misery* explanation was safer than *The Monster Squad* theories the kids favored about the Wellspring Center.

"By reprisals, you mean what?" said Mara's mom.

"I'm not really sure," I said. "I am using my imagination at this point. But better safe than sorry, you know."

"What's happened?" said Laci's dad. "Obviously something must have happened."

"Someone vandalized my dirt bike and is watching my father's house. Where I live. And remember the permission slips you signed for our hike in the woods yesterday? Someone threw rocks at us. But it's the stalking at my home that really has me worried."

"Rocks? Federico never said anything about rocks," said Mrs. Hernandez. "That happened when he was little, but since the show, there hasn't been any bullying. He's treated so well now."

"You still live at home, Miss Albright?" said Laci's dad.

"Is that pertinent—"

"You know they have a sponsored event this afternoon?" said Mara's mom. "They can't miss it."

"I know," I said. "But—"

"The sponsors made us sign a contract," said Mrs. Hernandez. "We're obligated to fulfill it."

"Mara wants to go to film school at NYU," said her mom. "These opportunities are really necessary for her application. Many kids have YouTube accounts and it doesn't mean anything. But channels with sponsorships? That's a big deal. I can't let her blow it off."

"It's not really blowing it off when—"

"I'll be at the event," said Laci's dad. "It's a public place. I'm sure it's fine."

OMG. This was total Vicki déjà vu.

"Please," I said. "I have a bad feeling—"

"I'm going, too," said Fred's mom. "Maybe we should get dinner after?"

"I'm up for it. But not pizza again," said Mara's mom. "And I think they have an AP art history test tomorrow."

"I didn't hear about that," said Fred's mom. "Federico doesn't tell me anything."

I broke in. "Be careful? Keep an eye out. Even at home. No more hiking. There's been a lot of crime lately."

"We don't helicopter, Miss Albright," said Laci's dad. "It causes poor self-esteem. They'll need to do a new show by this weekend, but no later. However, we can compromise with parental supervision. I'll take them into the woods."

"I want to go, too," said Mara's mom. "She never wants to do anything with me anymore."

"Detective Ian Mowry with Black Pine Police said no woods," I repeated. "Do not go into the woods. Stay off the mountain."

"I'm sure there's an area that's safe for them to film. They could just pretend. For the show. To keep up their ratings. Why don't you ask this detective where it's safe to shoot?"

The three would never pretend to look for Bigfoot. They were a lot of things but not sell outs. "The mountain is not safe. Maybe you should take them out of town for a while. They can look for Bigfoot in South Georgia. Okefenokee swamp? There've been sightings there. That should be safe enough."

"Ugh," said Mara's mom. "No swamps. Swamps are full of alligators. How is that safe?"

"She might have a point," said Laci's dad. "It could be good for ratings to have a change of scenery. Chandler kept focusing on the same area near the Wellspring Center. It was getting boring."

"Federico has marching band practice. They're still in competition season," said Mrs. Hernandez. "South Georgia is a half-day drive. I've got two other kids with all their activities to balance."

"I know what you mean," said Mara's mom. "We're trying not to let Mara's career overshadow things like soccer and orchestra. They're just as important."

"Except they don't have sponsors that expect new content every week," said Laci's dad.

"Easy for you to say when you only have one child," said Mara's mom.

OMG. "Okay, I've got to go." I'd talk to Mara, Laci, and Fred myself. And make their safety seem more important than anything else. Including looking for Chandler.

Good luck with that.

THIRTY-THREE

#ThePriceofThePrices #GamerOn

*L*aying my head on the desk, I thought about parents who cared more about their child's career than what might be good for the child.

Reminding me I still needed to call Vicki about the deer march down the aisle.

My spa rejuvenation had worn off. I was still an emotional hot mess. I no longer had a phone, so I couldn't do a selfie examination. I did a quick emotion check à la my ex-therapist Renata. Confidence and peace ranked low. Frustration was fairly high. As was uneasiness, confusion, fatigue, loneliness, and guilt.

Guilt. I was kidding myself that Mrs. Price's "help us" didn't bother me. Tiffany and Rhonda were right.

The front office door opened. I slowly raised my head. Lamar moseyed in and collapsed into the La-Z-Boy. "Just came from the hospital," he said. "Good to have Nash awake even if he's weak."

"Yes, it is." I drug out the to-do list. Added, "Visit Mrs. Price again." Then wrote, "Apologize to Tiff and Rhon." In small letters at the bottom. But added a heart.

"Did you see Nash?"

I nodded. The memory still made me feel nauseous.

"You should head over there before visiting hours end. Now that he's awake, he could use a distraction. The man hates inactivity."

"Did he have a lot of visitors today? Jolene was there earlier. Maybe he needs his rest."

I held my breath waiting for Lamar to deny Jolene's hospital activity. To tell me that after I'd left, Nash had dropped her hands, proclaimed his love for me, and kicked her out of the room. Without getting up from the bed, of course. I didn't want him to strain himself.

"I guess that's true," said Lamar.

My small hope crashed like a sugar high.

Lamar cocked his head. "You look different from this morning."

"I had some work done while I was at the Wellspring Center."

His eyelids fluttered shut. "That's...convenient."

"It's a weird place, Lamar. Armed guards, heavy fencing, and an amazing security system. They claim it's to protect their celebrity clients. Oliver showed me there's nothing to hide. But it just feels off."

"Is it the place or is it this Oliver that feels off?"

"Both. But you may be right." I rose from my desk droop. "I'll work on the flyers when I get back. I need to visit Mrs. Price."

The brown eyes popped open and he turned his head sharply to study me. "Leslie Price? Why? I thought you collected her check."

"I did. But something's going on there. Agent Langtry won't call me back. Neither will Leslie Price." I didn't want to worry Lamar. If anyone needed a spa day at Wellspring, it was Lamar.

"You look like you need some rest, Lamar. You've been running yourself ragged, helping us and staying on top of Dixie Kreme. I'll be back in a jiffy."

"No more ragged than you." He closed his eyes and folded his hands on his stomach. "You're a good 'un, Maizie."

. . .

I didn't feel like a good one. I still resented the Price's interference in my life. I felt like yesterday's ATF take-down should have been enough proof that the universe did not want me dealing with Mrs. Price or her crazy son. But somehow my guilt overrode that sensible conclusion.

In an hour or so, I had a group of teens to convince that they should skip town. I still needed to convince Vicki that deer don't march down aisles. Or at least to get an animal trainer and stop bothering my father. I hadn't edited the dang flyers yet. Jolene's clients needed vetting. I also had a broken heart that needed a serious ice cream fix.

And not from Wellspring. I was jonesing for some Mayfield's Butterscotch Fudge. On the couch. In my pj's.

But first, Mrs. Price. Teenagers. Missing person investigations. The business. And Vicki.

I would really need that ice cream after dealing with Vicki.

Before leaving the office, I tried calling Agent Langtry once again. Left a message that I would be dropping by the Price's to check on Mrs. Price. By knocking on the front door. Then leaving.

When I reached the Price's neighborhood, Lucky and I scooted up and down the street, drawing attention to ourselves. Hoping Agent Langtry would pop out of hiding and tell me to go home.

No Langtry. Figures.

In the Price driveway, I sat on Lucky and stared at Roger Price's torn up car. Willing myself to hyperventilate and pass out, there-fore justifying my inability to deal with the Prices.

Of all the times to get over my panic attacks.

I trudged from the drive to the house. Rang the doorbell. Waited. Rehearsed my story (I was delivering the good news about Nash). Knocked. Rang again. Told myself, "You can go home now."

Instead, I plodded around the house to the patio door. The kitchen blinds were open. No Leslie sitting at the kitchen table. No thug skulking in the background. I knocked on the glass. No one came running out with a gun aimed at me.

So far, so good.

I peered through the glass and noticed the pile-up of dishes in the sink. Empty containers on the counter. A pizza box on the stove. My skin prickled. The familiar buzz of anxiety sent an electric jolt through my body.

In all the times we had visited Leslie Price, I never saw a dirty kitchen. Sure, the tea glasses were old and fading. The entire house was old and fading. But it had always been clean.

I tried the sliding door. Locked. Circling the house, I knocked on curtained windows. Tried opening them. The house was shuttered and closed.

The wings of panic beat against my neck and fluttered in my stomach. I returned to the front of the house and looked for a key. No key. Paced the porch, glanced at the drive, then ran to Mrs. Price's car. Locked. But Roger's Sentra couldn't even close properly. I pried open the driver door and found the garage opener clipped to his sun visor. Pressed the button. The engine whined and the door lifted.

I darted into the garage and hit the button to close it. Inside, I walked past stacked tubs of Christmas decorations and lawn equipment. Spotted the empty space where Roger's fertilizer once lay. Forced myself to continue to the kitchen door marked by a neat row of pegs for coats. Knocked on the door.

All was quiet on the Price front.

I turned the knob slowly, opened the door quietly, and called out feebly, "Hello, anybody home?" Entered a narrow hall. A small laundry room and pantry stood opposite. The kitchen lay open at the end of the hall.

Taking a deep breath, I gathered my courage and a rank whiff of spoiled food.

Bypassing the messy kitchen, I glanced into the empty living room. A few scattered magazines on the coffee table. An empty beer can rested on a side table next to the TV remote. The echo of cigarette smoke still hung in the air. The beer can had been used as an ashtray.

I made a wild guess that it was not Leslie's Old Milwaukee.

Down the hall, I checked Roger's bedroom. His computer and gaming equipment had been confiscated. Also, his robots and electronic tinkerings plus the cluttered mess of tools. The guest bedroom and hall bathroom were empty. Leslie's bedroom was neat. Her bathroom was also clean.

No Leslie. But her car was still in the drive. And her son was in the local jail.

Maybe the thug had scared her away. She had run to a neighbor or a friend. A family member had picked her up and taken her to their home.

Or something bad had happened.

Leslie Price wouldn't leave an empty beer can in the living room. She'd told us that she kept Roger's bedroom closed because she couldn't stand the mess. If she tried to clean or straighten, Roger would argue with her.

I checked Leslie's closet and bathroom again. A suitcase sat in the rear of her walk-in. I had no idea if she had more than one. In the bathroom, I found her toiletries and OTC meds. But it meant nothing, not knowing if she kept travel-sized in her suitcase.

Returning to Roger's room, I stood near his bed and gazed around the room. The shelves opposite his bed held models, software, gaming books, and a few action-adventure paperbacks. His high school yearbooks were organized by year.

Had Roger robbed the bank to get out of his mother's home? Had he been talked into the robbery by his accomplice? Had they threatened his mother, forcing him to rob the bank?

We never saw him communicating with anyone other than store clerks and his online gaming buddies. He didn't even chat on Reddit threads.

Gaming buddies. Could one of them be the accomplice?

The ATF had all his tech. And we looked at those chats. A whole lot of cursing for tactical failures. Many riffs on "u suk," "gonna burn u," "did u see that," and "I'm awesome." All their identities were a combination of numbers, x's, and either ninja, assassin, dark lord, sniper, or lone wolf. Except for one "xxxI-heartunicorns1996xxx."

It would take the ATF time to track down the gamers. If that was even possible. Mrs. Price said some came from "foreign parts." Why would foreigners want him to rob a bank? I didn't believe Roger had any international political leanings.

I also didn't believe Mrs. Price had left on vacation.

And I couldn't believe that Nash and I would have missed something as obvious as clandestine meetings with bank robbers. Me, maybe. But not Nash. My heart squeezed at the thought. Nash would be struggling with this very issue now that he was awake.

I should see him, make sure that he knew that Roger had an accomplice. A young thug had inhabited Mrs. Price's house. Someone we had not seen in the week we'd been tailing Roger. Whatever had happened, the wheels had been set in motion before Mrs. Price had hired us.

Poor Nash. He'd still be agonizing over the situation. I could give him comfort.

Not ex-wife-style comfort, but apprentice-type comfort.

Maybe I should also talk to Roger. Maybe the girls were right.

But it was now the ATF's problem.

Except Mrs. Price had written "help us" on our check memo.

Shizzles.

I stepped into the hall, ready to leave, and heard the creak of an opening door. I froze, listening. The door shut with a muffled click. Afraid to look, but more scared not to peek, I edged down the hall. It had to have been the front door. Unless someone had been in the front hall closet the whole time.

Which would be so uncool.

And so scary.

In Julia Pinkerton's third season, episode nine, "Sax as a Weapon," she'd been in a similar situation. Snooping for clues in the house of a rival classmate (and marching band member) whom

Julia suspected to be in a black-market weapons ring. Selling weapons to high school students. Also uncool. And super scary.

Julia had crept down a hallway, too. Poked her head around the corner to spot the star saxophone player and his adult weapons dealer. Both armed, naturally.

I peeked around the corner of the hall and spotted a young man. The young thug from earlier. But not with an older guy.

But still armed. Naturally.

THIRTY-FOUR

#LittleRunAway #ExExploitation

*S*hizzalation. This was why one shouldn't break and enter.
I ducked back down the hall and evaluated possible
escape routes. All at the other end of the house. Lucky was parked
in the driveway. He must know I was in the house.

I turned a tight circle, evaluating rooms for hiding. Picked
Leslie's. As the master, it seemed to have more options. In Leslie's
room, I spun again like a demented top, trying to guess the most
unlikely hiding spots.

Leslie had a phone next to her bed. But it was attached to the
wall by a cord. I was claustrophobic. I didn't like closets. Or hiding
in bathrooms. I'd had a previous under-the-bed fail. This time I
wouldn't be dodging books. What else was there? The drapes?

The quickest way to lose when playing hide-and-seek. Remi
always poked at curtains.

Focus, Maizie.

In "Sax as a Weapon," Julia Pinkerton had wedged herself
between the walls near the ceiling while the weapons dealer had
strolled unknowingly beneath her. She sprung from above, tack-
ling him below. Disarmed him and used the weapon on the saxophone player.

However, I no longer had the stunt double or the abs needed for that scene.

I chose the drapes. Hopefully, it'd been a while since Young Thug had played hide-and-seek. And Mrs. Price had lined, faux-velvet drapes. I opened the curtains so they bunched loosely on either side of the window. Slipped behind the drapes on one side, curling them around me so I hid between folds. Stood on my toes.

Then realized where one door (or three) was closed, a window could open. Thanking Mrs. Price for living in a ranch, I opened the window, pushed out the screen, and climbed through. Behind me, I heard banging on the bedroom door. The door wouldn't hold against body blows. I ran to the neighbor's house. At the side where Agent Langtry had once tackled me, I paused to breathe. Heard the crack of the bedroom door frame breaking.

I dashed around the side of the neighbor's house and onto their porch. Hammered on their door. Rang the bell. Remembered the neighborhood was dead in the afternoon. Much like I would be if the man with the gun caught me.

Think, Maizie.

I hunted for a key. Not under the mat or above the sill. No plastic rock, garden statue, or flower pot. I dashed off the porch and pelted toward the next house.

He'd seen me. Surely. I looked over my shoulder.

Holy hellsbah.

I had been spotted. By an older man in the Price driveway. Arms folded. Bearded, sunglasses, and cap pulled low. Looking like every other local man from Black Pine.

Young Thug's father?

I turned my head. Kept going. My lungs were burning. My heart felt close to exploding. And my neck ached. By the next house, a new pocket of flames seared my lungs. My arms began to tingle. I told myself it was the adrenaline kicking in. Imagined the ice cream at the end of the rainbow.

A figure rounded the corner, blocking my path. Young Thug.

No gun in sight, but his hand sat on his hip beneath his untucked shirt. He'd headed me off at the pass.

My heart crawled up my throat. My stomach belly-flopped to my knees. I jerked to a stop.

"Why you running?" he said.

"So you don't shoot me," I gasped, trotting in place so my legs wouldn't seize up. And in preparation for a Roadrunner-style takeoff.

His eyes narrowed. "You need to come with us."

"I've got stuff to do. Huge to-do list."

He raised his shirt so I could see the handgun. Then he looked beyond me and waved at the man in the drive. I half-turned. The man had pushed Lucky off the drive toward a parked truck.

"Not Lucky," I cried.

"That's right. Your luck's run out." Chuckling, he pulled off his ball cap to scratch his head.

I used his casual scratch for my getaway. Sprinted across the street. One neighbor might be home.

The kid cursed. "Lady, you ain't going anywhere. Might as well stop. You're gonna give yourself a heart attack."

Lady? Did I look that old?

I quickly squelched the thought to focus on the big truck in the driveway one door down. I tripped over the curb, my arms flailing, and forced a sprint across the yard to the jacked-up truck in the drive. I careened toward it and slammed into its side.

No alarm.

"You got nowhere to go," said the kid. "Get in the truck and be quiet. We want to talk to you."

Talk, then shoot me. I reached for the tailgate and yanked. The alarm shrieked.

Jackpot.

Panting, I turned to face the kid. "This guy's home. And he's armed."

Behind us, the garage door rumbled.

"Shit." The kid whistled and waved an arm at the truck, then fixed his eyes on me. "We'll find you. We got your bike. Stay out of that house."

$\mathcal{U}$nderstandably, Monster Truck Man did not like me yanking on his tailgate, but he did allow me to use his phone to call the police and report my stolen bike. Particularly after he found me collapsed beneath his tailgate, wailing about men trying to kill me.

By the time Ian Mowry arrived in his Tahoe, I'd stopped crying. While Ian drove me to the police department, there was a litany of "I told you to go to Boomer's" and "how do you manage to get into these situations?"

At the office, I gave him a good description of the thug and a vague description of the other man. The truck was black. I had once again forgotten to get the plates, make, or model.

"I don't understand why you went back to the Price's," said Ian. "I thought you'd spoken to Agent Langtry. She did not want you there."

"I had some unfinished business with Leslie Price. But I left numerous messages with Agent Langtry. I told her I was going to the house."

"You're stepping on toes, Maizie."

"I'm not trying to get in the way of her investigation." I skipped the part where I had illegally entered the Price house. No need to give Ian or Gladys impetus to toss me in the can. "Let's focus on the important part. I was threatened with a gun. They said they would find me, Ian. And they want to 'talk' to me."

He drummed his fingers on the desk. "I don't get it. Do they think you know something about the bombing?"

"I have no idea. Maybe it's because I'd been sniffing around Mrs. Price's house."

"Sniffing around?"

"Knocking on doors and windows. Trying to see if Mrs. Price was home. And she was not."

Ian pulled out his phone and punched in a number. "Stay here. Let me talk to Agent Langtry so you can give this information to her. After this, I'm taking you to Boomer's cabin."

"I can't put Remi in jeopardy, Ian."

His lips zipped into a narrow line and he stalked off, holding the phone to his ear. I leaned around the corner of his cubicle, checked for nearby police buddies, then leaned forward to grab Ian's desk phone.

I punched the nine and asked to be connected with the Wellspring Center.

*I*n the Black Pine Police Department waiting room, Ian glowered at Oliver. I had to hand it to Ian. Oliver had greater size and swagger, but Ian's "don't mess with me" cop vibe was something to behold.

My bruised ego had a nice pick-me-up. My heart, however, still lay on the hospital floor.

Ian turned to me. "Why is he here?"

"I'm taking Maizie to the Wellspring Center," said Oliver. "She needs a place to stay. You said her office wasn't safe. And she doesn't have a ride."

"I'm her ride," said Ian. "To her father's house. Which has a great security system."

"Actually, the Wellspring Center has pretty awesome security," I said. "They have armed guards."

"So does the cabin. His name is Boomer Spayberry." Ian cut me a look. "Can I talk to you privately?"

"Ian." I placed a hand on his arm and gave him the sympathetic look I used in *While You Were Shifting* when my character broke the news to her were-dolphin boyfriend that his pod had migrated without him. "There are plenty of empty rooms at the Wellspring Center. Hardly anybody is staying there. I need to do my community volunteer work there anyway."

"I made a call to her probation officer," said Oliver. "It's all fixed."

"That's inappropriate," said Ian. "You're the reason why she has a probation officer."

"You called my probation officer?" I said sharply, then turned back to Ian. Back to sympathetic. I'd do morally outraged in a minute. "Please understand. I can't draw any more attention to Remi. And I need you to make sure the teens are safe."

"I get it. But I don't trust him."

"Understandably."

"What about Langtry?"

"You have my statement and description of the guys and truck. She can call me at Wellspring if she needs more." No way did I want to talk to Langtry. I had a feeling she'd drag out my breaking and entering. Which would get back to Gladys. I wasn't going to jail for the Prices. That kind of irony would be too cruel.

Keeping my hand on Ian's arm and my eyes on his, I shifted closer. Adjusted my voice to breathy. Ran my hand from his forearm to bicep. Making the subtle shift from sympathy to seduction. Not something I was proud of, but the request I was about to make needed all the help it could get. "And Ian, I need you to do something for me."

"What?" His eyes darted from Oliver back to me. Softened.

"I need you to get me an appointment to speak to Roger Price." I squeezed his arm. "I was wrong about who was watching my house. It has to be related to Roger. I think his mother is in trouble. If I talk to him, he might tell me who they are."

THIRTY-FIVE

#Teensploitation
#DeathDoesNotBecomeHer

"*I* don't think you should talk to Roger Price," said Oliver.

We rode in the back of a white Escalade with the Wellspring Center logo printed on the side. No paneled van shuttle for the Wellspring Center. No helmet-head, thigh-burning ride on Lucky either. But I'd left my were-dolphin sympathy with Ian and had shifted roles. This character was trickier since I needed Oliver's help but also needed him to chill on the alpha-male act.

I felt terrible about hurting Ian. It'd been a Vicki move to toss Oliver in Ian's face. But poor Ian was law enforcement and I'd crossed too many legal lines.

"Do you know who Roger Price even is?" I said.

"Isn't he the guy who blew up the bank last week?"

"He's unresolved business from a previous case. Tiffany and Rhonda were right, I've got to face him."

"Babe, if you're in some kind of trouble and it's connected to Roger Price, the last thing you should do is confront him."

I closed my eyes and counted to five. "Oliver, it's none of your business." I opened my eyes and leaned forward to speak to the driver. "Can you drop me off at the Outdoor Outfitter store?"

"Where?" said Oliver.

"I need to talk to Mara, Fred, and Laci. They're doing an event there. I don't trust their parents to deliver my message."

"I thought you were coming back to the Center with me." I detected a slight pout to Oliver's voice. "I was going to order dinner…"

Once again, I conjured up the *While You Were Shifting* heroine. Peace, love, understanding. This time I really dug deep.

I turned to face Oliver. Placed a hand on his thigh. And used my sincerest voice with an added dash of huskiness for good measure. "You're so sweet. But I have this to-do list that must get to-done. We'll catch up later."

Oliver placed a hand over mine. And used his sincerest voice with a matching dash of husky. "I completely understand. I said I would help you with the missing camper. I'll go with you to the outfitter shop. I just love those kids."

Great.

*I*t took some time getting through the throng to talk to the three. I hadn't seen a mob like this since the 2008 Teen Choice Awards when Hannah Montana presented. Oliver elbowed his way through the crowd of ten and up fans. The teens sat on a small platform stage behind a table piled with merchandise. The screen behind them ran a silent montage of their videos.

Catching Mara's eye as she signed a metal tumbler, I mouthed, "I need to talk to you three—asap."

She nodded, elbowed Laci. Laci gave me a nod and kicked Fred. Resuming her sardonic smile, Laci selfied with a middle-aged man who appeared inappropriately excited about their encounter. Fred glanced over, spotted me, and dropped a preteen girl's phone. Leaving the astonished girl, he bounded from his chair.

"Never leave your fans hanging, Fred," I said, eyeballing the girl's enraged mother. "We'll confab in a minute."

I hopped from the stage to find their parents milling next to a rack of sleeping bags. Got the thumbs up from Laci's dad, which meant...I wasn't sure. Mara's mom motioned me around her iPad as she videoed the teens autograph signing. Mrs. Hernandez scrolled through social media on her phone, looking bored.

"Any problems?" I asked her.

She looked up. "Yes. There was a big scene when we first got here. An angry crowd of women who were shocked when Chandler didn't show. They didn't even stay to hear our kids do the Q and A. Can you believe it?"

"But no stranger-danger-type stuff?"

She looked at me blankly.

"Did you see an older guy and younger guy? The older guy is bearded, wearing a hat and sunglasses. The younger guy is also bearded and wearing a ball cap."

She pointed to the customers poking around the sportswear section. All bearded men wearing ball caps.

I stalked back to the stage, slipped behind the kids, and grabbed the microphone in front of Laci. "The *Bigfoot Trackers* will be back in just a moment. Keep an orderly line. If you wiggle out, you lose your place. And no holding spots. Give us five minutes. We're going to refill their Sharpies."

Fred turned to me. "Sharpies don't—"

"Backstage," I whispered and pointed behind the screen.

We trooped off the stage and hunkered between the back of the screen and a stacked display of ginormous coolers.

"There are some armed dudes following me," I explained. "They've been watching my house and now they've stolen Lucky and threatened me. With guns."

"Real guns?" said Fred.

"How would they threaten her with fake guns, Fred?" said Laci.

I held up a hand. "No time for arguing. You three might be in danger, too. I told your parents it might be a lunatic fan, but now I think it's related to the bank bombing."

"But that doesn't have anything to do with us," said Mara.

"By association, it might. I don't know what they want, but you need to be extra careful. No more events. Stay off the mountain and out of the woods. Those are police-issued orders. School and home only."

They gave me the "that's so unfair" scowl.

"What about Chandler?" said Mara. "Any new leads?"

"I looked at the Wellspring security tapes this morning," I said. "And that night's footage is gone. Disappeared."

"Like Chandler," said Laci.

"Could be operator error." Oliver wasn't the best at technology. He might be the worst. "But I also saw the mysterious chicken coop and it's just a lab for drying herbs. The greenhouse is full of plants. Nothing exciting at all. We hit an impasse."

Laci's lip jutted out. Mara stared at her feet.

"Are you giving up?" said Fred.

"No, I'm going to stay at the Wellspring Center for a while. The ATF is in charge of the bank bombing. Hopefully, they'll catch Roger Price's accomplices and then I'll be freer to look for Chandler. But I've got to lay low for a bit."

Oliver slipped in beside me. "Hey, kids. What's going on?"

"What's he doing here?" said Fred. "You're staying with him?"

"Not really," I said. "But Oliver is helping me."

Mara yanked on my hand, pulling me away from Oliver. The three circled around me. Mara glared over my shoulder at Oliver.

"We don't trust him, Maizie," Mara whispered. "Don't stay at Wellspring. They're encroachers."

"You can stay with me," said Fred. "My mom won't mind."

I wasn't so sure about that. "It's okay. Wellspring has great security. Speaking of, they have security cameras everywhere. If they wanted to, Wellspring could get you in a lot of trouble for trespassing. You should be thankful they didn't."

"That's bogus," said Laci. "Something's going on."

Laci's dad poked his head around the screen. "Your five minutes are up. Did you refill your pens?"

Laci rolled her eyes.

"Watch your back, Maizie," said Mara. "Trust no one."

"Same goes for you three," I said. "Keep your eye out for bearded dudes of various ages. Call Detective Ian Mowry if you see anything unusual. And please don't listen to your parents. Stay home and stay safe. Better yet, convince them to take you out of town."

We high-fived and I slid out of the huddle. The three squared their shoulders and trooped back to the stage. The din from the mob swelled into a scream.

Oliver leaned into my ear. "A call was forwarded from the Wellspring office." He handed me his phone.

I strode away from the crowd.

"Maizie," said Ian Mowry. "I just talked to Agent Langtry. There's something I think you should know. This is under investigation, so please don't tell anyone. Langtry found Leslie Price. We've got an APB on your John Does. Oliver said you're at the outfitter store? If you're insistent on staying with him, I wish you'd get to the Wellspring Center and stay there for now."

"Where's Leslie Price?"

"Her body was found in the debris dumpster at the bank."

"Her body? The First National? Oh, Mrs. Price." My stomach clenched and tears stung my eyes. "I failed her, Ian. She wanted my help and I failed her."

Ian spoke in gentle, reassuring tones, but I couldn't pay attention. My thoughts began to slow, pooling into her written "help us" and the look of panic in Leslie Price's eyes when I asked about an accomplice. My breath jerked and sputtered. My chest felt hot. My neck clammy.

I really did fail her. In the worst possible way.

"Maizie, are you there? You're breathing really hard. Are you okay? Do you need help?"

"Ian," I gasped. "I really need to talk to Roger Price. Please."

THIRTY-SIX

#TherapyWhamSlam
#KeepingItInTheFamily

*J*lay on Dr. Trident's couch, alternately hyperventilating and crying. "I'm the worst private investigator who lived. I can't Sherlock. I can't even Inspector Clouseau. And I'm running out of plausible Julia Pinkerton episodes."

Dr. Trident murmured something about the ills of comparing oneself to fictional characters, but I barely heard him.

"Aside from the armed men threatening to 'talk' to me, I have no progress in my missing person case. Quite frankly, the teens on *Scooby-Doo* are better at gathering clues than I am."

Worst yet, I couldn't face my boss now that he was actually awake and out of a coma. I wanted to see Nash, pour my heart out to him. And to help him shave. Which was weird. But mainly to help him with any feelings he might have about the bank bombing. Or feelings about anything else.

Nash didn't even know about Leslie Price. My chest tightened. I grabbed another tissue off the glass side table.

My new therapist was not helping. But at least I could check off Gladys's boxes. That was the one positive in the whole fiasco of a week. And as a positive, it wasn't saying much.

"Tea, Maizie?" Dr. Trident checked the steeping leaves in a teapot. "Chamomile and St. John's wort. With a dash of ginseng."

For the first time since my real recovery, I wanted tequila. But I scooted into a seating position and accepted the tea. "I should be the bigger person and see Nash. Even if Jolene is there. But he's had a traumatic brain injury. He needs peace and calm, and let's face it, I'm a hot mess."

"You'll never find peace of mind until you listen to your heart."

"Wow. That's beautiful." I set down my teacup. "If I really care about Nash, I shouldn't be afraid to see him. Even if Jolene is there. He'll need to talk about the Prices, and I'm the only person who can do that for him. Whether I'm a hot mess or not, I should be there for him."

We rose from our seats. Dr. Trident gave me a namaste bow.

"Thank you," I said. "That was the best thing you could have ever told me. Not to insult you, but that was the sort of thing I got from Renata, my ex-therapist."

"No need to thank me. I was quoting George Michael."

"The singer?"

"Of course." Dr. Trident held up his phone. "Selfie?"

*T*issuing off my tears, I sped through the east wing hallway then stopped short, realizing I had no vehicle to take me to the hospital. But this was a spa. I didn't need a vehicle, all I needed was a driver.

Maybe Oliver had a point about working here. I could get used to this.

Hold up. What was I thinking?

I strolled down the grand staircase and asked reception for the driver to bring the car. Felt my stomach clench and my shoulders stiffen. The scent of Chanel No. 5 followed. Knowing retreat was not a possibility, I mustered some courage and turned to face Vicki.

She wore a Vaara unitard with a long sheer jacket. Something only Vicki could pull off with her tiny body and ability to wear silk chiffon without snagging. I recognized the Dior Célèbre red lipstick and the pursing that accompanied it.

"Maizie. How nice to see you after your not returning my calls."

"My phone was stolen."

She arched a perfect eyebrow. "For someone who works in a security and investigations office, the irony must be unbearable."

"Quite." I blinked. I'd gone from sci-fi romcom to period piece. Maybe it was the historical vibe at the center. All the heavy wood carvings.

"I've had a terrible week," she said. "And considering my only daughter has not been available for a simple phone call, I'd say you are to blame as much as anyone."

"I've had a lot going on. Bank bombing. Missing person. Injured boss."

"And seduction of an old fiancé." She placed a hand on a slim hip. "Oliver insisted on changing the wedding security detail from Sweeney Security Solutions to Nash Security Solutions."

"I didn't seduce Oliver. If anything, it's the other way around."

"Really?" she purred. Slipping a hand through my arm, she led me to a seating area. "Do tell."

Hang on. This was Vicki. Speaking to her was like playing chess with a nine-year-old Mensa protégé. Full of brilliant strategy and an underdeveloped moral compass. "Why did you bring Oliver here, Vicki?"

"Who said I brought him? He reached out. You wouldn't have any contact with him and he was distraught. He was full of remorse and wanted to make reparations. It's perfect, really. Because of your legal issues, he'd have to move to Georgia to see you."

"How did you even know about the Wellspring Center a month ago?" I sucked in my breath. "Wait a minute, are you an investor?"

Her blonde ponytail skimmed her shoulder with the shrug.

"You knew he'd invest, too, if you could entice him. By using me."

"Vanity is not pretty, Maizie. Oliver Fraser has always been a promoter of health and wellness. He cares deeply about alleviating people's physical pain."

"He was arrested for alleviating people's pain."

"We're not all perfect, are we? Aren't you here doing community service?" She smiled. "It all worked out in the end."

"What worked out? Your investment? Wellspring has barely been open and there are hardly any guests. I'm pretty sure you aren't paying for anything or you wouldn't be staying here."

She smiled. "You never did have a head for business. That's why you needed management."

"That's easy for my ex-manager to say. Are you getting out of the entertainment industry?" I sucked in my breath. "Has *All is Albright* been canceled?"

"Why would you say that?" she snapped. "We're still filming."

"Now?" I glanced around for cameras.

"I know your rules. Does it look like I'd be filming? I'm on my way to a workout."

I eyeballed her for a hidden mike. Impossible to hide in a unitard. "Then why aren't you managing Giulio's career?"

"Oh, him." She waved a hand. "I must get to my workout. I have a meeting later."

"*Him* is your fiancé. God knows why. He's upset with the way you've been treating him."

"Giulio's Italian. He's always upset." She rose and the chiffon made a pretty swirl around the unitard. "He's also young. He'll get over it."

"That's not fair to Giulio. Marriage is more than a contract, Vicki. It means something to him." What, I wasn't sure. Possibly more screen time, but I'd give Giulio the benefit of the doubt. Besides, it wasn't the point. She shouldn't be using sacred vows for career strategy.

"Really, Maizie. I'd think you were jealous. Choose one, make your move, and get on with it." Striding off, she called over her shoulder. "Text me when you get your new phone."

"What does that mean? Choose one?" Did she want me to make a play for Giulio? Or Oliver? And why the hey?

Never mind. I was getting on with it. To the one I had chosen. In the hospital.

THIRTY-SEVEN

#OtherWomaning #BedsideConfessions

*I*t was dinner time. My stomach seemed to know it before I saw the trays of Jello rolling by on carts. On Nash's floor, my smile to the nurses felt superficial and guilty. They'd probably seen Jolene with him all day and wondered why I had previously claimed his non-visiting-hours time with such urgency.

I was the other woman. A character I had never played, although I'd been offered the role in real life a few times.

And never accepted, by the way.

At Nash's room, I knocked quietly before peeking inside. His dinner tray sat on the swing table near his bed. His monitors beeped in a soothing regular rhythm. The TV ran muted sports news. Nash slept once again. His bed had been lowered. His breathing was even and steady, no post-traumatic stress stirring his slumber. His large shoulders still strained the hospital gown, but they looked more relaxed than before. More alive. Less... cadaver-ish.

Speaking of stiffs, no Jolene, either.

I let out the breath I had been holding, entered the room, and sank on the chair next to his bed. Looked around for Steve. Found him on the floor. Grabbing the stuffed armadillo, I placed him at the foot of Nash's bed. Then moved him to the crook of his arm. Now that I knew he was truly awake, I could no longer touch Nash, but it felt better knowing Steve could give him some physical comfort.

"I'm sorry I didn't come earlier. A lot has happened since I last talked to you. I shouldn't upset you, but I thought you'd rather know what's happened with the Price case."

This was harder than I thought. The scent of food drifted into the room as a cart squeaked down the hall, but I was no longer hungry. I felt chilled and squeezed my arms across my chest.

Just say it, Maizie. He's not even awake.

"I...well, in all honesty, Leslie Price asked for my help and I did nothing. And now she's been murdered. I'm pretty sure I know who did it. Or at least I've seen the men. They threatened me and took Lucky. They've been following me. Watching my house and poisoned one of our dogs. Remi..." I choked back a sob. "I put Remi in danger. I moved out of my house. I wanted to stay at the office, but Ian Mowry said it wasn't safe. I moved into the Wellspring Center."

Swallowing hard, I lowered my gaze. "I screwed up royally, Nash. I never found Chandler. I've let down the teens. I've put my family and the kids in danger. Didn't save a woman from murder. And I haven't saved your business. Although if Lamar uses the flyers I made, we might get a lot of calls. Probably not for PI work, though."

"What do you mean they threatened you?" He croaked.

I jerked my head up. "Mr. Nash?"

His eyes fluttered open. "Slow down, Miss Albright. They've got me on heavy pain meds and I can't catch all you're saying."

His hands patted the blanket and finding the remote, pressed a button. An engine whirred and his bed slowly brought him to an upright position. He picked Steve off the crook of his arm, looked at him, and smiled. "Remi?"

"Yes. She wants Steve back, but only when you're out of the hospital."

"Start from the beginning. No crying. And speak slowly, for mercy's sake," he rasped. "You look like hell, by the way. I want to know what's done this to you."

Pinching my thumb, I began with the teens, Bigfoot, and missing Chandler Jonson. Routed him through Chandler's brother, the boot, the rock thrower, and the motorcyclist's attacks on Lucky. Glazed over Oliver, but told him about the Wellspring Center, the ramped-up security, spooky Everett Lawson, and the missing videos. Then hopped back to Mrs. Price's check and my run-in with the bearded dudes. "I've been reporting to the ATF and Ian Mowry all along."

"Jolene's secretary tried to shoot you, too?"

I shrugged. "She might have trouble contextualizing sarcasm."

He frowned. "Roger Price had at least two accomplices. How did we not see that?" He rubbed his scruffy beard. "I want to shave. It's driving me nuts."

"I can help you with that," I said, then dampened my enthusiasm. "Like, get the nurse for you."

He waved a hand, refocusing on the case. "Your gaming theory is interesting. They could have used coded messages. Didn't we have the downloaded scripts from Roger's games? Did ATF take them?"

"I gave everything to Agent Langtry, but I made copies."

"Bring them to me. At least it's something I can do while I'm in here."

"The accomplices would have to be local. Maybe not Black Pine, but definitely not foreign. Close enough to be still hanging around and terrorizing Roger's mother."

"They probably use a VPN to route their IP address to a different location than where they actually live. It'd take the ATF time to track them down."

"The two guys looked local. They look like any guy you'd see at Tractor Supply."

"We could've missed them during our surveillance." Nash closed his eyes and winced. "Let me think about this missing person case, too. It's interesting. I understand why the police moved on. There's not a lot of quality evidence."

I chewed my lip. "I kind of suck at finding evidence."

He opened his eyes to give me a hard look. "But the circumstantial evidence is compelling. And unlike the cops, we're not building a case for court, so it's okay to focus on the circumstantial if it leads somewhere. I agree it doesn't make sense that he'd leave the kids at the campsite. Why go with them to the campsite in the first place? And why did he continue to camp in the same spot near the Wellspring Center?"

"The kids had a theory about it being an old chicken farm."

"For a TV show, wouldn't staying in the same spot get boring? And it sounds like Chandler knew what he was doing when it came to promoting and running that show."

"Yes." I moved to the edge of my chair. "And he was the star even though he didn't come off as a diva."

"There must have been a reason for him to continue returning to the area near the Wellspring Center. It's hinky. From what you tell me, sounds like Chandler is obsessive but smart." Nash shifted in bed and moaned.

"It must be hard for you to do this in bed."

"Do what?" He stopped moving and gave me an inscrutable look.

"Normally you pace while you sort your thoughts."

"Oh." He eyed me then scratched his beard. "That's true enough. I'm too dizzy to walk. And too damn weak. It's miserable."

"Can I do anything for you? I brought you clothes. From the office. And a shaving kit."

He looked down at Steve. Picked him up and turned him over. "Thank you, Miss Albright. That was considerate."

"I've been visiting you mostly at night or early in the morning. Lamar would come during the day."

"That's…" He nodded. "Thank you."

"I didn't want you to think I hadn't been here."

"I wouldn't have thought that."

I swallowed. "You wouldn't?"

He dropped Steve and leveled me with a look that penetrated through my insecurities. Yet still left me uncertain. "No, I wouldn't."

"Because this morning, I…I don't want to interfere with… anything. You've been through enough. And…Lamar and I've been trying to keep the business…running. We…" An unchecked tear squeezed out. I tried blinking it away. Pinched the skin between my thumb and pointer.

"No crying, Miss Albright. Especially for me and my crap situation."

I sniffled. "It's my crap situation, too."

"Come here, Maizie." He held out an arm.

"Rule number two. No hugging?"

"Near-death overrides rule number two, don't you think?"

I shot out of the chair. He pulled me into an awkward lean against his shoulder and held me, while I cried and made his thin gown wet. Then I pulled away to stare into the cool blue eyes I'd missed seeing.

"I'm supposed to comfort you, not the other way around."

He attempted a smile. "Listen, Mrs. Price's death is not your fault. Yes, you could have handled that situation differently, but so could she. If it's anybody's fault, it's her son's."

"I'm visiting Roger tomorrow. I want answers."

"You might not get them." The hand that lay on my back slid to the nape of my neck. He closed his eyes, then slowly opened them. "Sometimes you can't solve the mystery."

"But—"

"I'll figure out the business and the bills. Jolene and I are discussing what to do." He yawned and slid his fingers into my hair to gently rub my scalp. "You and Lamar have done enough. He's got a business to run. You have a missing person to find."

Jolene. My stomach felt hollow and another lump formed in my throat. I couldn't make myself touch that subject. Not with his fingers in my hair and his confidence in my ability to find Chandler. It was too confusing.

"You're not going to tell me to drop the case and hide somewhere?"

"Your hair is so soft." His eyes looked unfocused and he blinked. "Sorry. Are you carrying your .38? Taking safety precautions?"

Not really, but I skipped that question to thank the universe for Olaplex treatments. Then felt guilty about Tiffany and Rhonda. But set that aside to focus on his fingers in my hair. Maybe he and Jolene held hands when they worked on business arrangements. Maybe I should just ask him to clarify the current state of his feelings for Jolene.

Or not. He just woke from a coma. I should probably give him a minute.

Maybe I should kiss him.

Tears prickled my eyes. "I really missed you."

The fingers slipped from my scalp to my shoulder. I tossed Steve and sat on the side of his bed. I cupped his face, stroking his beard with my fingers. His arm dropped from my shoulders to settle on my hip. Leaning forward, I pressed my body against his and tilted my face, hovering above his lips.

"Nash," I murmured, then pulled back to study him. His eyes were closed and a faint smile had settled on his lips. "Nash?"

His chest rose and relaxed. I felt his hand jerk against my hip.

Okay. He had a head injury. He needed his sleep. Probably used up his energy listening to my long, drawn-out story about Chandler and Mrs. Price.

Hells, why had I used all his awake time on that?

OMG. What if he was just doped up and it didn't mean anything? When Jolene was here, he was completely awake while they held hands.

It's not like he had said much other than my hair was soft. Which was more of a fact than opinion.

A knock on the door startled me. I hopped from the bed and spun around.

Oliver filled the doorway. "There you are."

"Yes, here I am." My heart thudded inside my chest. "This is Mr. Nash. My boss. From Nash Security Solutions."

"Poor guy." Oliver ambled into the room. "How are you doing? It must be hard, seeing him like this."

"I'm—" I wasn't sure what I was. Confused, mostly. "He's awake. Or at least he was a little while ago. No longer in a coma."

"Great news." Oliver shook his head. "He must be in a lot of pain. He looks so uncomfortable."

"I suppose. He's pretty drugged up right now."

"I'll give you more time." Oliver's smile didn't reach his sorrowful eyes. "I came to pick you up. Wellspring's driver returned and told me where you had gone. You need to be more cautious, Maizie."

"That's very thoughtful of you. I know it's not easy for you. To be in a hospital."

Oliver opened his mouth. Closed it, then said, "Yes, well. It's nothing I can't handle."

I lowered the bed, hoping the noise and motion wouldn't wake Nash. It didn't.

"I'm ready. We talked," I said. "Tired him out."

"Poor guy," Oliver said again, holding the door open for me.

Allowing Jolene to step through.

THIRTY-EIGHT

#TheOtherOtherWoman #HotShot

*J*olene still wore the blue sheath dress, looking as fresh as she did earlier that morning. Her auburn locks cascaded down her back. Her makeup was on point. She also held a Styrofoam box that smelled of ribs, collard greens, and cornbread.

Nash's favorite meal. In my estimation that made her even more attractive.

Well played, Jolene.

The tight feeling in my chest returned and guilt spanked my cheeks with a flush to match the scrape on my forehead.

"Why are you here again? Wyatt shouldn't be stressed. No new cases." She glanced at Oliver. "Who's this?"

Oliver stuck his hand out. "Oliver Fraser. I manage the Wellspring Center. Maizie's friend from LA."

Jolene backtracked on the bitchiness to simper for a potential client. Particularly for one who'd meet her financial and hotness requirements. "Jolene Sweeney of Sweeney Realty. Did you just move here from California, Oliver? I assist most of our new residents with searches for their homes and businesses."

"Are you also Jolene of Sweeney Security Solutions?" said Oliver.

Smiling, she placed her free hand on her chest and drawled a "Well, yes, I am."

Oliver drew himself up to tower over her. "How dare you endanger Maizie, other clients, and your young staff with firearms. I can't even fathom the kind of person who'd tell a child to shoot a woman for entering her office."

Jolene's mouth was not so pretty when it hung open. She snapped it shut. "Is that what Maizie told you? You must have misunderstood."

"That's what I saw with my own eyes when I was in your office. And immediately withdrew our business."

Jolene set her tone to briskly apologetic. "I'm sorry you experienced that. We do keep firearms in the office. It's a security business, after all. But Sienna must have misconstrued my orders. I didn't tell her to shoot Maizie. That pea shooter is not even loaded. Sienna's only supposed to make it clear that Maizie doesn't belong in my office. As a competitor. Poaching is an issue in our industry."

She shot me a venomous look.

Guess Jolene had heard about my circular file rescue.

"It's okay, Oliver. Guns are kind of thing in Black Pine." I laid a hand on his arm.

"It's reckless and irresponsible." Oliver grabbed my hand. "You should sue her."

"I don't want to get Sienna in trouble."

"Excuse me, but I need to get to my husband." Jolene moved around Oliver. "Have your argument somewhere that's not a hospital. Wyatt needs his rest."

"You're married to Mr. Nash?" said Oliver.

"Divorced, last I heard," I said.

Jolene gave me another fierce glance, then pushed past me to Nash's bed. She laid the to-go box on the swinging table, tossed Steve on the floor, and stroked Nash's cheek.

"Poor Steve," I said. "Come on, Oliver. Let's go."

As I walked down the hall with Oliver, I felt some relief. But also plenty of shame for throwing myself at Nash when he'd only offered a shoulder to cry on. I didn't want to fight Jolene for Nash. They had a history. A history I did not understand. At. All. But I refused to play the role of homewrecker.

Sometimes histories were hard to overcome.

I looked up at Oliver, then realized my hand was still in his. Talk about histories. I slipped it from his grasp. "Thanks for sticking up for me."

"Of course," he said. "She seems like a horrible woman. No wonder your boss divorced her."

"I don't know why they divorced. He never talks about it."

I wasn't really sure about anything.

I convinced Oliver to take me to the office before returning to the Wellspring Center. I wanted to get the gaming transcripts to Nash despite what Jolene had said. I couldn't make much sense of them, but maybe he could find hidden bank robbery lingo among the "Kill! Kill! Kill's" and "Retreat! Retreat! Retreat's." I also wanted to check in with Lamar, whom I hadn't seen in ages although it had only been since the afternoon.

This was what insomnia did to you. Hours seemed like days. Days stretched like weeks. It hadn't even been a full week since Roger blew up the bank and it felt like a year.

"I should see Tiffany and Rhonda, too, but maybe after I see Roger Price," I said.

"You shouldn't talk to him," said Oliver. "We shouldn't be at your office either. It's too dangerous."

He was right. Which reminded me my .38 Special was in the office gun safe. I hated carrying it, which was why I left it in the gun cabinet. But Nash had made the request and he was still my boss.

For now.

I was dying to know exactly how Jolene would help Nash with the business.

We climbed the stairs to the office and found Lamar in the La-Z-Boy. He opened one eye, spotted Oliver filling the room behind me, opened the other, and pushed the recliner into an upright position.

Oliver introduced himself. Lamar's eyebrows quirked. He glanced at me, then shook Oliver's hand.

"We just came from the hospital," said Oliver. "Maizie wanted to get some things. She's staying at the Wellness Center for now."

"Is she now?" Lamar looked at me.

I explained what happened at the cabin and the taking of Lucky.

"You should be careful, too, Mr. Lamar," said Oliver.

"I'm an ex-cop. Don't worry about me." He rose from the chair. "Maizie, can I talk to you for a minute? In the office?"

We walked into the inner office and shut the door.

"What are you doing?" he said. "I don't like this situation."

"I'm trying to protect Remi and the teens. This is on the down-low, but Mrs. Price was murdered. Wellspring's the safest place to go."

"I think this Oliver is a little too eager to have you there."

"I can handle Oliver." I opened the big drawer in the desk and thumbed through the files. "Nash thinks Wellspring might have something do with Chandler's disappearance. If I can figure out the motivation for Chandler's obsession with Wellspring, it might help us to understand what happened to him. I'll do some digging there. But not literally."

"Maizie, I spoke to your probation officer. She called to check in with you."

I looked up from my file thumbing. "I've done as real as therapy gets with Dr. Trident. And Oliver offered to sign all my community service forms. The numbers are a little fudged, but I was available to work even if they didn't have anything for me to do."

"Here's what concerns me. Someone recommended you do your community service and therapy at the Wellness Center. It wasn't Gladys's original idea."

"You think it was Oliver?" I shrugged. "If Oliver pulled strings to get me over at the Wellspring Center, it was just so he'd have a way to see me. He still has feelings for me and wants to make up for what he did."

"I can't keep up with all y'all's drama." Lamar shook his head. "Nash and Jolene. You and this Oliver. I liked Detective Mowry, for what it's worth. He's a nice guy and a damn good cop."

I ignored the nice guy to home in on Jolene. "What's up with Jolene and the business now? Nash said we shouldn't worry about it. He said they were working something out."

"No idea, hon'." Lamar patted my shoulder. "Just focus on staying out of the way until ATF nabs these bank robbers. I'm going home. Tomorrow's coming early, and I want to catch up on sleep now that Nash is awake."

I hugged Lamar, wished him good dreams, and finished gathering the files and equipment I needed. In the reception area, I found Oliver on the battered couch, leafing through my copy of *People.*

"I'm ready." I slipped the Smith and Wesson into my belt holster and felt the downward tug on my Jean Atelier jeans.

Oliver dropped the magazine on the coffee table. "You're wearing a gun. And it's pink."

"Daddy gave it to me for my sixteenth birthday." I rolled my eyes. "I don't usually wear a piece. It's like an investigator thing."

He stood up. "That's kind of sexy."

"Um. Okay." My cheeks burned. "It's just for protection. Those bank robber dudes were armed."

"Right." He padded toward me, his eyes on my hip where the .38 rested. Reaching me, his gaze traveled slowly up my body. He spoke apologetically but something simmered beneath. "We have a no weapons policy at Wellspring, but you can leave it in my office safe. We'll go in through the back door and stop there first."

"Okey-dokey," I chirped, trying to get us back into the friend-zone. I ushered him out the door, locked it behind us, then charged down the stairs, skipping the step that sounded like gunfire.

Oliver approached more slowly. I took the extra time to poke my head into the donut shop. And spotted Young Thug sitting in the corner by the window, watching the street.

Sitting across from him — with a donut, coffee, and an open computer — was Crispin Jonson.

THIRTY-NINE

#PeaShootin' #LoversAndMadMen

I quietly closed the shop's side door and leaned against it. Oliver's foot hit the step that made the godawful racket.

Noticing my cringe, he took the last stairs in a leap. "What's wrong?"

Many things. I didn't know where to start. "The bank bomber guy from Roger Price's house is in the donut shop. He's watching the street." I had to process his table-mate. It would take too long to explain.

"What do you want to do?"

My heart jackhammered, and I suddenly had to pee. "Call Ian."

Oliver whipped out his phone and handed it to me. Behind my back, the doorknob jiggled.

"Shizzles." I grabbed Oliver's hand and tugged him toward the street door. "He heard the stair. We've got to get out of here or we'll be trapped."

I was not ready to shoot anyone. Especially in the tiny foyer of my beloved Dixie Kreme building.

The donut door pushed open. Oliver and I banged out the street door and shot down the steps. His BMW was parked in front of the donut shop. I yanked him the other way. We ran down the sidewalk. Glancing behind me, I spotted the Dixie Kreme shop door opening.

"Jolene's office is around the corner," I gasped. "We'll duck inside and call the police."

Oliver's long legs overtook my gallop. Grasping my hand, he pulled me along. We hustled around the corner. He flung open Jolene's door and yanked me inside. Sienna screamed. I locked the door.

"Sienna," I called over my shoulder. "Get in the back room and call the police. Two men, possibly armed, are looking for me. Give the police this location."

She screamed again.

Oliver spun around. "Quiet."

Sidling next to the window, I watched the sidewalk. "They're coming this way. There's no place to hide." I flattened against the wall. Oliver slid in next to me. Realizing I hadn't heard the back office door shut, I glanced at the reception desk.

Sienna stood behind the desk, pointing her tiny revolver at us. "Get out."

"Sienna, just go in the back, lock the door, and call the police."

"Jolene said you were absolutely not allowed in this office. You stole our client files. And you're bringing trouble here just like she said you would."

"I'm sorry I tricked you. Can you kick me out when there are not armed and violent men outside?"

"Out." She waved the gun. "I loaded the gun this time."

"Are you kidding me?" said Oliver. "Jolene Sweeney is crazy. She can't have you threaten people like this. You're a nice kid."

"Thank you." Sienna smiled at Oliver then drew her eyebrows together. "But Maizie is also armed. And Jolene said Georgia has 'stand your ground' law. If Maizie's armed, I have the right to defend myself."

"Sienna, my gun is in a holster on my belt. I have a concealed carry permit in my pocket. Just call the police and this will all be—"

A tapping sounded on the window. Sienna screamed.

Crispin stood in front of the window, peering inside. "Maizie, are you in here? Hey, can I talk to you? Can you come out?"

Oliver edged in front of me.

Young Thug elbowed Crispin out of the way and tugged on the door.

"Get down, Sienna," I shouted and pulled Oliver to the floor with me.

I couldn't watch Sienna and the window at the same time. Crawling backward, I prayed she wouldn't shoot me in the back. Oliver waited before edging back, using his body to shield me.

"Oh my God," sobbed Sienna. "I know him."

Young Thug rattled the door, then pulled his handgun from beneath his shirt. Pointing to the gun, he motioned for us to open the door. Crispin stared at Young Thug for a long moment and took off.

"What does he want, Maizie?"

I glanced over my shoulder. Sienna still stood behind the desk, holding the revolver and trembling.

"Get down." I sprang toward her.

She screamed and spun, holding the gun in both hands. A shot rang. I dropped to the floor, holding my hands over my ears. Looked up. Sienna's arms still stuck out rigidly, but the gun drooped in her hand. Her body shook, and her eyes had swallowed her face.

I leaped from the floor and threw myself at her, knocking her to the ground. Beneath me, she didn't move, but her body continued to quiver.

"Oliver," I cried. "Are you hurt?"

"I'm okay. What about you?"

"Sienna and I are okay. We're behind the desk. What's going on?"

"She shot a hole in the wall. The guys took off."

"Holy shiz." I pried the gun from her hand and rolled off Sienna. Stared at the ceiling. Sienna began crying. I patted her back. "They're gone."

"You're not supposed to be in here," she cried.

"I'm leaving. In a minute."

Oliver appeared above me. "I'm calling the police."

"Jolene's going to kill me," she howled.

Probably.

"You did good, kid," I said, using Nash's line. "Look, Jolene didn't prepare you for this exact situation. Next time, maybe duck and cover? But everyone's alive and the bad guys are gone."

Bad guys. I jerked to sitting. What was Crispin doing with a bank robber? "Sienna, you said you knew that guy. Which one?"

"Chandler Jonson's brother. He was a senior when I was a freshman. He was on the morning announcements all the time."

Hang on. Crispin went to Black Pine High School? He and Roger were the same age. "Did you know Roger Price?"

She shook her head. "I want to go home."

"The police are on their way." Oliver held out his hand to me.

I gave Sienna another pat, then took Oliver's hand and let him pull me to my feet. He swung me into his body. His arms wrapped around me and pressed me into his chest.

"Maizie. You were incredible. I never thought you could be like this. I mean, I've seen you do action scenes on your shows, but I had no idea you could do it in real life."

I let him squeeze me for a second more, allowed my head to rest against his chest, and permitted myself to be calmed by the erratic beating of his heart. I slid my hands up his chest and looked into his warm brown eyes. Which had grown even warmer.

Which spelled trouble.

I pushed away. "Oliver, I've got to get out here."

"The police—"

"That will take forever. Can you stay here with Sienna until the police come?"

"But Maizie—" His eyebrows pulled together, and his hands

tightened on my waist. "They're still out there. And what will the police say?"

"I'm sorry, Oliver. But I need a Black Pine High School year-book. And I need it now."

Sienna popped up. "I have them at my house. Let me call my mom and she'll bring them. What year do you want?"

*S*ienna's mom arrived with the yearbooks and found her daughter wrapped in a victim's blanket, giving the police her witness testimony. Her mom dropped the yearbooks into my arms, rushed to her daughter's side, and began sobbing.

Sienna gave her an "Oh my God, Mom," and continued her interview.

Jolene arrived thirty minutes later. Upon her entry, Sienna's mother darted toward the door, screaming obscenities, and swearing Sienna would never work for her again. An officer grabbed the mother so Jolene could hightail it into the back office.

"God, Mom," said Sienna. "Could you be more embarrassing?"

Sitting next to me, Ian Mowry muttered under his breath while I poured through the senior class photos. Oliver stood a little distance away, also watching me. His glazed expression made me wish my concealed carry had been a little more concealed.

I'd found Roger Price in the yearbook. Robotics Club. AV Club. His senior quote was, "I can't think of anything. Just put whatever."

Crispin Jonson was on another page. Senior quote, "You're going to regret not dating me in high school." Thespian society. Drama Club. And AV Club.

"Get the data from Crispin's video games," I said. "I bet he and Roger were on the same kill teams. They play the same battle games."

"No sign of the third guy, though?" Ian pulled out his phone and began texting. "Agent Langtry is leading a perimeter search right now. But if they were parked near the Dixie Kreme and were careful in their getaway, they had enough time to get out of town."

"There's still the older guy from the Price's house. Maybe Roger will tell me something he won't tell Agent Langtry. Especially since I know Crispin."

"If Langtry gives the okay, I'll take you to the jail in the morning. You're not her favorite person. Neither am I. But I'll do my best." He lowered his voice. "You know what this confirms. They *are* watching you."

"And I've put Lamar in danger if they're spying on the shop."

"I'm not worried about Lamar, I'm worried about you." He glanced at Oliver. "I thought you were staying at Wellspring and not the office."

"I was getting a few things for Nash. Oliver was going to drive me to Wellspring when we spotted Crispin and the other guy."

"I see." Ian flicked his gaze back to me. He looked disappointed.

I felt like I was in a local production of *A Midsummer's Night Dream*. But I wasn't sure if I was Hermia or Helena.

Or worse, Nick Bottom.

FORTY

#DisarminglyDisarmed
#UnscriptedSkulking

$\mathcal{B}$y the time Oliver and I reached Wellspring, my last burst of adrenaline had sapped the rest of my strength. In Oliver's office, I dragged my Smith and Wesson from the holster and handed it to him.

Watching him lock it his office safe, I felt a strange resentment at having to part with the revolver. I rarely wore it. Never wanted to use it. But I didn't like handing it over like this.

After locking the safe, Oliver turned to me. "Do you want to go to your room now?"

"Very much." I yawned to emphasize my point.

"Or would you rather stay in my apartment? I'd feel better. Your safety is my top priority."

I wasn't sure if it was my safety that was his top priority. And I never realized a pink gun could be such a turn on.

"Isn't safety why I'm here?" I said. "With all the fences and cameras? But if you're really worried, just let me keep my .38. I'll sleep with it under my pillow. Because that's all I really want to do. Sleep."

He padded toward me. "I can't let you keep the gun. House

rules. I have an extra bedroom. It's cozy and comfy. Egyptian cotton sheets and a feather duvet. I'll make us crepes in the morning with strawberries from the greenhouse. And coffee in my French press."

Oliver had a menu that could tempt Satan. "I could sleep on plywood and rocks. That's how tired I am."

"I can see the exhaustion. But you're looking better than you did this morning. Let me take care of you some more." He placed his hands on my shoulders and began kneading the knotted muscles. "I'm just thinking of your comfort."

"Oliver, I'm not getting back together with you. You hurt me too much. Badly enough that I let Vicki talk me into getting engaged to Giulio."

Oliver stopped kneading and dropped his hands. "But Giulio's engaged to Vicki."

"That's how messed up my life has become." Or maybe it already was, but that wasn't the point.

"But—" Oliver pressed his lips together and hung his head. "I understand. I'm sorry."

I touched his arm. He really was trying. "I'm sorry, too."

In my room, the bed was not made of plywood and rocks. Like Oliver's offered guest room, it also had Egyptian cotton sheets and a feather duvet.

What it did not contain was me sleeping. I stared at the ceiling. Then stared out the window at the beautifully landscaped plaza. Noted that from my fourth-floor room, the positioning of the gym, other buildings, and flower dunes created a visual barrier to the barren area and giant walled garden. Which bugged me.

Crispin's involvement in a bank robbery also gnawed at me. Or at least, his role as a friend to a possible accomplice and robber. Crispin, whose brother was still missing. Whose brother was obsessed with Wellspring's back forty.

If I was safe from bank robbers at Wellspring, I could get on with my actual case. Which conveniently meant snooping around Wellspring.

I dressed in Stella McCartney for Adidas. Black. With matching sneakers since I'd ruined my Golden Gooses. Slipped my ponytail through a black Barney's baseball cap. Perfectly on point for skulking.

The hall was lit and full of security cameras, so I ambled with purpose. Like I had decided on a late night bout of exercise. That anyone who knew me would find suspicious. But still.

In the elevator, I jogged in place. Keeping up the exercise appearances. On the first floor, I skirted the reception area and ducked into the west wing hall. Strode toward Oliver's office door. Pretended to knock and tried the knob. Locked.

Good. He was in his apartment.

I sauntered towards the security office. Knocked. And found it also locked.

Which it should be, considering the gun safe inside.

I needed to ask Oliver to let me look at the security videos again. Although spending time alone with Oliver was becoming an issue. He was eager to help me. Which was a nice change. And it wasn't his fault that he was gorgeous.

Hang on.

It wasn't his fault our shared history meant he knew how to please me. And he was available. Whereas other people were not so much.

Maybe we could look at those security videos right now. I could find Oliver in his apartment, not yet asleep.

I spun around and walked with purpose toward the elevator. Which unfortunately held Giulio. Fortunately, he wore more than a robe. But he carried an overnight bag.

"My darling, are you staying here?" He leaned forward to give me a double cheek kiss. "Let's have a drink in the bar."

"I thought this was a health spa?"

"Who can be that healthy?" He studied me. "But you are dressed for what?"

"Exercise. I'm headed to the gym."

He doubled over in laughter.

I elbowed him. "What's with the suitcase?"

He sobered and straightened. "I am leaving."

"On a trip?"

He shook his head. "I have finished with Vicki. I will return to California."

"She's not interested in Oliver, and Oliver's not interested in her."

"Perhaps not romantically, but this business of theirs." He waved a hand in disgust. "*Basta!* I can no longer take it. Am I not a man? Am I not to be the husband? I should be excluded?"

"You knew Vicki was like this. I thought you were okay with her running things."

"She takes me for the granted too much."

"I understand. I'll miss you, Giulio. Good luck in California."

He dropped his hands from their mid-air revelry. "What? That's it?"

"Isn't that what you want?"

He pouted. "It's not exactly what I want. I want her to drop these business dealings and return to the real drama. Theatrical drama. I am an actor, Maizie."

"Yes, I know."

"Vicki no longer looks at the dailies. She is not communicating with the other producers. She doesn't read our scripts and is disengaged during our scenes. How do I work under these conditions?"

"Because it's a job, Giulio. And sometimes jobs are hard." I didn't need any more reminders of that. I spun away and tromped down the west hall, past Oliver's office to the outside door.

A minute later, Giulio caught up with me. "Where are you going?"

"The gym."

"The juice bar is closed. Where are you really going? Is it the detective work? Let me come with you. I left the bag at the desk. What are you detecting?"

I knew better than to try to argue with him. And he was wearing dark colors. Dark gray satin sweatpants and a tight Fila T-shirt.

"You are walking quite quickly for you," said Giulio. "Maybe this is exercise."

I hung a right, following the outside wall of the Center and plaza outbuildings. At the gym's rear, I pointed toward the narrow gap between the building and the fence. "This is the only way to get in the back area, so why don't you act as my lookout? Pretend you are taking the evening air. Or play the actual lookout."

"I do not have the right props. They don't allow smoking here. I'll come with you. If you can fit in that gap…" He gave my chest a pointed look. "I can easily fit."

"We could get in trouble. The back area is off limits."

"Anything is better than the misery I have endured."

I rolled my eyes then squeezed into the gap. Giulio slid in next to me.

"This is not so bad because I have the slim hips," he said. "If you actually exercised, you would not be so smashed. But it is interesting to watch your struggle. There is a lot of…movement in your parts."

"I have a gun on the premises, Giulio. You better think about what you say next."

We spilled out of the gap, facing the giant garden fence and crumbling remains of the old farm.

"It is like I'm on a different planet," said Giulio.

"I know, right? Keep your head down. There are security cameras everywhere. Luckily, there's no moonlight."

We crept across the cleared area, avoiding the cameras on the garden and back fences.

"I want to poke around the cow barn," I whispered. "I saw some equipment in there earlier. And there's another building that Oliver didn't show me."

"It is so exciting," said Giulio. "But no cows, please."

We crept toward the shack where I had observed Everett Lawson enter the vegetable garden. Giulio peeked inside. "*Che schifo.* Disgusting. I will wait outside."

I slipped through the doorway. Hoped the bats were out for the night. Swept my tiny keychain flashlight over the walls and floors and returned to Giulio.

"Just gardening equipment. Shovels and the like."

He shuddered.

I led him across the field. Another old building lay near the thicket of trees that hid the gate where we'd met Oliver. This building had a better roof but appeared older than the barn. On the far side, a garage door had been retrofitted into the wall.

"It is odd, but not so interesting," said Giulio. "They keep the tractors inside."

"The gardeners have a building. I saw it when I looked for Everett Lawson." Whom I hadn't seen since the first day. Which was odd, but also not so interesting. "We can't get in this way."

I circled back to where the stone had fallen off. Shone my flashlight on the exposed areas. "See how there are gaps between the stones up there? Like a window for ventilation."

Giulio stood on his toes to see in. "It is very dark."

"Naturally." I handed him my mini flashlight.

"But the smell is less rank as the other shack. This one smells like gas and oil."

"Which explains the garage door."

After a moment, he said, "It is where they keep the small vehicles."

"Golf carts?"

He shook his head and handed me the flashlight. "The kind for the driving in the forest. Like your father uses."

"ATVs. Boost me up so I can see."

We struggled for a moment. Giulio bent his knees. I stood on his thighs while he grasped my waist and leaned his head against my butt.

"Hurry. You are not so light, Maizie. But at least you are soft in the right places."

I gritted my teeth and held on to a piece of stone with one hand. Raising my chin to see, I shone the light inside. "I wish I had a bigger flashlight."

"I wish for many things right now." He grunted and dug his chin into a butt cheek. "Hurry."

"Wait a minute." I trained the light on the wall behind the ATVs where debris had been piled in a heap. "That's my Campomaggi backpack. The one that was stolen."

"Maizie," gasped Giulio. "I think someone is coming. There is the noise."

I froze. A metal gate creaked. "Shizzles."

I pushed off his thighs and hopped to the ground. Giulio moaned and rubbed his quads.

"What should we do?" he panted. "Run? Hide?"

A figure appeared in the distance. A flashlight shone on the ground at their feet.

"I can't tell who it is," I whispered. "Too dark and too far away."

"But Maizie," he murmured. "Look at his shoulder. That looks like a—"

I squinted. The metal glinted in the faint atmospheric light. "A rifle. Craptastic. That must be Everett Lawson."

We ducked behind the building. Everett's footsteps grew louder but remained unhurried.

"I don't think he knows we are here," whispered Giulio. "Or he is prolonging the suspense."

"This isn't scripted. He's not a James Bond villain." I slid to the ground and peered around the corner.

Growing closer, Lawson swung the light over the building, then flashed it toward the woods. The light circled the perimeter before shining on the wall near the garage door.

I glanced back at Giulio with my finger to my lips, then peeped again.

Everett moved the flashlight to the hand holding the rifle and leaned forward to flip the key cover next to the door. The light beamed on the pad, shrouding his face in darkness. I knew it was Everett Lawson by the way he held the gun and trudged through the landscape. But he also reminded me of someone else.

The man in front of the Price home.

FORTY-ONE

#SharedHerstory #OliverTwisted

I rose, sliding up the wall next to Giulio. The garage door lifted. We flattened against the vibrating building, the stones rubbing against our back. Before the engine cut off, Giulio mouthed, "What now?"

I held up a finger.

We heard Everett moving inside the building, then start the motor on one of the ATVs. I grasped Giulio's hand. Ready to run, I pushed onto the balls of my feet and felt Giulio making a similar adjustment.

The ATV roared out of the building. Its lights cut through the gloom of the trees. A path perfectly wide enough for the ATV emerged. The building rumbled again as the door began to close.

"Hurry." I darted around the side of the building. I stood beneath the closing door, activating the safety sensor. The door hung above me, swinging like a guillotine.

In the darkness, the ATV continued on its trek into the woods. The motor slowed.

"He's probably at the outside gate," I whispered.

"You are very risky," said Giulio. "If I wasn't engaged to your mother, I'd find you incredibly attractive right now."

"Don't you start." I darted into the garage. Found my backpack and rooted in the other debris. "Mostly trash."

I held up my helmet. "Do you know what this means?"

"It means I am done with the snooping," said Giulio. "It is always exciting until we're almost caught. Now I'm thinking again about the bar."

"And I'm thinking about Everett Lawson and why a Wellspring caretaker is hanging out with bank robbers."

*T*he bar was closed. I sent Giulio back to his suite and took my backpack to my room. Mara's video camera and my phone were gone. But my wallet and keys were still inside. Also evidence of mice, including the protein bar wrapper they had partially eaten. After I screamed, dropped the bag, and scrubbed my hands and arms, I shoved the backpack in my closet.

After showering a second time, I redressed and went to find Oliver. I wanted information on Everett Lawson. I knocked on Oliver's apartment door and waited. Long enough to question my rationality. Did I *need* to speak to Oliver at this time of night? Or did I *want* to speak to Oliver?

Wait. Was this some sort of Freudian booty call on my part?

But it was too late. A slide of a lock broke the silence. The door swung open and there was Oliver. Looking demi-god-ish. Bare-chested. With sweatpants hanging mightily low on his hips.

I had forgotten about all the muscles. Holy shmizzles. I snapped shut my mouth and cleared my suddenly dry throat.

"Maizie?" He blinked fuzzily several times then widened his eyes. Grabbing my hand, he yanked me inside. "What are you doing up this late?"

"I don't sleep anymore. And I need to speak to you about something important."

His apartment was standard Wellspring Center sumptuous with luxurious upgrades like a kitchen and leather furniture centered around a fireplace with a mounted flat screen. He had several framed pictures on a console table behind the couch, but otherwise, the living area appeared impersonal. I approached the photographs. He and his parents in separate frames. Like mine, they were divorced. Oliver and his grandmother. Oliver and me.

Actually, five photos of us in one of those multi-picture frames. Cute couple pics and two of just me. One was from my *Maxim* shoot when he'd accompanied me and taken pictures behind the photographer.

I wasn't sure how to feel about the number of photos. Particularly the *Maxim* shot where I did not appear "girl next door" in the least little bit. I picked up the frame to study the pictures and felt Oliver's large presence behind me. He hesitated, then circled an arm around my waist. Pressed his body against my back and kissed the top of my head.

"I was hoping you'd change your mind," he said. "You can't believe how much I've missed you."

"Um," I said, drawing myself up, ready to pull away.

Which might have given him the wrong impression. His other hand slipped to my shoulder to pull back my hair. His lips descended on my neck.

"The thing is Oliver...I actually came to talk to you about the missing person case." I sucked in a breath. He found the sensitive spot on my neck that drove me crazy (in good ways) and began plundering it with his mouth. He hadn't forgotten which proverbial buttons started my engine. I groaned.

"Sure," he murmured against my neck. "Of course."

The lips continued their treacherous journey. My eyelids fluttered shut and I gripped his arm to steady myself. The solidity of his forearm motivated me to lean against him. Inducing Oliver to continue to burn a hot lips trail from my neck to shoulder. Prompting me to arch my back. Encouraging him to let his hand roam over my body.

"Oliver, I'm— It's just that—" I couldn't think of the words.

He didn't seem to care.

And I didn't either. It'd been too long. And he was too familiar.

This was early courtship Oliver in the wake of my biggest crash after I'd left *Julia Pinkerton*. When Oliver was an anchor in a churning Hollywood sea of vice and victimization.

I turned in his arms, dropping the frame. It crashed and splintered on the wood beneath my feet. Oliver swept an arm beneath me, swinging my body up and against his powerful chest.

"There could be broken glass," he said, gazing down at me.

"Very considerate," I replied, feeling very damsel-ly and light. Especially after Giulio's implied remarks about my weight.

He nuzzled my cheek. "It's good to have you back."

Wait. Was I back? I shifted in his arms. Which wasn't the effect I was going for considering the resulting expression on Oliver's face.

"I'm not necessarily back."

"Necessarily?" Angling his head, his lips hovered above mine.

"I've got a lot going on."

His lips nudged my mouth. "You're busy. I get it."

"It's complicated."

"You've always been complicated, Maizie." Our lips brushed. Then opened. And I forgot to breathe. Or think. But somewhere deep in the part of my mind that wasn't swimming in hormones, a memory of another kiss niggled. And a cloud of guilt spread, thundering through the lust to rain on my libidinous parade.

I was still in love with Wyatt Nash. My boss. Ex-coma victim. And perhaps soon to be not-so-ex-husband of Jolene Sweeney.

I was probably the biggest idiot who ever lived.

But what else was new.

I slid out of Oliver's arms — slow enough to not damage either of us — and stepped away. "I really did come here to talk."

He rubbed his face. "I thought that was an excuse."

"Possibly. But I need to focus on the missing person case. For my sanity. And for the kids."

Oliver collapsed into a leather chair. "I'm not firing on all cylinders, babe."

"You're preaching to the choir, Oliver. I figured out tonight that

Everett was the older guy at the Price house who accompanied today's gunman. That means he's involved in the bank robbery and I'm not safe at Wellspring either."

"What?" He straightened in the chair. "Are you sure?"

"I didn't recognize him at the Price's because I was running from him and he had his hat pulled down low and sunglasses on. With his beard, I couldn't tell him from any other older dude who hangs out at the feed and seed."

"Feed and seed?"

I waved a dismissive hand. "Anyway, I think you need to check your human resource files on Everett Lawson. And we should call the police. Maybe he's some kind of Fagin to Black Pine's gamers. A bank robbing crime ring. Maybe Crispin and Roger are nothing more than Oliver Twists. Except neither are orphans. They both live with their mothers. But whatevs."

"I have no idea what you're saying." Oliver mopped his face. "But okay. We'll go to my office. You're sure it can't wait until morning?"

"It's already morning, Oliver."

FORTY-TWO

#HellaciousHookUp #Mothercopter

In Oliver's office, I practiced Nash-like pacing while Oliver skimmed through human resource files on his computer. Giving an aggravated grunt, he pushed out of his desk chair and bent over a filing cabinet. Left the room without a word, then returned fifteen minutes later.

"Maizie," he said. "I'm sorry but I can't find anything on Everett Lawson. Are you sure that's his name?"

"I met him when I was with Dr. Trident." I sucked in a breath. "Do you think he works for Dr. Trident? Maybe Everett's a community service volunteer like me."

Oliver placed his hands on my arms and slid them to my shoulders. "I'm not waking up Dr. Trident, babe. It can wait until morning. You need to sleep."

"There's no way I can sleep now, Oliver. Everett Lawson's out there somewhere on an ATV doing who knows what and he could come back any minute. He didn't see me Oliver, but I saw him."

"I'll alert security." The deft fingers skimmed my back, massaging small circles along my spine. "If he shows, they'll call the police and prevent him from entering."

"What if he knows I'm here?" My voice had gone from troubled to breathy. "What could they want from me?"

"I'm not going to let anything happen to you." He sidled closer, sliding his hands to my waist. "I promise you that."

"I know you won't. But I'd feel better if I could have my little gun back." I tipped my head, feeling my hair swing against my shoulders. His eyes had gone fuzzy again. I slid my hands up to his shoulders. Pushed onto my toes and leaned into him. If that's what it took to get my gun back, I felt no shame in using what God gave me.

And, I had to admit, I kind of liked seeing how I could make his eyes go fuzzy.

"Please, Oliver. You wouldn't have to tell anyone. I'd just feel so much safer."

Oliver pulled me closer. "You're safe with me, Maizie. Why don't we go back—"

The office door banged open. I shrieked, and Oliver clutched me against his chest.

"Thank God someone's on duty," said Vicki. "I need another suite and I think your reception attendant is sleeping. Oliver, you need to do something about the service around here."

I leaped from Oliver and turned to face Vicki. She nonchalantly tightened the belt on her silk kimono robe, her gaze averted. But she'd seen everything.

"Perhaps you don't need your room, Maizie," she said. "You weren't there when I checked. Glad I found you here. With Oliver. This will save us time."

"Try the front desk again," I said. "I'm sure the receptionist is no longer asleep. The whole spa probably heard you burst in here."

"Give me the keys to your room," she said. "I can't spend another night with that man and his machismo."

I gazed at the ceiling, then the floor. Crossed my arms. "No. You can't have my room."

Oliver gave a small groan and returned to his office chair.

"You need to work it out with Giulio," I said. "You've been

taking him for granted. Either work it out or cut him free. Not just from the engagement, but from his contract. He deserves better treatment. You're wasting his time and talent when he could be working on other shows."

"Just because you quit *All is Albright*, doesn't mean you can pull everyone into your mutiny. We're having a tiff. When Giulio calms down, everything will be fine."

"It wasn't a mutiny, Vicki. It's called the terms of my probation."

"She used probation as an excuse to quit," said Vicki to Oliver. "Just liked she used partying as an excuse to bomb other projects. She wants to fail."

My libido jerked free from vanity's grip thanks to a kick in the butt from pride. "It wasn't an excuse. And I don't want to fail."

Wait. Did I want to fail? Is that what I was doing here instead of actually investigating? "What *am* I doing in here? With Oliver...Oh my God. I've lost my mind."

"Not your mind," said Vicki. "But perhaps your dignity. It's not like you're the first person to hook up with an ex."

"Oh God," I wheezed, my thoughts straying once again to Nash and Jolene. "So true."

"Calm down, Maizie." Oliver rose from his chair and rushed around the desk. "You're starting to breathe erratically again."

"Honestly, Maizie. Does everything have to be about you?" Vicki rolled her eyes. "Oliver got you into your current predicament. But he can get you out. You offered her the job, didn't you?"

"Wait. What?" I forgot to exhale and sucked in another breath. My lungs spasmed and I held up a finger, fighting to gain control over my body. Let out a shaky breath. "You told Oliver to get me the job at Wellspring?"

"I would have offered you the security position anyway," said Oliver. "We could work together. It would be perfect. Vicki just helped your probation officer get you in the door so you could get used to the idea."

"You set all this up, Vicki? Community service and my therapist? To give me a job until what? I quit investigations and start acting again?"

"Don't be ridiculous. I recruited Dr. Trident because I wanted you to have the best therapist. I am still your mother."

"Dr. Trident's not even pro bono? You're paying him?" I felt dizzy. "I couldn't even get a free therapist on my own?"

"Why would someone like Dr. Trident work for free?" She scoffed. "He only treats celebrities. Haven't you looked at his Snapchat?"

"And Oliver?" My lip trembled. "Did she pay you, too? Like Giulio?"

"Baby, of course, not." Oliver reached for me and I slunk away. "It's not like that, Maizie. Although I did come to Black Pine for you. Vicki knew I'd do just about anything to get you back."

"Oh my God." I closed my eyes. "Do you even realize how that sounds?"

"Stalkerish," said Vicki. "Poor choice of words. But get a grip, Maizie. You've been in much worse situations. Of your own doing, may I remind you."

"Maizie, why don't you sit down," said Oliver. "I'll get Vicki a room and we'll just talk. Get everything out in the open. You're having another panic attack. That's why you can't think rationally."

"Any more talking and I'll end up with more than a panic attack." I darted to the door. "I just want to think irrationally by myself."

I returned to my room, determined to focus on the case — any case, actually — and not on my love life. Or lack thereof. Everett Lawson was at large, armed and possibly dangerous. No one but Dr. Trident seemed to know him. I still had no good leads on Chandler Jonson except his crazy jealous brother was hanging out with Everett Lawson's young disciple. Which couldn't be good.

I hated calling Ian Mowry in the middle of the night, but Agent Langtry never picked up. It was like she was ignoring my calls.

Which possibly, because of the number of calls I left for her, she was.

"Mowry," he said fuzzily. "Maizie?" His voice grew more alert. "Maizie, what's wrong?"

"Everett Lawson is one of the guy's I saw at the Price house and he just took off on an ATV with a rifle."

"At Wellspring?"

"He left from a retrofitted garage in their hidden back area. I also found my stolen backpack with the ATVs. Mara's camera and my phone are missing but everything else was inside. Of course, after taking the valuables, my mugger could have dumped the backpack in the woods and someone else could have found it and left it in the ATV garage as trash. But I think it was Everett Lawson who attacked us."

"When you say mugger, are you implying that you hadn't left your backpack with your bike like you originally told me?"

"Um." This is why I didn't like lying. "Ian, let's just skip to the part where you put out an APB out on Everett Lawson."

"Did anything else happen tonight, Maizie? You're sounding a mite hysterical. Or at least more than usual."

Oh boy. I so did not want to get into my family melodrama with Ian Mowry. Getting caught lying was humiliating enough.

"Hon'? Is Oliver Fraser…is everything okay?" He took a breath. "You don't have to stay there. I've got Maddie here tonight, but I can send someone to get you. You can stay here. I'll take the couch. Until we figure out what to do."

His daughter, Maddie. Ian Mowry was playing domestic disturbance white knight when he had a six-year-old to think about.

I used that thought as the slap in the face I needed. I needed to concentrate on the objective: find Chandler Jonson. Let the police deal with Everett Lawson. I'd deal with Roger Price.

FORTY-THREE

#OvercomingHistory
#HoldingHandsAndTakingNames

---

*I*n the morning, I opened my door to find a tray of strawberries, muffins, and French press coffee. A single note read, "I'm sorry. Oliver."

I noted there was not a similar message from Vicki. Natch.

Before leaving the building, I sought Oliver in his office. He cautiously greeted me from behind his desk.

"Last night was my fault," I said. "I led you on. I tried not to, but I'm not thinking clearly this week. Sometimes it's hard to overcome history. I should probably bring it up at my next couch session."

"I got carried away, too," he said. "Can we start over?"

We shared niceties about breakfast, feather pillows, and French press coffee. Then the not-so-niceties of my suspicions about Everett Lawson.

"I called the police last night," I said. "I think he was the one who attacked me in the woods, too."

"What?" Oliver pushed out of his chair. "Sweetheart."

I held up a hand. I could tell Oliver wanted more hugging and as much as I hated to deny myself hugs, I had to stay on track. "Detective Mowry is taking me to visit Roger Price in jail."

Oliver crossed his arms. "I'm worried, Maizie. What if the other bank robbers learn you're still investigating?"

"The ATF is investigating, not me. I just want to know who's trying to hunt me down, so I can focus on finding my missing person." I shrugged. "And if I can help the ATF, I'll have accomplished at least one good thing this week."

"You've already accomplished one good thing," said Oliver and patted his heart.

If I wasn't overcoming history, I would have hugged him.

Ian arrived early enough to take me to the hospital before seeing Roger Price. I told Ian it was lucky I'd already grabbed the gaming transcripts and put them in my backpack when Oliver and I had been chased from the office.

Ian told me he wouldn't consider getting chased by a guy with a handgun lucky at all.

At the hospital, we found Nash arguing with the physical therapist. "I'm ready. I can walk."

"Like a drunk man," she said. "Give it another day. And don't even think about driving. Don't push yourself. Stay home and rest. Isn't your wife picking you up?"

My stomach twisted at the wife implication, but while riding in Ian's Tahoe, I'd mentally rehearsed my new role—the spunky sidekick. One who was not in love with her boss and only cared about keeping her job. And not getting killed by bank bombers.

Nash spotted us in the doorway and motioned for us to enter. "Mowry. Give me the latest in the bombing investigation. Maizie, how's your missing person case?"

"Don't wear him out," warned the therapist as she passed us. "He's cranky because he's tired and dizzy."

"I'm cranky because I'm stuck in here," he thundered.

I laid the gym bag on his bed. "I have the gaming transcripts and all the Price case notes for you. And the notes I've made on the

Chandler Jonson case. But I'm kind of behind on those considering people are still trying to kill me."

"What?" Nash grabbed my hand and released it. "Mowry? What the hell is going on?"

Ian recounted the incident at Jolene's office, then added my Everett Lawson reconnaissance. Nash's jaw tightened throughout Ian's monologue. When the veins in his neck began to bulge, I motioned to Ian to stop.

"Yesterday was kind of a long day," I said, trying to diffuse his anxiety. "But at least the teenagers and Remi are safe."

"Where's your sidearm? I told you to carry."

"In a safe at Wellspring. They don't allow weapons. Aside from the guards. And Everett Lawson, if you count him."

Nash rubbed his temples. A nerve ticked above his eye.

"Let's all calm down," I said with all the congeniality I could muster accompanied with my *Cosmo* cover smile. "Everything's fine."

"Stop trying to make this look better than it is," said Nash.

Ian moved closer and put a hand on my shoulder. "She's trying to make this easier on you, Wyatt. We don't have to report to you. This was a courtesy."

"Miss Albright's my employee. She does have to report to me."

Ian's hand tightened on my shoulder. "Watch yourself, Wyatt. Maizie's been through a lot."

"And what are you doing?" Nash narrowed his eyes. "Other than holding her hand and taking her to lunch?"

Ian's hand dropped from my shoulder and curled into a fist. "We're leaving, Maizie."

I slid between the two men. "No one's been holding my hand. Much. And I can't remember the last time I had lunch. Chill."

They both gave me the side eye.

"Don't leave," said Nash. "You have my humble apology. What's the intel on these jokers who're hassling Miss Albright?"

Ian sighed. "Everett Lawson doesn't officially work at Wellspring but seemed to have access to everything. ATF said they would handle the research and recon. It's only Maizie's testimony of seeing Everett Lawson at the Price house that links him to the bank and the death of Mrs. Price."

"What about the body you found on Black Pine Mountain?" I said. "Maybe that's related."

Ian shook his head. "Unrelated to the bank. GBI made the fingerprint match. The victim's part of an Atlanta gang involved in a drug cartel. We think it was a revenge killing or an argument between members that got out of hand. No evidence of anything more than the single victim."

"You had another murder while I was out?" said Nash.

"Technically, it happened Friday. About the same time as the bank. Someone found him on the peak near the lookout. He and the perp could've stopped in Black Pine while driving between Atlanta and the Carolinas. We're coordinating with Atlanta police. Anyway, I've been balancing that investigation with…" Ian looked at me.

"My hot mess?"

"Agent Langtry put me in charge of her key witness," Ian spoke soothingly. "Not that she'll let me do anything else."

"Langtry lumped you with me? I'm so sorry, Ian. I'm hurting your career."

Nash pinched the bridge of his nose. "Can we focus on the bank robbery? Why are they sticking around town? With the robbery blown, you'd think they'd have hightailed it until things cooled off."

"My theory is they think Maizie's an eyewitness and can testify," said Ian. "She was in the parking lot at the time of the robbery. Then she showed at the Price house and that made them nervous. Maybe they were parked near the bank and spotted her."

"Miss Albright was an eyewitness?"

"You don't remember?" I said. "You left me in the parking lot in your truck. Which Lamar won't let me drive, by the way."

"I don't remember anything about that day." Nash stared at his feet.

Ian and I exchanged a look of pity. Although Ian's pity was probably mixed with "Damn, that's witness testimony we can't get."

Considering the return of the tick and bulging neck veins, Nash did not care for our pity. "Mowry, what kind of FUBAR show is Black Pine PD running? I'm holding you responsible. You knew Miss Albright was an eyewitness and you've let her run around town. You know how she is."

"What does that mean?" I said.

"I'm going to let that pass, considering you've had a blow to the head," said Ian. "It wasn't clear that there was a threat to Maizie until yesterday."

"That's sort of my fault," I said. "I've had my probation officer all over me and I didn't want to get into trouble. I've been purposely vague with Ian. In certain regards."

Ian shot me a "we'll talk later" look but kept his tone patient. "Maizie's safety has been my priority. Her ex-boyfriend took on the role as a personal bodyguard and insisted she stay at the Well-spring Center. At the time, it seemed like a reasonable solution."

"Giulio Baloney?" Nash spoke through gritted teeth. "Why in the hell would you trust Miss Albright's safety to that idiot?"

"Not Giulio Belloni," I said. "Oliver Fraser."

"Who's Oliver Fraser? How long have I been out?" Nash collapsed against the mattress. "Cripes, my head is killing me."

I laid a hand on his forehead. "Please calm down. Everything is going to be okay."

"Lord Almighty." Nash stared at the ceiling. "I take a four-day nap and everything goes to hell."

"What's going on? Why is Wyatt so upset?"

Jolene. My breath hissed through my teeth. I slipped my hand from Nash's forehead and backed up a step. "We'll go now. I'm sorry for everything, Mr. Nash."

His hand shot out to snag mine. "Just a minute. Jolene, wait in the hall."

"I'll do no such thing. These two are upsetting you. You're in

pain. She keeps bringing work when you're supposed to be resting. Maizie, if you're not capable of doing the job, get into a new
line of business. You're going to need a new job anyway if I have
anything to say about it."

I flinched and tried to jerk my hand from Nash's.

Nash tightened his grip.

"That's uncalled for, Jolene," said Ian behind us.

"You, too, Officer Mowry? How many men is she seeing?
Honest to God, she must have a revolving door on her bedroom."

"That's Detective Mowry, ma'am. And the patient asked you to
step into the hall. I'll escort you."

"Wyatt? Are you going to let him escort me out of your room?"
said Jolene.

Nash ignored her. "Look at me," he muttered.

I swung my gaze to meet his. The polar blue had frosted over.

"Come on, Jolene," said Ian.

The door clattered shut on the rising pitch of Jolene's voice.

The icy eyes narrowed. "Miss Albright. When I met you, I
thought you were scatterbrained and silly. You proved me wrong.
You're smart and capable. So why are you trying to convince yourself you're not?"

"I'm—"

"I see right through you. You're better than this."

"But Nash—"

"Don't let anyone bully you. You've got a job to do. If your ass
is on the line, stop worrying about everyone else and take care of
that ass." He shook his head. "You know what I mean."

I knew what he meant.

FORTY-FOUR

#SilencingTheLamb
#GirlsWhoMakeBoysCry

---

*I*n *Julia Pinkerton, Teen Detective* season six, episode seven, "Cell Block Kango," Julia had to question a notorious exotic animal trainer. He'd been arrested for training his non-human accomplices — poodles, falcons, and a kangaroo — to aid him in a string of cat burglaries. Ironically, no cats. At the jail, they had the usual visitation scene. A row of windows separated into carrels. Julia Pinkerton and Cedric Pound carried on a dialogue through the plexiglass in a PG-13 homage to *The Silence of the Lambs*.

Mentally, I had prepared to speak calmly on the phone and give Roger my Julia Pinkerton via Clarice Starling private investigator poker face through the plexiglass wall. If Roger refused to give me the information I wanted, I would hammer on the plexiglass with the phone and tell him to "wise up."

That was my plan, anyway.

At Black Pine Jail, Ian checked me in. My heart pounded with each step to the visitation room. Sweat inched up my neck and into my hairline. By the time, Ian escorted me through the double set of doors to the visitation room, my teeth chattered. A series of vending machines ran along the back wall. Knee-high tables with connected stools were bolted to the floor. And the walls were rainbow-striped.

I whirled on him. "Hold up. Where are the windows and phones? This looks like a cafeteria for juvie kindergartners."

"We're getting video chat booths if the next SPLOST referendum passes," said Ian amicably. "But we'll continue to use this room for family visits, depending on the inmate's visitation rights."

"I don't want to talk to Roger Price in person. I want to talk to him on a phone through a window."

"Maizie, I've pulled strings for this. He's an ATF suspect," said Ian. "You have fifteen minutes and I'm really hoping you get some information from him."

"He's no suspect. He's the real deal. I watched him walk in that bank with a bomb."

"Hon'," Ian grasped my shoulders and forced me to look at him. "Why are you so afraid of Roger Price? He's a loser."

"I'm not afraid." I swallowed. Or tried to swallow, but my tongue had thickened. "This is me angry."

Ian looked doubtful. "I'll be right behind you if you need me."

I took a stool and waited with the other visitors. A buzzer announced the prisoners. I chewed on my thumbnail then spotted stocky, pimple-faced, twenty-one-year-old Roger Price. He looked like he'd slept even less than me.

And just saying, orange was not his color.

Roger stared at his feet until a guard forced him to my table. With his hands still cuffed behind his back, he slowly sank onto the stool across from me.

I cleared my throat. "We only have fifteen minutes. Let's begin."

"Who are you?"

"I'm one of two private investigators hired by your mother to follow you. The other is still in the hospital because of the bomb you set off in the bank. He saved your life. He was in a coma until yesterday."

At "mother," Roger began to cry.

This was not the reaction I wanted. Which was totally unfair. This week of hell was his fault. He'd gotten his mother murdered. Which I'd planned on reminding him, but now felt like I didn't want to mention it and cause more tears.

"Roger, I'm sorry about your mom," I said in my Clarice Starling-minus-the-West-Virginia-accent voice. "But Leslie wouldn't talk to me either. She wrote 'help us' on a check memo and I had no idea why. And before I could ask her, she was killed. I know you can tell me who did it. Justice for your mother, Roger. That's why I'm here."

Roger began sobbing. Loud enough that the burly inmate at the next table shot me a death glare.

I glanced over my shoulder at Ian. He raised his eyebrows but kept his expression impassive. I could not Clarice Starling Roger Price. We weren't going to get to the quid pro quo.

"Roger, please stop crying."

His sobbing intensified to bawling.

Abandoning my Clarice pretense, I reverted to plain old Maizie. "You've got to get a hold of yourself. Please, I need to know who you're working with."

He shook his head and tried to rub his snot and tears onto his orange shoulder.

"Roger, this has been the worst week of my life. I couldn't protect your mom. I couldn't help some teens find their friend. I couldn't wake my boss from his coma. His ex-wife did that. And now these men, your accomplices, are after me, too. My little sister was in danger. You've got to help me. Who worked the bank job with you? Was it Everett Lawson?"

"It wasn't meant to go off." His voice shook. "I wasn't supposed to rig it to go off. But I did anyway. I don't know why I did it, but I'm sorry."

He sounded sorry. I wasn't prepared for a remorseful Roger and felt my own tears stirring. "But Roger, who helped you? Crispin Jonson?"

"Nobody." He shook his head. "I made it by myself."

"Not the bomb. Who helped you rob the bank?"

"Nobody." Roger bent over and laid his cheek against the table. His arms stuck out behind him like ski poles. "I was alone."

"But Roger, I saw the men at your house. The ones who probably killed your mom. I know you didn't act alone."

"I was just supposed to take the bomb into the bank. It wasn't supposed to go off."

"What about Crispin Jonson? Did you work with him?"

Roger attempted a shrug. "We made a robot together in high school."

Ian tapped me on the shoulder. "Your time is up."

"Roger was going to tell me who told him to take the bomb into the bank. Weren't you, Roger?"

His face mashed against the table, Roger repeated, "It wasn't supposed to go off."

Ian sighed. "That's all he's said since he's been here. His lawyer can't get anything else out of him either."

"Roger, don't leave me hanging. I'm counting on you."

His head rose from the table. Tears rolled off his cheeks and plopped on to the laminate top. "Please, help me. I didn't mean for it to go off."

The guard collected Roger. Ian led me back through the double doors.

"I really thought he'd tell me," I said. "His mom basically said the same thing."

"Doesn't matter if it was meant to go off or not, that boy is in a lot of trouble. He built the bomb and he took it into the bank."

We took the breezeway from the jail to the police station and huddled at Ian's desk.

"Could he have been coerced or forced?" I chewed a nail. "Threatened?"

"If he had been forced, he should be squealing," said Ian. "It's obvious there are other people involved. He's scared. We keep telling him that we can protect him if he talks."

"Protected like his mother?"

While Ian attended morning roll call, I sat at his desk and phoned Lamar. Nash had checked out of the hospital and returned to the office. My spirits rose, then plummeted when Lamar said Jolene insisted on staying at the office with him to make certain he didn't work. Feeling low, I called LA HAIR. I needed my girlfriends. And their forgiveness.

"Where've you been?" said Rhonda.

"I'm at the police station," I said, then waited while jostling and grunting ensued. A few seconds later, I was put on speaker.

"Arrested again?"

"I'm being babysat until an arrest happens. I finally saw Roger Price. He told me nothing more than the bomb wasn't meant to go off."

"Well, that's stupid," said Tiffany. "Why would you build a bomb that wasn't meant to go off?"

"If I was going to rob a bank," said Rhonda. "I'd build a gun, not a bomb."

"Can you build a gun?" said Tiffany. "Don't you make a gun?"

"The point is who robs a bank with a bomb that's not supposed to go off?"

"Right," I said. "Roger said he wasn't supposed to 'rig it to go off.' Which means someone gave him those instructions."

"Who?" said Rhonda.

"He won't say who, but the ATF are searching for three suspects. And get this, one is Chandler Jonson's brother."

"No. Bigfoot Hottie's brother is a bank robber?"

"Crispin wasn't actually at the bank. I don't think. He's just hanging out with some dude who might have killed Roger's mother."

"This is very confusing," said Tiffany.

"Tell me about it," I said. "Hey, I actually called to say I'm sorry."

"For what?" said Rhonda.

"For getting angry at you two when I didn't want to deal with the Prices. You were right."

"Lawd," said Tiffany. "I didn't give it a second's thought. Rhonda's always mad at me."

"Tiff's right," said Rhonda. "She gets all up in my grill every second of the day. Maizie, you take everything so personal. You've got to let things go. Tequila helps with that. Just sayin'."

"But now Roger's mother is dead. Roger might be in danger if he doesn't let the police help him. It's all my fault because I was too caught up in my own stuff." I sniffled.

"Are you crying again? Rhonda, this girl cries way too much."

"Maizie, you might have let Roger's mother killed," said Rhonda. "And you can't do much about crazy Roger Price getting shanked…"

I winced.

"But you still have Chandler Jonson out there. If his dumbass brother is hanging with bank robbers, seems to me you need to get on that."

FORTY-FIVE

#SlippingInASlip #Grrrling

To get on with Chandler Jonson, I needed to get out from under Detective Ian Mowry's eye. When Ian returned, I asked for a release from his babysitting. "I'm going to cramp your style, sitting at your desk all day."

"It's not a problem." He swiveled in his desk chair and reached for a thick stack of files.

"I'll get super bored and drive you crazy."

"Everett Lawson is still at large. And your unnamed gunman."

"Your coworkers will think you have a thing for me."

"They know why you're here." He opened his laptop without looking at me.

"I'll act out Julia Pinkerton scenes in the break room. I'll flirt with the desk sergeant."

"We don't have a desk sergeant." He narrowed his eyes. "What are you up to?"

"I want to work on the Chandler Jonson case. There's a reason he hung around Wellspring."

"I thought the reason was Bigfoot and something about chickens."

"His brother was also involved with bank robbers. Or at least knew one. Maybe there's a connection."

"Between bank robbers and Wellspring?" He shrugged.

"You can't play innocent. You think so, too. Everett Lawson was hanging out at Wellspring."

Ian leaned back in his chair. "Which is why I'm not taking you back to Wellspring."

"Come on, Ian. Isn't ATF conducting an investigation there anyway?"

"Exactly, we'll be in the way. Agent Langtry has her chosen people and I'm not one of them." He sighed then leaned forward, settling his forearms on his thighs. "Look, let's say Chandler was interested in Wellspring for non-Bigfoot reasons—"

I bobbed my head. "Maybe it was because he wanted to know why his brother was hanging out with Everett Lawson. And Chandler was watching Everett Lawson."

"Hang on, you've seen Crispin eating a donut at the same table with the unnamed perp. And according to your testimony, the suspect shoved Crispin out of the way to try to enter Jolene's office. Crispin didn't run like the other guy. We picked him up. That's a tenuous connection between Crispin and Everett Lawson."

"According to Nash, I can work with tenuous because I don't have to prove anything in court. I just have to find Chandler."

"You think Everett Lawson is going to lead you to Chandler?"

"I don't know. Maybe." I sighed. "I don't have much else to go on."

"We questioned Crispin. He has credible alibis for the bank robbery and the Price murder."

"There had to be some reason Chandler was so obsessed with Wellspring. I want to talk to Crispin again."

"No." He turned back to his computer.

"Ian, you're no fun."

"I'm a cop. I think you forget that." He swiveled in his chair to face me. "You've lied to me, Maizie."

"More like I haven't told you the whole truth on several occasions. And I hated doing it. But I didn't want you to worry about me either."

"I think you didn't want to get in trouble. Did you illegally enter the Jonson home?"

"I'm taking the fifth. Remember I'm on probation." I gave him my *Maxim* smile and a slow wink.

He glared at me. "You're right. You're going to drive me crazy. Where else can I take you?"

"How about LA HAIR? No one's going to look for me in a beauty shop."

While Ian waited with his laptop and stack of folders in the waiting room, I slipped onto the salon chair closest to the sinks. On the far end, stylists Jenna and Shelly applied color and highlights to their clients while shooting Tiffany and Rhonda dirty looks.

Considering Tiff and Rhonda had abandoned their stations to crowd around me and gossip, I kind of didn't blame them.

Rhonda fingered my hair. "How'd they get your hair so soft?"

"You cheated on us." Tiffany picked up my hand and examined my manicure. "They did a good job."

"It was the spa at Wellspring." I batted them away from examining my skin. "I was doing an undercover thing."

Tiffany snorted. "Yeah, right."

"Okay, Oliver treated me." Rhonda opened her mouth, but I held up a finger. "I know what you're going to say. I don't have time. I need to get out of here."

"You just got here," said Rhonda.

"I need to get away from Ian. Detective Mowry. I want to go back to Wellspring, but he won't let me out of his sight. I'm going crazy. I need your help in giving him the slip."

Tiffany brightened. "I like it."

"Not because he's a cop. He's too worried about my safety. I'd ask Oliver to pick me up, but Ian's not a fan."

"I'm not a fan either," said Rhonda. "Take my car."

"Oliver's been trying to make things up to me. He's been really sweet."

"That's what Tiffany said about her ex-husband when she got back together with him the second time."

"Love makes you stupid. Don't be stupid," said Tiffany. "And don't date guys who say they're picking up pizza and rob a convenience store on the way home. Never works out."

"Fine, I'll take Rhonda's car. Thank you, Rhonda."

"What do you want us to do?" said Rhonda.

We bent our heads together, shifting glances at Ian who was, thankfully, ignoring us to catch up on paperwork.

Ten minutes later, Rhonda had covered my body in a cape, my hair in a towel, and slathered my face with mud. She walked me to the row of sinks and helped me to lean back against the porcelain. I fought the crick in my neck, closed my eyes, and focused on shallow breaths through the mud caked around my nose. Three minutes later, I sensed someone next to me. I opened an eye and spotted a caped figure also leaning back against a sink. Twenty seconds later, I heard a crash and roll of plastic bottles.

Taking that as my cue, I sat upright. Ian had bent under his chair, retrieving bottles of shampoo. A large box lay tipped on its side. Behind him, Rhonda kicked another shampoo bottle under his seat.

I hopped from the chair and darted to the door behind the sinks. Next to me, Tiffany slid over to the chair I'd occupied. Green mud covered her face. A towel had been wrapped around her blue ombré asymmetrical bob. A cape hid her body.

In the back room, I tore off the cape, rubbed the hardening mud from my face with the towel, and grabbed my backpack, conveniently left at the door by Rhonda.

I felt bad for deceiving Ian Mowry. He was a sweetie. But it was time to put on my big girl panties. I didn't need these men to hide behind. I'd played Julia Pinkerton and Kung Fu Kate. All Grrrl girls.

Well, okay, they were literally girls. Like twelve and sixteen. But still.

FORTY-SIX

#LookAtMeImSandraDee
#OliverYouForever

I knew there was some connection between Roger Price and Crispin Jonson. And in my bones, I felt that something was the reason Chandler Jonson was missing.

Ian wasn't stupid. I felt terrible about tricking him. I might have ruined our friendship. And got into more trouble with Gladys. It wouldn't take him long to figure out what I'd done. I sped to Crispin Jonson's house. Parked two doors down and watched the windows. Saw movement. Bolted to the porch and rang the bell.

A woman answered the door. I hid my surprise.

"Mrs. Jonson?"

She smiled.

"Is Crispin home?"

"Sorry, just missed him. He left town to be with his dad. Mike's shooting a documentary on butterflies in Mexico."

"Mexico?" How convenient. "When did he leave?"

"Early this morning. Flew out to meet his father. It was a big surprise."

I bet. "Have you heard from Chandler?"

"Not yet," she said. "But I'm sure it'll be soon. Chan had a ticket to Mexico. I'm sure he plans to hook up with his dad once he's done exploring."

"How can you be so sure? I've been looking for him." I explained the case with the teens.

"Oh my," she said. "I didn't realize they'd attached to Chan like that. He's a great guy but not always responsible. When his YouTube channel went viral, we were happy for him. But he gets bored easily, so it didn't surprise us much that he'd quit."

"I think it's more serious than that. Actually, I think something might have happened to Chandler because of Crispin."

"Crispin?"

"Crispin's been seen with an unknown man who's connected to the attempted bank robbery that happened last week. And possibly the murder of the bank robber's mother. They're about the same age."

"But—" she stopped. "I need to call my husband."

"Please, do. I'm sure the police told Crispin not to leave town. There's no evidence he's done anything, but the police are still investigating."

Her mouth rounded into an O and she paled. "Crispin didn't say—"

"Mrs. Jonson, are you going to be okay?"

"I'm sorry," she said, closing the door. "I really should call my husband. Oh Lord, and maybe our lawyer."

"One more thing, does Crispin know Roger Price?"

"Roger Price...I think from high school? Is he the kid who did all the tinkering? They built a robot together or something?"

"Are they still friends?"

She shook her head. "I don't know. Please, I need to make some calls."

*C*rispin had done something or he wouldn't have fled. I needed to give the police a heads up, but I still didn't have a phone. Also, I didn't want to talk to Ian. Yet. I thought I should probably give him time to cool down. Before he did something rash like call Gladys and have me arrested.

Instead, I parked at a gas station and used their pay phone to call the office.

"We're closed," said Jolene. "If you have security needs, I'll connect you with Sweeney Security Solutions."

"Let me speak to Wyatt Nash," I said in my best masculine drawl. "This is Steve from Black Pine Hospital. I want to ask him a couple questions to see how his concussion is affecting him."

"Shouldn't I bring him back to the hospital so you can run tests?" said Jolene.

"Only if he can't answer the questions. Put him on, if you would, sugar."

"Just a minute," she huffed.

A moment later, I heard Nash's deep growl. "I'm fine. I just have a headache. Which would go away if everyone left me alone."

"It's me, Maizie," I said. "Miss Albright. I'll call back another time."

"Not you. Just a minute." A door closed, and Jolene's squawking receded into the background. "Where are you? Mowry called here looking for you."

"At a gas station. I had to escape. He's very nice, but I couldn't sit and watch him do paperwork all day. Being safe isn't for me, I guess. What about you?"

"I feel like a stuck pig. They're treating me like I'm a damn child who can't do a dang thing for himself." He lowered his voice. "You want to break me out? Go on the run together?"

A delicious heat shot through me. I licked my lips. "I went to Crispin Jonson's house to talk to him. Do you know who that is?"

"I've been reading the case notes." He paused. "Trying to at least. That's giving me a headache, too."

"Oh, Nash," I said, then remembered I was the spunky sidekick. "Anyway, his mother was home. Crispin's flown the coop to Mexico where his dad is shooting a documentary. When I first talked to Crispin, he said he didn't know where his parents were, but obviously, he did. And everyone thinks Chandler went to Mexico."

"Ten to one Crispin doesn't show up at his dad's shoot."

"Ten to one Chandler didn't fly to Mexico and Crispin bought that ticket to make it look like Chandler did."

"Miss Albright, you're very sassy when you're on the lam."

I blushed and kicked a rock with my sneaker. "Thank you."

"You sound like you're doing smart and capable again."

I sighed. "I miss you. I mean…working with you."

"Come get me, Maizie."

I thought about how much I wanted to get Nash. How I'd pull up like Kenickie in the sleepover scene from *Grease.* I'd park Rhonda's Nissan around the corner from the Dixie Kreme shop and whistle for Rizzo through his office window. Burn rubber when he jumped in the car. Laugh as Jolene hollered at us. Then I'd wrap my arm around Nash's neck, pull him toward me, and give him a huge kiss.

But I wasn't Kenickie. I wasn't even Rizzo. I was a total Sandy. Wyatt Nash had a severe concussion and was still weak, dizzy, and in pain. He needed to rest. And no matter how much Jolene probably annoyed him with her helicoptering (which I secretly hoped she did), that's what he needed. Someone to watch over him. Like a wife should. Or an ex-wife, in this case.

"No, I'm not going to break you out," I said. "And you know why."

"You disappoint me, Miss Albright."

"Welcome to the club."

*M*y other available connection to Everett Lawson was Dr. Trident. I parked Rhonda's car and scouted the parking lot. The police vehicles were gone. The interviews and search for Everett Lawson must have concluded. I also didn't see Ian's Tahoe. He either looked elsewhere or had given up on me.

Guilt knocked on the walls of my heart. I ignored guilt and focused on finding Dr. Trident.

He wasn't in his office. I turned back to reception and learned of a staff meeting. In the west wing, I listened at doors until I heard the rise and fall of voices in Oliver's office. Continuing my stroll down the hall, I knocked on the security room door. And found it slightly ajar.

A note had been stuck to the main computer screen. Instructions for the police. I guessed with such few staff, someone had left the door open for the ATF helpers, rather than watch them check the security videos. Very trusting of Wellspring.

And I guessed that had been Oliver with his "nothing to hide" policy. And vanity. He wouldn't want to show the police his lack of computer skills.

Peeling the sticky note off the computer screen, I found the instruction book and typed in the previous night's footage. I watched Giulio and I argue before the elevator, then slide out of the narrow recess between the physical life building and garden fence. Saw our shadowy figures running across the field. And slipping into the ATV garage. Rolling my eyes, I thanked the moon for not showing that night. I changed screens and found Everett Lawson. Watched him exit the maintenance building and stop to talk to someone.

Dr. Trident.

I danced in my seat. My therapist did know Everett Lawson. And here was proof for the police. Maybe Trident wasn't in the staff meeting and Agent Langtry had already taken him in for questioning.

Wait. What did that mean for my therapy? Did it still count if Dr. Trident was connected to a bank robbery? Would I still get my probation points?

I left that thought for Gladys and swapped camera scenes as Lawson continued his trudge toward the back acreage of Wellspring. He unlocked the back gate hiding behind the flower mounds and stalked toward the ATV garage. Didn't even glance toward the side of the building where Giulio and I had hidden. I switched views to the hidden gate. And did another chair dance.

Waiting on the other side of the hidden gate, clearly visible in the ATV headlights, was Young Thug. The gate opened. An exchange took place between the two men before Young Thug climbed into the ATV with Lawson. They drove off into the woods. Happily ever after.

For now.

I wanted to kiss the video screen. Here was all the physical evidence the police needed to connect these men. Physical evidence that wasn't just my testimony.

Quite honestly, holding the only burden of proof was getting old.

Slipping out the door, I pulled it shut and felt the lock tumble. Grinning, I ambled to Oliver's office door. Then stopped.

Wait. Why did I want to celebrate my finding with Oliver and not Nash?

Horrified at my fickleness, I paused to do an emotional wellness check. But couldn't selfie without a phone. And considering my therapist was connected to bank robbers, I didn't find it appropriate. As I stood in the hall, sorting my feelings and feeling more confused, the door to Oliver's office opened.

Sam Martin strode out, blasting someone inside with a "check your priorities" over his shoulder. Spotting me, the Wellspring investor stopped short. "Maizie." He paused. "I understand you've had some difficulties."

"I'm okay, thanks. I think the bank robbers will be caught soon."

"Good to hear. You're friends with a police officer, aren't you? Does he have any news?"

"Unfortunately, the ATF is in charge of that investigation and they don't tell him much. And he tells me even less. Did the police bring in Dr. Trident for questioning?"

"Trident?" Sam placed his hands on his hips. "What for?"

"He knows at least one of the suspects."

"God." He rubbed the back of his neck. "I didn't know. Thanks for telling me."

"You're welcome." I grinned, then swapped it for a more serious expression. The Wellspring founder wouldn't think the questioning of his famous employee exciting. "Is Oliver inside?"

He cut a look at the door. "Yes. And tell him your news. He needs to know this."

I nodded. Oliver already knew about Trident and Everett Lawson after last night's epiphany. But I could still share the news about the video footage. I skipped through the outer reception and into his inner office.

Oliver sat slumped in his office chair, checking his phone.

"I have great news," I said, rushing around the desk.

He dropped the phone on his desk and lifted his eyes to mine.

"What's wrong?" I placed a hand on his cheek and leaned against his desk. "Is the Everett Lawson investigation disrupting the resort? Are guests complaining because of the police? I heard Sam yelling at you."

He placed his hand over mine and gazed at me. "Something like that. I'm the one who wanted to work here. You have to take the bad with the good, I guess." Sliding my hand to his lips, he kissed my palm and brought it to rest between his hands. "What's your good news?"

"Someone left the security door open, so I helped myself. I saw last night's security video feed. It shows Everett Lawson talking with Dr. Trident. Lawson took an ATV and met the guy who's been threatening me at your back gate."

Oliver closed his eyes and groaned.

"I know Dr. Trident isn't exactly good news. It's bad for business. But it's one more link toward apprehending these guys."

He tugged on my hand and pulled me onto his lap. I snuggled against him, fitting my head against his shoulder. "What else has happened?" he said, threading his fingers through mine.

I told him about Roger and Crispin. "It's coming to a head. I can feel it. It'll be hard to extradite Crispin, but if he does find his dad, maybe Mr. Jonson will turn Crispin in. I think he really has something to do with Chandler's disappearance."

"Can the police identify this guy who's been threatening you?"

"I'm not sure. He's kind of fuzzy on the security video because of the lighting. I knew it was him though."

Oliver stroked my arm. I tried very hard not to think about how comforting it felt to snuggle against him, nor how easily I seemed to console him. Or if Nash and Jolene did the same. And as much as I currently enjoyed snuggling with Oliver, how I still wished he were Nash.

I shifted to move from his lap, but Oliver's heavy sighed pulled me back down.

"This is nice," Oliver said. "Just me and you. Have you ever thought about getting away from everything? Living somewhere else?"

"Not really. I mean, the terms of my probation made it pretty clear where I had to live."

"What if we could fix that? We could live in...I don't know, Baja. Or Costa Rica. Maybe Europe? You liked Cannes, didn't you? I have the money."

"Don't be silly," I said. "You just got this job. You want to help people with all the holistic stuff, remember? This is more than just a spa, right? Even though you only serve the rich and celebrities, it's still a noble thing."

"We're going to reach more than just celebrities. They're just the start, to legitimize our branding. We have a long-term plan." Oliver kissed my forehead. "But right now, I just want to run away with you."

"That's very sweet." My face felt hot. I slipped from his lap. "But I also have a job. For now. I need two years of training to become a private investigator."

"You don't need any training to become my wife." Oliver took my hands in his.

"Your? Wait. What?"

"Let's get married, Maizie. We'll go file the papers today. Later we can do the big wedding. Or small and private. Whatever you want. But I don't want to wait. We could fly out to Vegas and be back by morning. Your probation officer wouldn't even miss you."

"Vegas?"

"Unless it's legal to do same-day weddings in Georgia?"

"I don't know," I stammered. "I've never looked into it."

"Of course, why would you?" Oliver's eyes danced. "I just thought of it. It's brilliant and will solve everything."

"Solve? But—"

Oliver dropped to one knee. "Maizie Marlin Spayberry, please do me the honor. I love you so much. You make me happy. I've been lost without you."

"Um—you know. It's just—"

"Is it moving? You want to stay in Black Pine? We don't have to move, sweetheart. You can keep your job. I won't try to convince you to work here. If we're married, we'll see each other every day anyway."

"Uh…it's a bit of a shock. And all very sudden. Very flattering, of course." I'd reverted to *Downton Abbey* again. "But, you see—"

He kissed my hands. "I don't have a ring. I'm going into town and buy you the biggest diamond I can find. But don't worry, we'll stop at Harry Winston in Vegas and do it right. Unless you're set on Tiffany?"

My mind reeled. I slipped my hands from his and gripped the desk. "We can't—"

"And a dress. Does Vera Wang have a Vegas shop? We'll call ahead. Don't worry, even if we do this on the fly, it'll be classy. Vicki would have your head otherwise. Don't worry about that." He stood and cupped my chin. Dropping a kiss on my lips, he murmured, "I'll protect you."

He darted to the door and paused. "Just stay here. I'll be back soon. With fried chicken and a ring. Vegan spa be damned. Nothing is too good for you."

I jerked out of my shock. "But Oliver, I haven't said yes."

Too late. He was gone.

FORTY-SEVEN

#PhonePriveleges #ItsOffToWorkIGo

My excitement had deflated, bringing on an escalation of heartache mixed with heartburn. I didn't want to marry Oliver — I didn't even want to date him — but I also didn't want to hurt him. I considered calling the girls, but they'd remind me about the stupidity of love, which wasn't what I wanted to hear. I already felt like I was two-timing Nash, even if our relationship only existed in my head. And three-timing Ian, though I had no intention of dating him, either.

How did I get myself in these predicaments? I looked down at my chest and felt some blame might lay there. But in all honesty, it was my lack of spine. And possibly my mixed-scruples upbringing.

Mostly my lack of spine. The same missing spine that always got me in trouble.

I flopped into Oliver's chair and spotted his phone still resting on the desk where he'd dropped it. Picking it up, the phone flickered to life. His code was too easy. My birthday. I checked his Facebook to make sure he hadn't updated his relationship status. Changing that back to "jilted" would be super awkward. No recent updates. And thankfully, none of our selfies appeared. Restless, I looked through his apps. Spotted the Wellspring security app and tapped.

Tiny screens with a scroll bar appeared. The first four video feeds were interior. I tapped and the hall outside his office enlarged. Empty. I minimized, then scrolled. Oliver had already left the building. Vicki and Giulio strolled into the lobby.

Thank God, they hadn't run into Oliver and heard about our non-elopement.

I scrolled until I reached the screens showing the back acreage. Back gate. Hidden gate. ATV garage. Garden gate. Spotted movement just inside the garden gate. No one appeared within the camera's angle. I grew bored waiting for a gardener to haul a load of tomatoes to Café.

Sliding the scroll bar, I found the last four screens. Dying corn stalks and bean teepees in the garden. The old chicken coop where herbs dried and Dr. Sakda's microscope waited for her return. A sunlit room full of tropical plants. And another greenhouse shot, where a teeny Dr. Trident spoke to a tiny Dr. Sakda near a doorway.

Rising from the chair, I tapped on the screen. The police had to have seen Dr. Trident speaking to Everett Lawson. Why wasn't he taken in for questioning?

I grabbed Oliver's desk phone, pressed nine, and dialed Agent Langtry's number.

"Langtry," she said.

Of course, she'd answer when it wasn't my number or Ian's.

I forced my voice to perky. "Agent Langtry, Maizie Albright." I explained the security video I'd seen and my confusion as to why Dr. Trident was allowed to roam free. "Have you talked to him?"

"The officers canvassed all the staff at Wellspring."

"But there's some kind of relationship between Lawson and Trident. Dr. Trident seems goofy, but I think he hides his intelligence. Or at least in our therapy sessions, that's what it seemed like. I mean, selfie therapy sounded like a sham to me, too. But once I tried it, there is some merit."

"Thanks for your concern," she said and hung up.

I stared at the phone and wondered about justice, warrants, and rights. And the possibility of the federal government hiring incompetent agents. And decided I needed a session with Dr. Trident.

Like now. Before he took off for Mexico with everyone else.

*W*ith Oliver's phone in hand, I skipped the gym bypass and hurried to the back gate. I'd found his list of security codes, handily typed in his Notes app, listed under "codes."

Before I broke off our non-engagement, Oliver needed a lesson on privacy protection.

At the gate, I entered the code on the alarm app and watched myself enter the back lot on the handheld security feed. I swiped to the greenhouse camera. Dr. Trident sat on the edge of a table, his leg swinging, talking with his hands. I could sense Dr. Sakda's irritation in the rigidity of her shoulders and jerky movements. She had her back to the camera, peering into a set of boxes that covered a long table.

I hurried through the barren area, theorizing the police had spoken to Dr. Trident and left thoroughly confused. Which happened when one listened to Dr. Trident. I had experience in making sense of his cryptic therapy-speak. Hopefully, I'd learn something about Lawson. Then, if it seemed there was more to the story, I'd use Oliver's phone to call Ian. The police could use me for an interpreter.

It felt like a good plan and maybe one where I could redeem myself in Ian's eyes by scoring him some brownie points at work.

An ATV and two golf carts were parked outside the garden gate. Using Oliver's phone, I unlocked the gate. I hurried toward the greenhouse, passing the bags of fertilizer. My heart hammered inside my throat. The sun glared overhead, baking the overturned dirt and steaming the bags of fertilizer. Sticky sweat broke out on the back of my neck.

The crazy security still bothered me. Why was this area such a secret? Farm to table was a thing to show off in our world, not hide. They should hang fairy lights from the razor wire and place picnic tables among the tomatoes.

Reaching the greenhouse, through the window I saw Dr. Sakda's white coat move among the plants. Where was Dr. Trident? I didn't want to charge in on scary Sakda.

I halted before reaching the entrance. Cut through the rows of corn to the side of the greenhouse. Peered through the windows. The kratom trees obstructed my view. Took out Oliver's phone and pressed the app for the security feed. And saw a group of teenagers enter the lobby and approach reception.

Fred, Mara, and Laci.

I checked the time and gritted my teeth. Those truants.

They huddled then moved toward one of the couches. Flopped and pulled out their phones. Oliver would find them and take care of them. Probably feed them my fried chicken.

While he wondered where his non-fiancée had gone with his phone.

Right. Dr. Trident.

I thumbed past the other screens until I reached the greenhouse. The security cameras were positioned at each end of the building. Dr. Sakda moved around the far end, checking the plants. Dr. Trident sat on a table near the entrance, swinging his leg and talking. To Young Thug.

Holy hellsballs.

Sliding to the ground, I squatted and chewed my thumbnail. Wished I had gotten my .38 from Oliver's safe before leaving his office, but it hadn't occurred to me until now that I might need it.

What the frigistan was Dr. Trident doing? And Dr. Sakda seemed oblivious. Maybe she was. She'd seemed totally fixated on her organic chemistry plantage whatnots.

Okay. I had a phone. I'd call the police and report the sighting of armed and dangerous. I thumbed through Oliver's app — *Why was it so hard to find the actual phone app on his phone?* — and heard the creak of a door. I peered around the edge of the greenhouse. Young Thug was leaving. Outside the entrance, he acquired an empty wheelbarrow. And a shovel.

Hang on, were Young Thug and Everett both garden caretakers? Working privately for Dr. Trident?

From my squat, I watched Young Thug push the wheelbarrow toward the bean teepees and begin to dig. His back was to me and I was out of security camera range, but I wasn't exactly hidden around the corner of a glass house. The shriveled cornstalks didn't obstruct my view of Young Thug, but they also didn't provide much cover.

I hunkered as low as possible and bore the numbness in my haunches. Young Thug carefully removed bean poles with the attached vines and roots. Setting these aside, he dug again. The earth was loose and loamy — probably thanks to all that fertilizer — and his dirt pile grew quickly. An oblong hole appeared. Bending over, he reached into the hole and pulled back a dirty tarp. Working quickly, he hauled out a garbage bag. Someone buried more than boots at Wellspring. Whatever was inside was lumpy. Like a body.

No, too lumpy. But I wished my mind hadn't jumped there.

Fighting off the cramping in my thighs and the ache in my back, I watched him lug out another bag and dump them in the large wheelbarrow. The dirt returned to the hole. The beans replaced. The earth tapped down. Young Thug pushed the wheelbarrow toward the gate. Striding through the rows of tomatoes and peppers, like one of Snow White's dwarfs rolling their mining cart.

Heigh-ho.

FORTY-EIGHT

#Tridont #KnightAgain

---

oung Thug hurried the wheelbarrow toward the gate and I slowly pushed off the ground, creeping along the wooden fence. I felt safe from security cameras. As long as Dr. Trident or Dr. Sakda stayed in the greenhouse, I wouldn't be seen. Young Thug focused on rolling the cart between vegetable beds. And because he was in a hurry, he had his eyes on the bouncing bags.

As he stopped to open the gate, I sank behind bags of fertilizer and flattened against the fence. Waited until he'd pushed the wheelbarrow through the gate. Glanced back toward the greenhouse. And spotted Dr. Trident moseying among the pepper plants.

Craptastic.

I had no way to hide from this angle. I rose and waved.

"Maizie," he called. "What are you doing in here?"

"Oh, you know." I waved my hand at the garden, playing vague to his cryptic. "What are you doing?"

He drew himself up, swinging his arms and sucking in the scent of dirt and vegetables. "Taking in the gloriousness of nature. Try it with me, Maizie."

"Yes, very glorious, but I should get going." I danced on my toes. "I'm in a hurry."

"No, I meant take it in. Not describe it." He rolled his hand. "Deep breath."

I inhaled the scent of fertilizer and coughed.

"Life-giving, isn't it? We should selfie. But not here. Walk with me to the Center."

I didn't know what tune Dr. Trident played. And considering with whom he gardened, I didn't trust him. "I'm good. Listen, there was a young guy just here. Do you know him?"

"Very helpful young man. Denver Crosby."

"Does he and Everett Lawson work for you?"

"Work." Dr. Trident cocked his head. "It means to toil or labor. Why do we call work, work?"

Digging in the garden seemed like toil and labor to me, but I couldn't tell if Dr. Trident's intention was subterfuge or just general nuttishness. "I meant, did you hire them personally? Or are they community service volunteers? What are they doing at Wellspring?"

Dr. Sakda leaned out the door. "Dr. Trident, who's in the garden with you?"

"I'm going to leave now." I scooted around the fertilizer, edging toward the gate. "Thanks for the session."

Trident looked over his shoulder. "Maizie Albright. Should we rap with her?"

Not waiting to hear Dr. Sakda's response, I shot toward the gate. Trident called after me. I waved, kicked the gate closed, and jumped into a golf cart.

Denver had left on the ATV. I had a feeling he headed to the hidden gate. I floored the cart. It whirred across the weedy waste-land past the old cowshed. Before reaching the ATV garage, I stopped. Snuck around the side and found the garage door closed. Ran back to the cart and motored through the pine grove path to the gate. Using Oliver's phone, I let myself through, then studied the trail leading up the mountain.

"Hey, Maizie."

Startled, I turned. Three figures broke through the vines entrapping a group of pines. Fred, wielding a pocket knife, followed by Mara and Laci.

Shiztastic.

"What did I say about hiking in these woods? Why aren't you in school?"

"We were worried about you, so we came to see you," said Mara. "Our parents wouldn't let us go to school today because you told them it wasn't safe."

"Why would it be safer here than at school?" I waved my hands at the forest. "Where are your parents?"

"My dad had to go to work." Laci spun a lock of hair around her finger.

"I didn't want to go to a swamp," said Fred, playing with his knife. "Neither did my mother."

"In other words, they left you at home and you snuck out."

Three more shrugs.

"Anyway, we got tired of waiting in the lobby," said Laci. "We overheard someone saying you were in the back area, so we thought we'd come this way and call to you through the fence."

Shizzles. I'd been reported. "This is like the worst place for you to find me."

"Actually," said Fred. "It's the best since we found you."

"I'm trailing Denver, the dude who's been threatening me."

"That's not safe either," said Laci.

"It's my job." They simultaneously raised their brows. "Okay, not my job, but it's somebody's and they're not doing it. I'm collecting evidence for the police. I'm going to lose him, so I've got to bounce."

"We'll come with you." Fred waved the knife. "To protect you."

"A knife won't do any good against a gun." I slid onto the golf cart. "Go home."

I whirred forward. Twenty yards up the trail, the cart jammed on a tree root. I mentally face-palmed.

"You need an ATV," called Mara. "Golf carts aren't meant for trail riding."

They reached me a minute later. "You'll need help with the trail," said Fred. "It's old and hard to see."

"I can't protect you if things get sketchy." Sliding off the cart, I marched forward. "Remember the last time we went hiking? You need to go home."

"We have experience in these woods you don't have," said Laci. "We've hiked to the peak lots of times."

"The police found a body on the peak. A dead one. You need to go home."

"Was it Chandler?" Mara grabbed my arm. "Did they find him?"

I patted her hand. "No. Nothing to do with Chandler." I gazed up the trail that led from Wellspring. *Maybe something to do with Chandler.*

"Let's go," said Laci, heading off the trail. "We can be stealthy. Better than you."

Mara darted into the woods after her. Leaving Fred to protect me with a Swiss Army pocket knife.

"Go after the girls," I said to Fred. "You need to convince them this isn't fun and games. This guy had a gun and there are at least two people dead. It's seriously dangerous."

"Okay, but they don't really listen to me."

"Fred, this is your time to shine. Be the knight. Save the damsels."

"They told me it's sexist—"

"Fred, go."

He disappeared into the woods after the girls. Continuing uphill, I listened for the kids and the ATV. Thirty minutes later, the area between my backpack and back had grown steamy. My calves shot stinging waves of complaint into the backs of my thighs. And I was starving.

"I am so never hiking again," I promised myself. "At least not uphill."

I needed a break. Denver was probably long gone. I moved off the trail to rest on a fallen tree. And immediately hopped off. The area behind the tree buzzed with flies and smelled like old garbage. I circled around the tree to look for another resting spot downwind and found a boot.

Again.

FORTY-NINE

#NoBootAboutIt #BigfootBounty

he boot in question was not a Keane. It was a brand of which I was not familiar. And attached to the foot of Everett Lawson, of whom I was familiar. In a way. And who'd been mostly buried beneath the fallen tree. Or not buried well and drug out by something. Hopefully not Bigfoot, but I didn't want to know just the same.

It wasn't that thought that sent me hurtling deeper into the woods to get sick. But it didn't help.

By the time I had lost the lunch I had not yet had and breathed shallowly against a tree, I looked around. I couldn't spot the fallen tree, much less the path. Above me squirrels frolicked, completely oblivious to the death haunting the forest. I had enough sense to mark the tree with a strip ripped from my Re/Done tee (which took some doing with their quality craftsmanship). Remembered I still had Oliver's phone. Which had no service on the mountain.

Frigorrendous.

I hollered for the teens. Who didn't respond. I set out in a dubious direction. Turned back. Tried another way. Turned back. And wished I'd paid more attention ten years prior when Daddy decided I should spend the summer learning outdoor survival. I'd spent the summer unlearning outdoor survival because I was fifteen and found the idea of myself lost in the wilderness ridiculous.

Which was exactly why Mara, Fred, and Laci should listen to me. Fifteen-year-olds don't know everything.

Because the ground sloped, I chose the uphill climb. At least in this direction, the mountain would peak as opposed to spread. I gave up on Denver and the ATV and focused once again on the back sweat and ache in my calves. I stopped. Behind me, a crackling of leaves sounded more human than squirrel. I whirled around.

Nothing but trees and bushes. And a possible snake that was more likely a stick.

I slowed my steps, listened, and again heard the dry rustle of feet treading on pine straw. This time I moved toward a large tree, passed it, then double-backed to hide behind it. The rustling halted. I hesitated, building my courage to peer around the tree. A thump resounded from the tree, followed by a scrabbling. I tiptoed from the tree. Took three running steps. The air stirred. And a body collapsed on me.

My scream ended as I slammed into a pool of leaves. Something lay on top of me, panting. I tried to roll, but the weight kept me pinned. I screamed again. My feet scrambled, trying to push off the ground. My hands clawed the dirt, trying to pull myself free. Then froze.

A male voice whispered, "Don't move. I have a knife."

I screeched and felt a sharp point dig into my armpit.

"Denver?" Butterflies beat inside my skull. Hummingbirds thrashed inside my rib cage. My hot, sweaty skin now felt slick and icy. My breath shuddered. "What do you want with me? I didn't see you at the robbery. I can't testify you were there."

"What robbery?" The tip of the knife poked through my shirt. "Was Crispin Jonson there, too?"

"Crispin?" I gave a cry feeling the blade knick my skin. "I don't know. I only saw Roger."

"Roger? Who's Roger?"

"The guy who blew up the bank."

The knife wielder fell silent.

"Who are you?" I said, my voice unsteady. "Can I roll over? I don't have a weapon."

My head was shoved into the leaves and I inhaled pine straw dust.

"No, who are you?" said the voice. "I saw you earlier. Going through the Jonson house and Chandler Jonson's apartment. And on the mountain. What were you doing with the *Bigfoot Tracker* crew?"

"Are you the guy on the motorcycle?" I glared into the dirt and dead leaves. "You vandalized my dirt bike. And almost gave me a concussion with your rocks and sticks."

He shook my shoulder. "Who are you? What are you doing with Fred, Mara, and Laci?"

"They hired me to look for Chandler Jonson. I'm a private investigator." I inhaled another round of leaf dust and hacked.

The pressure against my head and back eased and he rolled me over. I flopped on top of my backpack like an overturned turtle. And stared into the face of a bearded man. Looking more Leonardo in *The Revenant* than Bear Grylls in *Man vs Wild*.

I hiked in a breath and felt a strange thrumming throughout my body. "Chandler?"

His chin jerked. He narrowed his eyes, staring into the distance. Popping up like a chipmunk, he'd darted toward the tree, jumped, and hauled himself onto a branch. Climbing branch to branch, he hid in a heavy mass of browning foliage.

The drumming was the pounding of feet on the forest floor. I couldn't believe it. Chandler had left me to be caught by Denver.

"Maizie?" hollered Fred. "Where are you?"

I released the breath I'd held and sat up. The three appeared in the distance.

"We heard you screaming," said Mara. "Was it a snake or a spider?"

I pointed at the tree, not liking the tremble in my hand. "Chandler. I found Chandler. He found me."

"Did you hit your head again?" said Laci. "That's a tree."

The ground thudded and the three turned toward the tree. Rushing forward, they attacked Chandler. I waited while they exchanged numerous "dudes" and "where you beens" and "we were so worrieds."

"I knew you hadn't gone to Mexico," said Mara, her voice tuned to boy-crush. "I thought you were dead. Or kidnapped."

I supposed "believed dead or kidnapped" made the heart grow fonder.

"Almost dead," he said. "Some dude caught me at the Wellspring fence. A bunch of them were having some kind of meeting out in the dark. I was trying to listen. He and an older guy forced me to walk back to my car. The younger guy took off in my car. But first, they made me take off my clothes and boots."

I was so right about that boot. Not that it gave me any pleasure now.

"Why would they do that?" said Laci.

"The dogs would have a harder time tracking my body. I ran before the older dude could shoot me with his rifle."

"You were running around the woods naked?" said Laci. "Gross."

"I stole clothes asap. That *Naked and Afraid* TV show is bogus."

"I knew it was Wellspring," said Fred. "Did they interrogate you about our chicken farm theories?"

"It had nothing to do with Sasquatch, man," said Chandler. "I didn't want to tell you three because it was too dangerous. I was spying on Wellspring, but not why you thought. My brother's involved in major pharmaceutical sales with them. I caught him with a box of pills and began tailing him. He's dealing for Wellspring."

"I saw the capsules in his room," I said. "Those pills are herbal supplements."

"Those pills are as herbal as opium," said Chandler. "They're selling them."

"Kratom's not illegal. The police know about it. They've been in the greenhouse and they've seen the pills," I said. "I researched kratom. It's controversial and not regulated. The police don't like it and there are kratom-related deaths. In other states and countries, it's illegal. But not Georgia."

"Then why are they bringing boxes up the mountain on ATVs at night? I saw it all. Two dudes in a truck were at the tourist spot waiting for the delivery. I saw one dude get shot."

"Oh my God," I said. "That's the murder that happened last Friday. You saw it? Why didn't you go to the police? They've been trying to solve that crime. They didn't even find that guy's body until somebody reported it."

"That was me. I've been sleeping in a tree on the mountain. I hiked down in stealth mode, stole that bike, and reported the murder when I thought the coast was clear."

"Dude, you're like a total hero," said Fred, giving him a fist bump.

I wasn't sure if stealing a motorcycle and not reporting a crime properly qualified for hero status. "The police would have protected you. You should have driven that stolen motorcycle to the police department."

"I had to get my brother out of the situation first. What if they went after him, knowing I narced to the police? Then I saw you at my apartment and my house. I thought you were with them. I couldn't come out of hiding. Sorry about your bike, but I had to get away without you tailing me."

"That's epic," said Laci.

"Why would you throw rocks at us?" I said. "You could have hurt them. And you almost knocked me out, slamming me into the tree with that stick."

"Dude, I threw rocks to scare you away. I didn't want my team on the mountain with all this going on. But I didn't assault you with a stick. I'm not into violence. Especially against women. Get real." He shook his head, stroking his beard.

Mara clasped her hands together. "Of course, you wouldn't."

"You threw rocks then took off?" I could have used a rescue from getting clubbed, but whatever. "Did you see who hit me and stole my backpack?"

He shook his head. "It's not safe for me to be out of my tree for long. There's been a lot of activity since the shooting."

"Denver Crosby and Everett Lawson are the main culprits. Or at least I think it was Everett…" I paused. "I found his body in the woods. They sound like the men who abducted you and attacked me. Possibly Dr. Trident's connected. It's just unfortunate for Wellspring that they're using it for whatever they're doing."

"That place is evil, man. I don't care what you say. I don't like what's going on with my brother."

He had a point. And running to Mexico made Crispin look guilty of something. Roger's mother had thought he'd been involved in drugs, too.

"The mountaintop murder is drug-related. But these guys are also involved in the bank bombing. Maybe they planned two armed robberies?"

"I've watched *Breaking Bad*," said Chandler. "It wasn't a robbery. There was an exchange. Then a fight and that's when the dude was shot."

"Listen," I said. "Your brother fled to Mexico. It's time for you to come out of hiding. We're going to visit Detective Ian Mowry. I need to report Everett Lawson's body. Chandler, you're going to explain why you've been living in a tree."

"Dude," said Chandler. "The cops?"

The three glowered at me.

"I'm pulling my adult card," I said. "Denver Crosby may still be out on the mountain. We've got a man recently buried and a garbage bag full of who knows what. If the supplements aren't illegal, there must be something else buried under the beans."

"I don't understand what you're saying," said Fred.

"Doesn't matter." I set my hands on my hips. "We're going before it's too la—"

The growing drone of an ATV engine stopped my words.

"Run," I screamed.

FIFTY

#TreedAndCarated #AGirlsBestFriend

"We can't outrun an ATV," said Chandler. "Quick, the tree."

We darted toward the big oak. Chandler leaned over. Mara helped Laci climb on his back. While he boosted her, Laci grabbed the lowest branch, swinging her legs and pulling her chest onto the branch. Mara grabbed her calves and pushed.

The roar of the ATV grew.

"There's not enough time to get everyone up the tree." I feared the tree wouldn't hide everyone. Maybe two, three if you didn't look too carefully.

Mara climbed on Chandler's back and scrambled for the branch.

"Fred, run," I said. "Hide. Get down low. They might not see you."

"What are you going to do?" said Fred. "I'll protect you."

"They know I'm out here, but they don't know you are." I grabbed Fred by the shoulders. "Whatever you do, don't come out. Promise me. Do not try to be heroic. Do you understand what I'm saying?"

He nodded, blinking back tears.

"You have to stay hidden for the sake of the girls. And when they're totally gone, I want the four of you to get back to Black Pine and tell the police everything." I pulled him into a quick hug.

I ran uphill, toward the sound of the ATV. I hoped I could draw Denver away. Spotting the vehicle in the distance, I adjusted the angle of my dash. My arms churned. My lungs burned. Tree roots and hidden rocks threatened to send me sprawling. I zig-zagged, ducking around trees and bushes blocking my path.

Behind me, the ATV growled. Denver shouted.

He'd seen me.

I pelted toward a thicker grouping of trees. Pushing aside a vine, I climbed around a leggy rhododendron. And prayed for a lack of spiders and snakes.

The ATV engine roared. Inside, the thicket forced me to slow. I picked my way through the denser vegetation. Wondering if Denver would follow me inside or ambush me on the other side. Feeling a bit *The Princess Bride* in the Fire Swamp.

Minus Dread Pirate Roberts' help.

My breath wheezed, keeping time with my racing pulse. I moved between the trees, glancing over my shoulder. I couldn't hear the ATV. I bit my lip, praying he didn't find the *Bigfoot Tracker* team.

The dense wood broke into a small glen protected by a rock outcropping. I hesitated before stepping into the enclosed space. My heart walloped against my ribs. My lungs constricted. The granite wall had trapped me. I couldn't climb it. I'd have to find another way out. I backed into the tree line.

And felt the muzzle of a gun.

"Put your hands where I can see them," said Denver.

I held out my hands. His slid around my back and jeans. Finding Oliver's phone, he pulled it from my back pocket, then gripped my shoulder.

"Move slowly. To the left."

"Denver?" I babbled between gasps. "I don't know why you're doing this. Not exactly. I can't testify about the robbery. I didn't see you at the bank. I don't know what you're doing at Wellspring. You don't have to do this."

"Shut up." The gun jammed into my back.

I shut up.

We wound through the thicket to where the forest thinned. I squinted into the distance but saw no movement among the trees. We continued forward. Denver's breath warmed the back of my neck. The ATV emerged behind a large ash. Gripping my shoulder, he halted our movement. The gun eased from my back.

"Seriously, Denver. If you and Everett are into shady business, whatever," I craned my neck to see him. "I truly haven't figured it out. Just let me go. I promise I won't say anything."

"I know you're not going to say anything." His grip tightened.

In my peripheral vision, I saw the gun swing overhead.

"No," I cried, raising my arms.

The grip caught me behind my ear. The bone-jarring crack loosened my knees. Spots danced in my eyes. Pain shot down my neck to my fingers. I gulped. And blacked out.

J woke with an aching head and a sore jaw. With my eyes still closed, I evaluated my surroundings. A firm, yet soft cushion beneath me. My body felt intact. Except for my head. No bird calls or squirrel rustlings. No longer in the woods. The hint of tea and something herbal scented the air. The soft patchouli, lavender, and vanilla blend of Gentlemen Givenchy by Givenchy. I sniffed to double-check and slowly opened my eyes.

"Thank God," said Oliver, leaning over me. "How are you feeling?"

"Not so good," I said. "My head feels like I got pistol-whipped. Which I did. By Denver Crosby. Call the police."

Oliver stroked my cheek. He gently lifted me into a hug. I rested there a beat, mainly because I didn't have the strength to do otherwise. My head was on fire.

"Here." A brown capsule rested in the palm of his hand.

I eyeballed the capsule. "No thanks."

"It's great for pain."

"I'd rather have a couple ibuprofen all the same. And a phone to call the police." I took in the couch and the room. "Why am I in Dr. Trident's office?"

He shook his head. "I'm so sorry this happened to you. I'm taking care of everything. Look."

A small green box lay on the coffee table. Taking it, Oliver pulled back the lid and showed me the ring inside. Platinum. Or white gold. An emerald-cut trio on a band of tiny diamonds. The center diamond was at least three carats. I squinted, then realized what I was doing.

I snatched my hand back.

"We need to get you to the hospital to check your injury. Rest, sweetheart." He picked up my hand, slipped the ring on, and kissed my finger. "Everything is going to be okay."

"Um, Oliver?" I focused on not lifting my hand to examine the ring. I was going to give it back. In a minute. When I had a better idea of what was going on. Or something like that. "Where is Denver and Dr. Trident?"

Oliver kissed my hand again. "You really should take something for the pain."

"I'm confused as to what's going on. Why won't you tell me?"

"You probably have a concussion."

The door creaked. I tried to sit up, but Oliver patted my shoulder and gently pushed me down. He stood, blocking my view of the door.

"You're in here?" The voice sounded like Sam Martin.

I rolled over and pushed up, sending off an agonizing starburst inside my head. Oliver acted strangely. Although that may be due to me taking off with his phone to nearly get myself killed while he purchased this gorgeous engagement ring.

A ring I was totally giving back. In a minute.

I tried to see around Oliver's big body and could make out a sliver of Sam Martin near the door. Probably wondering what we were doing on Trident's couch. As Oliver's boss, I'd wonder why Oliver spent more time dealing with me than managing his wellness center.

But as a terrible employee myself, I couldn't cast stones.

"Did you take care of everything?" said Sam.

Oliver shoved his hand in his pocket and adjusted his stance. Creating a better view of Sam Martin. Sam was scrolling on his phone, not looking at us. Someone else stood behind him in the hall. Maybe they were about to have a staff meeting.

Sam Martin looked up and caught my eye. His eyes widened, then darted to Oliver. "What's she doing in here?"

I breathed out a sigh. Finally, we'd get some answers.

"I thought she was taken care of," said Sam.

Okay, that didn't sound good.

FIFTY-ONE

#Backsliding #TheProposal

*H*oping he meant "taken care of" as in "take care of her aches and pains in the spa," I waited for Sam to explain. Instead, he moved aside. Denver Crosby entered the room.

Chandler Jonson was right about Wellspring. Shizzilation.

"Oliver," I murmured. "That's Denver, the guy who attacked me. He has a gun."

I slowly rose, ignoring the pain and dizziness. My knees shook. I leaned against Oliver to gain purchase and focused on not falling over.

"That man ran me down on the mountain." I pointed at Denver with a trembling finger. "He knocked me out with his gun."

Denver folded his arms and rocked back on his heels. Sam glanced at him and shoved his phone in his pocket.

"We're engaged," said Oliver. He rested his hand against my back and lifted my hand with the ring. "By tomorrow, we'll be married."

We looked at Oliver, wondering if he knew how Cocoa Puffs he sounded.

I lowered my voice. "I don't think they care about that, Oliver. Who are they really? Everett, Denver, and Sam?"

Oliver shifted to face me. "Sam's the founder of Wellspring. Everett and Denver don't work here."

"The investor is asking why I'm still alive. The gunman is in Dr. Trident's office. And Everett Lawson is dead and half-buried in the woods."

Oliver paled. "What?"

"You've been duped. Big time. I didn't want to believe it either, but it's all related to Wellspring. This isn't about herbal supplements."

"Oliver," barked Sam.

"Just a minute." Oliver kept his eyes on me. "I'm not doing anything illegal, sweetheart. I learned my lesson. After we get married, it'll all be okay. I can protect you this way."

I closed my eyes, sighed, looked up at him. "So I can't testify against you? If everything is hunky-dory, why would I need protecting?"

"You have to trust me."

Says the man who got me arrested.

"It's too late, Oliver," said Sam. "She knows too much."

"The police know I'm here," I said. "I gave them Denver's name. They know about Everett and Dr. Trident, too."

Denver glared at me. Leaning back, he closed the door and pulled the handgun from beneath his shirt.

"Craptastic." Oliver's brow tightened. "Don't do this."

That was my line. But I had no time to be ticked off about stolen lines. I also had no time for a concussion. A mighty dose of adrenaline had replaced my pain.

We were in a room with one exit. A killer with a gun stood between us and the door. And there was nothing in Dr. Trident's room that could save us, unless I could *MacGyver* his herbal tea into something useful.

If only. But I did have something — calling it useful was a stretch — but I'd played someone who was often trapped in desperate situations. Although Julia Pinkerton could make a weapon from herbal tea (if the writers were especially creative), I'd focus on her cunning and wit instead of weapons.

And because Oliver had not thought to get my revolver from his stupid safe.

I eased from Oliver, ignored Denver and his Glock, and focused on Sam. My voice dropped into a lower register. "Did it occur to you I might want a cut? I mean, if I'm willing to marry Oliver…" I left my reasoning femme fatale vague.

"That's easy for you to say now," said Sam.

"Of course, I don't want to get shot." I cocked a hip and folded my arms. "But how long do you think this operation can last? Everett was a local connection and he's dead. You've only got Denver and his buddies, like Crispin. Crispin involved Roger Price. But the police will be watching all the Black Pine losers, right? I'm guessing you still have *product* to move. And at a celebrity retreat, who better to distract the public and the police than a real celebrity?"

Thankfully, I'd also seen *Breaking Bad* and knew drug cartel vocabulary.

This time Sam snorted.

I sashayed to stand between Sam and Denver. Deliberately putting my back to Oliver. "Look, Sam. I get it. When your delivery guy arrives at the peak for a pickup, you need a distraction for the cops. That's where Roger came in. Except that doofus built a real bomb instead of a fake one. While the cops were supposed to swarm First National, defusing a fake bomb, Everett and Denver would hand over your real product to your distributor."

Sam smirked. "Clever."

I gave a half-shoulder shrug. "This week must have been hell. First, Roger blows up the bank which did distract the police, but also brought the ATF up in your grill. Then your loose cannon, Denver, shot one of the delivery drivers. Which sent the police running to Wellspring again. And you had me at Wellspring, hunting for a missing person. Who happens to be the brother of one of your crew."

He nodded.

"So, how about a little win-win? Oliver offered me a job in security. I've got a criminal justice degree and have been mentoring as a PI. I also know the local police really well. As a household name, I can help you pull in celebs and finally fill this place. The job will ensure I can't give you up because I'd go down with you."

"I appreciate the offer," said Sam. "And you're almost right. The doofus was supposed to cause a distraction. Leave a fake bomb and get out. But we didn't have 'product to move.' Just a private meeting between my loose cannon and a criminal who asked for some subterfuge."

"But Crispin was dealing..." Wait. Chandler was wrong? "No, the gunshot victim was from a drug cartel."

"Crispin? I don't know him." Sam shrugged. "Kratom helps with withdrawals. Even though it can be addictive. I could see where an ambitious kid would want to make some cash selling our supplements. But it's not like Wellspring gave any to him."

"But—"

"Here's the thing, Maizie. I don't really care about filling Wellspring. It's better if we don't have a lot of guests." Sam smiled. "What we have in place works great. Oliver's a little overzealous. He spoke out of turn."

"What?" I glanced back at Oliver. "There wasn't a real job?"

Oliver's eyebrows pulled together, but he had his eyes on Denver.

"Why wouldn't you want more guests? There's hardly anybody here besides Vicki—" I bit my lip. I'd forgotten about Vicki and Giulio.

How could I forget my mother and my ex-fiancé-stepfather?

FIFTY-TWO

#DéjàDump #NotHubbyMaterial

I had to get us out of this room. And I had to make sure Vicki and Giulio were safe. The only thing keeping a panic attack at bay was the adrenaline. And the massive headache.

Silver linings.

While Sam Martin snickered at my failed job interview, I sidestepped toward Denver. Peripherally, I sized up the distance between us. Tried to formulate another plan. Clearly, Julia Pinkerton cleverness wasn't working.

"Fraser, we talked about this," said Sam. "You have a health resort to run. Our guests — people sick and in pain — are counting on you. Marriage is not going to keep her mouth closed."

"Maizie?" said Oliver. "If we get married, you can't talk to Roger Price. You should probably stop looking for the camper, too. At least here, anyway. It's not Sam's fault. Can't you see that these other characters just let things get out of hand?"

"The police are on their way." I hoped my irritation didn't show in my voice. Who used spousal immunity as a proposal? "Do you even know what happened to that camper, Oliver?"

"Let the police come, they're not going to find anything," said

Sam. "Denver's going away for a while. The only evidence against us is your testimony."

I wouldn't compromise Chandler, as much as I wanted to take the burden of testimony off myself. "How about the body of Everett Lawson in the woods?"

"Everett Lawson took his own life because an ATF agent was pressuring him to become an informant in the bank robbery. That's on the ATF, not us."

"What?" Oliver and I said simultaneously.

"Everett didn't bury himself. Denver took him out," I said. "I saw them leave together from Wellspring. And if he was going to incriminate you, Denver should have done a better job at making his death look like a suicide."

Sam gave Denver the side-eye. "We're not trying to hide anything here at Wellspring."

"Then let me marry Maizie." Oliver held out his hands. "It'll be just like she said."

"Listen, Oliver," said Sam. "You're doing great work here. You can help a lot of people. But we need to proceed as planned in order to fund your dream. She wants to stop us, and you'll end up in prison. Think long term."

"But—"

"If you have to bring fried chicken into a vegan resort to win her over, it proves she doesn't hold your beliefs. How long will she keep up the charade? She's an actress. She's pretending now."

Oliver's hands dropped.

"We talked about this," said Sam. "You know I'm right."

"I just hoped we could...before she..." Oliver plunged his hands in his pocket. "Let me give it to her?"

"Seriously?" I gaped at Oliver.

"I don't want to go to prison, Maizie. I haven't done anything wrong. This is my chance to really help people. You know this is my dream. I can't let an idiot like Roger Price blow it for me."

"Literally 'blow it.' As in a bomb, Oliver. Wellspring is into bombs, guns, and murder. How can you not see that?" I was having a *Twilight Zone* moment. Denver had hit my head harder than I thought. I had to be dreaming. "Oliver, they want to kill me."

"Not kill you. Just incapacitate you for a while. Until this blows over. If you had just waited for me, it wouldn't have to come to this. Sam was right. You escalated the situation."

My breath caught in my throat. "Oliver, you're not seeing this clearly."

"I tried to help you find the camper, but you had to go behind my back. I tried to protect you and you won't do the same for me. That's pretty clear."

"I thought you loved me."

"I did. Even when I could tell you didn't feel the same about me. But Sam's right. It's just not going to work, Maizie, is it?"

"*You're* breaking up with *me*? You're just going to let them kill me?"

"I keep telling you, they're not going to kill you. I think you're misunderstanding the situation."

"How do I misunderstand a Glock?"

A knock thumped behind us. Denver swung his gun at the door.

"Watch it." Sam held up a hand and checked his phone. "It's Sakda. Let her in."

Denver reached for the doorknob with his free hand.

Oliver swiveled and crossed the room, making Denver tense, drop the door handle, and steady his feet.

At Dr. Trident's desk, Oliver glanced over his shoulder. "Just something for the pain?"

"Sure. Really strong," sneered Sam. "And highly addictive, thanks to Dr. Sakda's amazing chemistry. I heard drugs used to be your thing, Maizie."

"Well, you got that wrong," I said in my best Julia Pinkerton snark. "The chemical most likely to kill me is triglycerides."

"You'll be more useful to us as a junkie. Word will get out about what you're using. Celebrities market certain products better than anyone. And if they OD, it doesn't seem to bother the consumer.

"Just incapacitate her for a while," repeated Oliver. "That's what you said, Sam."

Dr. Sakda knocked again. Denver leaned toward the door, reaching for the lever with his free hand.

Julia Pinkerton wasn't doing me any favors. And neither was Oliver. Time to revert to a preteen character, Kung Fu Kate.

I shifted to the ball of my right foot. Pivoted on my left. Struck my right foot out sideways. Caught Denver exposed in his wide-legged lean toward the door. Landing on my right foot, I shoved on the door, slamming it into Dr. Sakda. While she teetered, I thrust, elbowing her in the gut. She bent, gasping. I bounded down the hall, screaming "Fire" in my stage projection voice.

I hoped they didn't kill Oliver before I could get back to save him. Because after saving him, I planned to throw that ring in his face.

Scratch that. I was keeping the ring.

At the end of the hall, I yanked the fire alarm. The alarm blared. A gunshot rang from the office and behind me, the plaster wall exploded. I faltered, then picked up speed to the stairs. Running down the grand staircase, I windmilled into the lobby and banged into the reception desk. The young woman's eyes rounded as she looked up. Water rained from overhead sprinklers.

"Quick," I shouted above the alarm. "Vicki Albright and Giulio Belloni. Are they still here?"

Covering her head, the receptionist yelled, "No. They checked out." Her eyes darted to focus on something over my shoulder.

Craptastic. I could guess who was behind me.

"Go out the back," I said. "Make sure all the employees get out of the center. Emergency exits only."

I spun from the desk. Sam Martin had Denver's Glock. He held it against his leg, half-hidden from employees and guests. His expression had freaked out the receptionist. Freaked me out, too.

My heart triple-thumped. Where was Oliver? Had they killed him?

Sam Martin spotted me. I sprung across the wet wood, skidded onto the oriental carpet, and darted through the heavy wooden doors. In the parking lot, I headed for Rhonda's car. Patted my jeans and realized Denver had taken the keys with Oliver's phone.

Universe. Really?

The Center's front door crashed open. I crouched behind the car. Began to plot distances between my squat, the woods, and Sam Martin. Peering out behind Rhonda's car, I spotted him standing under the portico. Holding the gun in a two-handed grip. A mistake on Denver's part. I'd never have been able to kick him if he'd followed basic gun safety.

Sam glanced around the parking lot. I ducked my head. Leaned back against the car, trying to catch my breath.

How was I going to get back in to save Oliver?

In the distance, an engine growled. A vehicle ascending the mountain drive. The motor grew louder, accelerating into the Wellspring car park. I dropped to my belly and peered out. A pickup burned through the lot toward the front door.

My heart triple-thumped again.

Nash.

Wait. He wasn't supposed to be driving with that kind of concussion. And he might get hit with an unexpected bullet.

I popped out from behind Rhonda's car. "Hold up," I screamed, waving my hands.

The truck skidded to a stop. The driver's door flew open. Nash beckoned. I shook my head, pointing at the Center's entrance. He turned toward the passenger window and his hand moved to the gear shift.

Without taking his eyes off Sam Martin, Nash accelerated and cranked the steering wheel. The tires squealed. His door swung back and crashed against the frame. A shot sang. The truck continued the tight turn. The brakes cried and the truck jerked to a stop. I leaped toward the door. Yanked on the handle. Swung a foot onto the running board.

The gun blasted again. Nash stepped on the gas. I clung to the door, trying to gain my balance. One foot on the running board. The other trailing beneath the door.

Sam fired round after round. Metal screeched and pinged. The back window cracked.

"Hang on." Nash reached for me. "Grab my hand."

I shook my head, keeping my grip on the door. Using my body weight, I kicked my free leg backward and flung myself onto the seat. Nash grabbed the back of my jeans and gripped them while I hung half out the door.

"My arms are going to give out," I cried. "I can't shut the door."

"Leave it." He leaned toward me, then jerked back. My body slid toward him and I released the door. The parking lot disappeared. Cool pine air rushed into the truck. Nash took the corner onto the mountain road. The door swung back and banged against the doorframe.

I stretched to grab it, pulled it closed, then collapsed back on the seat.

"Are you okay?" He still gripped my jeans. My butt rested against his thigh and my legs dangled awkwardly below the seat.

I laid my forehead against the cool pleather. "Yes. But I have to go back."

"No." Nash patted my butt. "You've done enough. The police are on their way. Sounds like all first responders are on their way. Did you pull that fire alarm?"

"Yes." My ears tuned to the distant sirens. "Stop here. I'll cut through the woods. I can't just leave him like this. They're probably holding him hostage."

"Who? Your teenagers showed up at the office with Chandler."

"They never listen to me," I spoke into the seat. "I told them to go to the police first."

"I called the police. It's okay. They did good. You did good."

I shook my head, rolling from cheek to cheek. "I did lousy. I'm an idiot. I put a lot of people in danger. I got some killed. I was totally blind. And you should still be in bed."

The truck slowed and stopped. On the opposite side of the road, a police car roared by. A fire truck followed.

"Can you sit up, so I can talk to you? Not that I mind the view, but…"

I quickly scooted to sitting and faced him. Three more police cars shot past us.

"You found your missing person. You broke that case by yourself."

"Chandler found me. I don't think it counts."

Nash shrugged. "He's still found. Sounded like if you hadn't been wandering in the woods—"

"Like an idiot, chasing an armed man driving an ATV with bags of drug money."

"And convinced Chandler to turn himself in," Nash continued. "He would still be living in a tree."

"Doubt it." I crossed my arms. Uncrossed them. "Although he might've been found and killed."

"Well, there you go. In a way, you saved his life."

I pursed my lips, then bit them. My traitorous eyes brimmed with tears. "What about Oliver? What if they killed him because I escaped?"

"What was his role in all of this?"

"A not very good henchman. He turned a blind eye. Possibly he was keeping the books for them, laundering drug money through Wellspring. Sam Martin didn't care about having more guests or employees. That should've clued me in earlier." I sniffed and wiped a tear with the back of my hand. "Oliver really believed he was helping people with their pain. It sounded like Dr. Sakda was doing something to the kratom to make it stronger and more addictive. I don't know if Oliver knew or not."

"And you still want to save him?"

"We have a history." I glanced at my ring.

Nash's gaze followed and stopped on the ring. "Oh. I see."

I stuffed my left hand in my armpit and stared at the truck ceiling. "I don't want to talk about it."

"Okay."

Nash drew away to drum his fingers against the door. Another police car and an ambulance rushed past. A tear rolled down my face. I wiped it on my shoulder.

"Do you know what happened to Dr. Trident? My therapist?"

He kept his eyes on the windshield and shook his head. "We'll try to find out everything from Mowry when we can."

"Roger Price was telling the truth," I said. "The bomb wasn't meant to go off. He was supposed to distract the police while Denver and Everett arranged the drug money pickup. They drove their ATVs up the old mountain trail and met the delivery men at the lookout on the peak."

"Roger wasn't robbing the bank?" said Nash.

"Crispin was working with Denver. He knew Roger liked to build things. He connected with Roger and got him to do it. Except it wasn't supposed to be rigged to explode."

"I'll be damned. And we missed it."

I laid a hand on his arm. "If Roger had used a fake bomb like they wanted, you would have taken him out and none of this would've happened. You're still a hero."

Nash studied my hand on his arm. The diamonds sparkled in the flashing lights driving past. He drew his gaze up to meet mine. "I'm no hero. I've been weak—"

Something slammed into the passenger door and slid along the side. I gasped and turned toward the window. Nash placed a hand on my shoulder and pushed me down.

"Call the police." Tossing his phone into my lap, Nash leaned over me. Popping open the glove compartment, he fished out his .38. Checked the chamber. Grabbed the speed loader. Cracked open his truck door. "Stay in the truck."

It felt like déjà vu. The most horrible kind of déjà vu. Worse than the Oliver selling me out déjà vu.

"You're injured," I hissed. "You can barely walk."

"No, Maizie. Stay here."

"But Nash—"

"That's an order." He slipped outside. The door snicked shut.

"Hells-to-the-no. I'm not doing this again."

FIFTY-THREE

#SelfieShipFix #BigfootBeliever

Keeping his back against the truck, Nash held his .38 pointed at the ground and scanned the area. I slid to the passenger side window and peeped out. Saw nothing but the empty road curving down the mountain. I popped the door. A breeze rustled the trees. In the distance, alarms and sirens wailed. I listened for movement. Heard the scratch and slide of a foot on gravel.

And spotted a man bun peeping above the tailgate.

Dr. Trident.

Not knowing Trident's role in the Wellspring crime group— or even if he was armed like Sam Martin and Denver — I didn't want to call out and give Nash away. He'd ease around the truck and see Trident.

And they'd shoot each other.

Trident's back was to me. I tiptoed to the end of the truck. Panting, he stared into the woods. A rifle hung over his shoulder. But not in his hand. I exhaled and rounded the corner to face him. "Dr. Trident. What are you doing here?"

"Maizie?" He turned his head. "There's something out there."

Nash rounded the other side, his revolver aimed at Trident. "Drop your weapon. Miss Albright, get out of the way."

"Maizie, who is this?" Trident held up his hands.

"Drop your weapon," said Nash, swaying. "Lay it on the ground and step back. This is the last time I'm going to say it." He gritted his teeth and replanted his feet.

"Dr. Trident," I said. "Do what he says. He doesn't want to shoot you, but he will if you don't follow his directions."

Trident slipped the rifle off his shoulder, laid it on the ground, and stepped back. "Listen, I don't know what's going on here. What do you want? Money?"

"He's not robbing you." I bent to scoop the rifle and almost blacked out on the return trip. Blinking away stars, I stumbled toward Nash. I steadied a hand on his shoulder and whispered, "You're swaying, cowboy. You shouldn't be on your feet like this."

Nash slipped an arm around my waist but kept his gun gripped and ready. "You're swaying, too," he murmured. "And you look like hell, by the way. Like some kind of zombie who's been rolling in a hay pile."

"That's pine straw. And thanks to you, I haven't slept in a week." I refocused on Trident. "This is my therapist, Dr. Trident. Who, I believe, is not really a therapist. And to think I was doing selfie therapy until my phone was stolen."

"How can you say that Maizie?" cried Trident. "You hung my Ph.D. certificate on the wall. We've been working together all week. You've had breakthroughs because of me." He looked at Nash. "My YouTube series treating celebrity clients is quite popular."

"Okay, calm down." I didn't want to get into any supposed breakthroughs in front of Nash. "It's just that Sam Martin and Dr. Sakda were using Wellspring to make their hybrid drug and laundering the money. How are you not involved? You introduced me to Everett Lawson. And Denver Crosby. They do the exchange with the cartel guys."

"Drug cartel? No." Dr. Trident blinked a few times and rubbed his chin. "I don't like labels, Maizie. I also don't believe in judgment. And I can't believe this is true of Sam Martin and Dr. Sakda. We're hashtag-healing-revolution. Did you forget? Say it with me, Maizie, hashtag—"

"Let me point out something more compelling," said Nash. "You were carrying a rifle and running through the woods."

"For protection. There's something in the woods."

"Something like cops." He motioned with his gun hand. "Get in the truck. We're taking you to Black Pine PD."

"But I really don't understand what's going on," he said.

"Then they won't arrest you," said Nash. "But that's for the police to decide."

I held the .38 and rifle while Nash tied Dr. Trident's hands behind his back with a bungee cord. After Trident scooted into the passenger seat and Nash had swung into the truck, I handed Nash the .38.

"Get in," he said.

I shook my head. "I've got to go back. I don't know if he's alive or dead. I can't leave Oliver like this."

"Right, your fiancé." Nash nodded and cranked the ignition.

"Ex-fiancé," I said. "And after you drop off Trident, you need to go home. To your wife."

"Ex-wife."

"About her." I pulled my shoulders back and notched my chin up. "Do I have to look for another job?"

His polar blues considered me. He gave me a half-smile, one that spoke of remorse. Yet still warmed his eyes and made my heart gallop. "I honestly don't know. But I still want you for a partner."

"Wait," said Dr. Trident. "Are you Maizie's boss? We've talked a lot about you."

I stepped on to the running board to fix Dr. Trident in a death glare. "Even if you're arrested, we still have doctor-patient confidentiality, right?"

He nodded. "Of course."

"Good. This is Wyatt Nash. My boss." My cheeks heated. I kept my eyes on Trident. "And I'm in love with him. I don't care what anyone thinks. He can fire me if that's what it's going to take to be with him."

A hand closed around the nape of my neck, drawing me into the truck. Nash's lips fell on mine. The fire in my cheeks zipped through the rest of my body. I clung to his shoulders and teetered on the running board. His arm slipped around my waist, securing me, then he angled for a deeper kiss.

The dizziness had gotten worse in a good way.

Nash drew back. "I just fired you. Are you giving him back the ring?"

"Nope." I stretched to kiss his cheek. "And if he's alive, I'll visit Oliver in prison. Even if they don't give us a window. Are you going to be okay with that?"

"I may have to work for my ex-wife. Are you going to be okay with that?"

"Have you two thought of couple's counseling?" said Trident. "Check out my YouTube channel under Hashtag-Selfie-Ship-Fix. It's worked wonders for a lot of lovers."

I was so over hiking. But at least this time I had a song in my heart and a rifle in my hand. The Center's castle-like edifice rose above the trees. A cacophony of first responders created a buzz of background noise among the usual woodland sounds. I tuned it out to pay attention to my surroundings. Like the rustle of movement in the leaves behind me. I stopped and slid around a tree. Something large crashed through a bush. Birds flew overhead squawking.

Swallowing hard, I lifted the rifle and placed the butt against my shoulder. I blew out a long breath and pivoted to face the intruder. Among the trees, something moved. I looked over the gunsight but couldn't make out a person.

"Come out," I said. "I'm armed and have you sighted. The

police are here. You can't get away."

Narrowing my eyes, I scanned the landscape. But I couldn't pick out anything more than the browns and greens of the forest. I stepped sideways, trying a different angle. The woodland noise had quieted. No bird calls. No squirrel chatter. No crashing in the undergrowth.

An eerie howl broke the silence. Deep and long, imitating a wail.

My heart pounded inside my head, causing pain to spot my vision. I blinked it off, trying to steady the rifle. And decided I'd take a headache over whatever was out there. I spun and ran up the incline toward the castle.

At the edge of the forest, I handed my rifle to a deputy and entered the obstacle course of explaining who, what, and why, until I found Ian.

"Did they hurt Oliver? Is he alive?"

"He's in custody." Ian cut his eyes to a squad car. "Alive."

"I have to see him," I said.

"Not a good idea."

"We both need the closure. And I need to give him this." I flashed the ring.

Ian gave me a dark look. "You should probably keep it."

"It's a long story. But we're not engaged."

"We're not done questioning Fraser, hon'. It's going to have to wait. He'll probably be charged with at least aiding and abetting. We'll hold on to him for a few days before the arraignment. We want to get all the facts together."

"I can tell you everything as a witness. I've got it all, the bank robbery, your drug cartel victim, and what happened here today. But I need to have words with Oliver." I gave Ian my best Julia Pinkerton stare down. "The last time he sold me out, I refused to talk to him. This time, he's going to hear it."

"I might make an exception for that." Grinning, Ian winked. "Where was this resolve a week ago?"

"I found my spine, Ian. And I'm not giving it back."

FIFTY-FOUR

#ByeByeBae #ReboundGirl

*B*ecause I had dragged Ian Mowry to my probation meeting, Gladys was forced to listen to my longest excuse to date. Showing her irritation, she pulled out her knitting and kept the needles clicking through the entire story.

"I need to speak to Judge Ellis about your career choice," she said. "And I don't care if a drug mule steals your backpack and phone, you're still to report to me from a landline. That's a strike."

I buried my head in my hands.

"And you're not supposed to have a weapon," she said. "That's another strike. But the manager of Wellspring did fax over your community service hours and you're caught up there."

"Seriously?" I looked up. "Oliver did that for me?"

"Before his arrest for aiding and abetting. I'll have to double-check that's not an issue. You might need to get someone else to sign it."

Ian patted my shoulder.

"Now for the therapist. He's been released for now. It seems Dr. Trident was an outside hire and didn't realize what was going on at the spa." Gladys leaned forward. "But the police are still investigating. If Dr. Trident is convicted and has his license suspended, you're going to need a new therapist."

"I still have to see Dr. Trident?"

Gladys eased back in her chair and picked up her knitting. "I heard you're unemployed. I'll give you a week to find another job. No excuses."

I stopped chewing my lip to gnaw on my nails.

Ian stood up. "We have another issue. Did you meet with Vicki Albright, the mother of your probationer, one month ago?"

Gladys's gaze shifted from me to Ian. "I'm not sure. I'll have to check my scheduler."

"And did Vicki Albright offer you an acting role as 'probation officer' in the *All is Albright* television reality show? To which you agreed to be filmed?"

"There are no rules against that."

"And a few weeks later, did you then agree to use the Wellspring Center and a Dr. Trident for both Maizie Albright's community service and therapist? Through Vicki Albright?"

"They were recommended by Vicki," said Gladys. "It was clearly stated as a suggestion and not as a—"

"Bribe?" said Ian. "Because that's a serious offense."

The ball of yarn dropped from her lap and rolled across the floor.

"I'm keeping an eye on you and your business," said Ian. "Come on, Maizie."

I followed him from the office and into the parking lot. "Thank you."

"No problem. You'll be happy to know Agent Langtry is gone. She had to turn over her case to the DEA. Sam Martin's got a rep for using real estate to launder money for a drug cartel, the one connected to our Atlanta victim. He builds resorts on the West coast but moved here thinking it'd be easier to cover. He brought in Dr. Sakda to impress his boss with new drugs whose chemical makeup isn't technically illegal. Yet."

"It was the evil land developer all along. Hollywood screenwriters would love that villain," I said. "What about you? Do you get to assist the DEA?"

"Only to turn over my files. But I'm okay with that. At least they were polite about it." He smiled. "Back to small-town crime. Speaking of, even though I helped you today, you still need to follow your probation requirements."

"I know."

"And no more lying to me. That's obstruction of justice. I can't help you with Gladys in that regard."

I nodded.

"Maizie." Ian took my hands in his. "I really like you. But I think, it's best if we just remain friends. If you had a different job or didn't take such risks, I'd probably think differently. But I've got my daughter to think about. And my career."

"You're dumping me, too?" I pulled my hands from his. My second breakup in two days from men I wasn't even dating.

I had found my spine and lost my mojo.

I strolled from Black Pine Probation to Nash Security Solutions, enjoying a pace that wasn't an armed man chase. Also because Lucky was currently impounded as evidence. I popped into the donut shop, grabbed a bag of apple and pumpkin spice, then slipped through the side door. Backpacks, film equipment, computers, phones, bottles of Coke, and balled up bags of chips covered the stairs. As well as three teenagers, who had sprawled across what space wasn't covered in debris.

Checking the time on my watch, I opened my mouth. Before I could remind them of typical school hours, the three bounded down the stairs and fell on me. We group hugged. Then individually hugged. And I might have cried. A lot.

They took my bag of donuts, gathered their things, and followed me into the office. I fell into Lamar's La-Z-Boy while they ransacked the donuts.

"Chandler is getting treated for dehydration in the hospital," said Mara. "Isn't that cool?"

Not really. But I nodded.

"And we're going to do a special episode about drugs," said Fred. "As a public service project."

"We'll continue the show, but we're using new locations," said Laci.

"Sounds good." I hesitated, then decided not to share my possible Bigfoot encounter in the woods. Maybe after everything calmed down. And the Wellspring Center turned back into a chicken farm.

Instead, I popped the footrest. Folded my hands on my stomach. And relaxed.

I totally got Lamar's obsession with the chair.

"The police have everyone in custody except Crispin," I said. "His dad didn't want to turn him over to the Mexican police, so they hired a bounty hunter to bring him back."

The room burst in a cacophony of "that's so cools."

Which it kind of was. I smiled, then blinked my eyes open. The kids were gone. The door's creak had woke me. I popped the footrest back. Saw it was Vicki and Giulio and kicked back again.

"Really?" said Vicki. "At a time like this? What are we going to do for a wedding venue?"

I yawned. "Are you mad about Oliver lying to you or is it the loss of your investment that has you so angry?"

"My darling, what is that magnificent piece on your hand?" Giulio darted to the chair and picked up my hand. "Wrong finger. But nice ring. Tell me about the conjugal visits. It is something I have always wondered. Please help my imagination."

"As if." I snatched my hand back.

Vicki paced to the coffee table, picked up a *People*, checked the cover, and dropped it. "I suppose we're back to the old venue. And using Sweeney Security Solutions."

"Whatever." I closed my eyes. "I don't work here anymore, anyway."

When I opened my eyes, Vicki and Giulio had left. Replaced by a robust man with Paul Newman eyes, a small scar on his chin, and a bigger scar on the back of his head. Kicking the footrest back, I shot forward. He placed a hand on the back of the chair, steadying it, then leaned over me and kissed me slowly. Then pushed the chair back and dropped Steve into my lap.

"Sleep." Nash smiled, flexing the tiny dimple near his scar. "But when you wake up, we need to talk about the snoring. That might be an issue. Then there's the drooling. But that'll bother Lamar more since it's his chair."

"What's going on?" I struggled with the chair and hopped out. "Where have you been?"

"In a long meeting." He sighed, dropped into the La-Z-Boy, and pulled me onto his lap. "At Sweeney Security Solutions. With crazier people than you experienced at Wellspring."

I snuggled against him and stroked his scar. "What's the verdict?"

"Even with insurance, the hospital bills are astronomical. And thanks to Jolene snagging Black Pine's business these past months, it looks like I'll be deep in the red. I can't let Lamar invest in a bad business." He kissed my temple and rubbed his knuckle against my cheek. "You and Lamar tried your best this week and I thank you for it, but it'll take a lot more than fliers and Jolene's castoffs to save me."

"No. I can't fail again." I felt an onrush of tears but gritted my teeth instead. "We'll work harder."

"Don't worry." He kissed my nose. "I'm not going to let you lose your chance at getting a PI license."

"This isn't about me. This is your business."

He absently twined our hands together, then lifted mine to examine the ring. "It's a funny thing about comas. You wake up and see things differently. When I thanked the nurses, they told me how Maizie Albright came to my room early in the morning and late at night. Looking like something the cat drug in, which concerned them. But you'd still sit by my bed and talk to me."

"That's unfair," I said. "I had an Olaplex."

"Forget the business." He rubbed his cheek against my temple. "Nothing means more to me than that story."

I pressed my lips against his neck so he couldn't see my expression. "To be fair Jolene was there, too."

"To be seen as the wife of the bank bomb hero. That's Jolene for you." He sighed again.

I didn't like the sigh, but the weight on my right ring finger reminded me I had no room to complain. "What are you going to do?"

"I cut a deal. It's a terrible deal. But I couldn't hang you out to dry. You're still going to mentor with me, I insisted on that. But I won't be your boss. You're not going to like it. Neither of us will. But it's the best I can do. For now."

My stomach dropped. "Who's going to be the boss?"

I quickly chose a new mantra. *Don't say Jolene. Don't say Jolene. Don't say Jolene.*

"Vicki Albright."

he End.

Thanks for Reading NC-17

Thank you for choosing Maizie Albright's third case. This is my longest Maizie book and longest book to date. I'd vow to write less complicated mysteries in the future, but I know I'll never keep that promise. ;)

If you missed 15 MINUTES, Maizie Albright's first case, click here to get it!

And do sign up for my newsletter to get updates on new releases, discounts, giveaways, and events. All my newsletter subscribers get a free short story and are entered into subscriber-only giveaways, like to receive a signed advanced copy with each new release! I love my readers!

<3!

Larissa

For the Maizie stories, I wanted to explore a different topic in current entertainment. If you asked my (teenage) children what they watch on TV, they will cite a few series on Netflix. But they mainly watch YouTube. They listen to music on YouTube. They learn how to do whatever craft they're into on YouTube. My youngest loves "satisfying videos" which she calls ASMR. (She had no idea ASMR stands for Autonomous Sensory Meridian Response.) But then, much of what they learn in school is on-line now, so what should I expect?

I find this an interesting phenomenon and a little disturbing. Both of my girls are iGen (iPhone Generation), like Fred, Mara, and Laci. They don't remember a world without smart phones. Tapping an app, typing in a search, and clicking on a video is much easier for them than searching through channels on TV.

This phenomenon has opened a new avenue in entertainment and stars. There are YouTube channels that are pulling in millions of dollars in revenue. Without agents, managers, and producers taking their cut, these new celebrities are probably making much more than the average TV actor.

Of course, it's a Pandora's Box, like everything else in our digital world today. Which is great fodder for a mystery writer!

Thanks for reading! xoxo

Larissa

A Sneak Peek of The Cupid Caper

Sometimes it takes a con to catch a crook. It'll take an ex-con to catch this killer.

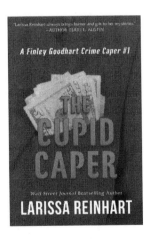

The Cupid Caper, A Finley Goodhart Crime Caper #1

Ex-grifter Finley Goodhart may try to stay on the straight and narrow, but walking that thin line becomes wobbly when she believes her friend Penny was murdered. The last thing she wants is to work with her ex-partner (and ex-boyfriend), the brilliant (brilliantly frustrating) British con artist, Lex Leopold. However, when it appears Penny's demise might be related to an exclusive matchmaking service for millionaires, Fin needs Lex's help to pull a long con to get the goods on Penny.

Romance is in the air for hustlers, gangsters, and their marks. Unfortunately for Fin and Lex, infiltrating the racket doesn't make for a match made in heaven. This Valentine swindle could stop their hearts for good.

One
The Approach

Wednesdays often brought the college boys to Jello's Pool Hall. Particularly in the winter. I'd call it cabin fever, except we were in Georgia. Still, too cold to drink on their frat house front porch rocking chairs. Too early in the week to host a party. The non-heathens would be attending Wednesday night church. The good students would be in class or the library.

But the bad boys would bring money to places like Jello's. Which was why I was there.

And how Lex knew to find me.

I had just racked a fresh round. Satisfied with the smooth lift of the triangle. No balls escaped. Feeling good about the roll of twenties tucked into the front pocket of my jeans. That gratification disappeared upon sensing a male presence behind me. The scent of his aftershave cut through the pervading smell of beer, stale smoke, and old fryer oil. I sniffed once. Recognized the cardamon and bergamot scent. Rested the cue stick on the table.

"Wanna make a wager? I'm having a lucky night." I bent over the table to place the cue ball. Angled the stick. Shot it backward. And turned to face him.

"Hello, love." Lex grabbed the stick. "Watch yourself. I'd like to remain a baritone, if you don't mind."

"Sorry." I didn't sound sorry. Didn't even get close. "Careful where you stand next time? Another town, maybe?"

He pushed the stick away. Grinned. Sidled forward. "Don't want me too deep in your pocket?"

I rolled my eyes, then studied the man. His thick, sandy hair had been trimmed to maintain an artful dishevelment. Smiling blue eyes. Sensuous lips held a relaxed smirk. His boy-next-door good looks never revealed anything but indolent charm and false promises. A real ace. Too careful and too practiced to show anything else.

"You look tired." I took a careful step to the side. Rested my hip against the table. "Tinge of blue beneath your eyes."

"Too many lonely nights."

"I bet. They have medicine for that, you know."

"Not the cure I seek. You're looking fit, though." His gaze traveled the room. "How'd you do tonight?"

"What do you want, Lex?" My hand reached for the cue ball. I rolled it beneath my palm.

His eyes snapped back to me and told me what I already knew. I narrowed mine. His mouth quirked.

"Relax," he said. "Gave you my word I'd leave you alone, didn't I?"

"Your word isn't worth much. And you just proved it, seeing as how you're here and all."

"When have I ever lied to you?"

I gripped the cue ball.

He raised his hand. "Right. But I am here out of the goodness of my heart. Thought I should see you about Penny Forbes."

"What about Penny?" I frowned. "Are you working together? Not interested."

"You haven't heard?" The mask fell. His face tightened and he appeared older, matured. "Fin, we should go somewhere private."

"Why?" I didn't like the mask, but I didn't like what he'd

replaced it with either. He looked worried. Lex never worried. The carefree charisma wasn't just an act. I was the worrier. "You know I'm on the square. If you and Penny have gotten yourself into a mess, y'all just get yourselves out of it."

"On the level but still dodgy enough to plunder these wankers," he muttered. "Finley, I'm serious. I don't want to tell you here."

"You're never serious." I turned. Settled the white ball. Chalked the cue tip. Moved to the side and leaned over the table. Sighted the ball. Placed the stick between my thumb and fingers.

Lex leaned over me, close enough for his words to buzz in my ear. "She's dead, Fin. Penny's dead." A hand fell on my shoulder. "I'm sorry. I didn't want to tell you like this. Finley, come with me."

I pulled in a breath. Ignored his hand and the clamor ringing between my ears. Gritting my teeth, I lowered my head. Centered my gaze on the space between the second and fourth racked ball. Brought the stick back and let it glide. The break rang. Two solids slammed into the back and corner right pockets.

Lex's hand shot forward. Caught a stripe as it raced toward the front left. "Sloppy. That's a scratch."

"Hey." I turned, swinging the stick with me.

He caught the stick again, pushed it aside, and grabbed my arm. "Love, did you hear me? I'm sorry. I didn't want to be the bearer, but God knows I can't...had to see you. News like this. I cocked it up." He shook his head. "Love. Fin. Are you alright? What can I do?"

"Nothing." I shook my arm free and fixed my eyes to a point on the wall behind him. I hadn't seen Penny for months. She'd been busy. I'd been hiding. But dead? She was too young — mid-twenties, like me. Car accident? Cripes, I hoped she didn't get sick. The fatal illnesses I knew that struck Penny's age bracket weren't pretty.

I sucked in a deep breath. Let it out. Hated how shaky it sounded. "How'd she die?"

"Let's talk somewhere else." He paused. Sighed. "Right. Drug overdose. Heroin is what I heard."

My eyes flew to his face. The blue eyes watched me. Soberly, with a hint of pity. I despised that look even more than the worry.

"No way on God's green earth. Penny's momma was a junkie. Crooked as she could get, Penny wouldn't touch a substance stronger than champagne. You heard wrong, Lex."

He shrugged. "I'm sorry, love."

"Stop calling me that." I felt my throat tighten and forced a swallow. "Don't call me that anymore."

"Can't help myself." His head tilted, the pitying expression deepening. "Let me at least buy you a drink. We should toast Penny. You've known her since, when? First time on the street?"

He reached for me, but I sidestepped. "I'm not drinking to that lie. She didn't overdose."

"Fin, it's hard to hear, but it's true. Heard it from Dot, then checked myself."

"Who found her?" I gripped my cue stick. My chest felt like it was going to cave in. Or dump out. "Police? Which one? County? City? The heroin could have been planted, Lex. You know she's on *his* list because of me. It's not beneath him to do something like that just to make...her look bad. He's got the county coroner in his pocket. John Prince's a drunk and a gambler—"

"What would be the point in that? Penny was taken to the hospital, love. Wasn't a bust or anything like that. Your da—"

I held up a finger.

"Right, come on." Lex glanced around. Spotted my cue case under a nearby chair. Pulled it out. Took the stick from me. Unscrewed the shaft from the butt, flipped the top open on the hard case and slipped the sticks inside. Slinging the long case strap over his shoulder, he cupped my elbow.

I had stuck on the word *hospital*, rooted to the floor. Absently, I'd reached for the ring hanging from the chain around my neck. At Lex's touch, I shook off my daze and dropped the ring.

"Where are you staying?" said Lex.

"Nowhere." My stomach squeezed. I allowed him to walk me to the door. "Motel on Thirty-Four."

"You're coming to my place." He glanced at me. "Don't worry, love. You can trust me."

"No, I can't." I could feel the tears forming. I swallowed hard. "I can't go home with you. I should talk to Dot."

"Let me go with you."

I shook my head. Before I could speak, a voice hollered from the rear of the hall. The shout intensified. We turned. A young man jogged forward, followed by a small herd of beefy minions. The insults thrown in my direction did nothing to faze the other patrons. Nothing new for Jello's. Behind the bar, Jello called out, demanding payment of the young man's tab. Jello didn't care about fights as long as his end was covered.

"Did you take him?" whispered Lex. "Of course you did." He spun us back toward the door. Hurried our pace.

"Wasn't much of a hustle," I said. "He saw me beat the pants off his friend first. He's drunk."

"Drunk, stupid, and big. Not a good combination, love." Lex handed me the cue case.

"He practically begged me to—" The obscenity the guy shouted caught me off guard. "Vile boy. Guess he's worked himself into a lather about it at the bar. I am a mere female, you know. A blow to his pride. Took him three large before he gave up."

"Right. Blighter. He's going to catch us in the parking lot. Student, yes?"

Before the doors, Lex stopped. Pivoted. Retraced his steps toward the ape. Lex put out a hand as if to shake, then used it to steady the gorilla. "Hey, mate. Couldn't help but hear you. Let me correct the situation."

Behind him, the man's friends — an indistinguishable line of baseball hats, college-branded hoodies, and beards — blundered to a halt, confused by Lex's friendly voice and relaxed candor.

"What?" bellowed the man. He shook a fist in my direction.

"She— Were you carrying her stick? She friggin' has her own cue? What the f—"

Lex cut off his drunken cursing. "Sorry, mate. Didn't catch your name? Drew, was it?"

"Yes, how—?"

"Your friend mentioned it." Lex jerked his chin toward the line of monkeys behind Drew. They shifted, widening the circle. One twisted away to wander back to the bar.

"Listen, Drew. She took you for a ride, did she? Are you upset," Lex's voice rose while seeming to drop, "that this young girl beat you in pool? You know, she's a brilliant mathematician. Really. It's all in the angles. Trajectories. That sort of thing. Her father's a professor. Maybe you had him. Physics. Genius, really. Doctor—"

"Williams?" offered Drew.

"You know him? You might know me as well?"

"You're British."

"Accent gave it away, did it?" Lex smiled "Yes, a doctoral student. I work for Williams. Unfortunate situation. His daughter." He gave a nod in my direction.

Leaning against the door, I shrugged. Gave Drew an apologetic smile.

"A bit touched. Explains the maths, yes? Can't help herself, you know what I mean?"

"What?" said Drew. "She seemed normal."

"We won't speak the words. Minor's right to privacy. So hard to tell sixteen from twenty-one these days."

Drew's eyes widened. "She's sixteen?"

"And Jello," Lex continued. "As all students know, looks the other way on such things. Fake IDs and the lot. Probably why you and your friends are here. I trotted over to find her. Mission for Dr. Williams. Campus Police are on their way."

"Security? They're not cops."

"No, but they report criminal incidents to the police. Under the Clery Act, I believe. Campus police is not mall security, Drew. The actual police will be just behind them. Nothing they love more than a fake ID bust. Identity theft and the like is a serious concern these days."

As Drew swayed, Lex dropped an arm around his shoulder and steered him toward a table.

"Let's chat, Drew. Dr. Williams has a protocol for these things." Lex pulled out a chair.

Drew sank into it. His remaining friends drifted toward the pool tables.

Hovering above Drew, Lex crooked a finger at me and raised his voice. "Miss Williams, we need to settle this. If you could join us, please."

I slunk to their table, doing my best imitation of sixteen-going-on-twenty-something.

Lex cupped a hand around his mouth and raised his voice. "Jello, how much does he owe you?"

"Fifty," called Jello.

Drew blanched.

"Heavy night for three dollar beer," said Lex. "Alright, Drew. Let's pay Jello first. Jello only takes cash. Doesn't like to pay those pesky credit card service fees."

Or taxes, but I kept that thought to myself.

"Can't." Drew pointed at me. "She took all my money. I told Jello she'd have to pay."

"You lost your bet," I said. "All six of them. After the first three times, you might have realized the odds were against you. Really, after losing the first two, it's sixty percent in favor of losing. A betting man should know these things."

"Miss Williams, what have we told you about speaking so bluntly? People perceive that as rude." Lex shook his head. "Sorry, Drew. Looks like I got here just in time."

He presented a clip of cash. Palmed the clip. Counted off what appeared to be fifty. Handed the folded notes to me. "Miss Williams, pay Jello. And tip him well."

I nodded meekly. Trotted to Jello and delivered the fold. "Payment for young Drew."

Jello scooped the bills into a meaty fist and dropped them in his till. "You're going to catch it one of these days, Fin."

"Not if they catch it first." I winked. "Drew had an extra Benjamin for you. Gratis. Also in case the others don't reconcile. These rich kids are the worst at paying their debts. Money spilling out of their pockets, yet too cheap to pay a tab."

"And too dumb not to see it fall out of their pockets and into your hands. I thought you went straight, hon'."

"I did," I said. "Can I help it if these boys won't let themselves believe what's right in front of their eyes? If I don't hide my skill, it's not a hustle."

"This is Lex's money then?" Jello's smile stretched, making his chins wobble.

"I didn't say that. Lex would never short you, any more than I would. But Lex would rather have Drew pay his own bill. As he should." I leaned forward. "Jello, what did you hear about Penny Forbes dying?"

"Thought you knew, hon'." Jello's chins quivered with a mournful shake. "Can't believe it. She was engaged, too, did you know that? Found a way up."

"Up?"

"Rich guy. Didn't surprise me too much. That Penny. Gorgeous and smart. A legend."

"Hold on." I checked on Lex. While drawing out a story with one hand, he slipped the money clip back into Drew's pocket. Typical Lex. Let Drew think he'd blown his cash when he woke hungover and broke.

I turned back to Jello. "Penny was engaged to a rich guy and OD'd on heroin? Doesn't add up Jello. She didn't use and she'd never pimp out. She was a good roper, but never let herself get too dirty."

"I reckoned the same. After her momma—" His chins shook again.

"Exactly. The rich guy, was he a mark? Or legit?"

"Dunno, hon'." Jello fixed his piggy eyes over my shoulder. "Lex is wrapping up."

I turned, catching the exuberant expression lighting Lex's face. He could be mistaken for a young, doctoral student. A highlighted lock had fallen over his forehead. His lean physique gave the impression of slightness. I knew the wiry strength that hid beneath his designer button down. He just needed a pair of wire-rims to complete the picture of slightly nerdy but cute grad student. Not that Lex had ever stepped foot in a college classroom. No more than I had.

At least I didn't think so. You could never be sure with Lex.

I wouldn't put it past him to audit the classes that interested him. And it wouldn't surprise me if he had somehow obtained a diploma. He was good at that sort of thing. Got his kicks from pitting his wiles against bureaucratic quagmires. Anything that frustrated a normal person, Lex loved to unravel and beat.

Including trying to lure me back into his questionable operations. And other areas of his life.

Continue reading The Cupid Caper on your favorite ebook device or in paperback.

A Sneak Peek of Portrait of a Dead Guy

A Cherry Tucker Mystery #1

In Halo, Georgia, folks know Cherry Tucker as big in mouth, small in stature, and able to sketch a portrait faster than buckshot rips from a ten gauge — but commissions are scarce. So when the well-heeled Branson family wants to memorialize their murdered son in a coffin portrait, Cherry scrambles to win their patronage from her small town rival. As the clock ticks toward the deadline, Cherry faces more trouble than just a controversial subject. Between ex-boyfriends, her flaky family, an illegal gambling ring, and outwitting a killer on a spree, Cherry finds herself painted into a corner she'll be lucky to survive.

* Winner of the Dixie Kane Memorial Award * Nominated for the Daphne du Maurier Award and the Emily Award *

One

In a small town, there is a thin gray line between personal freedom and public ruin. Everyone knows your business without even trying. Folks act polite all the while remembering every stupid thing you've done in your life. Not to mention getting tied to all the dumbass stuff your relations — even those dead or gone — have done. We forgive but don't forget.

I thought the name Cherry Tucker carried some respectability as an artist in my hometown of Halo. I actually chose to live in rural Georgia. I could have sought a loft apartment in Atlanta where people appreciate your talent to paint nudes in classical poses, but I like my town and most of the three thousand or so people that live in it. Even though most of Halo wouldn't know a Picasso from a plate of spaghetti. Still, it's a nice town full of nice people and a lot cheaper to live in than Atlanta.

Halo citizens might buy their living room art from the guy who hawks motel overstock in front of the Winn-Dixie, but they also love personalized mementos. Portraits of their kids and their dogs, architectural photos of their homes and gardens, poster"-size photos of their trips to Daytona and Disney World. God bless them. That's my specialty, portraits. But at this point, I'd paint the side of a barn to make some money. I'm this close from working the night shift at the Waffle House. And if I had to wear one of those starchy, brown uniforms day after day, a little part of my soul would die.

Actually a big part of my soul would die, because I'd shoot myself first.

When I heard the highfalutin Bransons wanted to commission a portrait of Dustin, their recently deceased thug son, I hightailed it to Cooper's Funeral Home. I assumed they hadn't called me for the commission yet because the shock of Dustin's murder rendered them senseless. After all, what kind of crazy called for a portrait of their murdered boy? But then, important members of a small community could get away with little eccentricities. I was in no position to judge. I needed the money.

After Dustin's death made the paper three days ago, there'd been a lot of teeth sucking and head shaking in town, but no surprise at Dustin's untimely demise from questionable circumstances. It was going to be that or the State Pen. Dustin had been a criminal in the making for twenty-seven years.

Not that I'd share my observations with the Bransons. Good customer service is important for starving artists if we want to get over that whole starving thing.

As if to remind me, my stomach responded with a sound similar to a lawnmower hitting a chunk of wood. Luckily, the metallic knocking in the long-suffering Datsun engine of my pickup drowned out the hunger rumblings of my tummy. My poor truck shuddered into Cooper's Funeral Home parking lot in a flurry of flaking yellow paint, jerking and gasping in what sounded like a death rattle. However, I needed her to hang on. After a couple big commissions, hopefully the Datsun could go to the big junkyard in the sky. My little yellow workhorse deserved to rest in peace.

I entered the Victorian monstrosity that is Cooper's, leaving my portfolio case in the truck. I made a quick scan of the lobby and headed toward the first viewing room on the right. A sizable group of Bransons huddled in a corner. Sporadic groupings of flower arrangements sat around the narrow room, though the viewing didn't actually start until tomorrow.

A plump woman in her early fifties, hair colored and high-lighted sunshine blonde, spun around in kitten heel mules and pulled me into her considerable soft chest. Wanda Branson, step-mother to the deceased, was a hugger. As a kid, I spent many a Sunday School smothered in Miss Wanda's loving arms.

"Cherry!" She rocked me into a deeper hug. "What are you doing here? It's so nice to see you. You can't believe how hard these past few days have been for us."

Wanda began sobbing. I continued to rock with her, patting her back while I eased my face out of the ample bosom.

"I'm glad I can help." The turquoise and salmon print silk top muffled my voice. I extricated myself and patted her arm. "It was a shock to hear about Dustin's passing. I remember him from high school."

I remembered him, all right. I remembered hiding from the already notorious Dustin as a freshman and all through high school. Of course, that's water under the bridge now, since he's dead and all.

"It's so sweet of you to come."

"Now Miss Wanda, why don't we find you a place to sit? You tell me exactly what you want, and I'll take notes. How about the lobby? There are some chairs out there. Or outside? It's a beautiful morning and the fresh air might be nice."

"I'm not sure what you mean," said Wanda. "Tell you what I want?"

"For the portrait. Dustin's portrait."

"Is there a problem?" An older gentleman in a golf shirt and khaki slacks eyed me while running a hand through his thinning salt and pepper hair. John Branson, locally known as JB, strode to his wife's side. "You're Cherry Tucker, Ed Ballard's granddaughter, right?"

I nodded, whipping out a business card. He glanced at it and looked me over. I had the feeling JB wasn't expecting this little bitty girl with flyaway blonde hair and cornflower blue eyes. My local customers find my appearance disappointing. I think they expected me to return from art school looking as if I walked out of 1920s' bohemian Paris wearing black, slouchy clothes and a ridiculous beret. I like color and a little bling myself. However, I toned it down for this occasion and chose jeans and a soft orange tee with sequins circling the collar.

"Yes sir," I said, shaking his hand. "I got here as soon as I could. I'm sorry about Dustin."

"Why exactly did you come?" JB spoke calmly but with distaste, as if he held something bitter on his tongue. Probably the idea of me painting his dead son.

"To do the portrait, of course. I figured the sooner I got here, the sooner I could get started. I am pretty fast. You probably heard about my time in high school as a Six Flags Quick Sketch artist. But time is money, the way I look at it.

You'll want your painting sooner than later."

"Cherry, honey, I think there's been some kind of misunderstanding." Wanda looped her arm around JB's elbow. "JB's niece Shawna is doing the painting."

"Shawna Branson?" I would have keeled over if I hadn't been at Cooper's and worried someone might pop me in a coffin. Shawna was a smooth-talking Amazonian poacher who wrestled me for the last piece of cake at a church picnic some fifteen years ago. Although she was three heads taller, my scrappy tenacity and love of sugar helped me win. Shawna marked that day as a challenge to defeat me at every turn. In high school, she stole my leather jacket, slept with my boyfriend, and brown-nosed my teachers. She didn't even go to my school. And now she was after my commission.

"She's driving over from Line Creek today," Wanda said. "You know, she got her degree from Georgia Southern and started a business. She's very busy, but she thinks she can make the time for us."

"I've seen her work," I said. "Lots of hearts, polka dots, and those curlicue letters you monogram on everything."

"Oh yes," said Wanda, showing her fondness for curlicue letters. "She's very talented."

"But ma'am. Can she paint a portrait? I have credentials. I'm a graduate of SCAD, Savannah College of Art and Design. I'm formally trained on mixing color, using light, creating perspective, not to mention the hours spent with live models. I can do curlicue. But don't you want more than curlicue?"

Wanda relaxed her grip on JB's arm. Her eyes wandered to the floral arrangements, considering.

"I have the skill and the eye for portraiture," I continued. "And this is Dustin's final portrait. Don't you want an expert to handle his precious memory?"

"She does have a point, J.B," Wanda conceded.

JB grunted. "The whole idea is damn foolish."

Wanda blushed and fidgeted with JB's sleeve.

"The Victorians used to wear a cameo pin with a lock of their deceased's hair in it," I said, glad to reference my last minute research as I defended her. "It was considered a memorial. When photography became popular, some propped up the dead for one last picture."

"Exactly. Besides, this is a painting not a photograph," said Wanda. "It's been harder as Dustin got older. I wanted to be closer to him. JB did, too, in his way. And then Dustin was taken before his time."

I detected an eye roll from JB. Money wasn't the issue. Propriety needled him. Wanda loved to spend JB's money, and he encouraged her. JB's problem wasn't that Wanda was flashy; she just shopped above her raising. Which can have unfortunate results. Like hiring someone to paint her dead stepson.

"A somber representation of your son could be com- forting," I said. Not that I believed it for a minute.

"Do you need the work, honey?" Wanda asked. "I want to do a memory box. You know, pick up one of those frames at the Crafty Corner for his mementos. You could do that."

"I'll do the memory box," I said. "I've done some flag cases, so a memory box will be no problem. But I really think you should reconsider Shawna for the painting."

"Now lookee here," said JB. "Shawna's my niece."

"Let me get my portfolio," I said. Pictures speak louder than words, and it looked like JB needed more convincing.

I dashed out of the viewing room and took a deep breath to regain some composure. I couldn't let Shawna Branson steal my commission. The Bransons needed this portrait done right. Who knows what kind of paint slaughter Shawna would commit. As far as I was concerned, she could keep her curlicue business as long as she left the real art to me.

My bright yellow pickup glowed like a radiant beacon in the sea of black, silver, and white cars. I opened the driver door with a yank, cursing a patch of rust growing around the lock. Standing on my toes, I reached for the portfolio bag on the passenger side. The stretch tipped me off my toes and splayed me flat across the bench.

"I recognize this truck," a lazy voice floated behind me. "And the view. Doesn't look like much's changed either way in ten years."

I gasped and crawled out.

Luke Harper, Dustin's stepbrother.

I had forgotten that twig on the Branson family tree. More like snapped it from my memory. His lanky stance blocked the open truck door. One hand splayed against my side window. His other wrist lay propped over the top of my door. Within the cage of

Luke's arms, we examined each other. Fondness didn't dwell in my eyes. I'm never sure what dwelled in his.

Luke drove me crazy in ways I didn't appreciate. He knew how to push buttons that switched me from tough to soft, smart to dumb. Beautiful men were my kryptonite. Local gossip said my mother had the same problem. My poor sister, Casey, was just as inflicted. We would have been better off inheriting a squinty eye or a duck walk.

"Hello, Luke Harper." I tried not to sound snide. Drawing up to my fullest five foot and a half inches, I cocked a hip in casual belligerence.

"How's it going, Cherry?" A glint of light sparked his smoky eyes, and I expected it corresponded with a certain memory of a nineteen-year-old me wearing a pair of red cowboy boots and not much else. "You hanging out at funeral homes now? Never took you for a necrophiliac."

This time I gave Luke my best what-the-hell redneck glare. Crossing my arms, I took a tiny step forward in the trapped space. He stared at me with a faint smile tugging the corners of his mouth. If I could paint those gorgeous curls and long sideburns — which will never happen, by the way — I would use a rich, raw umber with burnt sienna highlights. For his eyes, I'd mix Prussian blue and a teensy Napthal red. However, he would call his hair "plain old dark brown" and eyes "gray." But, what does he know? Not much about art, I can tell you that.

"I thought you were in Afghanistan or Alabama," I said. "What are you doing back?"

"Discharged. You still mad at me? It's been a while."

"Mad? I barely remember the last time I saw you." I wasn't really lying. My last memory wasn't of seeing him, but seeing the piece of trash in his truck. And by piece of trash, I mean the kind with boobs.

"You were pretty mad at the time. And I know you and your grudges."

"I've got more to do than think about something that happened when I was barely out of high school."

"Are you going to hold my youthful indiscretions against me now?" He smiled. "I'm only in town for a short time. You know I can only take Halo in small doses."

"If you're not sticking around, I can't see how my opinion of you matters. Not like you asked me about your sudden decision to join the Army and clear out of dodge."

"That's what you're mad about?"

Dear God, men are clueless. Why He didn't sharpen them up a bit has to be one of life's greatest mysteries.

Find my other books, including the Cherry Tucker Mystery series, at my website: www.larissareinhart.com

TV and Film in NC-17

In reference or literally mentioned.

"Cell Block Mango"*
"Sax as a Weapon"*
"Trust No One"*
A Midsummer's Night Dream
Breaking Bad
Casino
Creature from the Black Lagoon
Donnie Darko
Downton Abbey
E.T. the Extra-Terrestrial
The Fast and the Furious
Ghost Hunters
Grease
The Haunting
High Noon
MacGyver
Man Vs. Wild
Misery

Naked and Afraid
Oliver Twist
The Princess Bride
Say Anything
Scooby-Doo
The Shawshank Redemption
She-Ra
The Silence of the Lambs
Star Wars
Steel Magnolias
Stranger Things
Supernatural
Tasty
The Dark Knight
The Godfather
The Golden Girls
The Goonies
The Monster Squad
The Revenant
The Shining
The Wizard of Oz
The Twilight Zone
Tom and Jerry
Twin Peaks
*While You Were Shifting***
X-Files

   ***Julia Pinkerton, Teen Detective* episodes.
   **TV movie starring Maizie Albright

Also by Larissa Reinhart

Portrait of a Dead Guy, A Cherry Tucker Mystery #1

Still Life in Brunswick Stew, A Cherry Tucker Mystery #2

Hijack in Abstract, A Cherry Tucker Mystery #3

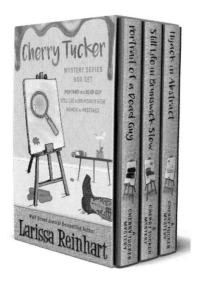

Cherry Tucker Mystery books 1-3 Box Set

Death in Perspective, A Cherry Tucker Mystery #4

The Body in the Landscape, A Cherry Tucker Mystery #5

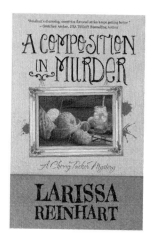

A Composition in Murder, A Cherry Tucker Mystery #6

Sleigh Bells and Sleuthing, Sixteen Christmas Cozy Mysteries
Featuring Women Sleuths (including "Christmas Quick
Sketch," A Cherry Tucker Mystery prequel)

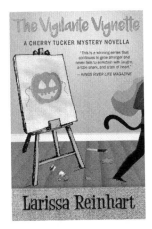

"The Vigilante Vignette," A Cherry Tucker Mystery Novella #5.5 (first published in Midnight Mysteries, 9 Cozy Tales)

15 Minutes, Maizie Albright Star Detective #1

16 Millimeters, Maizie Albright Star Detective #2

NC-17, Maizie Albright Star Detective #3

"A View to A Chill," A Cherry Tucker and Maizie Albright novella (first published in The 12 Slays of Christmas

The Cupid Caper, A Finley Goodhart Crime Caper #2

About the Author

Wall Street Journal bestselling and award-winning author, Larissa Reinhart writes humorous mysteries and romantic comedies including the critically acclaimed Maizie Albright Star Detective, Cherry Tucker Mystery, and Finley Goodhart Crime Caper series. Her works have been chosen as book club picks by *Woman's World Magazine* and *Hot Mystery Reviews*.

Larissa's family and dog, Biscuit, had been living in Japan, but once again call Georgia home. See them on HGTV's *House Hunters*

International "Living for the Weekend in Nagoya" episode. Visit her website, LarissaReinhart.com, and join her newsletter for a free short story.

Made in the USA
Middletown, DE
26 December 2018